I0831662

GRANGER'S RETURN

Books by Teresa Pijoan from Sunstone Press

American Indian Creation Myths

Dead Kachina Man
A Mystery

Granger's Threat
A Murder Mystery Laced with a Web of Lies and Familial Contempt

Healers on The Mountain
And Other Myths of Native American Medicine

Myths of Magical Native American Women Including Salt Woman Stories

Native American Creation Stories of Family And Friendship
Stories Retold

Pueblo Indian Wisdom
Native American Legends and Mythology

Water Stories of Native American And Asian Indians
Legends of Rain, Rivers and Lakes

Ways of Indian Magic
Indian Legends from the Tewa

GRANGER'S RETURN

A Novel

TERESA PIJOAN

This is a work of fiction. Names, characters, places and incidents either are the product of this author's imagination or are used fictitiously and any resemblance to actual persons, living or dead, business establishments, events or locals is entirely coincidental. The publisher does not have any control over and does not assume any responsibility for author or third party contents.

Cover art by Eric Halberg

Sunstone books may be purchased for educational, business, or sales promotional use.
For information please write: Special Markets Department, Sunstone Press,
P.O. Box 2321, Santa Fe, New Mexico 87504-2321.

eBook 978-1-61139-696-6

Library of Congress Cataloging-in-Publication Data

Names: Pijoan, Teresa, 1951- author.
Title: Granger's return : a novel / Teresa Pijoan.
Description: Santa Fe : Sunstone Press, [2023] | Summary: "The prodigal son
returns to the family fold, but this is no joyous family reunion for he is a manipulative murderer out for revenge"-- Provided by publisher.
Identifiers: LCCN 2023009609 | ISBN 9781632935335 (paperback) | ISBN 9781632937025 (hardcover) |ISBN 9781611396980 (epub)
Subjects: LCGFT: Novels.
Classification: LCC PS3572.A4365 G728 2023 | DDC 813.6--dc23
LC record available at https://lccn.loc.gov/2023009609

WWW.SUNSTONEPRESS.COM
SUNSTONE PRESS / POST OFFICE BOX 2321 / SANTA FE, NM 87504-2321 /USA
(505) 988-4418

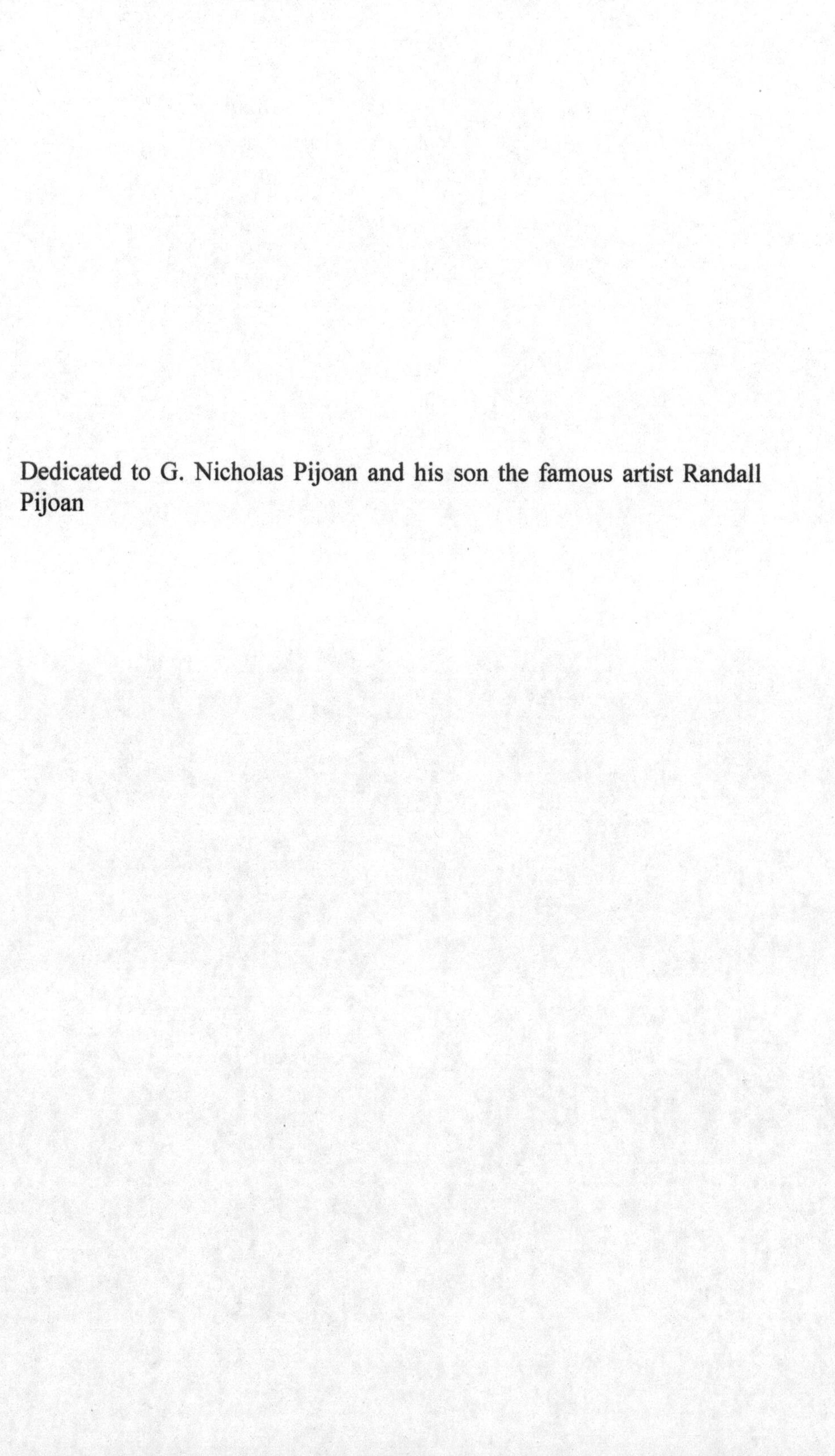

Dedicated to G. Nicholas Pijoan and his son the famous artist Randall Pijoan

Acknowledgements:

Diana Godinez for giving the world a clear vision of life; Cindy Clonch for her knowledge regarding drugs and herbs; Jorge Sedas, MD for his wisdom regarding medicine and physical ailments; Patricia I. Tapia for reading and rereading then editing this work; Nicole D. Garling for her patience while helping to type this work; Devin Casamero for his ability at humor and herbology; April M. Fitzner who holds the ears and eyes of the fields; Josefa Tarin who is a wizard with numbers and people;

And for the Mystery Men who make it possible for books to be published and for their ability to listen and give wisdom. You are the best.

"Life should be an aim unto itself; a purpose unto itself."
—Michel Montaigne

"There is no more beautiful life than that of a carefree man. Lack of care is a truly painless evil."
—Sophocles

Preface

Rosa washed the pinto beans in the yellow colander. The plump brown beans had soaked overnight. The pot was filled with hot water, on the stove that had started to boil as she dumped the beans into it. Bending low, Rosa turned the heat down. This would allow the beans to simmer throughout the day. At four o'clock she would add skinned green chili pods with the minced pork and carrots. This would be their typical Monday dinner. Her husband Roberto would be home from his work at the Senora's by five-thirty today. Together they would fry up the tortillas to sit down for this dinner. Their Monday evening feast was traditional.

The sharp knife felt heavy in her grip. It was sharp as it sliced through the fat onion with ease. Paper thin onion strips lay on the wooden cutting board. Opening her hand, Rosa smiled to see the letters R. M. burnt into the wooden handle. Roberto and their oldest son Berto had once spent a morning outside their small Mexican home with a magnifying glass and the sun to engrave their initials on all the wooden utensils and wooden handled tools. Rosa dropped the knife onto the counter. Studying the day outside the kitchen window, she noticed how still the air was. The sun broke through the clouds. The roses were blooming by the short fence in front. Gladiolas were still worrying about blooming. A neighbor's dog gave a short bark.

Metal smells of death permeated her nostrils. Her boys, both boys, were dead now. Not men anymore in her memory, but boys. Berto became an avid reader of Bible stories at the age of nine. Everyone said he was a bright boy to read so well at such a young age. His long curly hair fell over his forehead as his large brown eyes fell in love with God. Uncle Ishmael had given Berto a silver cross for his birthday when he was eleven and Berto wore it everywhere hanging from his neck by a long leather strip. Shoes had been a problem for those long legs with brown ankles bare between pant leg and shoe top. Berto had grown tall by the age of fourteen. Rosa smiled. It was Christmas after church at her parent's home. The tall backed wooden chair with wooden slats painted in colorful flowers and a woven cane seat was pushed back from the large round table. All sixteen of the family were sitting, eating, talking with love. The chair's movement had caught Emmanuel's grandfather's attention. The old man picked up his spoon to ding it against his water glass.

Nodding at Berto, Emmanuel spoke, "Hush, our grandson has an announcement to make."

Berto returned the nod to his grandfather. The metal smell. Sharp and intense was all Rosa could remember. His body laid out in the open casket for everyone to pray. Silence had filled the church where Berto wanted to be priest. Her beautiful little boy. Shaking her head with the odor of the onions permeating the small kitchen, she wondered what had returned that memory. Her hand felt the knife. It was sharp, very sharp still. Five knife stabs into Berto's chest and abdomen, he had bled out in the sacristy of the old church. Drugs. A gang of drug hungry youths wanted the donation money. Berto had confronted them. Her little boy of twenty one bled to death on the holy floor of the sacristy, alone.

Boiling water brought her back to the present. How alone they were here. Roberto and Rosa both in their fifties, alone. Little Manuel had gone soon after. How big he thought he was bragging to everyone that he knew who had knifed his brother. Little Manuel determined to find and kill his big brother's murderers. Caught in the night as he came home from a friend's party, kneeling in the dirt beside a stranger's wall, shot. The gun had been placed against the back of his head with no one to stop them. Quick kill, the cops said. It was quick, no pain. Little Manuel was only nineteen and ready to marry his sweetheart. A white coffin. No open funeral this time. No chance to see his face one last time. Flowers covered the full length of his plot the day after the funeral. One child left.

Ice tinkled in the glass as Rosa drank more of her herbal tea. The taste was nasty. She should live for her husband. They only had one another. The kitchen was full of humidity from the boiling water that cooked the pinto beans. Onions were tilted from the wooden cutting board into the bubbling water. Such grief was hard to survive. Roberto was her worry now. His face had aged. His hands shook and his eyes spoke volumes of pain. Their daughter Celestina had been their only joy left.

Celestina had Roberto's eyes and his laugh. Somehow she had allowed the death of her older brothers to wash over her. Fiestas, dinners and dances filled Tina's life. Stories of her social life entertained them each morning. Then fear. Tina's best friend was killed after a party at a fancy home not far from where they lived. Roberto wrote letters to his cousins who lived in New Mexico. Letters from New Mexico arrived with money, maps and plans. Rosa worked at a school and at night she took English classes. Roberto refused. He was a proud macho Mexican and there was no way he was going to speak English. People in New Mexico were Spanish. They spoke Spanish, he would be fine, just fine.

Jokes were told about migrants who tried to get into the United States. Her brother the priest kept telling the joke over and over about the two men with no education or skills. "These two men stood at the border. The Border guard asked the first one, "What would you do if you entered the U.S.?" The man said, "I cut wood. I can saw any type of wood. I'm your hombre for cutting wood." The border guard turned him away. The second man was asked the same question. He answered in his best English, "I pile it. I can pile it really good." The border guard was impressed, "We can use good pilots. Come ahead." Her brother had laughed and laughed. At the time she didn't believe his joke to be funny, but his laughter was contagious.

No cars were allowed. They were told if they drove to the border, the guards would take their car's title and as they filled out papers, the cars were stolen. If they had no title, there was no proof the car was theirs. Two thousand dollars was put into an envelope. Dollars not pesos were used by the Coyotes who helped them cross from Juarez into El Paso. Trucks, hotter than anyone thought possible closed and shuttered, drove for hours to an unknown town. Stale air and body smells filled their noses and their pores. Released, they were given water and a small paper bag of junk food and a chance to use a portable toilet. Tina was on her period and knew her body stank, but there was no place to wash. Another truck arrived. People jumped from the open back gasping for air. A mother held her dead small son in her arms.

Four days of travel. Roberto said if he would have driven they would have done it in one day. Eight hours was all it would have taken, but instead they had four days of being cramped in with strangers, sweating, hungry and tired. In Juarez the Coyote had given them papers. They were false documents. All three walked across the border in their filthy clothes with U.S. citizenship papers. Rosa knew she should be scared, but she was too tired to feel anything. Tina held her breath and Roberto spoke for all of them, "U.S. citizens." Water flowed easily under the bridge as they walked into America. There on the other side, anxiously waiting were Roberto's cousins. Aged great grandparents with white hair and wrinkles opened their arms to them. It was a year later, they were both dead from heart failure.

Beautiful Celestina melded with her peers. Her long red hair flowing around her shoulders. Young men fancied her. Other young women loved her free spirit. Only one man took her heart. He was a Gringo with lots of money and a nice car. Flowers arrived for her. A ring was placed on her finger when she turned twenty one. Roberto frowned at the wedding. His parents had insisted on paying for the bride's dress of layered white taffeta embroidered with pearls. The Methodist church was decked with flowers of every color. Roberto frowned even more. Tina changed religions, saying, "God lived in every person not in the name of just one religion." Berto would have been shocked to hear his sister speak such blasphemy. People came from all over to attend. Rosa and Roberto were the only Mexicans invited. Roberto didn't want to go. He was coerced with tears and promises of eternal love.

A black tuxedo was rented for Roberto. Strutting in the kitchen, he said he felt like a rooster with tail feathers. Rosa wore her old blue dress from her mother's Easter party several years ago. The black flats were polished, but they were worn and tired. Party goers flooded the recreational hall at the edge of Fourth Street. There were so many who drank and yelled. Tina had wanted to dance, but her new husband was too drunk to stand. Five months later it was over. Celestina's marriage ended. The pregnancy brought anger and threats. Her husband accused her of being disloyal, unfaithful. The phone call in the middle of the night crying. She was gasping for help, "Mama, help me! Help!"

Roberto drove through two red lights. Rosa's hands tensed in her lap. Roberto swearing under his breath, "I will kill that pendejo if he hurts my querida!" Landscape lights were blinding over the fancy garage door outside Tina's home. Running to the house's front door, it was locked. Roberto raced to the backyard, screaming Tina's name. Locked. A patio chair was thrown through the sliding glass door. Entry. The front door was flung open for Rosa as they ran to the back bedroom. Tina was on the floor. Blood gushed from between her legs. The toilet in the master bathroom flushed. Kenneth wavered in the doorway, "What the fuck are you doing here! Get the fuck out of my house, you dirty Mexicans!" Quickly, he turned to gag into the toilet.

Kneeling beside Tina, Rosa screamed. Her lively beautiful daughter was not breathing. Not missing a beat, Roberto called 911 using his best English he ordered an ambulance. Red and blue lights flashed, an ambulance siren echoed awake the wealthy neighborhood. Police held pistols on them as they entered the bedroom. Kenneth finally stepped from the bathroom. "They killed her. They're dirty Mexicans." Handcuffs, stinky cop cars and being separated into different stark white rooms, left Rosa feeling dead herself. A female cop found Tina's letter. It was on the bedside table. Tina had written it to send to Rosa telling of the verbal abuse, beatings and threats given to her by Kenneth. Fear was ripe in the letter accusing her drunken husband of his impotency when drunk. His shame of having to be totally dependent on his parents. Tina's words described her fear of Kenneth's beatings on her unborn child.

United after hours of dark pain at the police station, the two parents were released to return to Tina's home. They sat in the truck staring at the fancy house. Celestina had been so proud of her new home with all of the fancy utilities and she had had her own maid. Her body had been beaten to death. The unborn grandchild was dead. Somehow they drove home in the early morning. Roberto stopped talking or eating. He lost his job with the highway department. Rosa's crazy hippy neighbor got her a job at the high school cafeteria. There were bills to pay and they needed to take Celestina's body and her baby home to Mexico for the burial in sacred ground beside her brothers. Money was needed to live.

A car honked outside. Rosa shook her head to take another drink of herbal tea. Puckering her lips at the awful taste she thought of Roberto now. He had a good job working for three elderly Senoras. Working outside always made him happier and these older women paid well. They were old, but they were alive. Memories kept them going and Roberto took good care of all three women. Rosa had met them all briefly.

After another sip of the tall glass filled with ice and herbal tea, Rosa suddenly felt very tired. Their trip to Mexico had been a whirlwind visit since the Senoras only allowed Roberto three days off from work. The elderly women had been generous. The oldest woman gave them an envelope with three hundred dollars. Roberto did everything for this Senora since she had been home from the hospital. Senora Pino had helped Roberto learn English, helped him read the questions on the forms and let him borrow her truck for his citizenship swearing in at the courthouse. The citizenship party afterwards at Rosa's tiny adobe home had been grand. Neighbors and friends had arrived with their children to liven the festivities with a piñata and games. People overflowed into the dirt road in front of their house. Potluck food was rich and the leftovers had lasted them for days. Roberto's job at the elderly women's farms had been a godsend. Now they had money for the mortgage and the donations of money as extra gifts had helped on their trip south.

The aftertaste of the tea was awful, she winced as her tongue wanted to reject the liquid. Yerbas Medicinales were supposed to help her diabetes and high blood pressure. The elderly Senora Pino found the package in her cupboard and had given it to Roberto when he had expressed concern over Rosa's health issues. Evidently, the deceased husband had been a doctor who used herbs to cure many of his patients and this packet had been sitting in her cupboard waiting for her to use. Maybe Rosa should have shown the brown paper package to her priest. The neighbor Peggy might have misread the label. Peggy and her husband Carl were what

Roberto referred to as old hippies. Peggy's Spanish was learned eons ago in secondary school, but she seemed confident translating the directions.

The glass of herbal tea was placed on Rosa's small kitchen table. Every cell in Rosa's body felt swollen and tired. Exhausted. Smiling, she remembered the trip to Palma Azul and her parent's home. They were legal U.S. citizens now. Passports in her purse were proof. The bus ride south to El Paso had been lovely. She and Roberto had three seats in their row all to themselves. The packed homemade burritos were eaten before they arrived at the bus station. Her two cousins met the bus, helped them get their one suitcase into the old beat up Datsun. Singing songs they crossed the Juarez border into her country. Mexico. Home. Laden with presents from the cousins to her parents, they boarded the train. Chickens in cages, skinny dogs with rope leashes and crying children traveled cramped in their railroad car all the way to Villa Hermosa.

As the train entered the station, Roberto had held her plump waist as Rosa stuck her upper torso out of the train's window to search for her parents. There they were frantically waving. Her mother had tears in her eyes. Her father's face beamed with joy. Laughing and talking one over the other they had arrived home in her father's old truck. Rosa's youngest nephew Tino was in the kitchen studying for an engineering exam. Smiling, she remembered how young he was to be a college student. Her older sister had had four children. All of them had grown to adults.

Tino decided to live with his grandparents and go to the University in Mexico City. He had earned a scholarship and loved learning. Roberto had taken some of the three hundred dollars and he bought a cellphone in Villa Hermosa to take memory photos of the family. At this moment, right now, in her small kitchen Rosa wanted to hold the cellphone and stare at her parents in the photos. Each cell in her body felt bloated and heavy. Shuffling to the stove, she spooned two large spoonfuls of lard into the simmering beans. As she tapped the wooden spoon against the side of the pot, a piece of lard fell onto her barefoot. The sandals no longer fit. Her feet were swollen and ached when confined in shoes. Roberto thoughtfully bought her the sandals at the train station on the way north.

Roberto's feet were deformed from race horses stepping on them when he was a trainer for the Jefe in Mazatlán. The trainer had hired a shoemaker to design and sew special boots for Roberto, but then after their wedding Roberto had decided his feet had taken enough abuse. How handsome Roberto was back then. Back then, she was the plump housecleaner. The mayor's home was spotless for his two sons. The clothes of the rich family were washed, ironed, mended and proudly neat thanks to Rosa. Those days were crazy and fun with Rosa making the money while husband with bad feet stayed home to raise their children.

Now, Roberto was making twenty dollars an hour working for the elderly Senoras. He referred to them as the widowed women. He worked their old horses, cleaned the stalls and barns, fed chickens, and even walked one woman's dog. When they had parties he helped by sweeping the dirt around the farmhouses to keep them free from weeds and debris as well as helping with housecleaning. Certainly he was earning his wages.

Maybe the herbal tea was working, but Rosa felt tired, very tired. Hairpins were pulled from the tight braids wrapped around her head. Suddenly, she sat down in the wooden chair at the table. The straight back was uncomfortable, but she could no longer stand. Lifting her heavy arms, she crossed them on the table in front of her. Sunshine out the kitchen window reminded her of the beautiful flower garden of her father. The bougainvillea grew up and over the north side of her parents' large hacienda. Pastel pink blossoms had fluttered in the evening breeze. Hibiscus flowers bloomed all around her parent's picnic table. Tears formed in her eyes, she missed her mother the most. Her plump mother who sang the old songs as she danced on the back portal, swinging Rosa in a twirl. Everyone said that Rosa and her mother looked like twins with their sparkling brown eyes, flat noses and perfect teeth. Both of the women braided their long hair and wrapped it around their head to keep it off their necks. Home felt far away, too far.

Her attention returned to the beans simmering on the stove. Rosa thought for a brief moment that they should be stirred, but she couldn't move. "I'm a fifty-eight year old woman." Feeling too heavy to sit upright, she bent forward to rest her head on her folded arms. Her body was exhausted. She attempted to reach for her herbal tea, but her arm wouldn't move. Brown eyes shut. Breathing stopped. By four o'clock the beans were burned and the kitchen was filled with smoke. Monday night dinner was ruined.

1

Driving south out of the huge city of Albuquerque, Sophia studied the interstate. Eighteen wheelers roamed down this interstate roaring their way to Socorro and the railyards. The long straight stretch of gray asphalt shot due south without wavering thanks to the highway department who dynamited the lava mesas. She smiled remembering her Tio Manuel's visit several years ago. Her uncle Manuel had clapped his hands when he saw the never ending flatland of brown earth surging all the way to the horizon. The landscape flowed nonstop to the eastern high mountains. He laughed saying, "An ocean of brown flows across this desert, how fine! This is an ocean with rabbit bush, chamisa, and dwarfed juniper trees and it goes on forever!"

She had never thought of this flatland as an ocean, but certainly it did have waves engraved by the blowing winds through the caliche dirt. The ripples in the dirt appeared as wavelike features only interrupted with bovine hoof prints and well placed cow paddies. The reservation owned by the Isleta Pueblo proper held the land sacred. There were no buildings, no off ramps leading to picnic hideaways. The casino brought in the high stakes money. High flying ravens, a solitary pair flew in the high wind currents, weaving in and out amongst the cloudscape above them. The long drive with Uncle Manuel had given her a different perspective of her land.

He had remarked at the beauty of the unmarked landscape that went forever, long and flat until it dipped over the edge of the earth. Then the mountains appeared on the right with the ancient dead volcanoes. The vista was interrupted by the metropolis of Albuquerque. Manuel decided then that he wanted to fix her girls a spectacular Argentinian dinner. Driving to the turnoff close to the high mountain forest, they had turned with the traffic into their small town of Rincon. Manuel had remarked about the tall ancient cottonwood trees and the spindly growth of the tamarisk trees. Taking the bridge over the interstate into Rincon, he was amazed at the small trickle of water in the famous Rio Grande. Once in town, Manuel had insisted on walking down the sidewalk to peer into all the shops' windows. They had only entered one other shop beside the grocery store and that was to buy a tall Kachina doll carved from a cottonwood root for his new wife who was sixteen years younger than he.

In the grocery store, Manuel was taken aback by the lack of fresh produce. Scolding her for not taking her to a better grocery, he had decided to make South American spaghetti with fresh tomatoes, onions, mushrooms and chili. The clothing area in the store fascinated him for he thought in America more people would wear only cotton and not so much nylon. Their dinner that night had been such a delicious feast! Every pot and pan in her kitchen had been used. Sophia's daughter Sybil had contributed by making flan from the fresh eggs their hens had laid that morning. Manuel was surprised Sybil loved to cook and he complimented her over and over again. In the morning, Sophia had allowed Sybil to stay home from school to show Manuel the sights on horseback.

All three of them had saddled up the horses after brushing the equines down with gusto. Manuel had regaled them about his two oldest sons. Paolo who had just turned seventeen and was interested in becoming either a medical doctor or a veterinarian and loved being outdoors and his next oldest Carlo who wanted to become a librarian and had a great love of books. They had cantered down the ditch road only to jump the turnouts when necessary. Then Manuel's voice was lost as he continued to brag to Sybil about his life on the Tung Leaf farm on the hundreds of acres in eastern Argentina. The saplings had been brought over by his grandfather. Tung oil was used in everything from paints to healing oils. Sophia felt he was seriously flirting with his daughter and loved it that Sybil was taking all of his stories in her stride. Once at the river's edge, the talking stopped. The horses walked single file as Manuel watched the long necked cranes wade around the fat geese. Ducks flew beside them for a time and then for some unknown reason would squawk and take flight, spooking the horses.

Manuel's smile never gave way to a frown the whole time he had visited them. When Sybil clicked her tongue to urge her horse Teddy up the side of a foothill, Manuel had challenged her to a race. Shaking her head, Sybil pointed below them at the shifting sands of the barrancas that could leave a horse lame. Zigzagging down the foothill, Sybil led them to the Lost Miner's Cave. This was one of Sybil's favorite haunts. Flinging her leg over her horse's rump, Sybil jumped down. Teddy stood stock still with his head hanging low. This gelding was well trained to not move until spoken to or led by his reins. Manuel cautiously dismounted, watching Sybil as she raced up the side of the sandy foothill to disappear into a cave. He had turned to nod at Sophia who had laughed and pointed to the cave. Sophia had chosen to remain mounted, for Sybil would tell Manuel the story of the Lost Miner and she didn't need her mother there to guide her words. Sophia knew that every time Sybil told the story, she would change it to make it spookier or more frightening as it fit her mood.

Sybil's story had certainly worked its charm, for soon Manuel had raced out of the cave with his eyes sparkling and his hands in the air, shouting wildly. "Your daughter knows how to scare an old man!" He had quickly mounted his mare and was turning her in circles until Sybil stepped from the cave. "Mom, the lost miner is still in there only now he is screaming for help!"

Sophia had shaken her head, "I'm not going in there to hear him! Come let's ride our way home for the sky is turning gray."

They had galloped along the river's edge, cantered up the ditch road to home. Manuel was not anxious to leave, but he had a necessary flight to Denver for a convention on natural arbor oils. Sybil was given the chores to do while Sophia drove Manuel back to the airport. She hated to see him go for he had brought such joy to their little group. Sophia had wanted Donna to meet him and take the horseback ride with them, but Geoffrey the Divorced One had insisted Donna not miss school. Geoffrey's lawyer had explained how the court judge had asked Donna who she wanted to live with until she was of age to leave home. The lawyer stated emphatically that Donna wanted to live with her Dad during the week and not with her and Sybil. Somehow, Sophia would have made it work. She could have driven Donna to her new private school in Albuquerque, but Geoffrey the Divorced One wouldn't have it and he was paying the tuition for the private school.

Coming back into the present, Sophia slammed the car door hard as she braced herself against the blast of cold wind. The flat parking lot cemented all around the Prison was surrounded by worked farmland. Rains had stopped mid-August and now it being October, the farmland was specked with dried alfalfa fields of gold in rows of brown. A high wire fence surrounded the internal structure of the Minimum Security Prison. The wire reached at least twenty feet high with rolled razor wire at the top. There was a lookout tower in the center of an open area behind the prison of gray cement. Today with the gray-blue of the sky mixed with the washed out fields, the prison blended in with the scenery. Sophia felt her throat constrict as she pulled her plum-red wool beret tight over her ears.

Tall prison walls of cement block gave her a feeling of terror. The thick collar of her heavy beige overcoat pulled up as she stepped purposely into the prison's discharge door. Sophia jerked the heavy metal door open to step inside the front room of gray cement block. The metal door clanged shut to lock behind her. Now she was dedicated to getting Granger released. There was no other way she could leave for the locked door of thick metal had her confined within this space. Ripe body odor confronted her along with the feeling of claustrophobia. She walked directly to the black plastic phone bolted onto the cement wall. Beside the wall phone was another military metal door. It was locked with a stenciled sign: NO PERSONS ALLOWED BEYOND THIS POINT. Sophia had no desire to walk through that door. Turning to the black plastic wall phone, she lifted the handset. A sticky substance coated the handheld device. There was no dial tone. Suddenly a deep male voice barked, "Who are you and who are you waiting for?"

Startled, Sophia answered, "This is Sophia Pino and I am waiting to take my brother Granger Pino out of here." Her voice maintained indifference.

"One moment." There was a bang as the phone was dropped on a hard surface. Voices conferred, then the male voice returned, "He's being processed. Wait for further instruction." Dead sound.

Sophia hung up the phone on the wall cradle. Speaking out loud, she said, "Well, thank you very much and have a lovely day!"

Straight legged she walked back and forth from one cement block wall to the other opposite cement wall. The leather heel of her new boots hammered down on the cement floor. She liked the sound her boots made. A sound of control and power. Walking from the cement wall at the front of the room to the internal cement block wall, she counted six of her long-legged steps. Then she stood in front of the metal door, staring at metal bar across the door. It was shoved into the frame by a mechanism. She decided to shove on the metal bar and see if it would open. It didn't.

Peering at the square glass window panels that had a thick wire mesh behind them, she studied her reflection. There she was a forty-three year old woman with short curly brown hair with streaks of white around her temples. Her hair was held flat with a maroon red wool beret. Her brown eyes were outlined with her latest green eyeliner pencil and her lips were chapped. The skin around her lips and eyes wrinkled when she smiled. Sophia stopped smiling and the wrinkles disappeared. Otherwise she was a medium build, medium height, and middle-aged woman waiting for her medium convict brother who had murdered her father and attempted to murder her mother.

Sophia hugged her brother's black leather jacket. When he was arrested he had worn his every day summer clothes. Today with the north wind blowing in winter he would most certainly need his jacket. Their mother Margaret had insisted Sophia bring this particular jacket. "Leather," her mother had said, "keeps the wind out. It's not that cold, it's just wind. Take the leather jacket, the black one, it's his favorite." Margaret had thrust the jacket at Sophia as she stood in her mother's farmhouse.

The red aluminum walker with the drop seat bent forward held Margaret upright. Granger's loosening of a motor part in Margaret's car had caused their mother's severe accident killing a small girl and physically damaging the other drivers. This accident broke their mother's spine, punctured one of her lungs and ripped her left hip from its socket while smashing her left leg into pieces.

Margaret had insisted Granger was not to blame. Her precious son was not stupid except when it came to vehicle's motors, but he was not responsible for any of the damages. Granger's and Sophia's mother Margaret had, without a thought to finances or the legal system, worked tirelessly to have her perfect Granger released from jail. Most of the money inherited from Margaret's mother and Margaret's deceased husband went into gaining Granger's freedom by hiring expensive lawyers. "Granger is my only son. He cannot be left in jail. We must get him out and have him honor his namesake."

Sophia thought her mother would come with her to retrieve Granger since Margaret had paid handsomely to have Granger legally released early from this minimum security prison. He was being held there for good behavior. Granger had only served six years for attempting to kill their father and the nurse who cared for their father and the vehicle accident on the interstate that almost killed their mother. Those who had actually done the killing at Granger's request were in for twenty years. They had done the deed. Granger's greed had motivated his associates to accomplish what he could not. His health clinic associate and his wife had pointed the finger at Granger giving excellent proof Granger was behind the killings.

Sophia stood straight with her back against the gray cement block wall. Leaning against it, she counted the cement blocks in the wall opposite her. There were twenty-two horizontal blocks. Above her were two florescent lights embedded in the ceiling with wire mesh for protection. There was no chair, there was no furniture. Just the phone bolted into the wall and the two metal doors opposite one another. The one went to freedom outside, the other went to incarceration. Neither would open for both were locked at the moment. Sophia tried to hear noise from inside, but there was only the quiet, not even the outside wind penetrated these cement block walls. Then she noticed high above her in the ceiling, covered with a fine wire was a camera lens. When she moved far to the right, the lens followed.

Sophia walked to the opposite wall, leaned against it to study the opposite block wall. Down by the door leading out to freedom there were colored scratches. They looked like a children's crayon drawing. Probably a creative child with a crayon had waited for a parent to be released with an adult. Too bad they didn't add more color to the drab walls. Sophia thought of the colored pencils in her purse that hung from her shoulder, but the lens was watching. She shook her head as she leaned back to stare at the internal door.

Six years Granger had been imprisoned. He had gravitated toward the other men by somehow manipulating them into doing the dirty for him. Margaret had refused to meet with the psychologist who had notified her of her son Granger's discharge. It had been mandatory for someone from the family to meet before his discharge would be completed. Sophia had gone in her place. "We remember the good ones and somehow we can't forget the bad ones. Your brother Granger Pino will be definitely remembered for being a manipulator. He's a menacing soul. Causes trouble and takes none of the blame. Be sure he checks in with his parole officer regularly and you, yes, you be careful with him. Don't let him control you or push you into something you know in your gut is wrong."

The psychologist shook his head, "He shouldn't be out. He's going to do something again equally vengeful. Yes, you and your family best keep your distance from Granger Pino." The fifty something year old man stood to open the door for her. Thanking him for his advice, she smiled to say, "I was already well aware of Granger since I grew up with him." She departed his office. Now, she was going to bring him out into the world. Her world.

The inner door clicked. Sophia jumped, watching the metal bar slide back from the door frame. Granger appeared, slamming the door open for it to clang against a metal stop. Granger walked out with his head held high. "Hey, here's my baby sister Sophia! You really are a trooper to come and spring me! Thanks." The leather jacket was taken to sling it over his shoulder. "Let's go. I want to never see this place again."

He dipped his head while his eyes darted about. "Come on. We don't have to wait because they didn't find anything in my cell or they wouldn't have opened the door." Granger turned and kicked the locked metal internal door as he whispered in a mocking voice, "But, Sir, I'm innocent." There was a loud click as the outside door jumped open. Granger yelled, "Sophia, let's GO!"

Granger pushed Sophia ahead of him, shoving her out the door. Cold air hit their faces as the wind blew across the flat farmland. "Move, Sophia, for God's sake move!" His eyes narrowed announcing the high mindedness of their owner.

Ten feet from the building, Sophia stopped, "Hey, you're free. We don't need to run. Legally and legitimately you are free!" His pale face was clenched. Large brown eyes glared at her. The prep school hair cut was tussled by the fast flowing air. She noticed tight skin around his eyes and lips. Below his mouth, there was no chin. His body shrunk in on itself, his shoulders rounded. Fists were clenched, "What, Sophia, what?"

"Hey, Granger, it's me, your sister! Can't we at least have a hug or a congratulations?" She worked on her warm smile.

His dark brown eyes glared at her. For the first time she felt frightened of him. Granger grabbed her upper arm, his strong fingers bruised her upper arm through her thick coat. Quickly, his right arm grabbed her shoulders in a dead lock as he pressed her into his ribs. His side hug felt like an attack. Inches from her, Granger's face was cold and hard as the wind, "Where's my Mercedes? You came in my car didn't you?"

Pushing him away from her with all of her might, Sophia jerked free of his arm. "No! No, no, no Mercedes! Hell, no!"

Granger slapped down his leather jacket onto the parking lot tarmac, "What! Sophia, why did you even bother to come and get me! Huh! Why? Where the hell is my Mercedes?" The temper tantrum brought his right foot down as he whirled about in the wind, "Damn! Damn it! Where the hell is my Mercedes!"

Lifting her head high, holding onto her purse's long leather strap, Sophia continued to walk away from him. She shouted over her shoulder, "Fine, you can walk home. I'm leaving for my work is done. You can stay here and have a fit with all these cameras watching you, I'm going!"

Grabbing his leather jacket off of the parking lot tarmac, he raced after her, "Sophia, Sophia, ah, come on! Tell me, tell me, please tell me, where is my Mercedes?"

Sophia shook her head as she hurried to her vehicle, "You want to talk, right? Okay, we'll talk in my SUV. I brought a bag with all of your stuff. Your wallet, some money and your pants pocket things. Just in case you wanted to take me to lunch, you know, since I have been coming to see you for over six years, bringing you toothpaste, cigarettes that you don't smoke and all the other stuff. You know as thanks?" The Amtrak train blew its whistle as it rattled through the small town to the left of the prison.

Sophia shook her head trying to release her anger. She arrived at her pre-owned SUV with its faded yellow paint that was now a dull beige from age. Granger ran up to her to jokingly shove her against the side door, "Hey, you look good for a little sister! How come your hair is curly and mine is straight? Your hair has gray in it and mine is still a fine chestnut brown. What's with that anyway?" He grimaced, "Sophia, please, where's my Mercedes with the gold radials, leather seats and surround stereo sound?"

Clenching her jaw, Sophia stared at him. Calmly, quietly she answered him, "No. No Mercedes. Your car was sold ages ago to help pay for the legal fees to get you out of here." Sophia let her voice rise barely above the wind as she studied Granger. His face had hardened. Lines creased his forehead and his welcome was now harsh.

He pushed his arms into his leather jacket. "What! WAIT! No! I killed for that car! What was mother thinking? All I thought about was having my Mercedes back and my life regained from this place of nothing but losers!" He studied the flat parking lot with its freshly painted white lines, "So which used vehicle is yours?" Walking forcefully away from her down the cement path to the open parking lot, he noticed there were only four vehicles. Two trucks, a VW bug and the yellow SUV where Sophia stood. Disappointment clouded his eyes, "Oh, you came in the classy truck, right?"

Disgusted with his attitude, Sophia clicked her car alarm. The yellow SUV beeped. She opened the driver's door, quickly jumping into the seat. Sophia gripped the indoor handle firmly, pulling the door shut before the wind would take it. Granger stood outside the front passenger door as if waiting for her to open it. Pressing the automatic window down, she called, "Your door is open! Are you going to get in or do you want to stay?"

He jumped into the passenger seat as he tugged on the door. "Sophia, couldn't you get a classier vehicle in your divorce? This is a piece of junk!"

"Granger, close the door! You're really being impossible! I may just leave you here!"

He slammed the vehicle door shut and locked it. Leaning over the middle console, he puckered his lips to peck her on the cheek. "No, you wouldn't leave me because then you would have to come back here every week to visit me. Where's Margaret?" He pivoted to inspect the back of the vehicle. "Why didn't she come? Is she embarrassed by me?"

Shaking her head, Sophia sighed "No, Mom didn't want the hassle of getting her walker in the car and out of the car. That's her excuse. Besides she doesn't care for the wind now that she's fragile. She's very thin as you noticed the last time we came. She needs to be careful with the cold." Sophia put the car in reverse and then drove forward to the main street. "So, where to? Do you want to get a cold beer and see some women? I have four hours until I need to pick up Sybil from middle school."

Granger snapped the seatbelt to stare out the side window as Sophia drove onto the main street, "No alcohol. The prostate surgery turned me off to anything alcoholic, anything with sugar and anything with meat. Glad the surgery was on the government's dime and not mine. Damn, that was an ugly operation."

Turning onto the interstate from the prison road, Granger's smooth sultry voice reminded her of her life of hell. Family duty had slammed her, destroyed her marriage and radically suffocated her. Her brother leaned his elbow on the door's arm rest. "So, what are you thinking about so pensively? You know my life will be filled with the same old story over and over again." Mocking his mother's voice, Granger pursed his lips. "'Granger tinkered with my truck believing it wouldn't start, but it did start. I drove to my now ex-daughter-in-law's home for my little granddaughter Shirley's sixth birthday. We had such a lovely lunch.'"

Flipping his hand from the wrist, Granger continued to mimic his mother, "'Only when I floored the truck to cross the interstate at the base of the Negara hill, my truck died.'" His face took on a strange contortion of horror. Slapping his cheek, he went on, "'my truck died in the middle of the interstate! I was blocking three lanes of fast moving traffic.'" He laughed. "Am I right or am I right? She'll play this for all she's worth with her little girl helpless look. Right?"

Sophia shook her head, "Granger, you are disgusting and it isn't funny! What happened to all those people wasn't a joke!"

He clapped his hands, "Oh, she'll say this over and over again, right?" Then he continued trying to copy his mother's voice, "'Oh, I tried turning the key! I pushed on the gas pedal. The engine did not turn over and the wheels did not move.'" His foot slammed down on the floorboard trying to startle Sophia. She worked at ignoring him.

Continuing in his mother's voice he went on, "Six vehicles plowed into me and my small truck! Bones ripped and broken, ribs pierced lungs and skulls were smashed. Bodies destroyed. Wham!" He slapped his thigh to make the impact. Sophia shook her head to stare ahead as she drove. Granger's voice took on the persona of a television newscaster, "Ladies and gentlemen, when the EMT's arrived the woman was lucid and awake, saying over and over again, 'I turned the key. I am pushing on the gas pedal, the engine will not turn over and the wheels aren't moving. The EMT's had to remove the key from the ignition for the elderly woman wouldn't let go.'""

Poking Sophia in the arm, Granger's voice took on an accusatory tone, "You know Mother Margaret is going to say this to everyone when we are together in public? 'Please, please, turn over! Please, please, wheels move!'" Granger laughed at his own cleverness.

Shaking her head, Sophia swallowed hard, "You've been practicing this in prison?"

"Damn right! I entertained the other criminals. I'm a hard ass rightly so!"

Tumbleweeds blew across the highway. Dark clouds hovered over the Sandia Mountains. Eighteen wheelers roared around her as they sped north to their destination in a hurry. A gust of wind blew sand from the flatland to pelt the passenger side of the vehicle. Glancing into her side mirror, Sophia remembered the courtroom photos of her mother's body that showed blood oozing from Margaret's left shoulder and side. It was only when the EMT's had parked in front of the hospital emergency room area that Margaret finally fell into a coma and they had called Sophia. Duty, a life of duty came to Sophia. Life radically shifted, dropped, ripped and plummeted from the reality Sophia had known for fourteen years as an adult daughter and a happily married wife in her middle thirties into hell.

Six years and seven months ago, it was at the hospital where Granger was arrested for attempted manslaughter. Followed by court room proceedings that were a nightmare with lawsuit after lawsuit. Sophia was the only family member available to be legally responsible. Granger had power of attorney for their mother, but he was on trial for murder. Granger's ex-wife Emily and his daughter would have none-of-it. Sophia sat alone in the courtroom watching family after family relate their horror of the accident, of families' medical bills and of their tragedies caused by Granger. No amount of money would compensate for these people's losses. How the families had glared at her. Some had even come up to her with threatening anger while others had come to her and spoke of how horrible her brother was. She did not deny this. No, there was no way she could deny this.

In the courtroom Granger sat at the front table with the insurance carrier's lawyer. His face chiseled as if in stone. A handsome man in his late thirties dressed in his expensive suit and dark blue tie with polished black shoes. Sophia believed her father Dr. Mark Pino would have been proud to see how fine Granger appeared in this professional setting. Yet what a complete disappointment Granger would be to her father as the loser who not only brought about Papa's death, but had tried to kill Margaret as well. Between the court dates and her mother's needs in the hospital, Sophia felt lost. Where was she in all of this? She had two daughters who needed her. She had a husband who all of sudden decided he could no longer be part of the Pino clan.

Geoffrey who had been her rock through so much of her life finally chose anger and hostility. No longer would he help her with the girls. No longer would he share his day with them, but instead drank miniatures of bourbon, lots of small whiskey bottles rolled around on the floor of his truck. Geoffrey's anger came fast and crazy with no warning. One morning as Sophia was combing Donna's hair in the bathroom, they heard Geoffrey screaming in the kitchen. Racing down the hall, they came face to face with Geoffrey holding a coffee mug filled with boiling hot water. He was ready to pour it on top of the puppies who were dutifully sitting as ordered.

Sophia had grabbed Geoffrey's wrist as he was about to pour the hot water over the puppies. "What are you doing? What is this?" She carefully held his wrist still away from the puppies.

"Hell, this pup dug up my vegetable garden. Ripped the plants right out of the ground, damn dog!" Geoffrey flung his hand free from her hold on his wrist. Hot water flew out of the mug onto the floor behind her. Donna screamed as the boiling hot water landed on her bare leg.

"Get out!" Sophia yelled at Geoffrey. "Get out and stay out until you can be human again! Go! How dare you!"

Donna raced back into her room and had slammed the door. Hesitantly, Sybil stood in the hall outside of her room to stare at her parents. Quietly, Geoffrey shoved the puppy with his foot into the living room. "Sophia, you and your damn dogs and your spoiled daughters can go to hell! I've had enough of the Pino's." He had grabbed his satchel from the couch and walked out the front door, slamming it behind him.

Shaking, Sophia had returned the empty coffee mug to the kitchen sink. She watched as Geoffrey drove out of the driveway onto the dirt road. Then she burst into tears. Sybil had come up behind her putting her arms around her mother's waist. "Mom, don't worry. We're here for you. Dad's a drunk and he's not paying the bills."

Sophia turned to kneel by her oldest daughter. "Honey, your father is under a lot of stress. This trouble with your Uncle Granger is making us all crazy."

Sybil shook her head, "Mom, no. Dad got a call yesterday from Grandma Margaret's lawyer. I answered the phone in the kitchen when he picked it up there in his office. The lawyer told Dad he was going to be taken to court because he hasn't paid one dime on this house's mortgage to Grandma Margaret since we moved here."

Twisting, Sophia had fallen to the floor with her knees popping. "What? What do you mean? Daddy hasn't paid on our mortgage to Grandma Margaret?"

Sybil lifted her mother's hands, "Mom, the floor is dirty with mud from the puppies. I think you should get up now."

Standing, Sophia's emotions had caved in on her. Quickly going to the black plastic wall phone, she dialed a number she knew well. Her mother's lawyer Mr. Kramer's secretary answered on the second ring. Sophia quizzed her about the mortgage and as she listened, she stared at Sybil. "Thank you, Carla."

Sybil stared at her mom, "Well, what did she say?"

Gulping for air, Sophia pulled out a kitchen chair to abruptly sit, "Sybil, this is grown up stuff, but, but, yes. Dad has told me over and over again how short of money we are since he has to pay such a huge mortgage payment to the Pino family. Yet, in the three years we have lived here, he hasn't made one payment. Carla felt I should come in and speak with Mr. Kramer. This court business is expensive and he needs Dad to make a payment or else…."

Donna came into the kitchen. Her face was red from crying. She held a wet washcloth against her leg. "Mom, I think I have a bad burn." The six year old pointed to her leg just below her knee. Pink socks were turned at the ankle. Sophia took the washcloth from Donna to study the dark red mark on her daughter's leg. "Oh, dear. Yes, we had better call your pediatrician. Let's put cold water on it and a bandage." Donna's freckles covered her face. The puckered lips of the unhappy daughter reflected Sophia's life. Motherhood took over in automatic control along with the crazy unconscious days of fixing breakfast, packing lunches, driving the girls to school, driving to court to sit and watch other people's pain being played out. Then her cellphone would chirp and her mother needed toothpaste at the hospital and when was Sophia coming to talk to the doctor who would be in Margaret's room around lunch time.

Lawyers filled the empty spaces of Sophia's private time. Divorce. Geoffrey's hate and greed hit her like a ton of bricks. This man who was the father of her two daughters, a man she had loved and chosen for a life partner was now her enemy. His lies came out. He was spending huge amounts of money, but he wouldn't tell anyone on what. There was no energy to fight. Geoffrey got the house with an outside mortgage lender. He wanted everything except Sophia's and the girls' clothes and Sophia could keep the preowned SUV. The children would stay with her to have visitation with him one weekend a month.

Sophia had studied her husband Geoffrey's face as he turned red when he yelled about his rights, his ownership of their past and his disgust with her family. He sat in a slightly stiff manner on the attorney's upholstered chair. The room was a shade of beige up to waist height and then a shade of pale yellow above that to the tiled ceiling. The floor was covered by a hardwearing carpet of beige. The room was quite small, about fifteen feet by fifteen feet. Geoffrey sat filled with his anger, he was tall and balding, with squared gold rimmed spectacles holding thick lenses. Geoffrey was almost at state retirement age. The loose fitting Green Bay Packard jacket was unzipped, hanging loose open to his woolen brown plaid shirt. The buttons were not in order as he had buttoned it. Geoffrey's brown corduroy trousers were wrinkled and on his feet were heavy black shoes. Sophia said nothing as his lawyer handed papers to her lawyer. She agreed to his demands. She signed the papers and walked away from this strange person who was once her best friend. The reality of being alone hit her when she walked down the steps out of the lawyer's office. Hugging her coat tightly around her, she stared at the city as if for the first time. When her vision perceived her vehicle, she wanted to hold onto it as if it were her only friend at the moment. Behind her the heavy wooden door opened, Geoffrey and his lawyer were laughing and shaking hands. Sophia ran to the SUV, beeped it open and jumped in to sit and stare. "The girls, the girls must be told!" But at that moment her mind went blank, empty, nowhere to go. There was a huge hole in her life.

Sophia's bank account was her own for her father had engrained in her to maintain her own private financial life even while married. At the time, she had thought her father callous and cold, but now she was appreciative of his wisdom. Sophia was a full professor at the university and Geoffrey had agreed to pay her alimony. The lawyer had insisted on it as well as child support. Again, Geoffrey fought for her to not receive half of his social security when of age. The lawyers explained to him, he had no authority to withhold this money. It was hers. After all she had taken care of him for fourteen years. That had been her job and she was deserving of it. The lawyers with Geoffrey had given Sophia and the daughters exactly one month to move out, find a new home and depart from his life. Go!

Feeling motion beside her, she jerked. Granger's voice brought her back into focus. "Hey! Sophia, where are you girl?" He put his hand on hers as she held the steering wheel. "Wow, you're like a million miles away!"

Her voice was terse, "Oh, yes, Granger, I was miles away remembering how you arrived in prison and now you're here in the vehicle with me in my vehicle after six years and seven months, right?"

Granger's left leg began to shake as it did when he was nervous, "Let's not talk about prison. Hey, I'm out and not going back there. So, where are we going now?" Patting his midsection he added, "You know I really could use some green chili and a tall glass of cold lemonade. How about the Ristro for lunch and I'll buy?"

Sophia turned to quickly study him, "Wow, you'll buy, huh? Have you even opened the bag there by your feet to check out the contents? Maybe you should be sure you have enough money. That place isn't cheap. Check out the bag." She pointed to a white plastic bag on the floorboard between his feet.

The bag was retrieved and the wallet opened. Flipping it to his driver's license, he was pleasantly surprised, "Hey, I can still drive. Good for me, I was ever so thoughtful to get my license for eight years. It was expensive, but now I am pleased I put out the cash for this." Searching further into the plastic bag, he opened his black leather wallet. "Mother Margaret put five twenties in here. We can afford lunch and then some." Twisting in the seat, he lifted his butt to shove the wallet into the back pocket of his pants. He turned to her, "When did mom decide she wanted everyone to call her Margaret?"

Studying the traffic as she drove onto the interstate, Sophia shook her head, "What a day that was. I raced to the hospital when I received the call they were discharging her. I was cleaning her bedroom at her farm. Granger, that house of mom's is a mess. She has mice living under the brick floors and in her lower desk drawer. They're eating all of her cancelled checks and making a huge nest in the drawer next to her bed. Her room reeks of mouse poop and pee. I was putting the vacuum away when she called."

Clicking his tongue, Granger interrupted her, "She loves those mice. I hope you didn't get rid of them?"

Grimacing, Sophia shook her head, "No, they're still there. But she called and I drove. Her orders are to be fulfilled. Running down the corridor to her hospital room, I passed the discharge nurse. For some reason I stood outside the hospital door to her room and I froze in fear." She put on the blinker and moved over three lanes of the highway to take the exit ramp into Rincon. "Granger, now that she's home she is more demanding than ever. At least when she was in the hospital she was taken care of by the nurses and had three meals a day."

Suddenly, Granger slammed the dash, "Stop! Sophia, stop!" Two things happened instantly. The radio screamed out a song and Sophia put her foot on the brake to hurriedly slow down. She checked all rearview mirrors. "What? Where, why should I stop?" She drove the vehicle onto the shoulder of the off ramp and stopped way over on the dirt shoulder. The passenger side tire was almost in a small arroyo beside the runoff from the road.

Rolling down his window, Granger shook his head as his voice softened, "No, I didn't mean for you to stop! I just don't want to hear about Margaret!" Grinding his teeth, Sophia flinched. He continued, "You know she said the hospital was a prison for her! She had it easy compared to what I went through! Please! Don't talk about how difficult life was then or now, please!" Tall chamisa blew wildly beside the passenger door. Yellow pollen blew from the long stems. The shorter rabbit bush flayed as the wind ripped at the stalks. Cold air filled the cab of the vehicle. Fluffy gray clouds floated high above them. The dirt brown landscape filled the horizon.

Groaning, he went on, "You weren't stuck in prison and you weren't cut into by angry surgeons who wanted to castrate you! It was hell and beyond. One of the worst levels of Dante's hell! Man, I don't know if I can ever have sex again." His fingers pushed his brown bangs back from his face, "You women have it easy, because…"

"Hey, enough! I'm taking you back to Margaret's. Enough of this discussion. There are some things I seriously do not need to know. Even if I am your sister, I don't want to know." The blinker on, she merged back onto the small highway going through Rincon. "Granger, damn it! You scared me by screaming! Please, let's not have an accident!" Turning her head, Sophia glared at him.

Silence filled the cab. Silence pushed them apart as daggers of emotion were felt. Granger stared out the passenger window at the blowing tumbleweeds. "You know if we don't get some rain soon we won't have any irrigation water. It looks like the world is already drying up and blowing away." Sophia studied the cars racing the other way to get onto the interstate. Heavy gray clouds floated in front of the sun darkening the foothills and the tall Sandia Mountain to their right. The siblings sat inches apart, yet were miles distant. Raw cold emotion resonated within the vehicle. Granger reached into the white plastic bag for his watch. They both heard its loud ticking as he attached it to his wrist.

"Hah!" Granger let out a deep guttural laugh. "It would be best if she just died. Why can't the woman just die! She's a burden to all of us. But, hey, she who holds the purse strings is she who holds the power, right?"

Sophia stared into the middle rearview mirror. She didn't want Granger in her vehicle. She didn't want to know him, be related to him or be nice to him. Slowly, she lifted her hand to turn off the radio. The sound was now of static. It was irritating. "You're not going to kill our mother and you know it!"

"No, I don't know it. There are many ways to kill someone that are untraceable. I learned this in prison. It's amazing what knowledge can be gleaned while hanging out with druggies, murderers and rapists."

Clicking her tongue, Sophia admonished him, "No, I don't believe you have the courage to kill the woman who gave birth to you. I don't."

The passenger window lifted with his pushing the automatic button, "Hell, yes! Suffocation is brutal and I think too kind. Then there is the stabbing and the shooting of people." He waved his hand in the air, "Did you know that on television when they shoot someone and they promptly fall over, that isn't true. People don't just BAM fall over dead. The blood and oxygen has to stop in the brain. It can take hours for someone to die from a bullet, it's painful and awkward."

Clearing his throat, he illustrated further, "A knife wound has to be precise. You can't just stab someone willy-nilly. There is an art to it. A vital organ or a major artery is a must in the attempt. No, the best and the absolute best way is using poison. When you poison someone it can takes months, sometimes years, but the end result is the same. Death. Lovely, innocent death. No one would be able to prove who or when the person was poisoned. Sophia, did you know there are some poisons that cannot be traced?"

Words were spit out of her mouth, "Granger, really? You're planning on killing your mother with poison? Seriously?" Sophia glanced in the rearview mirror, "I thought poison was a woman's choice for murder?"

"Well, no, men can poison people, too, and that's the beauty of it. The law will believe a woman poisoned the victim. One has to be patient using poison for death does not happen right off the bat. You see it has to be tried and proven to work? One can't just go out and pick Datura to put into tea or something. It has a rancid taste and would be best tested with different foods or drinks. One has to figure which poison to use. There are even legal medications one can use. Too much of a good thing can kill a person." He rubbed his hands together, "Would you mind turning on the heater? Does this old can of junk have a heater?"

Her fingers turned the silver knob under the dashboard from vent to heater with the fan on full. The air blasted Granger's face. "Yes, I guess the heater works, huh?" He turned the vent slats away from him.

Sophia remained quiet. Rincon village was twenty minutes south of Margaret's farmhouse. Granger reached forward and turned the radio to play music. He flipped from station to station until Sophia put her hand on his to say, "What are you doing? Can't you leave things well enough alone?"

"Oh, you mean like you?" The radio was turned off. Granger's voice became soft, smooth and empathetic, "Sorry, I didn't mean to be nasty about your divorce. Sorry, but I knew eventually you would not be able to live with Geoffrey. How're the girls?" The automatic window button was pushed to let in cold air.

Sophia stared straight ahead as she drove. Granger mocked her in a high pitched voice, "'Granger, they're doing all right. Sybil is soon to be fifteen years old and is helping me with the horse boarding and Donna is moody, she wants to stay with her father. Donna was twelve years old last month and she's a pistol. Donna wants to become a vet. Sybil wants to be independent and powerful like all the Pino's.'"

Sophia shook her head. "Granger, you're disgusting. Absolutely disgusting."

He sat sideways in his seat to stare at Sophia, "So, what is old Geoffrey doing now? Is he still busy with his designs and inventions? He really is a dry bird, Sophia."

As they drove through the outskirts of Rincon, Sophia pulled into a parking lot. "Look Granger, I'm trying to believe prison was an inconvenience for you. Now, you're out and you can take care of mom.

You can deal with all of the bills and her doctors. I have a life and now you can be her caretaker." She stared ahead. "Mock me all you want, I've done a good job with mom. Now it's your turn. Tough shit!"

"Wow! Prison! An inconvenience!" Granger slapped his leg, "An inconvenience! Prison was hell, beyond hell!"

Spit flew from his lower lip, "Sophia, I was almost raped, beaten and threatened continually! Do you know what it's like to not be able to sleep for six plus years? Huh?" His hand grabbed her shoulder. His fingers dug into her, "No! You can't imagine what it is to live in total fear constant fear and not be able to take a shower without being on your guard constantly! Sophia, I paid my dues for what I did! Don't think for one minute I don't regret what happened to mom!" He leaned back, "Hell, I regret she's still alive to continue making my life hell! Hell, hell, she should be dead! "

Clearing her throat, Sophia choked out, "Really? Really, you regret that she's still alive? After all she did to get you out of prison? Why, Granger? Why do you regret she's still alive when she has given her all to get you out of the hell hole?"

Picking up the white plastic bag he blew into and then popped it between his hands, "Well, let's see." Lifting his finger he wiggled them over the center console between them in the front seat, "If she would've been able to drive a stick shift, she wouldn't have been in the middle of the road to be slammed by oncoming traffic. But since Mom never learned how to shift, I believe and I have thought long and hard about this, she was stranded in the middle of the interstate because she stalled the vehicle." Pointing his finger in the air, he further illustrated, "Not because of me or what I had done to her engine, I don't know a thing about engines. She stalled because she's stupid and didn't know how to shift!"

Pulling off her plum colored beret, it dropped onto her lap. Sophia turned down the heat. Her fingers combed through her short hair. Curls lifted around her head. "Granger, you're beyond irritating. If Margaret is such a threat to you, why didn't you just kill her like Papa? You were constantly here at her farm. There was more than ample opportunity for you to just hit her over the head. Seriously, Granger, if she's your arch enemy, why didn't you just do her in, then and there and avoid going to prison? You're a clever man. A bale of hay could've landed on top of her and crushed her or a platter from high up on the hutch fallen on her to cut her head open, right? Why didn't you just kill her when you had the chance there at her farm? You could've claimed you found her dead and bloody?"

Rolling the plastic bag around his fist, he ignored her to go on, "She's an idiot. That woman stood in the doorway of our bedroom and watched us be beaten alive as children. She refused to divorce Papa when he had numerous affairs. She treated you like dirt because you're female. Shall I go on or is this enough?" Ripping the plastic bag into pieces, he groaned, "Why didn't Papa just beat the shit out of her and leave us alone!"

Emotional tears rolled down Sophia's cheeks, "Granger, the accident was your fault! It was proven beyond a reasonable doubt in the courts! You were there! Those people suffered miserably because of you! Still you want your mother dead! You're a piece of work!" She stared ahead as she drove her SUV, "Margaret is your mother. She gave birth to you, without her you wouldn't be here wanting to kill her. Really!" Pulling into a turnoff by the road, she glared at him, "You know what? I'm taking you to your new prison with Margaret. You think life was hell there in prison, well you ain't seen nothing yet."

Turning the wheel, the vehicle moved back onto the road, "And good luck to you." Sophia wiped the tears from her face with the back of her hand, "Karma is a bitch, Granger, a real bitch and it's coming for you!"

They reached Margaret's farmhouse in silence. The vehicle bounced over the speed bumps, going to Margaret's dry alfalfa fields. A tall cottonwood in the middle of one of the fields had been struck by lightning. A blackened tree trunk reflected the mood within her SUV. Granger ripped the plastic bag into small pieces, they were now all over the vehicle's floor. Sophia ignored him. As she drove down the bumpy driveway to the front of her mother's farm house, she said, "Listen, mother wants you to stay with her until you get settled since you have nowhere else to go. You two can get reconnected since I need to go the school and pick up Sybil. How's that?"

Granger put his hands over his eyes, "Oh, God, I have to stay with dear mother? What happened to my things? Where's my house? Aren't Emily and Shirley going to welcome me to freedom?" He peeked out at her from between his fingers at the wrought iron gate that lead into Margaret's property. "I thought we were going to lunch?"

Sophia answered, "No and no. Your house was sold and the funds went to Emily since you were not able to pay child support. Emily has since paid mom for the house in Negara, which is now legally Emily's and Shirley's. Emily is in a new relationship with a very nice man who is not an ex-con. Shirley is in fourth grade and doing well. She doesn't need you in her life or your hate. You know all of this. We told you this when we visited you last. Please, Granger, leave them alone!"

Granger dropped his hands into his lap, "What! Wait, I'm her father! Shirley needs me and I need her! First thing I'm going to do is get mother dear to hire a lawyer so I can get full custody of Shirley. She should be with me, not her whoring mother Emily! Shirley and I have lost six years of life together." He stared out the window. The strong wind blew at the dead bushes alongside the high adobe wall surrounding their mother's farm. The stucco on the adobe wall was cracked, reflecting the pathetic condition of Margaret's property.

"No, Granger, what you need to do is get your life in order. You are an ex-con who has just been released. You still have one year of parole to accomplish. Also, you need to get a job. If you hate it here then get a home and get your life in order! No more manipulating mom."

"Hah," he pushed his brown bangs back from his forehead. Sophia noticed he was now graying at the temples. "Sophia, I'm going to be a good boy from now on." His attention went back to the forlorn looking house, "Papa was ill. You know this? He was dying slowly, a horrible death. All I did was save him from years of horror and silent pain. I did the right thing letting him go. You know this?"

Biting the inside of her lower lip, Sophia shook her head deciding to be silent and say nothing.

He studied a white plastic bag. It was stuck on one of Margaret's prickly pear cacti planted along the cracked brown stucco wall. "Enough with the arguing, tell me about Mom. What's she like, how's the horse?" Nodding at the horse in the field in front of them, he continued, "I see Geordie is still alive. He must be over thirty years of age. Is she taking care of him?"

"She has help. Charlotte who's her neighbor talked her into hiring this great fellow Roberto. He trained horses in Mexico. He and his wife Rosa live on Fourth Street not far from here. Roberto comes every day to feed Geordie, clean the stall, throw seed at the chicks, collect the eggs and please Mom."

"So, she likes him around? That's strange. Usually she won't let anyone close. Does he ride the old horse?" Granger appeared to have let his anger slide away.

"No, Geordie is ancient, but Roberto does take Geordie for walks down to the ditch roads for exercise. Roberto's father was a famous race horse trainer in Mexico. Near Hermosa, I think. Anyway Roberto was the youngest of nine children or something, he followed his father around the horses. When he was nineteen, as the story goes, he was given a wild Thoroughbred colt to train. This horse was loco-loco as he puts it. One day he went into the stall to put the halter on this loco caballo and this colt reared up to slam down on his feet. He had on boots, Roberto not the horse."

"What happened to his feet? That must have been painful." He faced Sophia.

She went on, “He said he just sucked it up and went on to halter the horse. Then out in the working arena he had had enough of this wild colt. He jumped on its back and rode it until it calmed down. There was an audience who watched.”

Shaking his head, Granger agreed, “Hell, yes, if Roberto couldn’t walk he’d better ride!”

“Roberto didn’t tell anyone about his broken feet. He kept working beside his father until the day he went to the Jefe to ask him for a raise because he was getting married.”

“Married? If he had deformed feet and worked all the time with horses, when did he have time to find a woman?” Granger continued to study the white plastic bag stuck on the cactus plant.

“Ahhh, yes, the hired help of the jefe was a Rosa who worked as a housekeeper for the big man and his wife. She helped raise the boss’s kids and they would come out and watch Roberto ride.”

“Poor guy to get married with broken feet. What happened then?”

“Well, the jefe noticed Roberto’s limping and asked. Then the boss man had a special bootmaker form boots for Roberto’s feet. This cost a lot of money, but Roberto had become a great and wonderful horse trainer and the jefe needed him.”

“How did they end up here? Working for our broken down Mom and her pathetic farm?”

“Don’t know for sure although he works for Charlotte, Mom’s neighbor as well. Once she met him over at Charlotte’s, Mom became enamored with him. He’s about sixty and he’s a little fellow. Small boned, light, not tall and he has a terrific smile and laugh. He limps around here and takes care of anything she needs. He even does housecleaning for her and grocery shopping.”

Granger stared at the flapping plastic bag. “That bag appears to be alive desperate for freedom and yeah, if he was training race horses, he’d need to be light and small. Is Roberto here now? I’d like to meet him.”

Shaking her head, Sophia explained, “No. He and Rosa left for Mexico a couple of days ago. Roberto and Rosa arrived back to Albuquerque late last night. I came early this morning to feed Geordie horse and the chicks. He might come by tonight to feed Geordie. Roberto is dutiful, that’s for sure.”

He brother continued to stare at the flapping plastic bag. Sophia paused, then added, “Also, I came early for Mom to give me your stuff and your leather jacket. Roberto and Rosa only were gone for few days to Mexico. I don’t think Rosa is well, something about high blood pressure and diabetes.”

Granger continued to watch the plastic bag, “I hope they don’t get deported? You know with all of this ICE trouble about illegals, do you think they will be?"

Laughing, Sophia smacked his leg, "He's legal. Both of them are legal. Mom paid for Roberto to learn English and to take the exam. There was a huge fiesta at their home on Fourth Street. I took Mom." The plum colored beret was lifted from her lap to be placed back on Sophia's head. "Charlotte paid for Rosa to become a citizen a couple of years ago. Or Charlotte's husband did, the honorable doctor. Charlotte's husband Danny was a promoter of citizenship. When he retired from his medical practice he spent all of his time working with illegals to get them legal."

"He was into healing then, huh?" He turned in the seat to ask, "Mom paid for the Roberto's fiesta, huh?"

"Oh, yeah, she went. I took her with her walker. She hates that steel walker, but she can't walk on her own. We loaded up the walker and some presents for their home and drove over there. Must have been at least seventy people or more there with food, presents, children and dogs. Babies and grandparents all laughing and singing with the Mariachis as they celebrated their citizenship." Sophia turned on the windshield wipers to clean off the dirt.

"What's the wife like? Rosa?"

"She's quite beautiful. Her long hair and it must be very long, is braided and wrapped around her head several times. She had paper flowers in her braided hair. Her large brown eyes sparkled and she's plump, but beautiful in her own way. Everyone was hugging them and congratulating them. It was quite wonderful."

"Did Mom take credit for the party? You know how she does?" His attention was back to staring at the plastic bag in the wind.

"Actually, Mom was demure. She pulled her little girl face all innocent and provocative."

"Oh, I hope she didn't wear her jeans with the frayed hems and the old stained work shirt!"

Relaxed now that their conversation was like old times, Sophia answered, "Mom dressed nicely. She wore her olive green squaw skirt with the colorful woven sash belt and her white peasant top with the lace. The old black pumps were polished just for the occasion. Although, Roberto hadn't had time to take her to the beauty parlor to get her hair trimmed. It was longer than she likes it and wiry, but she had it fixed nicely with hair spray."

He turned to stare at his sister, "Beauty parlor? Hair spray? What's that all about? Mom abhorred anything vain! What's going on here? Is she hoping to seduce this guy?"

Glaring at him, she spoke harshly, "Granger! Get serious! No! Mom knows her hair is best short in her bowl cut. She can't cut it herself, really!"

Smiling, he pointed to his own head, "You could do it. Just put a bowl on her head and cut around it. Hey, I could do this for her or Roberto."

Sophia sighed, "There was this black man in front of us at the party that I remember. We were sitting at a picnic table, they had made room for Mom and me to sit there, on the bench. The place was packed. Every chair was taken. There was this tall man, he must have been about six feet seven or more, wearing blue and black soccer shorts with his hairy long legs and huge sneakers. He stood in front of us. We couldn't miss him. He put his Styrofoam bowl of pasole down on the ground, bending from the waist with his butt in the air he then he folded to sit on the grass. He was graceful as he sat in the lotus position to lift his bowl of pasole and delicately eat it. He was amazing. That's about all I remember from the party although there was a piñata, a band and presents opened with singing. Mom totally enjoyed the whole event."

"Seriously? Miss Prim and Proper let her guard down?"

"She didn't really have to speak to anyone except the Mendoza's, Robert and Rosa that is. Her Spanish classes at the Senior Center came in handy. You would have been proud of her. She practices her Spanish with Roberto. They laugh to go over the words when she works to get her pronunciation correct."

Pointing to the front gate, Granger brought Sophia's attention to their mother. "What about Charlotte? Wasn't she in attendance? I mean she could have taken Mom, right?"

Smiling at Margaret as she stood at the tall wrought iron gate, Sophia answered, "No, Charlotte was in Korea with her son and daughter-in-law. She became a grandmother for the third time. She was excited to take the trip and visit her daughter-in-law's village, meet her folks." Glancing at the apple orchid next door to Margaret's property, Sophia pointed, "Roberto took care of Charlotte's property while she was gone."

Margaret waved at them. Granger spoke to the closed vehicle door, "I guess I better get out of your van and face the dragon."

"Granger, Mom worked hard to get you out of prison early. The least you can do is be kind to her. She's weak and frail. Please, please be polite to her and respectful. She's devoted to you!"

Shaking his head, he turned quickly to face her, "No!" Granger's anger returned, "No, she's not devoted to me, she's dependent on me. Just because I have the correct genitalia she believes I have all the answers, all the God given wisdom she doesn't have. How did Papa put up with her? I hate this, Sophia, I absolutely hate her neediness. It makes me sick!" His face was red as he spit out, "I'm out of here as soon as possible! Just you watch!"

Then he turned to kiss Sophia on the cheek, "Hey, Sis, remember I love you and I won't let anyone hurt you ever again. Remember, I love you!"

The vehicle's door slammed shut as he ran directly to the white plastic bag, swerving around the wrought iron gate. He ripped the bag free from the cactus to hold it open for the wind to fill. Then he quickly popped it and let the torn bag fly into the neighbor's field. Sophia shook her head as she backed up and drove away.

Sophia's deed was done. Glancing at the rearview mirror, Sophia watched as Margaret hobbled around the walker to embrace Granger. Her mother's gnarled arthritic fingers grabbed at Granger's leather jacket as if her life depended on holding him. There was no purpose to be gained by Sophia staying and listening to their strange conversation. Sophia had a teenager waiting for her at the middle school. Shaking her head, she tried to get the image of Granger's angry brown eyes out of her mind. They were cold and calculating while his voice worked at being endearing. The conflict in his eyes and his soft tender voice was revolting. The wind continued to blow hard against the side of her vehicle as she drove north to Rincon and her daughter. Whispering to herself, Sophia said, "Please, Universe, help them get along."

2

There was a long line of cars at the middle school. The harsh wind kept the parents from walking around the school, sharing, and talking. Sophia took an old towel from the backseat of the vehicle to wipe off the front passenger seat and the radio knob. She picked up the pieces of the torn plastic bag and shoved them into the waste packet on the backseat. A loud bell shrilled and suddenly middle schoolers straggled out of different doors with their hoods up or their jacket collars lifted to their ears. She watched to see Sybil in her new bright blue parka walk outside with two other girls. They were staring into the middle girl's cellphone. All three girls appeared to be concerned and then they laughed and shook their heads. Sybil searched out the line of parked cars to find her mother. The teen shyly waved as she said something to the other two and ran to jump into the passenger seat beside her mother.

Sophia asked Sybil, "What was that all about?"

Sybil shook her head. "Drama. Everything at school these days is about drama. Somebody saw somebody with their boyfriend and freaked. She threw her coke at the other girl and someone put it on Snap Chat. It's really stupid."

Sybil threw her backpack into the back seat of the SUV. "Hey, Mom, you're here on time! Amazing Grace! Do you think we could get an ice cream before we head home? I'm starving and lunch today was soggy sandwiches in the cafeteria. They must make the sandwiches days in advance. The mayo soaks through the bread. It's disgusting."

Pulling around the other parked cars at the school, Sophia smiled quietly. Sybil knew how to handle herself in middle school. Sophia was proud that Sybil was more interested in her classwork than in having relationships with boys. "Sure, we can cruise around to the ice cream shop. Unless you would like to get a burger and fries or something more substantial?"

Sybil shook her head, "No, tonight I'm thinking of making spaghetti and meatballs, that is unless, you're going out with Jack again?"

"No, I think that's cooling off for now. He has classes and students to deal with and his own kids are coming for the weekend. I don't really want to push this relationship into something serious. It's fun having someone to go to the movies with and to a concert, but our lives are complicated enough."

Laughing, Sybil coughed, "Oh, wow, I almost forgot! Didn't you get Uncle Granger out of the jail house today? Is he at our house or is he with Grandma Margaret?"

Poking Sybil's upper arm, Sophia snorted, "Our house? Why our house? What would he be doing at our house, young lady?"

"Ah, well, if Grandma Margaret didn't want a convict at her perfect abode, she would send him home to us, right?" Sybil feigned an English accent, "I don't want a tarnished man living with me, since I am so perfect!"

Parking in front of the ice cream shop, Sophia clapped her hands, "You did that quite well. You actually sounded just like my mother!"

The ice cream cones were still being licked as they entered their large adobe home at the edge of Alcon. The small village had once been a stagecoach stop for travelers going to and from Socorro to Santa Fe. Historically, Rincon had not been anything more than a few farmhouses. As more conquistadores and pioneers moved north from Mexico, Alcon had developed from a stagecoach stop to a village with a post office. Today, the Alcon B&B advertised a weekend getaway for people who lived in Santa Fe or Albuquerque. The Rio Grande River trickled on the west side of the B&B with an isolated hot tub under tall cottonwood trees. The B&B helped with the local employment and now Alcon was a developed village with a small mom and pop store and an elementary school. Inherited farms surrounded the village, developed hundreds of years ago from conquistadores who had moved north from Mexico with Onate and Coronado. Each farm had once been hundreds of acres, but with each son born, the land had been divided into strips. Each area of land started at a ditch channel, fed from the river's tributaries. New Mexico is famous for its numerous channels, ditches and diversions fed from the ever flowing Rio Grande or Big River. Massive quantities of cottonwood trees spread along the river, giving an aerial map of the river's meanderings. Every April brought deep layers of cottonwood tree cotton floating down from the cottonwood trees, giving the appearance of snow along the farms and the river's banks. This was followed with humans having asthma and allergy attacks.

Sophia Pino's home was also a horse boarding farm. This was her way to bring in extra income aside from her university teaching job. The divided two alfalfa fields and thick bales of hay in the barn brought a feeling of safety to Sophia. She had grown up on a farm rented by her father on San Geraldo Pueblo. Her mother's dream was to raise her children on a farm miles away from any town or civilized population. Margaret was born in New York City. Margaret's mother had been an avid man hunter, especially for men with lots and lots of money.

Sophia's grandmother or Margaret's mother had divorced her first husband, who was an accountant with a large government firm, to rake in alimony enough to live like a queen. A nanny raised Margaret and her little sister as they traveled from east coast to west coast and back again during the war. On their travels mother Margaret had fallen in love with the Pueblo people and the New Mexico landscape. Even though Margaret was twenty-one years younger than Sophia's Papa, Margaret worshipped him for treating the Native Americans in the outback of Arizona. Sophia's Papa wished to please his young wife Margaret who assisted in his practice with his medical magic on the reservation.

Granger had been born in Arizona in the tuberculosis clinic where Papa worked. Then Papa was offered a job near San Geraldo Pueblo. They moved when Granger was only months old to an old adobe home with half the front adobe wall of the old house missing and snakes in the open living room. Margaret was pregnant again by then with Sophia. Papa was loved by his patients who he cared for doing house calls. A bunch of Papa's patients would arrive on the weekends to rebuild the missing part of their house. Sophia was born in the hospital near Rincon.

Later, Papa, Granger and Sophia built their first barn on the reservation homeland. Papa had measured and strung the line for the barn. He had the wood delivered. The main barn structure's frame was built with Granger's help, but there was a hurry to put up the barn roof to protect the two by four frame. Sophia smiled, remembering.

Papa tied a number of two by fours with a rope. The rope was thrown up and over the barn roof trusses to the other side of the barn frame. This lose end of the rope was tied to the back of the tractor. Standing up high on the truss framework of the roof, Papa called to Granger to slowly drive the tractor forward. This would lift the wood slowly up to Papa where he could hammer it in place. Granger was nine. He had had his first tractor driving instruction earlier that morning. The tractor's gas pedal was far from the tractor's seat for Granger's legs couldn't reach. When Granger got the signal to step on the gas that is exactly what he did. He slid down from the tractor seat to push hard on the gas pedal. The tractor shot forward into the field. The two by fours flew into the air, smacking her Papa who then flew to land in the sand pile used for making adobe bricks. The two by fours slammed to the ground and were dragged until the tractor stopped. Granger was terrified. There was no end to Papa's 'spare the rod, spoil the child' punishment. Papa sat up on the sand pile. He didn't move. Then waving, he found his footing, brushed himself off and laughed. Sophia didn't know what had happened next for she had run into the house to hide under her bed. Later, once the barn was completed, she found solace hiding around the large bales of alfalfa. There in the barn loft she was well protected from her Papa's or her brother's emotional outbursts.

Sophia's youngest daughter Donna loved the fields of alfalfa and the horses as well. She helped her mom every weekend. During the week, Donna stayed with her Dad in Rocoso at the old house. Geoffrey worked in town and drove Donna to and from a private school. This appeared to work well for all concerned since Sophia taught at the university in the opposite direction.

Sybil followed her mother into the farmhouse, "Mom, would you mind if I didn't help with the horses tonight? I have an algebra exam in the morning and seriously need to study. Do you think you could deal with those hairy beasts while I study? I'll fix supper?" Sybil called their dog Shonac into the house with her. "Shonac can stay with me, protect me from the ghosts in Donna's bedroom!"

Sophia laughed as she called to her daughter, "Sure, no problem don't want those dead crazy sisters to hassle you while cooking. The hairy horsey beasts will have to be ignored by their princess. This old queen will feed and muck out the stalls." Nice shoes were kicked off as Sophia pulled on her barn boots at the farmhouse door frame. These comfortable boots smelled of manure and had cracked with age and were not worn for teaching or off the farm.

Two of the horses were already in their stalls waiting for dinner. They whinnied as Sophia walked to the large open barn. Two of the horses remained at the far end of the two acre pasture. They appeared busy grazing on tall grass by the stretched hog wire fence. Grabbing a tin bucket off the hook outside the pole barn, Sophia slapped it with her open hand. The sound had the proper affect, the two far horses lifted their heads, but then chose to ignore her. Sophia called to them, "Come on, come! Canter to your stalls. Come on!" Her voice fell on deaf horse ears. Gates to the stalls were shoved wide open while she grabbed a good handful of alfalfa to throw into each of the feeding bins in each stall. The two remaining horses in the field lifted their heads, whinnied only to stay put and continue to graze.

A movement at the opposite side of the open field caught Sophia's attention. A long lanky man leapt over the white pole fence on the west side of the field. He ran straight at the two horses. His hands clapped as he raced at them. Startled by the sudden noise and attack, they galloped across the field into their stalls. Sophia laughed. She loved the smell of horses and fresh alfalfa opened from the bale. Better yet she liked the swiftness of these sleek animals who obeyed. The man followed, to swing the stall gates shut with a loud clang. He shoved the bar shut onto the wooden beam.

"They're in! Thought you could use some help and I needed the exercise." He wiped his brow with the back of his hand. "We've met before, don't know if you remember? I'm Don Juan Calderon the eighteen wheeler driver next door."

"Don Juan Calderon, thanks. I've had a tiresome day, wasn't eager to run down there and back. Your work is appreciated." Sophia smiled as he came into the barn to stand next to her. "No problema."

The wheelbarrow was lifted as the two of them scooped and dumped the day's old manure into it and then wheeled to the compost pile that was growing taller each day. Stretching out her back, Sophia asked Don Juan, "You really didn't need to help me, you know? How did you know the horses didn't come in?"

"Young lady, these farms have ears and eyes. We watch and wonder. Also, we take care of our own." Bending, he knelt to tie the loose shoestring on his sneaker. "Say, not to be nosey or anything, what was all the commotion about with the sheriff cars about two months ago? Everyone was worried when you didn't come home for two days and the young one was here alone?" His forehead was wrinkled in concern. He stood to face her. His eyes were blue green.

"Oh, that." Sophia pulled the plum colored beret down on her forehead.

"Yeah, that?" His voice was firm, he wanted an answer.

"Well, yes, that." She shook her head, trying to think of an innocuous answer. The whole of the neighborhood didn't need to know their secrets. She stood tall, letting her voice carry weight as she spoke, "My youngest daughter Donna, do you know her?"

Don Juan smiled, "Yes, she rides like the wind with Griego Wallace. You know he was a real brat until Donna showed up with the horses? Then he became mister macho and for the first time took an interest in his horse Guaco. As a matter of fact we haven't seen Donna around lately, where's she at?"

Sophia stared over at the horses. Don Juan put his hand on her shoulder, "Look, I may sound like a snoop and maybe I am, but this is mostly concern. We look after our own out here on the farmland. It's good to know what's going on with our neighbors so we can help."

She shook her head, fighting back tears. She and Sybil were alone in this trouble. There was no way she could speak of what happened. Sybil and Sophia had swallowed the horror of that frightening night and were trying to come to grips with it. Still, there was no way she was going to share their life story with Don Juan. She would give him a watered down version. "The counselor at Donna's school was convinced that I was letting Donna sleep in the barn with the horses. The counselor felt this was abusive and reported me to the sheriff and Children Youth and Family Services. They all surrounded the house at dinner time and removed her."

"So, what? You went to find her and were gone for two days?" He rubbed his chin. "Anna my wife said her sister saw you in the jail in Rincon. Is this true?" Empathy oozed from his soft voice. For a minute Sophia remembered Granger's smooth voice that he used when he wanted information. She shivered. There was no way Sophia could lie if she was seen in the jail.

Turning away from him, she leaned against the stall, "No, I was in jail." She spoke to him over her shoulder, "They felt I might be a threat to Sybil my fifteen year old. Also, that perhaps I was a flight risk or something and would miss the court date for Tuesday morning." Remembering the horrible terror of those nights in jail gave her a cold sweat. Sophia watched the horses to let her fear subside.

Don Juan shook his head as he leaned his back against the stall next to her, "But you participate here at the Alcon Elementary School on Tuesday afternoons, right? Isn't Sheriff Salazar's grandkid in your class? Even the judge knows you, right?"

Sophia shook her head, "Yes, but the law is the law. Anyway, the horror is over. Now, we're back to normal and life goes on without the counselor. I was found innocent, obviously since I'm here." Taking a deep breath she put her courageous face forward.

Don Juan was taller than Sophia and he was determined to be the interrogator, "But where's Donna? Griego is going to be a pain if she isn't around. He's totally in love with her and her horse. Is her horse this one?" He pointed to Tracey the sorrel mare who was scarfing down her food with gusto.

"Yes, Donna loves Tracey. This was the worry, she was spending all her time with the horse and not doing her homework or her chores." Sophia leaned across the white pole fence to pat the mare's nose. Tracey jerked her head away to grab Sophia's beret and toss it onto the stall's dirt floor.

Don Juan burst out laughing as he reached forward to touch Sophia's hair. She put up her hand to block him from touching her head, "What're you doing?"

"Your hair is sticking straight up in the air. I don't want the neighbors to think we were doing anything untoward." He was still chortling.

Shocked, she pushed her fingers through her short curly hair,

"Untoward? Neighbors? Oh, yes, the farmland has eyes and ears!" Bending over she grabbed her beret from the stall floor and shoved it back on her head.

Her voice became short and prickly, "Donna's with her father during the week. She's going to a different school without a nasty counselor!" Sophia turned to shove the wheelbarrow against the internal barn wall. Moving the scooper into the bucket, she added, "A school she likes. She's here on the weekends to ride like a madwoman." Her voice stayed stern. She was not to be interrogated especially by Don Juan Calderon.

He stepped back as if slapped, "Hey, no hard feelings okay?" His hands went up as a gesture of innocence, "Just worry, that's all, just worry. Glad I could help with the horses. Aren't you going to give them some oats?"

Quickly turning on her heel with resentment that he should tell her how to feed her own horses, she went into the oat room. This was her favorite room. The sides were sealed with corrugated-steel wall pieces buried deep into the ground rising up to the barn's roof. An enclosed room of corrugated steel protected the oats from mice, rats and snakes. The rich smell of oats permeated the air while dust motes floated in the air around her movement.

Don Juan called from outside, "Hey, I'm going now. Glad to help." His voice drifted away.

Shutting the thick wooden door behind her as she stood in the oat room, Sophia straddled an empty saddle wooden frame. The quiet allowed her to let go of emotion. Tears fell, her nose ran as she heaved in sorrow and anger. This room, made of steel walls would echo if she screamed and then all the neighbors would know of her frustration. She was tempted, but then she whispered into the silent room, "Why! Why? I'm a good mother! What's happened to my life! Why am I being punished?" The wind rattled the walls reminding her of her other daughter inside the farmhouse. "Damn! Damn and damn again!" She threw her beret on the dirt floor.

The old coffee can was filled four times with raw oats. Each stall had oats dumped into horse bins. "You guys, I love each and every one of you and I appreciate your love back. This is the life I've dreamed of and I'm not going to let that man Don Juan or Granger or Geoffrey or anyone else ruin it. You understand?" Then she climbed the white pole fence to check the gates behind each of the horses. It was vital to keep them safe within their individual stalls for the night.

As she entered the adobe house, she could smell spaghetti boiling on the stove and onions frying. Sybil was an excellent cook. Sophia realized she was seriously hungry. Three foot thick adobe walls kept the wind out of the old farmhouse and the warmth inside. Sophia had not taken Granger to lunch and she had completely forgotten about food until the ice cream. Barn boots were yanked off at the outside door frame. As she entered the main room in her stocking feet, Sophia called out, "Hey, when is dinner going to be ready? It smells divine."

Sybil's voice called back from the kitchen, "In about half an hour. I'm studying and cooking, should be an interesting meal." There at the long kitchen table sat Sybil hunkered over a thick math book. She had a wooden spoon in one hand and a pencil in the other. The frying pan was simmering on the old gas stove and a pot of boiling water was on the back burner. "Hey, Sybil, I'm going to take a quick shower. Take your time with the cooking, although it smells delicious."

"Hey, I do anything to help, right?" Waving the wooden spoon, Sybil didn't bother to look up but continued to work on a problem in her notebook. Her waist length hair flowed behind her over the back of the chair like a cloak.

In her large bedroom, Sophia sighed with fatigue and concern about Granger. He could take all of this away from them in a heartbeat. This was the one concession she had to make with her mother. The bank. The mortgage. Mr. Carlton the chauvinist bastard. The divorce had not been completed when she wanted to buy this property. There were two other interested parties, so said the realtor. Desperate to get herself and her children out of Geoffrey's life and out of the old house, Sophia had had to ask her mother to co-sign the mortgage. Mr. Carlton the jerk had said, "No, your mother's name must appear as owner and you co-sign the loan."

Margaret's joy was more than noticeable. She was needed again by her independent daughter. There was a brief moment when Sophia thought of asking Geoffrey to sign, but the thought was quickly dismissed. He'd ruin her and destroy the family more than he had already. Geoffrey the Divorced One hated the Pino family and Sophia had taken back her maiden name. No, it was more than hate. Geoffrey held anger that was a loathing beyond any emotion known to humankind.

Sophia was making all the payments. Usually her deposits were ahead of time. There was safety in knowing the bank held the title. Valuable stocks her father had left her upon his death, had been sold. All she needed to pay off the property was seven thousand dollars. Her concern was if she did pay off the mortgage, the title or deed would go to Margaret. It would be in Margaret's name. Granger had power of attorney for Margaret's affairs. If he asked her mother to put the title in his name, Margaret would do it in a heartbeat. After all, Granger was her perfect son. His mother believed fully and erroneously that Granger would never hurt anyone, especially her.

Sophia allowed herself the opportunity to cry in the shower. Lifting her head to let water run down her face, she whispered, "Granger loves me. He said he would never hurt me, but I wonder."

Water cleansed the filthy feeling she had from being with her own brother. How could she be related to these strange people – her mother and her brother? They didn't feel connected. Somehow she felt estranged from them, unable to love or even care about them. Ever since she was a small child, Sophia believed herself to be an orphan adopted by these bizarre calculating people. Her mother's idea of a hug was to hold onto someone's shoulders, at arm's length and stare at them. Her Papa gave everyone a bear hug. Papa kissed, hugged and seduced everyone with his warmth and kindness. People loved him devotedly for his charisma was true. As a doctor his patients spread the word of his medical expertise and folks had come from hundreds of miles away for his help. A nurse's costume was given to Sophia when she was ten years old. House calls were made with her in tow to carry her father's black medical case. His death had put a hole in her soul.

Yet her mother Margaret had helped Sophia through the divorce by finding this farmhouse. Margaret put out the word of Sophia's horse boarding and within a week the two empty stalls were filled with paying customers. Her mother even floated her the down payment money to buy this place. How was it that Sophia could not feel any connection at all to her own mother? Margaret's affection toward Granger was more than obvious even to total strangers. Margaret's friends complimented Sophia on being so much like her mother. Margaret's eyes were a white chalky blue and Sophia's eyes were a deep chocolate brown like Papa's. Sophia had absolutely no freckles on her face. Margaret's face was completely dotted with them. Besides, Sophia hugged people and listened to them. Definitely, Margaret did not. Not at all. Sophia's mother was a cold fish with an alternative motive. Margaret took notes and kept them in her famous black notebook.

There was a knock on the bathroom door as a cold breeze flew into the hot shower room. "Mom, there's a phone call from Grandmother Margaret and dinner is about ready. You better eat before you return her call. She sounded as if she'd been crying." The door shut with a bang.

Dinner was eaten in silence. Humidity filled the room from the boiling water. Fog covered the long kitchen windows. Shonac slept under the table. Cats resided on the spare chair mats under the table. Silky the only gray house cat sat in the kitchen window staring at her own reflection. Sybil sucked up her spaghetti only to stop in mid slurp to complete an algebra problem. Blue notebooks were placed at Sophia's left. In front of her was an open blue book. Students were required to turn in a research essay every week. She preferred to give her tests with blue book essays.

Her hope was that by the end of the small blue book each student would finally get to the correct answer. A green correction pen was poised in her right hand ready to circle or strike a work or a phrase in the blue book.

Sybil tapped her eraser pencil on the blue book in front of her mother, "You know you don't teach spelling? Why's that word circled, huh?"

"Hey, I'm the professor and I get to circle what I want. This student misspelled 'civilization.' If she's going to take a civilization class, it would be wise to spell it correctly since she reads this word constantly. That's why it's circled."

Sybil smiled, "Really?" Lifting in her chair, she bent over the table to see the word. "That's how she spelled it? Seriously, she misspelled 'civilization?' You taught me to spell 'civilization' before I could even write my own name!" Her long hair fell forward onto the table. Sybil's bright green eyes sparkled as she stared at the page in front of her mother.

Tapping the end of the green pen on Sybil's notebook page filled with algebra problems, Sophia quipped, "Ah, yes, do you wish for me to check your answers?"

"Hah! Mom, you wouldn't know the answers anyway. You failed algebra twice, remember?" Sybil wrapped more spaghetti around her fork, "Anyway, do your own work, Dr. Pino, Ma'am." She slurped her spaghetti, hoping to get Sophia to laugh.

Breaking off a piece of homemade bread, Sophia finally broke the silence, "Hey, I'm not going over to Grandmother Margaret's. Not tonight, I'm not. She's on her own with Granger. He's there to take care of her. I'm done with the Grandma Care unit."

Sybil shook her head, "Sure, Mom, you believe that, but you know it isn't true. She thinks she owns you. She believes her strings are still attached to you especially now that you and Dad are divorced. Margaret knows you are her slave and she's not afraid to jerk your chain."

No sooner were the words out of Sybil's mouth when the phone rang. The piercing sound penetrated through the old farmhouse's adobe walls and wooden floorboards. Sybil hunched her shoulders, daring her mother to answer the phone. Sophia stuffed a torn piece of her homemade bread into her mouth, "Don't get up, I'll get it."

Usually the only person to call them on the land phone was Margaret who believed cellphones caused brain cancer. Landline to landline was Margaret's belief. Even then she yelled as if she was using a tin can and a very long string to connect with others via the modern phone line. The home phone in the farmhouse was on the front hall table near the kitchen's interior door. This was the only phone plug in the sprawling adobe. The other plug was in Sybil's room.

This was a suspicious plug, but they tried it out anyway. Telegraph wires were needed for this plug, however, for no other plug worked. The science teacher had loaned Sybil an old telegraph semaphore machine. It worked! Although they had no one to send a telegraph message to nor did they know how to receive one. Telegraphs were now obsolete, which seemed unfortunate. Especially out here on the farm. Electricity had a tendency to disappear at random times, but then the telegraph wouldn't have worked either. Evidently, it needed electricity as well.

Sophia pulled on the telephone cord as far as she could to the kitchen. "Hello?" She made funny faces at Sybil as she said, "Mother, oh, sorry Margaret, hello." There was silence for a time and then Sophia said, "You know Granger is a grown man who's just out of prison. Give him some space. If he took your truck and went into town, he's probably seeing old friends and just needs some time to feel his freedom." Sophia ran her fingers through her short curly hair, "Margaret, he's only been gone for three hours. Let him be. He has his cellphone with him, right? Uh-huh, call him and find out if he's all right then."

Empty plates were removed by Sybil from the kitchen table and placed into the chipped porcelain sink. She ran the water until it was hot, choosing not to listen to the phone conversation. Sophia reached from the doorframe to pull a kitchen chair closer to the stretched phone cord. Abruptly sitting, she quietly said, "Mother Margaret, oh, sorry, Margaret, if he knows you're fixing him dinner, he'll return home. I have no idea where he is nor do I wish to know where he is. Margaret, relax and eat your dinner. Enjoy your solitude, he'll be home soon. No. No, I'm not driving over there. I'm tired and have classes in the morning. Fine, then, good night." Carefully the black plastic phone was returned to its cradle on the small wooden side-table.

Washing the dishes, Sybil smiled at her mother, "Wow, Mom, I didn't know you had it in you! Good for you! Although, I bet you didn't muck out the stalls by yourself, did you?" Extra spaghetti was spooned from the serving bowl into a plastic container. "You didn't even tell her you loved her. That's a first for you, huh?" Left over spaghetti sauce was poured into a jar to be placed in the refrigerator.

Wrapping her arms around her fifteen year old daughter, Sophia admitted, "Nope, I'm not going over there. No way, not tonight. There's work to finish here on the table. Also, I didn't muck out by myself, but you already knew this, didn't you?" She kissed Sybil on the top of her head. "You were keeping an eye on your old Mom, weren't you, dear daughter?" The faded dishtowel was in Sophia's hand as she started to dry the washed dishes in the drain board. "Did you know that the farmland has eyes and ears? Everyone around here knows what we do and when we do it?"

Soap suds were flung at Sophia from Sybil's wet hand, "Yep, know all about ears and eyes. Its ears and eyes, Mom. At school the Acosta kids know all about what we do, when we do it and usually even how we did it. They try to get me angry and fight them, but I won't. I don't care. Who cares what we do anyway?" Wind rattled the kitchen window. Silky cat leapt over the counter to the floor. Minutes later a hard rain hit the bubbled kitchen window glass. Donna had been the one to explain that glass was a liquid. This window bubbled toward the bottom because after a hundred years the liquid glass had fallen with gravity, pulling air into the layers. As a family group they decided not to replace the bubbled glass. Sophia was relieved. There was no money for such an expense anyway.

Dishes were dried and put away in the slated cupboards. Cupboard wooden planks that made up the doors of each cupboard had cracked over time. Yellow lacquer had worn off the cupboard doors where the knobs were from wear. Sophia had wanted to replace all fifteen of the cupboard doors, uppers and lowers, but again the expense had turned her away from the idea. The old gas stove had an oven door that would not stay shut. Bungee cords held the chipped white porcelain door shut. Cords were strung from underneath the fat oven to over the stovetop hooking to the high back. Cooking with the stovetop burners meant the cords had to be released and the cook needed to keep the oven door shut with their knees. Many a bizarre meal had been made on this old gas stove.

Mabel was the name the girls gave this oven. "Mabel is able, but she's not always willing." Every now and again, Mabel would turn off the gas feed. She didn't leak gas, she turned the gas off all by herself. Homemade bread half-baked would be found hours later. Cold loaves with a hard outer crust and gooey dough remaining inside was Mabel's forte. This had happened enough times for them to keep an eye on her when bread was placed to bake.

The kitchen chair returned to the kitchen table, Sophia picked up her green pen to ask about the neighbors, "What do you mean about the Acosta's? I thought they were your friends here in the valley, aren't they?"

Sybil's freckles stood out on her pale complexion, "Hell no! So, maybe they live over there on the other side of our ditch and, hey, they claim they know every time we wipe our butts. Hey, I bet they use binoculars to watch us. I bet all our neighbors use binoculars or telescopes. It's as if we're the latest goldfish to watch and gossip about!" Sybil dried her hands, but she didn't sit down at the table. "We're the latest to move into the neighborhood, right? So, we're the latest goldfish bowl to study."

Sophia put her hand up, "Sybil calm down, please, let's discuss this reasonably." She was taken aback by this sudden burst of anger from her daughter.

Sybil's voice rose an octave, "Mom, I hate it here! I really hate living here!" She grabbed her notebook and slammed shut her algebra book. "Mom, just for you to know, this place is far from sane. Look what happened with Donna! My friends don't live anywhere near here! I hate it here." Sybil stomped into her bedroom. Suddenly stopping, she turned to glare at her mother, she screamed, "Mucking out stalls is not my idea of a good time!" The bedroom door slammed shut. A crack in the adobe wall above Sybil's bedroom door widened. Dust fell in a pile to the wooden plank floor.

Sophia clicked her tongue, "Damn and I thought everyone was ever so happy. Boy, did I get that wrong." Cynicism dripped from her voice.

Late that night, Sophia pulled out her diary. She wrote for about an hour and then decided she needed to go over her notes for tomorrow's ethnology classes. There were only twenty-two students in her first class at the university, but each one of them was seriously interested in Egypt's Golden Age and the linguistic base that evolved from that time. She didn't want to have to stand at the podium and read notes. Sophia prided herself on spontaneity and to keep her students engrossed in the moment. This meant she must know her subject well. Tonight she felt prepared for all three classes.

3

The sound of the chainsaw broke the stillness of the morning. Sophia rolled over. The bedside clock showed it was five-thirty five. Not even the rooster had had time to crow. "What's going on?" Shoving two of her cats off of her legs, Sophia plodded to the bathroom. There was no heat in the bathroom and it was bitter cold. Avoiding the mirror, she thought there was no way she was going to check her appearance in the vanity mirror. It was too early to look good or to care. Three of her five cats sat on the bed glaring at her as she entered the bedroom. "No, I don't want to get up either. Don't give me that look!"

Sweatpants were pulled on to tuck her short nightgown in at the waist. Her sweat shirt was pulled over her head to cover her upper body. At the corner of her room, she slid her bare feet into her old brown leather clogs. Clomping her way into the kitchen, she noticed Sybil leaning against the kitchen sink, staring out of the window with her spectacles smudged with fingerprints. The black frames were bent. Evidently, Sybil had not put her contact lenses in yet.

"What's going on outside?" Sophia moved to stand next to her daughter.

Sybil's voice was soft, "It's Uncle slime ball Salamander. He's sawing up our home. He's destroying our lives. He's a pustulant sore on civilization and we've inherited him. His pus is oozing this morning. He's a nuisance and a bacterial hazard of rot. Call the hazmat crew. Get rid of him, Mom." She returned to her bedroom.

"Wow, don't let your feelings out, Sweetheart." Sophia spoke over her shoulder, "Hey, where's Shonac? He should be barking or eating Granger? Where is he?"

Sybil mumbled from her bedroom door, "In here with me. You must be a heavy sleeper, Mom, Shonac woke me with his loud barking. He had Granger trapped in Margaret's truck. Shonac even tried to bite the slime ball, but the salamander kicked him. I called Shonac into the house. He's stuck in my room. We don't need a lawsuit and you know Granger would sue us to death!" Her voice faded, "I'm going back to bed."

Clomping over the old farmhouse's floorboards, Sophia opened the heavy wood door. Bright sunlight blinded her. She stood for a minute as her eyes adjusted. In the field next door, Don Juan was racing his horse around orange barrels. He flowed easily in the saddle as his horse cantered. His horse totally enjoyed being ridden. Maybe she could offer to ride with him as an offer of forgiveness. Stepping back from the open door frame, she let in her large orange male cat Fergus. Lifting him into a hug, Sophia whispered, "Damn, ears and eyes. Oh, well, everyone will finally get to view me at my worst. I don't really care." Fergus was put on the floor as her fingers tried to comb her curly hair flat.

The chainsaw stopped. Granger called out, "Hey, Sophia, over here!" She shook her head. There was no way she didn't know of his presence. The chainsaw noise woke the whole neighborhood. They wouldn't know who this man was maybe they thought he was her lover. Granger would give them something to talk about over the gossip fence.

Standing in front of him, she pointed at the long boards beside him, "What are YOU doing? This is my wood!"

Granger jerked his chin to the house. His left gloved hand held a one-by-four and the other held the chainsaw, "Your roofing fascia needs to be put up. Mom told me about your new roof and how you've been too busy to put up the fascia border. Thought I'd come and do some hard labor, help out my little sister." His smiling white teeth glared at her.

"Oh, so Mom explained to you about the trials and tribulations of the new roof, huh?" The roof had taken two weeks to replace. The old roof had holes the size of basketballs and the floors had grown mold from the leaks. As the roof was being replaced, Sophia and the girls had carefully removed each plank of the old pine floorboards to place them outside in the exact same placement. This made it easy to put the floorboard pieces back inside once the wood had dried, was cleaned and oiled. These three farmhouse dwelling females had lived in Donna's bedroom. The one room closest to the bathroom at night was jammed with everything they needed to survive. Mold smells, dust motes and falling rancid tarpaper entrenched every aspect of their home life. Cockroaches, spiders, mice and deserted bird nests became fellow roomers. The vacuum cleaner ran nonstop once Sophia came into the one room. Sweeping out piles of sawdust, the thousand rusted bent nails and chunks of rotted wood was done by the girls before nightly showers. Anyone within close range could smell them.

Roofers with a radio had appeared at six in the morning for two weeks. It had felt like eons of time that would never end. Despair and exhaustion showed in their faces. Sophia had been staunch in her determination when with the girls. Yet when she was alone or with her mother, she had let down her guard to show her frustration. At the time, she knew this would be used by Margaret for emotional blackmail. This release of emotion would come back to haunt her, just like the ghosts inside the farmhouse.

Granger stood there with a carpenter's pencil behind his ear. His thinning hair pushed back from his forehead. The blue chambray shirt was tucked into his old jeans with a measuring tape clipped to his leather belt. His brown boots were covered in saw dust. The stubble on his chin showed he hadn't shaved. His moustache was thick and waxed to curl up from his mouth.

"Sophia?" Granger interrupted her thoughts, "Where are you? Huh? Do you want to help me or what?" Moving to stand beside her, he nudged her shoulder with his shoulder. "You know you fade out every now and then. Have you been tested for dementia?" His white teeth smiled at her. The chainsaw was still grasped in his other gloved hand.

Eyeing him with cold contempt, she frowned, "Oh, yes, I'm tired that's all. Granger, I have classes this morning. I can't help you today. Could we do this maybe tomorrow? Tomorrow is Friday. I'm free and we could make a day of it. I could buy you lunch or something tomorrow?" She added, "Donna comes home, here, tomorrow late afternoon for the weekend. We like to spend it together, alone."

Granger's white teeth set, his jaw was firm, "Nope, doing this today. You go on and do your little lectures. I'll do this myself after all I promised Mother Margaret I'd do it." The chainsaw whirled in his hand as he bent to force it through the two by four board. The blade perfectly followed the mark he had made with his pencil. Glancing up at her as he bent to hold the board in place, Sophia felt his disappointment with her. Tough, she had responsibilities and he was not going to destroy her life.

Just as Sophia pushed open the house door, the chainsaw stopped. There was a clang and then footsteps raced up behind her. Turning, she bumped directly into Granger. Shoving her into the front room, he jokingly said, "Hey, how about a cup of coffee and a piece of toast for the handyman?" Evidently, he wanted friendship. Clomping loudly into the kitchen on her clogs, Sophia raised her voice as a warning to Sybil, "Sure, Granger! Glad to fix the handyman a cuppa and a piece of toast. Don't mind if I do!"

Granger sat in Sybil's chair at the long kitchen table. "I remember this table. Didn't Papa make this for you when you got married a long time ago?" He patted the table as he removed his leather gloves. "It still looks good, you take care of it with oil and stuff?"

Ignoring his jovial mood, Sophia plugged in the kettle. "Nope, not Papa's. I was married only fourteen years ago, Granger. Geoffrey the Divorced One kept Papa's table. This table was here when we arrived.

Evidently, this kitchen is haunted by a wife whose husband murdered her. That happened only a hundred years ago. It's believed a true man cannot enter this kitchen without getting his hackles up in fear for his life. This kitchen does threaten real men, don't you know." Sophia smirked as she turned her back to him. Thick slices were cut from the homemade bread loaf on the kitchen counter.

Slapping the table, Granger announced, "Hell, I'm not scared of ghosts! Mom told me about the hangman's tree outside. It's a beautiful cottonwood. A shame so many men hanged from its high branches. She said on a night of the full moon you can see the bodies swinging in the moonlight. Is this true or fiction?"

Sybil's bedroom door opened. Hugging her clothes to her chest, she hurried by him saying, "Yeah, it's true and hi, Uncle SSSSS Granger." She disappeared through the kitchen door and into the cold bathroom at the end of the cupboard hall.

Granger turned in the chair, "What was that all about?"

Sophia laughed, "Who knows, she's a teenager. Say, I don't have a toaster, but shall I use the oven to toast the bread?" Bungee cords were unhooked. The porcelain door fell with a loud thud. Buttered bread slices were laid on the oven's inside shelf. Granger stared. Sophia didn't care what he thought, she had places to go and things to do.

Sybil was dropped off at the Middle School. Her daughter appeared taller than most of the other students. Reddish brown hair flowed to Sybil's waist giving her fifteen-year old long lines as well as beauty. Sybil disappeared into the school's front door just as the last bell rang. Their freedom was a moment of joy for both of them, the feeling of escape from the shackles of the family's tedious reality.

Parking her vehicle in the lower lot at the University allowed Sophia the chance to mentally review her lectures in her head. Today the first class's focus was on Egyptian fashion during the Golden Age. Ethnology dealt not only with the cultural linguistics but also with the styles and the habits of the people during that era. She had all of this on her thumb drive and was ready to show the use of makeup and dyes. Many of which were poisonous but when used correctly, beautifully enhancing. The males in her class certainly would be entertained with the vanity of the kings and their makeup and the women with their breast reductions. Sophia was proud of her lectures, her students and the awards she had won in teaching university level. This was her terrain and she loved it.

The Egyptian Golden Age lecture was in the small classroom with only twenty-two students. Surprisingly most of the students were female. Five male students enjoyed and flourished with the female attention. After her first class, Sophia gathered up her notecards into her notebook and backpack to get to her next lecture. This was the big one with seventy-eight students in the large lecture hall. It was the first hall built to hold a high population of students. The red velvet theater seats were well worn. Some of the theater chair frames were cracked or broken. Brown industrial carpet fibers had been cleaned so many times over the years that the pile was worn to the thin cloth below. Sophia flipped on all the light switches to bring the large room into life. Twenty students were already seated. Some appeared to be proof reading their papers due today. Young women were in conversation, giggling. This was her U.S. Ethnology class. The colonists, wars and the pioneering days were enlightening to many students. The high school history classes had been dry of the cultural developments that had occurred.

Sophia fully believed people brought history alive, made the events relevant. Historical choices of different socioeconomic classes enlightened the past, bringing in a more personal awareness. Her students appeared to appreciate the development of history through the eyes of those who had lived at the time. Over the last three years, her students had nominated her for teaching awards and she had received them!

Today, her talk was on the class struggle at the end of World War One, the Big War to end all wars. Celebratory highs brought on the crash of the stock market. Rude emotional effects were suffered by women after the return of their men from war. Quickly, the theater chairs were filled as the clock ticked the beginning of class. Sophia stood in the moment, studying each of her students who now she knew by name. There were four missing. One had a dental appointment and had told her of it. The other three had been constantly absent. She would have to e-mail them and if no reply, she would call. A sign-in sheet was passed for each to sign just to verify her memory of who was present.

Storytelling was her strength. She held the class's attention with her telling of the return of soldiers with trench fever. Medical professionals used bizarre and strange techniques on the emotionally wounded. Women's strengths once used in the work force were now stripped. Her power point illustrated the desperation on the faces of the men and women who stood in long lines at the soup kitchens. Fear with the loss of hope was entangled in the joy of homecoming. Money gone in the stock market crash and locked banks that had stolen what little anyone might have had to survive for a day or a week were illustrated with her stories. Pride of the Great War being won was lost to a country found floundering. Sophia finished half an hour before the end of class to call four students up to the front. This was her signature teaching style.

Two females and two males would give their own empathetic rendition of the times referred to in this lecture. The four picked were students of different ages and different socio-ethnic standing. One of the male students went first, he was excited and eager. The forty year old father student took on the persona of a proud soldier coming home to no job or money with fear of losing his family to illness, starvation or homelessness. Next, a young female student spoke of her pride in counting bullets in the factory and of wearing a uniform of pants, doing work that before was socially unacceptable. Once her fine husband arrived home alive and appeared whole, how they celebrated, but then he screamed in the night bringing tears to her eyes.

The second male student was about twenty years old. As he stood front forward, he stooped his shoulders and dragged one leg behind him. He spoke of coming home to no one, having nothing and wishing he had died in the war. Finally, the last student who was a grandmother went over to him and hugged him. She spoke of opening the soup kitchen and her pride in helping out the poor. The audience of students stood to clap.

Sophia thanked the performing students, allowing them to return to their seats. Then she surprised her students by saying that here in New Mexico most of the people did well. They had land to grow food. PTSD soldiers had large extended families here and curanderos who knew of mind fevers and the use of herbs and psychology. Class was over. Students gathered their items to flee to the next class. Picking up her notecards in a pile on the podium, Sophia was surprised to find four students waiting in a line in front of her. The first male handed her his research paper, "I want to ace this class and my first paper was horrible. Can I rewrite it and turn it in next class?"

Smiling at him, she nodded in the positive, "Definitely. Each of you deserves to ace this class for putting up with me and my stories. Research is the key, remember research and write from knowledge gained not emotion."

His paper in her hand, he shook his head, "I thought history was boring. When you told us history means knowledge in Greek, hey, that was a turning point. Your class is wonderful, everyone should be required to take it. Thanks."

The next woman was in her late fifties, plump and appeared tense. Her research paper was held close to her chest. Her heavy winter coat was button closed and a lovely silk scarf was wrapped around her neck. "Dr. Pino?" The woman stared down at the worn pile of the brown carpet.

Sophia knelt slightly to be more at eye level with the woman, "Yes?"

A man who had been sitting way at the back of the lecture hall suddenly stood to walk down to them. Sophia didn't remember him as a student. He was more this woman's age. Again, the woman said, "Dr. Pino?" Then with anger in her voice and tears in her eyes, the woman shouted, "Dr. Pino, I hate you! I hate you!"

The two students behind the woman turned to stare at the woman. Sophia placed her hands on the woman's shoulders to quietly ask, "Why? Catherine, right? Isn't that your name?" Smiling as she bent to study the shaking woman's face, Sophia asked, "Why is there such anger here?"

Catherine's body shook as she burst into a flood of tears, "I hate you because you brought me back to life! Your class brought me back! When my son was killed with the Marines in Iraq…he was killed. Dead. He's dead. My life died." She wiped her hand on a handkerchief pulled from her coat pocket, "I stopped feeling! I died inside. I just existed and then here in your class, here, you woke me up!" She grabbed at her handkerchief as her tears endlessly fell. Sophia put out her arms and Catherine fell into her embrace, muffling words as she spoke into Sophia's chest.

The man put his hand on Catherine's back. "I'm Ben, her husband. She wanted me here today. Cathy was afraid she would fall apart if she told you." Then he mouthed, "Thank you."

Laughing through her tears, Catherine pulled away, "I did, too. I fell apart. Dr. Pino, I'm so sorry. I thought I was happy to just function, but now with your stories and your empathy for the people, you, you, brought me back. You woke me up and now I hurt! I hurt!" Shaking her head her permed curls bounced. Sucking in air, she stared at Sophia, "Hurt! I hurt now all the time!" Pounding her chest, she whispered, "It feels good, but it hurts."

Sophia nodded to the students behind Catherine, "Come on, let's do a group hug."

Bent over his notebook, a young male student scribbled on a piece of paper. He handed it to Catherine, "Here, here's my cellphone number. Keep it and if you want to talk, give me a call. I'm a math major and can't be late for my next class. I lost my older brother in Iraq. We can talk."

Flinging his class paper at Sophia, he said, "Here, Dr. Pino, here's my research paper." He darted up and out of the lecture hall. Catherine took the torn piece of paper with the phone number on it to stuff it into her coat pocket, "He's my son's age or the age my son would be if he were still alive. Thank him for me, would you?"

Ben enveloped Catherine into his arms and led her out of the lecture hall as he carried her backpack. The remaining female student was Annie. She kept Sophia, "This is my paper. I worked really hard on it. It's important for you to know I don't write well, never did well in English classes, but I like your class and I hope you enjoy reading my paper. It was hard work. I even checked the spelling with spell check because I didn't want to find all those green circles." Cautiously the paper was handed over to Sophia. "Please, remember I worked really hard on this. I want to get an A in this class."

Taking the research paper, Sophia held it in both hands. "Yes, this will be read with loving care. Now, I really have to go." Annie smiled and quietly walked up the lecture hall stairs to the door beside Sophia. In the hall she smiled, "Have a good weekend, Dr. Pino."

United States Ethno History was in a smaller classroom packed with sixty one students. This eight week class started today. Sophia carefully went over her syllabus after the students had introduced themselves and mentioned their interest or disinterest in this history class. Some only needed the credit and felt history was totally boring, a dead concept. Rain pelted the large eastern window. Bullet sized drops echoed into the room. A microphone would have helped carry Sophia's voice, but all she could do was speak loudly, "Our country was founded by warriors and brave adventurers. Soldiers fought for the freedom of the poor and repressed. Democracy came at a huge cost of lives, money and trade economy. Politics were based on the rights of all, rich or poor. Today, our country is based on an oligarchy. This country is controlled and owned by the rich. The poor no longer have a voice and the middle class is becoming obsolete."

Thunder shook the building. Sophia laughed, "Read the syllabus. If you want to buy the books recommended for this class and can afford them, do so. But, if you enjoy research use the library. There is a list of library books on your class internet file. You can check them out for free. All you need to do is have a student I.D. and a library card. Enjoy your weekend, sharpen your gray cells. You'll need them!" Most of the students disappeared. Several moved to sit in the front of the class to ask her questions. Once their curiosity answered, she closed up the room, turning off the light. She was relieved to have a few serious students to help this class move forward.

Sophia worked in her office cubicle to enter into the computer her roster and notes regarding the classes and the students who had turned in papers. Those who didn't provide papers would be fined points from their final grade. Then realizing it was time to get Sybil, she shut down her computer. The paved hill to the lower parking lot was slick with rain water. Her cellphone chirped. Glancing at it, the caller I.D. read her mother's name. The cellphone continued to chirp. The wind was strong. Dust devils swirled in the desert dirt. Tree branches whipped in circles. People ran from building to building with backpacks held over their heads. Heavy dark clouds were close to the earth. Bolts of lightning struck out on the hill behind the university buildings.

Cold air blew into her face with a blast of wind. Sleet sheered down, white and cold. Vehicles in the lot soon became covered with the white slush. A deep puddle of water was around most of the cars. Sophia stepped over it with her long legs as she jumped into the van's driver seat. She needed to shake off her smart professor mode to become a dutiful daughter if she was going to call her mother. Reaching for her blue plastic water bottle, Sophia took a deep drink. It was hot and stuffy inside the vehicle. Freshly vacuumed by the girls, the interior was clean. Lavender oil had been used by Donna to clean the dashboard. Car wax was polished onto the exterior windows to keep rain from sticking. This vehicle may be old, preowned when she bought it, but it ran like a charm and was loved.

Her fingers rubbed the leather steering wheel cover. A Christmas gift from both of her beautiful daughters. Leather gave this cracked plastic steering wheel some class.

Now the wind battered the front windshield with dirt. Closing her eyes, Sophia pushed the automatic dial on her cellphone for her mother's home phone. Immediate picked up, "Sophia, where are you! Do you know your brother left home early around dawn? I don't know where he is and I don't know what he's doing! He's probably selling his herbs to illegals!" Gasping, she continued, "Sophia, Granger didn't come home until after midnight last night. Where's your brother? Find your brother for me! God, I hope he's not dealing drugs or buying guns! Do you think he'd shoot somebody?" Dial tone. Margaret had hung up on her.

Again, the automatic dial went through and Margaret picked up immediately. Angrily she shouted, "What? Did you find him?"

Calm oozed from Sophia's voice, "Margaret, Granger is at my farm. He is cutting and staining the boards for the fascia around the outside of the farmhouse by the roof. He's been there since dawn. He woke us up and tried to kick my dog."

A terse tone dripped from Margaret's voice, "Why didn't he leave me a note? Huh? Why all the secrecy if he was going to be at your farm?"

"I don't know, Margaret. You will have to ask him. He has his cell with him, why don't you call him? Why did you call me?"

"I don't like to pry into his private life. He might hate me and leave. Then I'd be all alone! I didn't want to pry and get him angry at me. Besides you know where he is. There was no need for me to call him, right?" Margaret's tone was now of a shy young girl.

"Mother Margaret, yes, you are still my mother, I just finished teaching classes here at the university. You could have called him. He wouldn't mind. After all, you were the one who pushed him to put up the fascia. It was your idea." Sophia was tempted to scold her mother, but there would be no gain, "Please, relax and eat something. I bet you haven't eaten yet today?"

Dial tone. Sophia carefully placed her cellphone on the front passenger's seat. She patted it, "There you go. We did it. We defused the situation." The vehicle easily started. It was time to get her daughter. Then they could go shopping for tomorrow was wonderful Friday. Donna was to be picked up at Geoffrey's tomorrow late afternoon and would spend the weekend with her and Sybil and the horses. They loved the weekends together for this was the time they felt most whole. Suddenly the sun shone through a break in the fat black clouds. A stillness came across the land. This was a very good sign.

Fifteen year old Sybil jumped into the warm vehicle to dump her backpack on her feet. "Hey, Mom, you're late again. I got an A on my algebra test! Time for ice cream, yes?"

Sophia let Sybil's love fulfill her. "Yes! Ice cream is an excellent idea!" Turning onto the main street, Sophia informed Sybil, "Since we left in such a hurry this morning, I thought you should know about family affairs. Your Uncle Granger did return last night to Margaret's. Late. After midnight. Grandmother Margaret was not happy about his forgetting her fancy cooked meal."

Interrupting her mother, Sybil let out a gut laugh, "Hah, I wouldn't want to be in that house right now! I bet it was Chicken Kiev straight from the freezer and scalloped potatoes au gratin." The seatbelt was pulled tight over her shoulder, "What a conversation! Wonder who's going to win in the contest of 'my life was worse than yours' concept. Bet Grandmother Margaret wins, she's a professional at guilt and manipulation, right Mom?" Sybil bounced in the seat when she saw the ice cream shop.

"Oh, daughter mine, how fickle you've become in your old age. When did you become so wise, huh?" Sophia parked in front of the ice cream shop. The wind continued to blow hard and steady. The heavy clouds were moving to the northwest.

Jumping out of the vehicle, Sybil yelled at her, "Mom, you're raising me smart. You know this? Come on, I'm so hungry I could eat all the ice cream in here!"

Sybil stirred her cardboard bowl of ice cream all together. She had chosen three different flavors, but her favorite of all was the mint chocolate chip. "Mom, what's going to happen now with Granger? He's not going to come live with us is he?"

"Nope." Sophia licked her Jamaica almond ice cream cone, "Absolutely not. He's going to have to stay with and live with Grandmother Margaret. He has no house, no car and no other family who will take him."

Churned ice cream turned into real cream as Sybil smiled, "You know, Mom, I really like Emily's new man friend. I like his horses, too. Do you think Granger will try to remarry Emily? Because I think that would be awful. Shirley is having fun with George. He's warm and fun while your brother is as cold as ice."

"Um, what was it you called Granger?" Sophia studied her daughter.

"A salamander, but that was Donna. Donna seriously will throw up if she sees Granger again. Mom, I might throw up, too, if I have to deal with him. This morning was awful." Sybil licked her pink plastic spoon laden with multi-colored ice cream. "Do you suppose he's still at our farmhouse, sawing up our wood? Destroying our lives?"

Frowning, Sophia asked, "Do you think Shonac is still tied up in the barn? You know we have to go grocery shopping after this? Donna comes tomorrow and you girls will have one evening of no chores." A white napkin was used to clean the table in front of them.

"Nope, Donna will clean the barn as soon as she gets home. Please, please, don't let Granger come over. We'll help with the boards. I can carry the ladder even though I won't go up it. Donna's good at hammering. Please, Mom, no Granger, please." Sybil put both of her hands together as in prayer.

More customers entered. The door to the ice cream parlor opened with each bringing in the cold wind. Suddenly, the soft patter of rain hit the sides of the windows. People spoke of the climate change. Last summer had been the hottest anyone could remember. The peaceful calm between the ice cream customers ended with a loud remark regarding Donald J. Trump, the president of the United States. Mother and daughter quickly finished their ice cream and with several others exited the shop. Winter coats were appreciated as the frigid air hit once outside.

Grocery bags filled with food were placed in the backseat. The drive home was spent in idle chatter about Sybil's school friends. "You know the girls at my school are stupid. They fight over the boys and the boys have no clue. Today, one of the girls slugged another girl in the bathroom. She walked right up to her and slugged her in the nose. Blood and screaming, drama and for what? There was no reason. Teens are stupid. I'm glad you're my mother. You taught us violence is dumb." Sybil patted her mother's shoulder.

The vehicle was parked under the hanging tree. Sophia turned to Sybil, "Those girls don't attack you do they? You would tell me wouldn't you?"

"Mom, they're afraid of me. I'm tall. My metal teeth scare them. Besides they know you're my mother and you would eat them for breakfast if they tried anything." The backpack was lifted from the floor of the vehicle, "Since you substituted, hey, the others know you. When you told them you raised in Espanola, they freaked. Then when you said, 'don't mess with me or I fill you so full of holes like Swiss cheese' they believed you." Laughing, the grocery bags were grabbed. Racing into the kitchen through the rain, the two were soaked.

There was no sign of Granger. Stained one by two's were placed lengthwise on top of bales of alfalfa. Sophia gave a sigh of relief. They put the food away to change into their farm clothes. Sybil fed the horses on the right side of the barn while Sophia threw flakes of hay to the other side. Grabbing the pooper scooper, she dragged the wheelbarrow behind her to clean out each stall as the horses munched on their alfalfa. Sybil returned to the house to feed five hungry cats and Shonac dog, do her homework and put the leftovers from the night before into the oven. Life was peaceful here, uncomplicated and pleasant.

After Sybil was in bed with lights out, Sophia took courage to call her mother. Margaret was not happy with Granger. No surprise. Margaret wanted Sophia to come by after Sybil was dropped at her school the following morning. Sophia had an open day since she only was at the university on Tuesday and Thursday and taught a Wednesday evening two hour class on early Egyptian ethnology at the community college. Tuesday afternoon was her elementary school storytelling. Next term she would request more classes.

The morning brought a clear bright blue sky. Sandia Mountain was covered with snow. Long necked cranes pecked for worms in the alfalfa field behind the barn. That's where she found Sybil leaning against the white pole fence by the horses. "Mom, look. Granger put up all the fascia all around the house yesterday. He did it. We won't have to see him ever again. Not ever. We're done with him forever now, right?"

Stained boards under the roof gave the farmhouse a completed affect. As Sophia examined the boards, she noticed there was no sign of the nails used. He must have stained over them as well. It was certainly professional. "Hey!" A man's voice called to her from next door. Don Juan waved, "Looks great! I was going to help your man, but he said he didn't need any help. He did work hard all day until the rain came. Finished fast, huh?"

Sophia waved back and smiled. Sybil grabbed her mother's arm, "Come on, I don't want to be late for school. Stop flirting, Mom, it isn't becoming!"

Margaret's farmhouse was forty minutes from Sybil's school. Forty minutes to find composure and balance her emotions before Sophia would have to deal with her mother. Turning off the engine in her SUV, Sophia took a deep breath. The adobe wall around her mother's farmhouse was cracked and the stucco was falling off onto the half dead plants at the base. The window frames of the house were peeling paint and had separated from the adobe wall. Granger could fix this. He was able and smart. The problem was her mother's money. Money. It would take a lot of money to spruce this place up into being what it once was. Or not. Her mother didn't seem to care.

Turning the door handle on the back kitchen door, Sophia found it locked. She knocked on the wood as she peered through the panes of door glass. All she saw was the cleaned kitchen table her father had made from dark mahogany. It was more of a conference table than anything and too many nasty family conferences had occurred at that table. Beyond the table was the living room area. The green leather chair had been Papa's. The chair her father had expounded his stories from sat empty. He had been deceased for almost seven years. Extinguished by his son, his ghost had yet appeared. Peeking to the right side of the door, Sophia noticed her mother's tea cup and an empty plate on the counter. Sophia knocked harder.

The rattling of her mother's steel walker was heard moving toward her on the polished brick floors. Around the corner came Margaret. Puffing for air, she appeared haggard. Her dry hair was bowl cut and flying around her head. She gritted her teeth as she lifted and lowered the red walker, sliding her feet laced tightly in her black walking shoes. Sophia noticed for the first time how wrinkled her mother's face had become. The red lipstick was furrowing up each wrinkle from her mother's lips to the sides of her cheeks. Margaret stopped moving, lifting her hand and waving with a half-smile, she rested. Her mother's head bowed down to her chest. Margaret was puffing with pursed lips. It appeared to Sophia this would take time. She moved away from the door to wait.

The unlocked door clicked open, "Sorry, I was in the back bedroom resting. I forgot to unlock the door after the nurse disappeared." Margaret put her gnarled boney hand on Sophia's shoulder to give Sophia a half hug.

Pleasantness oozed from Sophia's voice, "How nice to have the visiting nurse come to help you, Mom." Sophia shut the door behind her as she moved into the kitchen.

"No. No, not at all. I lock the door to keep the visiting nurse out. I don't want strangers in my home. She calls and knocks and threatens, but I won't let her inside my castle. I hide in the bedroom after I lock all the doors. Eventually, she goes away. Then I get nasty phone calls from my doctor's office saying that I have to let the woman into my home. I won't have it. She's not coming inside and that's that." Margaret set her teeth and shook her head.

"Oh. Mom, if you don't let her help you, they can put you back in the hospital. You still aren't strong enough to be on your own. You know this, right?"

"No, I'm fine. Granger is here. Well, he was here. He's not here now. Granger is going to live with me and help me. I won't need a visiting nurse. The yellow paper they gave me at the hospital states clearly that if I live alone the visiting nurse is a requirement, but if someone lives with me and can help then no nurse. Granger's here now." Margaret was leading Sophia to the back bedroom. "Sophia, you are to call me Margaret, not mom!" The puffing of air continued as the metal walker was lifted and dropped with each step. It really made a lot of noise hitting the brick floor.

"Margaret, watch out! Don't hit the cat with your walker!" Sophia reached around her mother to lift the elderly cat. The cat weighed barely an ounce. A bloody raw stomach crusted with dirt covered the cat's belly. "Mom, your cat is half dead. Look at her stomach! She's lost all of her fur and it's raw from dragging on the floor. Her eyes are all yellow and goopy. Look?"

The walker continued to clang its way forward. Margaret kept sucking air, "I don't want to look. Put her down, call me Margaret. When you call me mom it makes me feel old. When she dies then she'll be at peace. Put her down and come in here." The steel walker stopped at the huge bed frame. Margaret pivoted to collapse on her double king-sized bed. "Oh, I didn't think I'd make it. My heart is racing. Sophia push the walker to the wall, would you?" The walker was pushed to the side. All four pillows were shoved under Margaret's back as she reclined with her legs dangling off the side of the bed. "Can you help me, Sophia, and lift my legs onto the bed?" Her small waif like body was held by thin arms wrapped around her waist.

Both women were lying on the bed. Both stared up at the vigas in the ceiling. Spider webs decorated the corners of the room. Intricate patterns hung from the vigas to the walls. The harsh wind blasted sand against the two bedroom windows "It's the wind, it makes me tired. The constant sound throttling my poor home leaves us both to whither inside." A tear fell from her left eye to drop on her pillow.

One window beside her mother's bed wouldn't close properly since the adobe wall had settled years ago. The other was painted shut and was at the far right side of the room. Dirt and dust particles floated in the air around them. Sophia rolled over onto her side to ask her mother, "Where's Granger? Isn't he supposed to be here for you?"

Margaret sniffed, "He's busy. I gave him some money, well, I signed a blank check so he can get a vehicle of his own. He doesn't like my new truck. He's busy." She looked vacantly up at the ceiling.

Gasping, Sophia commented, "Well, your truck just needs to be washed. The bird's nest is in the tree above where you park. Bird scat is baked onto the windshield and is removing the paint from the hood. It's highly decorated with foul poop. Don't know how you can see out of the windshield, it's filthy. Mom, I mean, Margaret, why did you want me to come this morning?"

The elderly cat meowed. Pointing to the oriental carpet on the bedroom floor, Margaret asked, "Sophia, pick up the cat would you and put her on the bed?" Sniffing, she continued, "You teach at the university about cultures and their traditions, but you don't know anything about your own family history. I thought it was time for you to get a grasp of what life was like for the women in your own family. It's time for you to know where we came from and how hard it has been for us."

Petting the elderly cat by her side, Sophia questioned, "I have asked and you told me to wait, right? Is it time now?"

"You always make things difficult, don't you?" Margaret huffed, "Sophia, you have always been a difficult person to please. Yes, it is time for me to explain to you how difficult our life has been."

Margaret explained how Sophia's great grandmother had been married to a railroad man who was as sober as the day was long until he went on a long four month extension to California through the Rocky Mountains. Great grandmother was left alone with eleven children to care for in the early spring. She made lye soap for washing bodies and clothes. While mixing the lye in a glass, one of her children ran up thirsty and drank the lye by accident. It was a horrible death. A neighbor had come to help her, a woman who was expecting any day. This woman's husband worked on the train, too. This poor woman had lost babies in five miscarriages. While this extremely pregnant woman was helping great grandmother, she had another miscarriage. Great grandmother being pregnant herself, gave birth to a fine fat baby boy a week later. This great grandmother was exhausted and overwhelmed with all the children she already had. Late at night, she took her new infant to the grieving younger woman to give her the newly born baby boy. No one was to be the wiser, but this story was passed down from generation to generation. Grant grandmother was a kindly Christian woman who believed in God's work. Strict Baptist law was also instructed into all of her children.

"Once great grandpa was home, he arrived with alcohol on his breath and a long story of being trapped in the Rocky Mountain snow storm. The train was stuck for ten days with no hope of being saved. They had run out of food and only had strong drink to survive. The man was frazzled, questioning his railway work and the people who were supposed to know of weather and emergency conditions. Great grandmother smelled the alcohol on his breath. Good Christians did not imbibe alcohol. Their marriage was over. She was a temperate woman with a mantra that any man who drank was not to live with her nor touch her or her lips. She packed up the ten remaining children to load them all on a train. Her husband worked on the railroad, their trip was free. They arrived in New York City with her savings and ten suitcases.

"Great grandmother realized she was able to be self-sufficient. Buying a brownstone three story building, she turned it into a Christian boarding house. Slowly, she married off her girls and had her sons help support her once they moved away to form their own families." Margaret grimaced, "My grandmother realized how difficult life was without a man. She instilled in all of us, or those who knew her, that a woman cannot live well without a man."

Sophia blew cat hair off of her fingers as she stroked the cat, "Margaret, women don't need a man to survive. Look at history. Greek woman thrived and did well while their men were away fighting wars for ten years. Roman women practically ran the country while the politicians ran amuck."

Pushing the cat away from her, Margaret shook her head, "No, Sophia, women need men. We cannot survive without men. We are weak and not as wise as men, listen…"

As if on cue, a well-built man with striking reddish-brown hair and piercing black eyes strode into the room, "How come I wasn't invited to this slumber party?" Granger tossed a check at his mother. The piece of paper missed the bed to float to the brick floor. "Margaret, there isn't enough money in your account for a Mercedes! I could only find a preowned vehicle with shoddy tires for this amount. This won't do! I had a Mercedes when I went into the pokey and now I want my Mercedes back!" Slovenly, he sat on the edge of the bed to pout.

Both women stared at him. Noticing their silence, he chose to lean against her bureau at the far side of the room. "Listen I have been in hell for over six years and seven months! I have endured almost being raped, stabbed and manipulated by big ugly guys! I deserve to have the vehicle of my dreams, I paid my dues!" He slapped his thigh and left the room.

Margaret gasped, "How can I please him? Get me the phone. Hand me the phone and the black rolodex. I'll call my stock broker. Somehow there's got to be money for a new Mercedes. Oh, Sophia, he's angry at me." She looked nervously from Sophia to the bedroom door.

Sophia picked up the check that was lying upside down on the floor. It was for ten thousand dollars. "Wow, Mom or Margaret, this is a chunk of change! Are you sure you want to do this for him? Isn't he supposed to get a job and find his own way to make a living and support himself?"

Boney fingers grabbed the check from Sophia's hand. Margaret leaned over the bed to retrieve her purse. In a timid voice, she pleaded to Sophia, "He's right. He does deserve to have his Mercedes. I don't have a clue how much things cost now a days. Before I call my broker, would you go and ask him how much a Mercedes cost?" Putting up her hand, Margaret smiled, "Don't fight me on this, Sophia! Please, don't fight me! I don't want to fight with anyone right now."

Placing her hand on Margaret's arm, Sophia smiled, "He's supposed to make his own way. They told us this at the prison when we spoke with his parole officer. You're not to spoil him, he's supposed to learn from his mistakes. There are consequences to his actions and spoiling him isn't going to help."

Grappling to sit upright, Margaret replied in a slow and steady voice, "No, Sophia, he's my son. He didn't know what he was doing. He's not a mechanic. This is all in the past now, it's time for us to move forward and enjoy life. Please, no, don't fight me on this. Go and get your brother. I don't know why you hate your brother so much! Just go and get him, please." A tear fell from Margaret's eye.

Sophia hesitantly found Granger in the kitchen making himself a sandwich. "Hey, Margaret wants you. She could use a sandwich, too? I'm out of here, got things to do. Bye." She grabbed her purse and headed for the door.

Granger called out, "Hey! Wait a minute!" He walked with her from the back porch to her vehicle. "You didn't tell her I wanted her dead, did you? Because that would be a very bad idea. She would twist your words around to believe you were the one who wanted her dead, right?"

Disgusted with him, Sophia smirked, "Of course not! Why would I say something like that to the frail woman? Come on, Granger, you are completely dependent on her now. She's dependent on you! Give it up!" Sophia huffed in anger, "If anything were to happen to her, well, you would be suspect and back in prison before you could blink. I know you're not stupid!" Pulling the driver's door open, she waved him away from her, "Go back inside and fix your mother lunch! Damn it, Granger, be kind to her. She bailed you out and stood beside you for all these years. Be nice to her."

He hurriedly followed her to hold the door handle to keep her driver's door open, "She sold my Mercedes! No one gave her permission to sell it. Besides, if she does die all of her money is mine. I have regained power of attorney. At least I will have it once my probation is over. Sophia, don't ruin this for me!" The car door slammed shut. "Also, don't forget he who holds the deed holds the house." As he walked away, he kicked her front tire.

Sophia spoke under her breath, "Damn you, Granger. You seriously could use lessons in decency!"

As she drove home, Sophia knew she had to call her mother's doctor about the visiting nurse. Perhaps it would be better if Margaret were to return to the hospital. Granger was only going to rob her blind. Sophia knew her mother didn't have much money left after all the lawsuits and court cases. At least Sophia was separate with her own income and no longer was dependent on anyone but herself. Except there was the issue of the farmhouse and her title. Granger's words echoed in her memory.

At seven years of age, Granger had threatened to take revenge on their parents. The two children had shared a room in the old farmhouse on the reservation. Papa had rented fourteen acres of land with an old adobe farmhouse for ninety-nine dollars a year right on the edge of the Pueblo's reservation. The barn they built housed hogs, pigs, chickens, five beef steers and two milk cows. Sophia's mother Margaret had been raised on the road with her wealthy mother and her older sister. The nanny had been the surrogate mother who hugged Margaret and complimented her regardless of the thick glasses she wore and the chipped front tooth. Papa was the one who paid for the tooth repair. The velour front teeth had cost a fortune, but Papa wanted his wife to feel comfortable with her appearance.

The Pueblo reservation home had been a place of hell. Each night when Papa would arrive home late from the hospital, the children would instantly awaken. Margaret and Papa would loudly fight. Margaret screaming at him to be a real father, to be home and punish the children when they had misbehaved. The list in her black notebook was shoved into his face. Wrong doings, misdeeds and inattentive behaviors were listed in her printed hand clearly written with a black fountain pen. Her sharp tongue would push him into the children's bedroom. He would first grab Granger. Slugging him in the stomach, throwing him onto the floor, kicking him and condemning him for something Margaret had ratted. Then, Sophia knew it was her turn. Papa was less forceful with her, but still the fists and the kicking hurt. They were silent during this escapade for to cry out or scream only caused more punishment.

Margaret would lean against the door frame, smirking. The children didn't know if she was proud of Papa for punishing them or she was gleeful at their pain. Although, Granger had said their mother believed in the old Bible. She had told him that to spoil a child was a sin. "Spare the rod, spoil the child is the word of God." Regardless, Granger had sworn at the young age of seven to take revenge, "Someday, they will pay for what they did to us."

Granger had grown to be a strong, educated man with the constant reminder of those days. His bruised and broken ribs ached still to this day. There wasn't a holiday shared where Granger didn't repeat his threat. "Someday, they will pay." Papa had expired thanks to Granger. Everyone knew this. Papa had abused pain killers after his open heart surgery and back surgery. Drinking down two or three tablets of Demerol with straight scotch, his brain fried. Three years of being a skeleton covered in skin, curled in a fetal position in the hospital bed of his big bedroom on his farm had left their tall, drop-dead handsome father a vegetable.

Elevated the hospital bed kept Papa alive with his I.V. drip and catheter. He had to be elevated or he couldn't breathe. Margaret and Granger had lowered the bed one windy night to let Papa aspirate and die. Everyone knew they had done this. No one did anything. Not even the sheriff or his posse. Sophia shook her head, the memory of her father's dead body being zipped in the black plastic mortuary bag still terrified her.

Sybil waved as Sophia pulled into the lineup of cars at the Middle School. The frown on Sybil's face spoke volumes of failure. "Mom, would it kill you to get here on time at least three times a week? All my friends feel sorry for me! My science teacher was going to wait with me, but I told him to go on because who knows how late you would be, right?" Folding her arms across her chest, the fifteen year old daughter glared straight ahead in her passenger seat as they pulled out onto the main road.

Sophia tried not to smile, "How about an ice cream then?"

Sybil pushed up her black framed glasses. There were smudge marks on her left lens. "Oh, you're going to resort to bribery?"

Ice cream finished, the two women completed the grocery shopping just as the rain began to fall. Running back and forth from the vehicle to the house with bags of groceries, they both became soaked. Sophia put the groceries away watching the clock the whole time. Sybil changed out of her school clothes into her comfort clothes. "Mom, go and change! We have to go! Leave the canned stuff, we can put it away later. Come on, Mom, we've got to go and get Donna!"

Rain slid down the front windshield as the wipers flung water back and forth. Sybil was nervously wrapping one hand around the other as she wished the vehicle to go faster. Then she laughed and pointed to Sophia's feet, "Mom, you didn't wear your stinky boots! What's Dad going to think?"

Sophia patted her side jean pocket, "Damn, I forgot the cellphone. It's on the kitchen table or on my bureau. Oh, well, let's not have an accident."

"Yeah, Mom, let's just get there and be gone. That house gives me the creeps. Dad has become a real hoarder and the house stinks of cat piss."

"Sybil, such language!" Sophia put on the blinker as they turned off the main interstate onto the highway going up the hill to Rocoso. Returning to this house always gave her the jitters. This was where she was almost blown up along with Sheriff A.J. Salazar on the afternoon Granger's bomb exploded in Geoffrey's truck. Sheriff Salazar had thrown his body on top of hers to protect her. Shrapnel had almost blinded him. Those times were bad times, bad memories. As they pulled into the driveway, Sophia glared at the house. She parked, turned off the engine to say to Sybil, "Do you mind? I don't think I can face him." Staring off at the vista to the north of high flat topped mountains, called mesas, Sophia remembered how she loved this house. The house was cleaned twice a week because it was small, there needed to be a constant care effort. Now Geoffrey didn't clean at all. Donna was the one who tried, but Geoffrey shrugged off her efforts saying he enjoyed a comfortable home not one that was sterile. Turning her attention back to Sybil, she noted her daughter watching the driblets of rain slide down the windshield.

"Are you going to get your sister?"

Sybil frowned, "I don't want to go in there either. Especially now that I know he isn't my real father. It's filthy in there. Last time we were in there, we both got sick." Sybil's attention was deferred to movement from the front door. Donna raced to the vehicle, slid open the back door and jumped in. "Go, Go! Dad's in a mood and we better hustle or he won't let me leave. Go! Mom, go!"

Twisting in the front passenger seat, Sybil confronted her sister, "What's going on? Why's Dad angry or pissed or whatever?"

Sophia turned on the ignition, "Shouldn't we tell him we're going?"

Donna screamed, "NO! GO!"

The ignition on, Sophia watched as the front door opened and Geoffrey came racing toward them. He was yelling something, but the windows were up because of the rain and they couldn't hear his words. Geoffrey's shirt was buttoned askew, his fly was down and he was in his stocking feet. Red faced anger showed. Terrifying emotion came at the vehicle.

Donna's voice became even louder, "Mom! PLEASE GO!" Geoffrey ran at the vehicle to slap the hood. This movement alone frightened Sophia. Pressing down on the gas pedal and letting off on the brake, the vehicle shot backwards onto the paved road. Sophia gasped with relief to see there were no cars on the road. Geoffrey continued to race after them. He had a beer can in one hand and the other was frantically waving at them as he screamed. His clothes drenched with the falling rain.

Sophia put the vehicle in drive as they took off quickly down Rocoso road to Rincon and home. "What's going on, Donna? What is with your father?" Sophia's voice was soft.

Donna collapsed back into the seat with relief. "I don't know. While I was packing my stuff in this good old backpack, Mom, I need a new one, there was a phone call. Dad answered. At first I didn't listen, but then his voice got loud. He was talking to Sheriff Salazar. The sheriff needed your new address, he didn't know you guys were divorced. I guess he hasn't spoken to you since Granger's court case. Anyway, Dad started yelling about how the Pino family was nothing but a bunch of murderers and thieves. Then he charged into my room. Donna put her knee into the front passenger seat back, "Sybil, you know how he charges about?"

Sybil's shoulder was pressed into the front passenger seat, pushing back against her sister's knees, "Yeah, go on."

"Well he charged into my room, grabbed my backpack and threw my stuff all over the floor. 'You're not going anywhere! You're not going to die in that Pino house! You're staying here, do you understand me? You're staying in this room and you aren't allowed to leave until I say so!' Then he went out and slammed my door."

Sophia watched Donna's expressions in the rearview mirror. "Why was he so angry? What happened?"

Shrugging, Donna went on, "He tried to lock my bedroom door. Good luck with that, right? So, he went into the kitchen and while he was in the kitchen, I put all my stuff back in my pack." She patted her faded demin backpack. "I snuck down the hall. He was gulping down out of his tall whiskey bottle, I don't know what was in it but he drank a lot!" She stopped to take a breather.

Sybil filled in the silence, "Yeah, when he's stressed he drinks. What was he stressed about?"

Waving her hand in front of her face, Donna continued, "All I know is Dad then tried to call Mom on her cellphone. There was no answer. This made him even madder. He pulled a can of beer from the fridge, screaming out, 'Damn that woman and her rotten family!'" Donna clapped her hands and smiled, "I hustled around the kitchen, down the hall to the front porch. Then his small dog Freddy started barking. I was holding him inside between the door and the hall when you guys showed to get me." She turned to look behind them at the road. "I hope Freddy's inside now, I hope. I hope Dad didn't leave him out. Dad forgets about the dog and Freddy pees and poops all over inside….along with the cats." Donna held her nose between her index finger and thumb.

Sophia put her hand up for Donna to stop, "You know, young lady, you can clean out the kitty litter boxes? Why do you expect your father to do it when you can?"

Shaking her head, Donna lifted her chin in the air, "Dad won't let me! He says I use too much kitty litter and that I'm wasteful. Whenever I try to do the dumping of extreme poop, he gets angry. Dad has one emotion or maybe two, he's either totally pissed or he's braindead. It's one or the other." Donna unzipped her backpack to pull out a large plastic horse.

Sybil put out her hand to take it, "Whoa, Donna, this is the Breyer horse you always wanted. Did Dad get it for you?"

"Yeah, I refused to go to school until he bought it for me. He stood in the store grinding his teeth, fiddling with his change in his pocket, but I wasn't going to budge. I wanted it and if he didn't buy it for me, I wasn't going to go back to school."

Running her fingers over the smooth plastic neck of the horse, Sybil smiled, "Hey, Donna, you're getting smart. Good thing you have an older sister to teach you how to get what you want, right?"

Sophia cleared her throat, "Hey, you guys, you know I am right here, don't you? The driver, the mother, the enforcer is within listening range."

Pointing down the Alcon Road, Donna said, "Hey, Driver, watch out for the tumbleweed monster. It's coming straight at us."

The tumbleweed flew directly at the front grill of the vehicle. Sophia shouted, "Take that, Monster Tumbleweed!" As it hit the vehicle it broke apart into thousands of little pieces.

Sybil laughed, "Wow, Mom, you're radical!"

They ran through the light rain into the farmhouse all together. The girls did their routine of both trying to get through the door at the same time, giggling, laughing and racing into Donna's room. Shonac barked, wagging his tail to follow them. Sophia leaned against the doorframe to kick off her clogs and pull on her barn boots. Burning pine smoke from neighboring fireplaces filled the air. Soggy earth was knocked off the soles of her boots. They were filthy. Dropping the boots, Sophia slid back on her old leather clogs. Then she remembered the cellphone, perhaps Geoffrey had left her a message about his troubles. On the corner of the kitchen table sat the small device. Lifting it, she saw the blue light blinking. There were five missed calls. Four from Geoffrey. "Oh, my!" Returning the small phone to the kitchen table, she called to the girls, "Hey, I'm going to feed the horses and make sure they're all in the stalls. Do you guys want to come help?"

Yelling in glee, the girls ran down the hall and out the front door, "Mom, we'll do it!"

Sophia pulled out a kitchen chair and sat. Her eyes scanned the kitchen cupboards, "I could use a stiff drink right now, too." Hitting the voicemail button on her cellphone, she waited to view the list of callers. The battery light went on and then the cellphone went dark. "Hah! Not even this guy wants to hear anger!" Trudging into her bedroom in her clogs, she plugged it into the wall socket.

Suddenly, a siren pierced the air. Shonac's barking was sharp and frantic. Racing to the kitchen window, Sophia saw a sheriff's vehicle. Red and blue lights flashed. Shonac growled as he raced around the driver's door. The flashing lights were suddenly off. Sophia watched as Shonac turned his attention back to the barn. Swiftly turning, he ran full speed into the barn. Frantically looking beyond the official vehicle, Sophia eyes sought to find her daughters. They were nowhere in sight, but then the poor light of dusk and the dripping rain off of the barn's tin roof made it difficult to see clearly. Clogs echoed as they pounded to the front of the farm house. The front door knob in her hand was flung open. There stood Sheriff A.J. Salazar with a clipboard. He inhaled quickly to step back startled by her sudden appearance.

Sophia gasped, "What? What is it? Where are my girls? Did you take my girls?"

"No!" His voice was firm as Sophia tried to get around him, he put his arm out to block her. "Sophia, I'm not the enemy here. Please, calm down. I'm just here to speak with you. Calm down, calm."

Glaring at him with full distrust, she noticed the scars on his face. His life was forever marked from trying to save her. His left eyelid drooped. His left eye now blind thanks to saving her life. Brown eyes softened as he watched her reaction. A.J. was her friend for life. If he said the girls are fine, then they must be fine. "A.J., I need to find my daughters. Please let me pass?"

His brown jacket was zipped halfway up and was rain wet. He had a plastic cover around the brim of his official brown hat. Rainwater fell off the brim onto his brown work books. Pulling off the dripping hat, his brown and gray hair had flattened with his bangs pressed against his forehead. Standing to the side, he let her pass by him. He was only an inch or so taller. Sophia ran into the barn. Bending low she peered around each horse. The smell of wet manure and horse hair was strong. Lucky the gelded bay stomped his hoof. Whispering loudly, Sophia called, "Sybil, Donna, where are you? Girls, where are you?" Two of the horses whinnied. They were hungry. The oat room door opened a crack, "Mom?" It was Donna. "Mom, what is the sheriff doing here?"

Sophia let her shoulders relax, "I don't know, but stay in here. We'll be in the house. You guys feed the horses, but stay out here just in case."

"O-kay, Mom. Come and get us after they leave." Donna pulled the door shut.

As Sophia turned, she heard Sybil's older voice barely call out, "Mom? Hey, Mom, should we muck out or leave it until morning? I mean what if they try to take us away?"

Knowing Sybil probably already had a plan of escape, Sophia leaned back, "Sybil, muck out. Evidently there is something afoot with Granger and Grandma. Take care of the horses. Then stay here in the oat room.

I'll come for you once A.J. is gone. He is our friend, remember?" The oat room door quietly shut with giggling.

Sheriff A.J. Salazar stood outside of the front door waiting, watching Sophia. Rainwater dripped from the hat now returned to his head. Then the side door of his official vehicle opened. A tall woman stepped out into the rain. She wore the same brown uniform as the deputy sheriff aside from black leather pumps and A.J. wore heavy brown work boots with laces. This blonde haired woman held a brown clipboard over her head as she ran to stand beside A.J. Salazar. Sophia walked slowly through the drizzling rain to the door. Rainwater dribbled down the back of her blue work shirt. "Go ahead inside." A.J. pushed the door open and let the women walk in ahead of him. Sophia led the way into the warm kitchen. Last night's frying onion odor still permeated the air.

As they sat at the table, her cellphone chirped in her bedroom. Then the landline phone in the hall rang. Sheriff A.J. Salazar shook his head, "Ignore those. We need to talk."

Glancing at the land phone, Sophia saw on the caller I.D. had Geoffrey's name. The room felt crowded as the woman sat beside Salazar at the table. Three mugs were taken from the side board. Sophia asked, "Tea? Coffee? Would you like something hot to drink after the long drive out here?"

A.J. laughed as he turned to the strange woman, "Be prepared. Sophia enjoys serving tea." Smiling at Sophia, he added, "Yes, a hot cup of tea would hit the spot."

Nodding, the woman agreed, "Yes, I'd love a mug of tea. Do you have any ginger with lemon tea, if that isn't being too pushy?"

Cupboard open, Sophia took down the yellow box of ginger and lemon tea. "Here we go. I agree. A.J. is it the same for you?"

He placed his hat flat on the table. "Yes, two tea drinkers? Who would've thought?"

Bending over the table, the woman put out her hand, "Hello, I'm Inspector Detective Clem Thompson homicide. International division."

Hot water boiled in the electric kettle on the counter. Mugs were filled and set on the table with a small milk-glass pitcher with matching sugar bowl. Fat slices of homemade bread with a butter dish were placed in the middle of the table with linen napkins placed at appropriate places set with spoons. A.J. nodded his appreciation, "Clem, this bread is divine. In the old days, Sophia used to fatten us with chocolate and cookies. This is a step up, right?"

The kitchen chair opposite the two was pulled out. Sophia sat down to stir her tea. "I aim to please, especially when visited by the law."

Pointing at the old gas stove, the stranger asked, "Does she still work?"

Turning, Sophia answered, “Yes, Mabel is able but she’s not always willing. At least that’s what the girls say.”

As if approving, Clem said, “Growing up with my grandparents, they had a gas stove like that. Agreed, it baked the best bread ever. Your home is beautiful, but I bet it’s hard to keep warm in the freezing winters?”

The kitchen was cold, but then Sophia decided she wasn’t going to turn on the heater. This was a formal affair. They would have tea and bread. Questions would be asked and answered.

Silence filled the large kitchen. Fergus cat wandered into the room, howled and jumped into Sophia’s lap. He was hungry. Salazar smiled, “He’s a big cat. How much does he weigh?”

Stroking his orange fur, Sophia answered, “He’s about fifteen pounds. He likes to eat fast food in the barn, known as his mice. Then he comes inside to eat everyone else’s canned food.” She frowned, “Why are we talking about the cat?”

Clem Thompson set her clipboard on the kitchen table. “We have a suspicious death on our hands and we think you can help us with it.” Sophia noticed the woman’s plain gold wedding band.

A.J. Salazar lifted his hand with his palm toward Sophia. His words were carefully chosen, “Sophia, this isn’t about you or the girls, not directly.”

Staring at him, Sophia asked, “The girls? What would the girls have to do with a suspicious murder? They aren’t old enough to know how to murder anyone?” Her mug of tea was pulled closer to her.

“No. They’re not.” He demurred to Clem Thompson who was buttering a piece of bread on her napkin. Not waiting for a reply, Sophia sat straighter to ask, “Is it Granger? Has he killed someone already? He’s just out of prison, just yesterday or maybe the day before, how could’ve he killed already?” Somehow she sounded protective of him.

Papers with black and white photographs copied onto them were taken out of Clem’s clipboard. Carefully, they were placed in a straight row across the table in front of Sophia. Clem’s voice was no longer friendly, but now firm, “Do you know of a Rosa Mendoza?”

Falling against the chair back, Sophia studied the sheriff woman’s face. Clem Thompson was about Sophia’s age. Her blonde hair was pulled back into a low ponytail fixed under her hat. Clem wore no makeup. Her eyes were a chocolate brown. Her thin pointed nose had a few freckles. The thin lips were chapped and dry. She asked again, “Are you familiar with a woman named Rosa Mendoza?”

“Sophia!” A.J. spoke loudly interrupting Sophia’s silence. She stared at him, “What? Of course I know Rosa Mendoza. I don’t know her well. She’s Roberto’s wife. He’s the guy who helps my mother. Granger and I were just talking about him. He's a great help to my mother. She would be totally lost without him. Why? What happened?" Sophia caught her breath, "What does a suspicious death mean?"

Clem Thompson cleared her throat as if she was irritated with Sophia. Salazar interrupted his fellow sheriff before she could say anything more, "Sophia, please. Rosa is dead. She died at home, in her home. Roberto is beyond frantic to find out what happened. His adult children were all killed under horrible circumstances and he's terrified. We're working on finding out what happened to his wife."

Stupidly, Sophia kept nodding her head at him as if she was trying to understand what he was saying. He continued, "There's an autopsy being done on Rosa right now. There are suspicious circumstances, but we don't think her death is gang related. It appears to be more personal." He leaned back and pointed to the woman beside him, "Clem is from Albuquerque, she works with immigration regarding unusual deaths." He put his hand back in his lap, "Please, humor us and just answer the questions."

Shoving one of the pieces of paper at Sophia, the female sheriff pointed to a particular shape within a photograph, "Do you know what this is?"

Squinting at the poor quality of the picture, Sophia gasped. "Yes, I know what this is."

Raindrops suddenly hit the window reverberating like bullets on a metal plate. Clem jumped, then stared at the kitchen window, "It's really coming down now, huh? All right, can you tell me what you know about this?"

Pushing her wet bangs from her forehead, Sophia appeared apprehensive. Her work shirt was wet. She was cold and worried about the girls. "Why? What's so important about this package?"

Clearing his throat, Salazar shook his head at her, "Come on, Sophia. Answer her."

"Well, this package is a brown bag resembling a lunch bag. The brown bag has a logo on it that is from Granger's old clinic. The symbol of eternal life from India or somewhere like that. Why don't you ask Granger?" Her attention turned to Salazar, "You know this is Granger's logo sticker from his clinic, right? Why don't you ask him?"

Clem's voice took her attention from Salazar, "Ma'am, we need to hear from you. Please, what else do you know about this picture?"

Sophia sucked in air, "Don't call me Ma'am! My name is Sophia Pino. You can call me Sophia or Dr. Pino, but don't call me Ma'am!" She pushed back the chair and stood as if urging them to leave. They didn't move. "Listen, my daughters are out in the barn. It's cold and getting dark. I need to bring them inside. Would you mind leaving us, please?" Sophia reached back to the kitchen wall to flip on the six hanging lights over the kitchen table.

The two officers didn't move. They remained seated at the long wooden kitchen table. Removing his brown hat, Salazar shook the water off of the plastic cover of the brim of his hat. The rainwater sprinkled on the kitchen floor. The overhead lights made the droplets of water look like sparkles. "Sophia, sit. Down. Talk to us. Then get your daughters. Sit."

Putting her hands on the back of the kitchen chair, Sophia remained standing. Her fingers were wrapped around the wooden slat backing of the kitchen chair. Her voice was hoarse now as she rattled out, "This bag contained herbs. Medicinal herbs. My brother Granger was an herbalist who worked at healing people who were ill. His specialty was Chinese herbs or local herbs. This package obviously came from his clinic." Suddenly, Sophia sat down. Shaking her head, she kept talking, "My brother Granger has been in jail for six years and seven months. His clinic was closed. His herbs, well, I don't know, maybe were destroyed?" She shrugged her shoulders, "I have no idea? Both my brother and his partner ended up in jail. If these herbs were used by someone, they were stupid."

She shrugged her shoulders, "Obviously, herbs only last so long. If someone was using these herbs or were given these herbs they should've looked for the expiration date on the bottom of the bag. That's all I can tell you. Now, will you please leave?" Sophia started to rise from the chair, but then A.J. put his hand out for her to stay put.

Another piece of paper was pulled from the lineup on the table. Clem lifted the paper, "Look, read this. What does this say?"

The white paper with a blurry photograph was picked up and held close to Sophia's face. She squinted to read the small print from the poor quality copy. The photograph was of the bottom of the brown bag. Salazar quietly spoke to his partner who dug into her carrycase to pull out a magnifying glass. "Here, this might help."

The woman's face smiled, but Sophia kept her expression rigid. Taking the magnifying glass, Sophia sternly read aloud the words, "E-x-p twenty-twelve-two-nineteen. This date is this coming February. How is this possible?" Exhaustion was noticeable in her face. Her forehead wrinkled. "What? What can this mean? Who is using my brother's herbs?" Frowning, she quizzed Salazar, "Where did this bag come from? Is this print from a printer or someone who is good at copying a hand held date printer?"

Salazar and Clem peered around Sophia as they heard giggling and a door softly closing. Sophia frowned, "I guess my daughters have arrived."

Clem Thompson gathered up the papers on the table returning them to her clipboard. Quickly, A.J. was on his feet and out the door following the girls' voices. "Hey, Donna, Sybil? Where are you both?"

"Here, we're in here!" Donna opened her bedroom door, screaming out, "Uncle A.J.! What are you doing here?"

Standing, Sophia whistled for Shonac who came directly to her. His tail wagging in friendly greeting. Clem bent down to rub Shonac's ears. "He's a beauty, this one. What is he?"

No matter what words came out of Clem's mouth they always ended in a question. Sophia smiled down at her, "Shonac is a Russian Wolf hound mix with some Australian Shepherd. He's extremely protective of us. Although, he likes to chase the eighteen wheelers, which is dangerous."

"Yes, I would believe so." Clem continued to scratch Shonac's head. "Why do you chase those big things, they can kill you, you know?"

A.J. disappeared into Donna's room eager to hear the story of the two ghost sisters who visit Donna each night at three in the morning. It was impressive that the girls remembered him from seven years ago.

Sophia took the mugs to the sink. Curiosity got the best of her, she turned to ask the woman who was rubbing Shonac's ears, "Where does your name originate? Clem is an unusual name, isn't it?

"Oh, yes. Well, not terribly unusual. My full name is Clementine Amity Rutherford. The guys I work with at the station found Clementine to be difficult to say. Men's mouths can't work around all those syllables. Yet, they can say Geraldo or Tostito, but not my name?"

Leaning against the porcelain sink, Sophia put her finger up, "Ah-hah. An old English name, but not a modern name. Probably your family is from an old British colony."

"Go on, so where do you think my family lives?" Clementine's interest was piqued.

"Well, my degree is in ethnology and solving riddles is part of my work. Let's think a minute. British colonies during the seventeen and eighteen hundreds were most prevalent in Australia or southern Africa, perhaps India. But you're tall and have the Anglo coloring, so I would believe your family lives down under?"

Clapping her hands, Clem was impressed. "Yes, my father's family were prisoners who were transferred to the southern isle. Aye, you're ace, bloody dead-set for I'm dinky-di the fair dinkum. Did you know you have a Sally in your kitchen?"

"How fun to hear the real slang from a real thunder gal." Sophia turned to fill the sink with hot sudsy water to wash the tea mugs and spoons. "Clementine, tell me how in the world you arrived here in the outback of New Mexico? Certainly this is a long way from your down under farm?"

She handed Clementine a dish towel hanging from the refrigerator handle. Clementine took a wet washed mug from Sophia to say, “It’s nice to have another woman to share with here. Since I arrived four months ago, it has been hard to make friends. Especially in my line of work where people are worried they’ll say something incriminating. Can you believe it?” Setting the dried clean mug on the counter, she relayed her story.

“There is an Army base near Sydney where I went to University, there in the center of Sydney. A tall drop dead handsome man was doing research in the library at the same time I was there. He was interested in the legal complications of working with radioactivity. Australia has thirty-three percent of the world’s uranium deposits. At that time I was interested in law. Can you imagine a young Sally interested in maintaining the law in a definitely male environment of predators?”

She held up the dried mug, “Where do you want me to put this?”

Sophia nodded to the hooks on the side of the cupboard over the sink, “Australia has uranium?”

Clementine nodded, “Yes. This handsome man and I met often for coffee and we fell for one another. Then he had to return home to Fort Bliss in El Paso where he was called to continue his work on the amounts of radiation at White Sands Missile base. He left and suddenly I was shattered for I believed in our true love. Then one Christmas I received a phone call from Roger. He asked me to marry him over long distance. Some gentleman, huh?”

Sophia laughed, “How romantic. No kneeling down with an engagement ring for him, right?”

“Right. My grandparents were there, listening in on the call. I lived with them since I was a poor student. He sent me a plane ticket. The Army said he couldn’t get leave to come to me. Sight unseen I flew with two large suitcases of gifts to El Paso, Texas. My heart in my hand. Surprisingly, I wasn’t frightened or worried. You know my mother would have killed me if she knew?”

“Brave woman. How old were you?”

“I was twenty-two years old and never been truly in love before. Roger was thirty, a widower with a nine year old daughter. This was a huge step, also, I had never been on a plane before. There was the hurried hassle of getting a passport and a work visa, all the political paperwork before going. Brave and naïve, hope your girls are smarter? ”

Putting the mugs and the clean spoons away, Sophia smiled, “I hope he was there to meet you?”

“Oh, yes, and his young daughter Elaine. She was tall for her age, almost as tall as I am. She was more frightened than I was.” Shaking out the dish towel Clementine placed it back through the refrigerator’s handle to dry. "We lived in his Army married housing area after we had a justice of the peace wedding. It was just us, Elaine and two of Roger's buddies from his work area on base. Our marriage was a success. Our love was rich and wonderful, one of those ever-after marriages you read about, do you know?"

Frowning, Sophia faced her, "What is this past tense reference?"

"I'm sure you don't want or need to hear my horror story. Certainly, we have taken up enough of your time here. Really, you want to hear the story of my life in pain?" Clementine's face was now a red blush.

Staring out the kitchen window, Sophia said, "The rain has stopped. A.J. is being entertained by my girls. Unless duty calls, I certainly want to hear what happened." Pulling out a kitchen chair, Sophia sat down pointing to the chair opposite. "Oh, please, don't leave me hanging. Now that I know you, I want to hear your story, please."

Clementine took off her sheriff's hat to pull loose her blonde hair from the rubber band of her ponytail. Her hair fell down to her waist. "Roger worked at White Sand Missile Base on recording and measuring radioactive activity. He and Elaine would catch small creatures in a butterfly net. When Elaine was small he took her with him to play in the sand, run and slide, eat picnic lunches and spend the afternoon. It was four years and eleven days after our marriage when Elaine came into our room to show us a rash she had on her back and her tummy. At first I thought it was a change of hormones, don't girls go through some of those times?"

Clementine held a linen napkin in her hand, "We took her to her GP and he felt the rash was an allergic reaction to soap or food. We changed everything, but the rash wouldn't go away and it got worse. Soon, even her clothes hurt her, to touch her skin. We ended up taking her to Phoenix to Mao Clinic there. It was brutally hot in July. The sweat on her skin made her cry out from the pain. Can you envision her a fourteen year old curled up in a ball of pain?"

She took a breath, "It turned out to be a form of skin cancer. Soon it spread and within three months, she was dead." Clementine wiped her nose with the linen napkin in her hand. "Fifteen years old and her life ended. Then everything happened quickly. Roger wouldn't eat. He didn't go to work. They gave him some time off for a mourning period, but he wouldn't return to work. I tried everything to get him to move, to go outside, to go to a movie with me, something! He sat in our bedroom with the curtains pulled, in darkness. Roger wouldn't shower, wouldn't eat or drink and this seriously frightened me. The curtains were closed all the time because he said the sunlight hurt his eyes. The sun hurt his eyes?"

Twisting the linen napkin in her hands, she stared at it, "Finally, I called one of his mates from work. Everyone was worried. We made an appointment for him to be seen in Phoenix at what we called 'the death clinic. 'Roger's best friend John drove while I sat in the backseat of our small Toyota. Don't you like trusty Toyota's?"

Clementine wiped her face, "It was then. Then in daylight while I sat next to him in the backseat of the car, that I saw Roger for the first time in months. All of his hair was gone. Large dark splotches covered his skin, all over his skin even on top of his bald head, on his face and arms, hands. His eyes were sunken. He resembled a starved prisoner of war. I tried to hold his hand, but he pulled away from me. Shaking his head, he said 'You know I love you?'"

She untwisted the twisted linen napkin to flatten it in front of her on the wooden tabletop. "Then I knew. I knew I had lost him. He was gone. How was it the cancer took longer to hit him?"

Sophia put her hand on the table by Clementine's, "Cancer?"

Nodding her head, she answered, "Yeah. Horrible, terrible cancer. It was in his vital organs and all over his body. He must have been in horrible pain, but he never complained. If one doesn't say something how is one to know, right?"

Putting her hand to her mouth, Sophia mumbled, "Oh, poor man!"

Studying the flat linen napkin, Clementine whispered, "Yes, ten months after I had buried my stepdaughter, I buried her father. He had become a skeleton with no voice, no hope and no choice. When I drove back to El Paso with John, I made up my mind to make the Army pay. John knew of a lawyer who would help me. He texted him to meet us the next day. I never went back into our bedroom after that return. The house felt jinxed, right?" Glancing up into Sophia's eyes, Clementine continued, "Of course I was tested, oh, yes, all kinds of medical tests, but I was free and clear." She knocked on the table with her knuckles, "Please, let it be so?"

"What happened with the lawyer?" A white linen napkin was picked up by Sophia. She was now twisting it into a tight ball.

Clementine's voice gained in depth, "The lawyer was a wonderful man named Gary Smith, of all names. We put together a plan. My anger was front center, I was living on anger! After the funeral and the guns going off, the flag folded and handed to me, I was ready to spit bullets at the whole of the Army." Now Clementine's face was flushed, her freckles were dark against the white skin of her face. "We concocted this excellent plan to notify the newspapers, the El Paso Sun and all the television stations of the disregard for human safety when they sent Roger out there with Elaine. John illegally found papers stamped with his orders from years before Roger had come to Sydney. Roger was one of the main people working at White Sands for years. Really, you want to hear this?"

Sophia stood to fill the water kettle and plug it on. "Go on, please."

"We met one morning on base. It was a conference room with this long table. I can still see it. There were enough chairs for at least sixty people, but only seven of us were sitting at one end. The black laminate table was polished to a mirror shine. There were clipboards, a container filled with pens and sharpened wooden pencils and a tape recorder. It was an old fashioned tape recorder, an ugly large black monstrosity. They quizzed us and one large man, he was round with many medals pinned on his brown uniform jacket spoke loudly, 'You do understand that your husband was a scientist. He knew the complications of going out in a radioactive hot field without a hazmat suit. He knew the risks. He took them anyway and with his precious daughter. His precious daughter?!"

Shaking her head, Sophia gasped, "What did you say?"

Clementine slammed her fist on the table, "I didn't say anything. I wanted to jump across the table and strangle the bastard. Gary put his hand on my arm to stop me. He said something back to the man, something calm and forceful. I don't know what it was for my mind was in a state of shock. The general was correct. Roger should have known, he wasn't stupid. He knew the risks, certainly he did. All I could think of was how stupid I was and nothing. Nothing we would do, nothing could bring Roger or Elaine back to me. At that point, I seriously considered getting up and walking out to leave all of this behind me. How could I leave?"

Questioning her, Sophia asked, "Do you think Roger knew how hot the area was? Really did he believe it was dangerous?"

Shrugging her shoulders, Clementine's voice was firm, "How could I know? He was dead." Her voice became sharp, "There was no way to ask him. I felt shot down, defeated and wanted to quit. My stomach hurt and my eyes wouldn't blink, they were dry and hot. I really wanted to leave, just walk away. Gary kept his hand on my arm, he kept talking. Suddenly, I heard a woman's voice. I had forgotten there was a woman at the table hidden by that large man. She was in a brown uniform with many medals. I was shocked. There was a woman there?"

Smiling, Sophia shook her head, "It must take a lot of time to pin on all those medals."

"Right. This woman spoke clearly directly at me, she asked me, 'What do you want out of this? What do you hope to gain here?' I wanted to say something to her, but I didn't know how. I really didn't know. Gary wrote something down on a piece of paper and shoved it over to her. She read it and nodded then passed it around to the others. The last man who took the paper was thin, he didn't look well either. He shook his head, took a pencil from the middle container and wrote something else. Again, the paper was pushed around the group. Each signed their initials at the bottom of the paper. It ended in front of Gary. He smoothed down his red moustache, cut short and neat and nodded in agreement. Somehow we stood, shook hands and walked out to never return. What else could be done, right?"

The kettle clicked off. The water was hot. Sophia brought two mugs back to the table with fresh teabags. She poured the hot water and waited to hear the ending. Clementine dropped the teabag into her steaming mug of water, "It was a monetary amount for life. A type of retirement fund for me. I was the sole remaining survivor. Money is what they gave me! A stipend for killing my husband and my stepdaughter. At first I was livid. I didn't want money, I wanted Roger. Gary took me to dinner and explained how the military works. I mean how would I know?"

Sophia stood to retrieve the spoons and a small dish for the teabags, "Then what did you do?"

"I completed my degree in forensic science. Decided that isn't what I wanted to do. I had had enough death and dead bodies. I turned to police work, wanted to be a detective and solve suspicious cases. Then I got out of Dodge so to speak. There was an opening here, I took it. Moved up here, met A.J. and his family. They adopted me. I'm renting one of his houses and have a small kitten who loves me devotedly. Don't you love kitties?"

Clementine stood to gaze beyond Sophia, "Is the bathroom back there? All this tea is going straight through me, may I use your facilities? I really didn't mean to bend your ear! Is it through here?"

Laughing, Sophia stood to hug her, "No ear bending here. I'm glad you could share your story with me. Thank you and yes the bathroom is here." She walked Clementine through the hall to a narrow wooden door with scratches along the bottom third. Cracks followed from the top of the door to the base. "This is an old house. The bathroom is remodeled to be modern, but it may not be very clean."

"Thank you, I won't pass judgement. At least it isn't an outhouse hole, right?"

"No. It has a toilet and running water. It's just all three of us use this one most of the time and it gets a lot of traffic."

"No worries. I'll not mess it up." Clementine moved around Sophia into the small bathroom. "Is there someone inside?"

"No, they're talking in Donna's room." Sophia walked into her bedroom and turned on the bedside lamp. The window glass glowed. There were no curtains on any of the windows in this room. The girls had insisted on curtains with a lining in their bedrooms. Sophia never thought of her own room since the windows faced the open land to the barnyard. Kicking off her heavy clogs, she reached for her sneakers. The four cats on the bed watched her. They were sitting up now, glowering at her. "Yes, it is time for your dinners. Probably past time for your dinners, but hey, we have company."

Sitting on the bed, Sophia leaned over to tie her sneaker laces. Clementine appeared at the door. "More kitties! I love kitties. Dogs are lovely, too, but dogs need to be loved and entertained. I'm never home and so I have one kitty who sleeps all day and tries to keep me awake all night." She came over to the bed to stroke Marmalade. Gathering him up in her arms, she sat on the bed next to Sophia. "What's this one's name?"

Double knotting her lace, Sophia sat upright, "He's Marmalade. Sybil's cat. He's usually in Sybil's room, but her doors closed to keep the heat in it."

"It's cold in this house. The thick adobe walls must help some though. How thick are the walls? Three feet?" Clementine cuddled Marmalade close to her.

"Yes, three feet thick in most places. Let's go in the kitchen and I'll turn on the gas heater. Believe it or not, this old home was updated last year to have central heating." Sophia pointed to the vent in the ceiling. As if on cue someone in the kitchen turned on the heater for it gasped and went on. At the closet, Sophia reached up to pull down a small brown paper bag. The logo was broken on the front, but it was the same logo as the bag in the photos shown to her earlier at the table. The small bag was handed to Clementine who put the cat gingerly down on the bed quilt beside her.

"Is this the same type of bag?" She held the bag between her index finger and thumb as if it were a dead rat.

Nodding, Sophia replied, "Yes, that's one of the bags from Granger's clinic." The two women walked into the kitchen. Donna was standing on a stool with white flour on her nose. "Mom, A.J. and I are going to make a super deluxe pizza. We found Sybil's leftover spaghetti sauce with meatballs in the fridge. He knows how to make pizza crust!"

Sybil was kneeling on the floor beside Shonac. The cat bowls were filled on the side table, "Sybil, call the kits. They're in the bedroom waiting for food. I guess they didn't hear the can opener."

The teenager raced into the bedroom, returning with her arms filled with cats. She placed them on the small table in the corner where immediately they chowed down. Fergus scarfed his food in a heartbeat. Sybil lifted him quickly before he had the chance to infringe on anyone else's food. Twisting, she handed the fat cat to Clementine who delightfully took him into her arms. "Well, you are a big fellow, huh?"

Sophia couldn't help herself, she laughed, "Do you know, Clementine, that you finish every statement with a question?"

"No, I don't. No, that's not true is it?"

At the kitchen counter A.J. laughed. "I never thought of it before, but yes, it's true! Hah! So, how thick do you guys want your pizza crust?" The rolling pin was pulled out from a long drawer beside the duo.

Clementine studied the kitchen as she walked around holding Fergus who was loudly purring in joy. "This is an ancient oven or stove, right? How old is this grandma oven? You call her Mabel, right?"

On cue, Sybil unhooked the bungee cords and lifted the top of the porcelain stove top. "Look, she has the date on her."

Bending sideways, Clementine read the date out loud, "Nineteen hundred and forty three. Sixty nine years young, right?"

Still in good humor, A.J. threw the pizza crust in the air, whirling it around to land back in his open hands. "The woman's good at math. Say, when I walked into the kitchen I felt a hostile breeze coming at me. What's that all about? If I didn't know better I would say there is a ghostly presence in here. Someone who doesn't like company."

White flour was rubbed on Donna's chin as she told the story, "Yes! You felt her! Uncle Granger evidently came in here and didn't feel anything, right Sis?"

"Right, Donna. Granger the Salamander walked right in and sat right down and wasn't even fazed by the hatred thrown at him." Sybil knelt on the floor by Shonac.

The flour laden hand of the twelve year old, waved in the air as she spoke loudly, "There was a man who lived here way before our time. He beat his wife and was super nasty to her. She resented his attitude and one morning while he was out in the field doing whatever he was doing out there, she put poison in his pancakes. Frying up the bacon and boiling his water for coffee, the wife smiled at the thought of doing in her nasty husband."

Sophia interrupted her, "Donna, we don't know if she smiled."

"Oh, yes, she did!" Donna went back to her story with great panache, "The husband came into the kitchen. It was filled with steam and the windows were frosted over, like right now. See?" She jerked her chin to the kitchen windows that had filmed over with moisture from the heat of the room. "These windows are the same windows that were here when she was here way back then. Anyway, the husband came in and he sat at the table. She knew, that's the wife that he would yell at her if she didn't get his pancakes and bacon on the table pronto."

A.J. asked again, interrupting, "You guys want a thick crust or a thin crust?"

Sophia nodded to Sybil, "I like a thin crust, really crispy and thin."

"O-kay, Donna, go on." A.J. took the rolling pin from Donna's hand to roll the dough. Donna turned around to lean back against the sink. She was standing on the stool beside A.J. "So, oh, yeah, so the wife puts the plate of food in front of her husband. She's only set one place setting just for him since he's such a bastard."

"Whoa, daughter mine, watch the language!"

"Mom, I'm telling this story. Stop interrupting me. Anyway, she put down the plate of food and her husband dug right into the pancakes. The bacon never was eaten because he fell face first into the plate of syrup and food. The coffee mug in his hand spilled to the floor all over his boots. His boots were muddy and yucky. The wife knew she would have to clean those, too."

Shaking her head, Sybil whispered, "Every time she tells it we get a new version, right?"

Clapping his hands, flour floated around the counter. A.J. smiled at Donna, "You are an excellent storyteller, Missy. That was an impressive tale. Why then are men afraid of coming into this kitchen?"

"Because, "Donna frowned at him as if he should have guessed, "A man was killed in here. Revenge is mine, sayeth the woman. Right, Mom?"

Nodding at her, Donna continued, "Even the other men who came to remove the dead husband's body were fearful of coming in here. The wife supposedly was not charged with the murder. The man had a history of heart problems and the belief was he died from a heart attack. Right, Mom?"

Sophia nodded for her to continue, "Donna, finish the story."

"Yes," the eleven year old's voice took on a very serious tone, "The woman kept a diary. She hid it in the floorboards of Sybil's bedroom. When the floor was being fixed from the flooding that came a couple of years after the wife died, they found the diary. We have it. It's in Mom's bedside table drawer if you want to see it. We read it. The wife admitted to killing the bastard husband because he continually beat her." Taking a breath, she finished the long story, "The wife died only a year after her husband. She didn't want to leave the house, she was afraid. In her own hand she wrote that she didn't even go to his funeral. She gave the priest money for the cheap coffin and the service, but she didn't go. No one visited her and she died alone in her bedroom which is Sybil's room now. I think she must have had a really hard life."

Donna jumped down from the stool. "Mom, light Mabel so we can cook the pizza."

Shaking his head, A.J. asked, "She buried her husband in a cheap coffin?"

"Yeah, the cheapest one they made way back then." Donna pulled a cookie sheet out from one of the lower cupboards, "Here, you can put the crust on this." While Donna entertained Clementine and A.J. with a tour of the old house, Sophia chopped lettuce, tomatoes, black olives and walnuts for a big salad.

The five feasted on pizza and salad. Sybil apologized for not having a desert while she gathered the dirty plates, taking them to Donna who was once again standing on the wooden stool ready to wash. Sophia asked, "This has been bothering me, but shouldn't you two be back at the office or doing something Sheriffs do? You both have been here almost two and a half hours, we don't want criminals to be running rampant in Rincon while you two are here keeping us company."

At the side of the kitchen table, A.J. wiped the brim of his hat with the cuff of his shirt, "No, there aren't any criminals running rampant or we would have heard about it. We all have cellphones now. Immediate notification." He patted the leather case on his belt. "No worries, it has been good to have time to catch-up on news and Clementine to meet someone local who isn't a criminal, at least we haven't proven you are a criminal yet." He smiled at Sophia.

Clementine lifted the small brown bag from the end of the kitchen table to examine. Sybil gleefully rushed to sit beside her, "Do you want to see my beads? I put all my special beads collected from the river or found outside on the ground in here. Let me show you?" Sophia quickly handed her daughter a shallow round bowl made of wood. The beads were poured into it.

Clementine shook her head, "I thought this bag was filled with medicinal herbs? Isn't this why you gave it to me?"

"No," Sophia took the dish towel from the side drawer. "No, the herbs are long gone. Check out the bottom of the bag. You'll see an expiration date stamped. That's what I was talking about. No one who can read and has half a brain would use the herbs that are out of date. They would be toxic or spoiled. In other words, do not use these herbs if past this date."

Taking the emptied bag into both hands, Clementine turned it over. "Yes, but this stamp isn't the same as the one on Rosa's bag. Look?" She reached for her clip board that had been placed by the cat bowls on the side table. A piece of paper was pulled free and handed to Sophia. Sliding into a kitchen chair opposite, Sophia studied the two different dates. The one on the bag was printed with an inked stamp used in stores for stamping price or dates specifically. The stamp on the bag in the photo was stamped with a computer printer. The ink was thinner, shallower and even. Whereas the ink on Sophia's bag had bled into the paper since the ink was thick when the stamp was used.

"This is obviously not the same type of ink." Sophia handed both back to Clementine. "What do you suppose this means? Granger wouldn't have used a printer. He's a greedy man. He wouldn't waste computer printer ink on each bag. He used the old date stamp from a store my father owned on the reservation. This appears modern."

Donna crouched in front of the sink, "Mom! Mom!" Her whisper was loud and cautious, "Mom! There's someone here!"

A.J. returned from the bathroom wringing his hands over the gas heater in the corner. He crouched as he stood beside Donna at the kitchen sink, peering over the deep shelf of the window. "Sybil, quick turn off the kitchen light, would you?"

Everyone's attention was now focused on A.J. and his directives. Sybil bent low, flipping off the kitchen light switch by the door. Clementine took her hat from the corner chair, placing it on her head. Her blonde hair was pushed back behind her shoulders. "Were you expecting company tonight?"

All three of them answered, "No!"

A.J. physically turned Donna toward her mother, "Go, and stand over there. This is now our scene." Dusk had fallen. The blue gray sky showed the fireplace smoke hovering close to the ground in the wet cold evening air.

Sybil strolled into the kitchen to loudly announce. "Guys, I looked out the window by the front room. It's Grandma. She's here in her poop truck and she can't get her walker out of the back of the truck. I think she's crying."

In a heartbeat, Sophia ran through the house, out the front door and to her mother. "Margaret? What in the world are you doing here? Why didn't you call me?"

Margaret leaned against the back of her truck. She appeared resigned to defeat. "I did call you. I called three times and left messages. You never returned my calls. Geoffrey called me. He said you were going to kill the girls. He was drunk, that was obvious, but he worried me. You didn't return my calls. Why didn't you return my calls?" Tears ran down her cheeks and her nose ran to drop on her shoes.

The two girls ran to stand beside their mother. Margaret shook her head, "You both are still alive, amazing grace! I drove all the way over here in the dark, almost was killed by an eighteen wheeler that turned in, up there and everyone one of you is still alive!"

Sybil smart mouthed, "Are you disappointed? Would you rather we were dead?"

Glaring at the fifteen year old, Margaret huffed air to say, "Probably." She sucked air in through her nose as she turned to Sophia, "You have a disrespectful daughter, Sophia. She should get a good whipping!"

Sophia tried to lift her mother's steel walker out of the flatbed of the truck. It was too heavy. She went to the back of the truck and tried to release the handle on the tailgate. It was stuck. "Damn, Margaret, this truck is not only dirty but impossible."

Smirking as she lifted her chin, Margaret stated, "I know. Roberto is the only one who can open the back tailgate. He has a knack for things like that. Leave it alone, you won't be able to open it. Roberto is the only person who can get that handle to work."

Slowly walking to Sophia, A.J. lifted his hat, "How do you do, Mrs. Pino."

Gasping at the sight of a full grown male, Margaret fluttered her eyelashes and with a sudden display of meekness softened her voice, "Hello? How do you know my name? How is it I am unfamiliar with yours?"

He put out his hand to take hers in a gentle caress, "I am Sheriff A.J. Salazar. We met in the hospital seven years ago. Although at the time I was in a hospital bed with a bandage on my head and had only one eye uncovered."

Margaret jerked her hand away, "You! You're the cop who arrested my son! Leave! Get off my property now!" All of her charming grace turned defensive.

His soft voice and lowering of his head appeared to be natural for him. "No, now, let's think about this for a minute." A.J. walked over to Sophia and with one quick jerk of his hand, the tailgate fell down with a clatter against the back bumper. "This needs straps. You don't want this to hit someone. It shouldn't fall any further than the height of the flatbed." He jumped up into the back of the truck and handed Sophia the walker. She opened it to place the steel device in front of her mother. "Mom or, ah, Margaret, A.J. was in the hospital when Granger was arrested. He wasn't anywhere near Granger or the arrest. It took five months for A.J. to be well enough to return to work and he's still having issues with his left eye. Don't blame him for what Granger did."

Puffing air in and out as she moved the walker to the house, she said over her shoulder, "Are you here to arrest Sophia for attempting to kill her two daughters? Is that what you're doing here?"

Trying not to laugh, A.J. answered, "No, Ma'am. We were here for dinner and listening to Donna's wonderful ghost stories." He hung back to be with Sophia to whisper, "I thought this place was yours. Does this farm belong to your mother?"

Shaking her head, Sophia whispered, "It's a long story. Another long story. Leave it."

Clementine met Margaret at the door. She had on her wide brimmed brown hat and held her clipboard in her hand. "Hello, Mrs. Pino." As if ready to be accused, Clementine added, "I didn't arrest your son either. We're just leaving. Have a good night." She skirted around Margaret and the red walker to join A.J. who had beeped the doors open on the sheriff cruiser. "Hey, thank you, for the lovely evening, we'll be in touch."

Clementine called to Sybil, "I have the brown bag. I hope you don't mind? I'll bring it back when I'm done with it." She waved.

Sybil ran to Clementine, "Can I go with you, please?"

Sophia yelled, "Sybil, that's enough. Get in here, now!" She wanted all of her girls beside her to face her mother.

Sophia, Sybil, Donna and Margaret stood at the door frame to watch the sheriff's cruiser backup and out of the driveway, disappearing down the narrow Alcon road. Suddenly, startling everyone, Margaret screamed out, "Charlotte, come inside now. The sheriff's gone and you did say you wanted to see the house!"

A flashlight from a cellphone glowed in the barn, moving quickly toward the women. Charlotte trotted up to give Sophia a hug, "Hey, I wanted to visit the horses first. You know how I love horses. Roberto takes care of my two horses, well, now I only have the one horse since Shadrack died two months ago. I miss him like crazy. All right, that's enough about me, show me this wonderful home!"

Sybil glared at her. Donna shoved the red steel walker aside to slip into the front room and disappear down the hall. Sophia grunted at her mother, "Oh, dear, Margaret, really it's late and the house is not prepared for a tour!"

Margaret snorted, pushing the muddy walker wheels forward through the front room. It was long and deep. The six windows on the far side facing Alcon road had no curtains, but the window glass was clean. Since the room was dark, the houses across the road were seen. A right turn in the front room brought them to the long hall with cupboards all along the left side. Deep wonderful cupboards to store anything and everything out of sight. The cupboard doors were white, clean and reflected the glow from the kitchen lights. Margaret's walker wheels left a mud trail behind her. At last in the large kitchen, Margaret huffed and puffed her way to the closest chair. Pulling it out, she plopped down with a soft moan.

Charlotte was still noticing the cupboards in the hall. She went straight to turn on the light in the old bathroom. "Whoa, this bathroom has a tub that seriously needs refinishing. How old is this bathroom?"

Sophia hurried to her, "This bathroom is hardly ever used. It has no heat and is older than God. Come on in the kitchen and I'll fix you some tea?"

Charlotte flipped off the bathroom light to walk to the kitchen counter by the sink, "This is a beautiful huge kitchen! I love it! But I would put curtains in the window. Certainly everyone in the neighborhood can see in at night." She moved to the gas heater. 'Nice, Sophia, this is nice. Your mother is a dear to buy you this old farm, isn't she?"

Gritting her teeth, Sophia tried to smile, "Yes, but I am paying for it not her."

Margaret shook her head, "Let's not quibble. Listen, we have to get back. The sheriff from Rincon visited us, the young one, what's his name? Garcia, Martinez, something Mexican?"

Her hand balled in a fist, Sophia answered curtly, "Cruz. His name is Deputy Sheriff Cruz, Mom."

Her hand on the steel red walker, Margaret pulled herself to stand, "Well, whatever his name is, he came by to tell us Rosa Mendoza is dead and Granger probably killed her."

Charlotte giggled, "No, Margaret! That isn't what he said at all! He wanted to question Granger about some herbs. He was interested in finding Granger, that's all. Margaret, you make everything so dramatic."

Slamming the walker on the wooded kitchen floor, Margaret went on, "Well, it was the same as an accusation. Then he went on to ask if Roberto worked for me and how do I think Rosa got a bag of Granger's herbs. How the hell should I know? Granger has been in jail forever and it took all my money to get him out early!"

Sybil came out of her room, moved around Charlotte to use the bathroom in the hall, "Grandmother, you know Granger kills everyone he meets." She ran into the bathroom and slammed the door.

Shaking her head, Margaret responded by saying, "Sophia, that girl is going to knock the house down with her door slamming. Let's go Charlotte. I have nothing further to say or see here. Let's go!"

Holding on to Margaret's elbow as the duo made their return to the truck covered with bird poop, Sophia called out to the girls, "Someone here needs to call Geoffrey and let him know we are all safe and no one has died." Tilting her head over her shoulder, she called out, "Donna? Call your father, please! Margaret and Charlotte are leaving now."

Sophia put the red steel walker behind the front seats of the double cab truck's backseat. She shoved it in sideways, showing Charlotte how to pull it out once back at Margaret's farm. Margaret huffed and puffed in her pain as she pulled herself up and onto the driver's seat. "I'm driving home. Charlotte, you almost hit the eighteen wheeler over there. Shut up and let me drive!"

Shrugging, Charlotte jumped into the passenger's seat, in her soft rasping voice she stated, "Sophia, next time let's have tea and you can tell me all about this wonderful old house. I think it's beautiful! Good-bye." She wiggled her fingers at Sophia and slammed the truck door.

Standing aside, Sophia watched her mother backup and with great discomfort turn the steering wheel with both hands. Her elbows sticking out at right angles with a lot of huffing. Then she backed up again, almost hitting the white pole fence of the barn. Slowly, the steering wheel was twisted around the other way, huffing and puffing, her mother's lips pursed with her face in pain. Slowly, the truck inched forward and then with a jolt raced out of the driveway onto the road. Sighing, Sophia returned to her kitchen. Margaret's muddy walker tires left tracks.

Donna and Sybil confronted Sophia, "Mom, this is an old blue sheet. You used to put this over our beds when we were sick, remember?" They held a faded queen sized sheet out to her.

She took it from them to pat it, "Yes this was known as the Blue Sky Sheet of Good Health. What about it?" Sophia felt how soft it was after years of washing.

Donna nodded to Sybil, who asked, "Mom, we want to hammer this sheet over the kitchen windows. There are four windows over the sink, we never open them. You said they were painted shut. At night…"

Donna interrupted her sister, "Yeah, when we were outside watching you in here with A.J. and Clem and we were in the barn, we noticed that you can see everything inside when the light is on. We could see…."

Sybil nudged Donna with her elbow to add, "We could see all the way into my bedroom! My room! When the door to the kitchen is open, you can see me undress!"

Donna not to be out done, shoved the sheet to Sybil, "Yeah, Mom, we need the ladder, some nails and the hammer. Please, Mom?"

Sophia unfolded the sheet. Holding it up to the kitchen lights, she pointed to the fabric, "Look. This lovely sheet is so old and worn, you can see right through it. We need something with substance. Something solid and less opaque. Maybe Sybil's underwear?"

"Really, Mom!" Sybil ran into her room and slammed the door. Dust fell from the adobe wall's crack over her door frame.

The two in the kitchen stared at the pile of dirt on the floor. Donna gasped, "Mom, you need to say something to her. The door might fall out of the wall if the crack gets any bigger."

Acknowledging the pile of dirt on the floor, Sophia shook her head, "You know she would just get angry and slam the door again. Come on, Donna, let's rummage in the cupboards in the long hall. Flipping the light switch on, the white cupboards were opened. Donna searched in the lower cupboards while Sophia stood on a step ladder to go through the higher ones. "Ah-hah," Donna pulled out an old blanket. It had a picture of a unicorn on it. "This was my old Girl Scout blanket when I went to Camp Barker. It's thick and long, let's use this. The folks looking in will see this pretty picture of a unicorn."

Sophia jumped off the step stool, "Yes, great idea. Now the hammer and the nails are a bit over the edge. Let's try tacks."

By the time the unicorn blanket was set in place, Sybil had returned and gave her full approval. "Hey, Donna, tell Mom what happened when you called Dad."

All three went into Donna's bedroom. Donna was now in her pajamas, Sybil was in her long thick nightgown and Sophia had on her comfortable sweats. Shonac was sleeping on the floor at the foot of the double bed, while Fergus and Silky were cuddled up in Donna's quilt at the head of the bed. Donna took on her grownup voice, "Dad wasn't happy. He wanted to drive over here right away and pick up Sybil and me. He said he's going to back to court to take us away from you. He wants Sybil to live with him full time and me to not ever have anything more to do with you or the Pino's."

"Yeah," Sybil interjected, "I could hear him yelling at Donna over the phone. He believes he can take us all away from you, move to Alaska, right? Was it Alaska, Donna?"

The twelve year old's face pouted. Her metal braces sparkled from the bedside table lamp, "Alaska and if that wasn't far enough to move back to Germany. He was totally pissed. He said Granger is going to kill all of us. Then he said something that neither of us knew about. Mom, he said Sybil was adopted and she wasn't his real daughter. Is this true?"

Turning to Sybil, Sophia nodded, "Sybil, you know we have had this discussion. Do you feel it is time to share with your sister?"

Sybil jumped on the bed, standing tall so she could reach the ceiling. "Yeah, all right." Sybil's long hair was loose, flowing around her thin body as she jumped on the bed. "So, Donna, this is what happened. Mama was in love with this guy who is a real jerk. She got pregnant with me, divorced him because he tried to run her over with his car and when I was born he came into the hospital nursery and tried to shoot me with his gun. He was in the military. So I have her looks, her smarts and he is long gone. Right?"

Sophia smacked Sybil's leg, "Not exactly. He's still around, but he isn't interested in having a family. He is a declared bachelor. He gave you to me as a lovely gift and I am most grateful to him forever. But 'yes' Sybil was only a few months old when I married your Geoffrey and he adopted Sybil and has loved her as his own ever since. Geoffrey had never denied you anything, Sybil, and you know this? He loves both of you equally."

Now standing next to her sister on the bed, Donna tried to touch the ceiling. She started jumping, "What about me? Is my father someone you met, fell in love with and he gave me to you forever? I want to be adopted, too."

Shonac was now barking at the girls as they stood tall over him. Sophia reached out to pull Donna to her, hugging her by the waist, "Yes! I fell in love with Geoffrey who is a great dad and someone who loves you with all of his heart, too. It's just now we aren't agreeing very well. Evidently, Granger has shoved a wedge between us. You both are not in any way a problem, it is Granger!"

Both girls jumped up and down on the double bed, shouting, "Salamander, Salamander!"

The old clock in the front hall chimed eleven. Clapping her hands, Sophia announced, "It's time for bed! Donna, you know Griego will be over here probably before dawn to see you and want to go riding. Sybil you and I have to deal with this problem of who poisoned Rosa and probably have to have a talk with Granger. No argument, young ladies. Bed time."

Outer doors locked, lights out. Sophia found two old twin sheets in the linen cabinet. The tacks were used to put up the folded twin sheets over both of her windows. Immediately the room felt warmer. Her diary was taken from the bedside table and she wrote in it until she was too tired to continue. Shonac snored in the kitchen on his bed blanket as the hall clock ticked away the night time.

4

A hand shook her shoulder. Gasping from the sudden shock, Sophia sat upright trying to focus on the person in front of her on the bed. "Mom, Mom, Dad was here. What should we do?"

Sybil's young face was filled with fear, "He was shouting. I don't think he could hear the television, but we sure did hear him. He was screaming that he was going to get Donna and take her home! Mom, he was screaming, loud! Everyone in the neighborhood could hear him."

Swinging her legs over the bed, Sophia hugged Sybil, "Where's your sister now? Did Geoffrey leave? Is he still here?"

The fifteen year old knelt on the bed beside her mother, holding her tightly, "I think he left. We didn't dare look out of the window. He was right there, screaming at the side windows by the front door!"

Freeing herself from Sybil's tight embrace, Sophia stood, "All right, we need to figure out what to do. Where's your sister?"

Pointing to the bedroom door, Sybil said, "She's in her room. She's crying."

They hurried into Donna's bedroom. She was hugging Silky cat with Marmalade, Biscuits and Oscar peeking out of the heavy quilt by Donna's stockinged feet. Sybil rolled over Donna to be on the far side of the full sized bed. Sophia knelt on the floor rug next to Donna, "What's going on, Donna? Why are you so scared of your father? You do know he is concerned for your safety, right?"

Sniffling as she wiped her nose on the back of her hand, Donna looked at her mother through her wet eyelashes, "No. No, he's not. He just wants to prove you guys are bad. I'm usually late to school because he sleeps late. He drinks a lot at night after I'm in bed. I do the laundry and the house stinks of cat pee. It's nasty, I don't want to go back there!" She fell over onto the cat, crying.

The phone in the hall rang. The sound echoed into Donna's room. Shaking her head, Sophia mumbled, "I better get it. You know who it is." Sybil hugged her crying sister.

Cold black plastic was lifted to Sophia's ear. The phone was held in her hand as she hesitantly spoke, "Hello?" She glanced at the large hall clock. It was a quarter to eight in the morning on the Saturday that was supposed to be a pleasant quiet day.

Her mother yelled, "Sophia! Why don't you answer your phone? This is your Margaret! Do you know where Granger is? Sophia, the cops were here searching for him, again! They went through the whole house, flashlights in closets and they even flashed my horse!" Margaret stopped to huff and puff, then continued, "Sophia, where are you? Where's Granger? What's going on?" Margaret had begun this dialogue with a frantic pitch, but it ended with a little girl's voice.

A pause, then Sophia answered calmly, "I have no idea where my brother is, nor do I care. You find him. I'm already having issues over here. Please, Margaret, just call his cellphone." Carefully, Sophia placed the phone back into its cradle.

Two faces peered at her around the doorframe. "Good for you, Mom." Donna opened her hand to give Sophia a bunch of jellybeans.

The three of them returned to Sophia's queen sized bed. She realized she had slept later than usual because her room was dark with the sheets over the windows. "Come on, girls, it's time to make a plan. Your father may return with the law or he may return with a battering ram, we don't know. Perhaps, I should call him. Act like a grownup."

Shaking her head, Sybil whispered, "He was drunk. I think he's been drinking since we left his house and probably all night. He was slurring his words and he was really mad."

"O-kay, but we are warrior women not victims. A.J. Salazar left his business card on the table. Think I'm going to give him a call. He has a cellphone. First let's get dressed." The girls noticed the covered windows and gave Sophia a thumbs up on her decision for privacy.

Standing at the front door with a mug of hot tea in her hand, Sophia watched her girls feed the horses. Sybil started to muck out as Griego rode up on Guaco his gelded horse. Donna dropped the oats from her hand into Tracy's bucket and raced to him. Sophia smiled. The two were best friends and all to do with horses. Sybil didn't even turn, she kept right at her task of scooping manure and dumping it in the wheelbarrow.

The phone rang four times before A.J. picked up, "Rincon Sheriff's office, A.J. Salazar speaking."

Sophia kept her voice calm, "A.J., its Sophia Pino. Thought I should ask for your advice since you are oh so knowledgeable about this crazy family."

He gave a quiet laugh, "Hey, I'm just a man trying to multi-task. What can I do for you?"

She sighed, "Geoffrey was over here this morning yelling loudly at our locked doors and windows. He wants to take me to court and remove the girls from my guardianship. He feels the Pino family will kill them. He's adamant about taking them away from me, perhaps today."

A.J.'s voice lowered, she could hear him walking on a hard floor in his heavy boots, "Not today, he's not. The courts are closed. It's Saturday. Even if he files with the law here, there isn't anyway the Child Services would do anything unless they were found to be physically abused. Have you physically abused your daughters as of this morning?"

A gasp, "No! I would never and you know this! What if he comes back and physically tries to remove them?"

"Then you call me. Do you want to have a deputy drive by your place every now and again? We have a deputy you know. Deputy Cruz is in your neighborhood vicinity today. He's watching a particular area for illegal activity. I could ask him to call you and have him give you his cell number, would this help?"

Relaxing, Sophia agreed. A.J. told her to wait about ten minutes before using her cellphone again in case it took that long for Deputy Cruz to return a call to her. She noticed Griego had tied Guaco horse to the tie down. The three young people were walking to the house. It was time to think of breakfast.

Eggs, bacon and plenty of toasted homemade bread with honey was quickly eaten. Griego insisted on washing up and Donna insisted on drying. Sybil went into her room pouting because she didn't want to be stuck with her mother all day. Sophia heard her cellphone chirp, "Hello?"

It was a male voice, "Hey, beautiful lady, how're you doing? This is Cruz, your favorite Deputy. I understand you have a problem over here in Alcon. Didn't know you lived here? What's going on?"

Sophia explained Geoffrey's behavior and anger. Cruz appeared to understand how things could easily get out of control when booze and family problems mix. He told her he would drive by the farm, he knew where it is, about every half hour. He gave her his cellphone number, adding, 'If you leave the farm, let me know. If Donna and her friend Griego go riding, they need to have a cellphone in case they are confronted by Geoffrey. It would be wise for them to stay at Griego's house than alone at your farmhouse. Please, keep in touch with me, hey, we go way back!"

Sophia smiled at the memory, "Hey, I heard from A.J. that you're married now and have children. How wonderful. Who did you marry and would I approve?"

Cruz agreed, "Yes, you would approve. Let me know when you're able to see my photos of family?" There was some radio static, then he continued, "Saw your Mother yesterday. She hasn't changed, there's just less of her."

Sophia swallowed hard, "I know she gives you a hard time, I'm sorry. She doesn't mean to be cold, she just wants to defend Granger." The call ended.

Donna and Griego took off. Donna on Tracy and Griego on Guaco Taco as he called his gelded horse. Sybil had made arrangements for Sophia to drop her off at a friend's house on the south side of Albuquerque. It was out of Sophia's route to her mother's, but it was important for Sybil to feel safe and enjoy her Saturday. The pay-as-you-go track phones were charged and each daughter had one. The batteries lasted about six hours, long enough for them to regroup. On the long drive to Albuquerque, Sybil was quiet.

Once they entered city limits, Sybil spoke up, "Mom, be careful with Granger. Don't let him try to fool you or make you do something you aren't in agreement with because you know? That's what he does." Pulling the track phone from her jean pocket, she added, "How about I call you in two hours and ask you to come and pick me up? That way, Margaret can't hold you hostage with her shhhhh…..stuff."

Slapping Sybil's leg, Sophia laughed, "I know what you were going to say and 'yes' I agree. Call in two hours or maybe two and a half hours. It will take me half an hour just to get there. Have fun, enjoy your friend. Glad her mother was eager to have you visit. She sounded nice."

They drove into a neighborhood watch area. Tall Ash trees lined the sides of the paved street. The sidewalk was cracked here and there by tree roots. There was an area of rolling lawn about the size of a football field. It was trimmed and manicured to perfection. Birds chirped and hopped around one area where an older man was throwing out birdseed. Sybil studied the street signs as they moved from one Stop Sign to the next. Finally, she jumped in her seat, "There, there, Mom! See the house on the corner with the large boat in the backyard? That's it. Stop! Mom, Stop!"

Laughing at her eagerness, Sophia pulled into the driveway to park behind an old blue truck. Quickly, reaching over, Sybil gave her Mother a peck on the cheek, "See you!" Sybil was out of the car. Her friend Jennifer was standing in the doorway with her Mother. The older woman hugged her sweater to her waist as she ran to meet Sophia, "Hi! I'm Robin, Jen's Mom. If you want Sybil can spend the night. It's all right with us, we love Sybil. She and Jen are the best of friends. Just give us a call and let us know how things are going, o-kay?" They waved at Sophia as she backed out of the driveway. "Now, to the house of doom."

Tumbleweeds continued to blow battering against the side of the old yellow SUV. Sophia drove north from Albuquerque to Calavera Village.

The streets were covered with the blowing sand from the higher foothills. The large industrial center on the hill above, continually chugged out white smoke. Tumbleweeds hung on lopsided barbed wire fences with horses standing around open barns. Tall cottonwood trees blew back and forth like dancing girls along the empty ditches. As Sophia entered Calavera Village proper, the traffic picked up its pace. The post office parking lot was full. The local bank had people standing around outside talking, there was a yellow tape across the drive through area. The Senior Center parking lot was filled with buses and the Pizza Café had Christmas lights still strung up outside from last December. The colored lights banged hard against the stuccoed adobe wall. In the wind. It was October, only two more months and these lights will be ready for the holiday. An old dog with gray fur on his muzzle stared at her as he walked across the narrow street from the Pizza Café to the post office. Finally, the double wooden pillars appeared. Sophia put on her blinker, noticing an old VW bus was right behind her.

The paved road to Margaret's was once dirt with ridges. Many of the elderly people who live down the road became angry when their cars started to fall to pieces as they drove fast and sometimes way above the speed limit. They petitioned the Village Council of Calavera and the dirt road now is paved. The smooth road brought complaints written up in the local paper for now the younger people who have moved in the area are speeding on the paved road. The seniors are worried their pets will be run over or horses will be hit while riding. There didn't appear to be an answer for there were those who had an argument at the ready for either way.

As Sophia turned to the left, entering her mother's long driveway, she noticed the truck was parked faithfully under the tree with the bird's nest. More bird poop would be added to the decorative work already done. Slowing and then she stopped at the high adobe wall, she noticed A.J. Salazar standing outside the wall. She rolled down the window to call out to A.J. Salazar, "Hey, thanks for the help from Cruz. By the way, Granger is back at my mother's here in Calavera. I'm here now, too. Do you want me to keep him here until someone can come and interview him?"

A.J. laughed, then snorted, "No love lost between you and Granger, huh? Sure, I'm just now with Clem. We're close by and should be there within ten or fifteen minutes. Can you keep him entertained?"

Now, it was Sophia's turn to smile, "Yes, no love lost. Yes, I'll start an argument. We'll be here."

The old SUV was parked far from the dropping tree by her mother's truck. Sophia let herself in through the wrought iron gate and walked around the side of the house to the backdoor. Turning her head, she could hear Margaret and Granger yelling at one another. Slowly, she turned the door knob to stand just inside the house, by the small kitchen. Mother and son were in the back bedroom.

Margaret screamed, "Granger! Don't you dare let that nurse in here! I swear you won't see another penny if you let that woman in here! Granger! You better not!"

A loud laugh and then Granger yelled back at his mother, "Hell, Mom, I'm not going to wipe your ass! If you fell down, you better get up! I'm not going to wipe your ass and I'm not going to pick you up!"

Then there was a blood curdling scream that came from the back rooms, "Granger! I'm hurt! I can't help my body functions! Get back here or I swear you won't see another penny of my money!"

Granger hurried around the corner of the hall into the kitchen. He jumped when he noticed Sophia standing there in her coat, her purse still hanging over her shoulder. "Sophia! How serendipitous that you're here! Mom, tripped over the rug in her bedroom. She crawled into the bathroom, but she can't stand upright and she pissed all over herself. She stinks like a septic tank!" He slapped his thigh, "I'm not picking her up and I'm not wiping her ass or changing her clothes! She's my mother for God's sake!"

Dropping her purse into one of the kitchen chairs, Sophia stared at him, "Well, at least did you call for an ambulance? For instance, she could have broken her hip or her pelvis or maybe she's losing her mind because she lives with you? Did you think of any of those things?"

Frustration oozed from his mouth, "Shut up, Sophia! You're a bitch. A chip off of the old block!" Granger leaned against the side of the stove. "So, what the hell do we do now?" He ran his fingers through his hair, "You know they'll blame me for this? They will! They will blame me because I tried to kill her once, now they'll think I did it again. Damn!"

Unzipping her coat, Sophia pulled it off and placed it on the chair beside her purse. "We need to take care of Margaret. If everyone knows what a dear and kind person you are, well, then there will be no blame." Slapping his shoulder lightly, she said, "All right," she sighed, "show me the patient. Let's see what we can do?"

They moved down the dark hall into the back bedroom, there was a soft weeping heard behind the closed door to the bathroom. The bedroom rug only five feet from the bathroom door in Margaret's bedroom was flipped. It was easy to see how the walker's back wheels had pulled the rug upright and Margaret had tripped. The red steel walker was on its side. It appeared to have hit the heavy wooden desk filled with mice and rolled to the floor.

Granger shook his head. His voice soft yet stern, "I wasn't even in the room! Sophia, I wasn't even in this room! I was taking a nap. I'd been out all night searching for my Mercedes! Damn!"

There was a pounding on the front door. Granger jumped and started to run down the hall. Sophia grabbed his shirt and then the belt buckle on his khaki jeans. "No! No, you don't! Come on, let's see who this is and answer some questions! You're not guilty, don't act guilty! Come on!"

She jerked him to her side, hugging him as he tried to twist away from her, she reprimanded him. "Act civilized! Remember, you're not guilty! You have done nothing wrong. Now open the door with a smile and a kindly handshake!"

She shoved him toward the front door. Rarely did anyone use the front door and the key was constantly placed in the key hole. Granger turned the key, pulled open the door to find Sheriff A.J. Salazar and Detective Inspector Clem Thompson. "Oh!" Granger stepped back onto Sophia's toes.

Shoving Granger off of her foot, she smiled, "Hey! How nice to see you guys! We have had an emergency and this is excellent timing, isn't it Granger?" She poked him in the back.

"Yes, yes!" Granger turned to glare at Sophia, but when he turned back to the sheriff there was honest concern on his face, "My mother fell. She's in her bathroom. Sophia and I think she may have broken a bone or something. She's anorexic and has fragile bones, also, she is still recovering from her bad traffic accident."

A.J. took Granger by the arm and led him into the living room. Clementine nodded to Sophia, "Let's go and check on your mother. Better women involved with a fallen Grandmother than two men with no tact, right?"

Sophia gently shoved the bathroom door to open far enough for the two women to squeeze into the small chamber. Margaret was lying on her side, quietly sobbing. Her arthritic hand shook over her wrinkled face. Her right foot was trembling. It was obvious from the smell that Margaret had wetted herself and more than likely had a urinary tract infection. "Margaret, "it's me Sophia. I've brought help. You remember Detective Inspector Clementine from last night? She's here to help me help you. Don't move. Let's see what's going on with you."

Clementine was kneeling beside Margaret's feet. She was untying her sneakers and carefully, gingerly removing them and then Margaret's socks.

Kneeling sideways with her back against the toilet, Sophia took her mother's hand that was shaking, "Margaret, have you eaten today?" Pinching her mother's wrist, she lifted the loose skin. It stayed up showing how dehydrated the woman was.

Sobbing with her eyes shut in pain, Margaret answered, "No, I wasn't hungry. Your brother tried to get me to eat some cereal, but I wasn't hungry. He's gone so much of the time. I worry so and then I don't have an appetite."

"Mom Margaret, where do you keep your hard candy? Can you tell me?" Sophia nodded to Clementine, "Mom is hypoglycemic and if she doesn't eat, she gets the shakes."

A soft whisper came from Margaret, "They're in my bedside table. Just pull out the drawer. My favorite are the cinnamon twists, just a few, don't bring a lot."

The two women managed with great care and tenderness to remove Margaret's foul clothing as she sucked on the hard candy. They washed her with a wet washcloth and then carefully dressed her in clean underwear, sweat pants and clean socks. Margaret's right foot had swollen to such an extreme that they knew the shoes would no longer fit. Clementine recommended they lift Margaret upright, but Margaret let out such a blood curdling scream that they left her on her side.

The scream brought A.J. and Granger. A.J. was told of Margaret's pain and the problem with the rug. "Mrs. Pino, would it be possible for us to call for an ambulance? They will have to remove the door from the bathroom, but they would be able to get you to the emergency room with less pain than the four of us."

Terror creased the old woman's face, "No! No, no ambulance! I'll be all right. Let Granger help me to stand. He can carry me to my truck and we can go in my truck, right Granger?" Margaret's strength appeared to have returned.

Granger shoved his bangs back from his forehead, "Mom, no! I can't carry you. You are nothing but skin and bones, but you have a hefty amount of metal as well! An ambulance is a good idea!" He backed away from the group to sit on her bed.

Another howl from Margaret when Granger moved out of her sight. The group agreed, the four of them would try to lift her to stand. They would be able to get her into Sophia's SUV on the long backseat with someone holding her head and shoulder upright and her legs and feet resting on the seat. The dedicated four were determined to please Margaret. After two hours and a lot of crying, sobbing and swearing, Margaret was in Sophia's family SUV. Clementine held Margaret's upper body in her lap in the back seat. Sophia drove. Granger sat in the passenger's seat with his mother's purse in his lap. A.J. Salazar led them in his cruiser with his siren going and lights flashing all the way to Presbyterian Westside Hospital. A team of nurses with a gurney met the SUV as Sophia pulled up in front of them. A.J. showed them his badge, explained the situation and only then did they come to the SUV's sliding door to retrieve Margaret.

A.J. met Granger as he stepped out of the passenger door, "Hey, you better go in and give them your mother's information. I have a feeling she's going to give them a hard time. Since you are her prince charming, you're on, buddy!"

Sophia ran around the vehicle to give her brother a hug, "Granger, be nice, do well and remember you're not on trial here. Show them what an excellent son you are!"

Twirling around to face her, Granger's eyes darted around the hospital's entrance, "Where are you going? Don't think I'm going to stay here all night! How am I supposed to get home? Huh?"

Sophia quickly put her arms around him for another hug, whispering into his ear, she said, "I'll go park and come back, how's that, big guy?"

A.J. and Clementine watched the two siblings. Finally, Clementine walked over to Sophia, "How about I come by tomorrow to your farm in Alcon and we can have a mug of tea? Say about four o'clock? Does that work for you?" Her wide smile gave an acknowledgement as to what was going on between her and Granger.

Sophia nodded, "Yes, four o'clock is good. If not, I'll let A.J. know or Cruz." She watched as the Granger strode into the emergency room before she turned to A.J. "Did you get a chance to talk with Granger about the herbs?"

Shaking his head, A.J. answered, "Yes, but he doesn't appear to know anything. He has no knowledge of where the herbs went after his arrest or who might have them now. He wasn't convincing, maybe you could ask him. He trusts you. His eyes were kept down toward the floor the whole time we spoke in your mother's living room. He's a tricky one, your brother is one tricky fellow." A.J. and Clementine walked to the cruiser and drove away, disappearing into the blowing dirt of the west mesa.

In the hospital there were different colored taped markers to follow for whatever department one was hoping to find. Granger was found sitting outside of two swinging doors. "She's in x-ray. The E.R. doc believes she fractured her pelvis. Every time they open and close the door to her cubicle, the door slams into her right foot and the right side of her pelvis is where they believe the break is. The nurse tried to get blood from her collapsing veins, but the nurse is totally fruit loop. That woman couldn't get blood out of a blood turnip. I offered, but she would have none of it." Shifting in his white plastic chair, he mumbled, "We shouldn't have brought her here. We could've just left her there and disappeared."

Loud foot falls came toward them from around the corner. A tall man approached them. "Hello, I am Dr. Sibas visiting from the Middle East. I am here doing my internship here in New Mexico. I have reviewed your mother's x-rays and here, let me show you." He held in his hand a tablet. Flipping it open, he punched in some numbers to turn the monitor to them. Bending over Sophia, he explained, "It is a fractured pelvis, clean and neat. This should heal if she remains still and doesn't do any fancy foot work for about three months. Although, she appears to have serious osteoarthritis and osteosis." He flipped the tablet shut to stand erect, "Margaret Pino has not taken good care of herself. She is deficient in calcium, iron, and well most everything. Also, she has a urinary tract infection. She's probably had the infection for some time, her kidneys are in congenital failure as well as her heart."

He stepped back to lean against the far wall, "We are going to keep her here for three of four days and try to build up her body and her immune system. She is severely dehydrated, not drinking water, huh?" Sophia nodded, "She refuses to drink water. She says it tastes awful, like metal."

Dr. Sibas smiled, "Yes, but once she is home she will need constant care. This means she will need to use the bedpan and need to be washed probably in her bed. She shouldn't attempt to stand or sit upright for at least three weeks."

Granger groaned putting his hands on his head, "No, no, no, and no."

Sophia smacked him on the leg, "Doctor, we shall find a way. Is there the possibility of a visiting nurse or someone we could hire to stay in the house with her?" Granger sat up and looked hopeful.

The doctor smiled, "Yes! She has good Medicare coverage and has Blue Cross and Blue Shield extra. So, I can set up a nurse to stay with her during the day and another nurse to be with her during the night. Also, we shall give her exercises she needs to continue at home. She has very little muscle strength. Does she walk or do any physical activity? Is there availability for someone to sleep on a cot next to her bed in her home?"

Granger jumped up from the chair, "Yes, we have a cot. It's a nice cot. I know because I have slept in it many times. My mother's room is long, as long as this hall and about as wide. There's plenty of room!" He put out his hand, "Thank you, doc, thank you!" The two men shook hands.

The doctor shook his head as he walked away. Granger was overjoyed, "Sophia, we should have done this ages ago. You didn't need to be over there every day, you could've gotten a nurse to sit on her!"

Shaking her head, Sophia quietly answered his joy, "Just you wait and see. She doesn't want anyone in her house except family. She's going to have a fit, Granger, you just wait and see."

"Too bad, I have power of attorney and I have the legal hand here.

She cannot be left alone. Period, the end. She has to be monitored and a nurse must monitor her. I will monitor the nurse, how's that?" Granger and Sophia walked out of the hospital to the car park. It was time for everyone to go home. The heavy gray clouds had filled in the cold clear sky. The wind was now a heavy gale and the dirt from the mesa top pelted the windows of Sophia's vehicle. As she jumped into the driver's seat, her cellphone chirped.

"Mom, Sybil here. How's it going over there?" Sybil was yelling over some loud music.

"Grandmother Margaret broke her pelvis. Granger and I are just leaving the hospital on the west side. I'm going to take him back to his house and then I can come and get you?" Sophia smiled at her thoughtful daughter.

Sybil squealed, "Mom, can I spend the night here with Jennifer? Her mother is making us sloppy Joes. Please, Mom, please? Jen and I wear the same size clothes and she's going to loan me some pajamas, please, Mom, please?"

Sighing as she watched Granger shove his seatbelt into the catch, she said, "Sure. That sounds excellent. Any news from your sister?"

"Nope, I bet she's at Griego's and they're watching t.v. Donna really, really doesn't want to go back to Rocoso with Dad. Maybe she could spend the night with Griego?" The music was finally turned down at Sybil's end of the conversation.

"You have a good time with Jennifer. We'll talk later. Love you, bye!" Sophia clicked off her cellphone.

Granger turned to watch the blowing wind ripple buckets of soft moving sand against the side of the hospital. "They must put in new windows every summer. These fall winds destroy those glass windows facing west. So, what's the news with your daughters?"

Shaking her head, Sophia said, "They're busy those two. I had better drop you off and get home, do you mind?"

A guttural laugh was with his reply, "Hell, no! Finally! I can have a night to myself. Hey, if he keeps her in the hospital for some time, I can finally have space for myself." He shook his head, "You know I went straight from being in a bunkroom with three other guys to coming home to demanding Margaret. Don't get me wrong, I'm glad to be out, but now I will have my own space. I can sleep late, stay up late and eat whatever I choose. This will be like Heaven!" He jumped out of the SUV with a wave as he slammed the passenger door. The farmhouse appeared forlorn with all the lights off and the cracked stucco on the front wall falling to dust on the cacti plants.

The rest of the drive was in silence aside from the wind. It was dusk by the time Sophia drove into Griego's driveway in Alcon. The heavy dark clouds threatened rain. The wind had not let up and the trees along the river were dancing wildly in the evening air. She parked beside Griego's mother's station wagon. A group of dogs came out to greet her, all wagging their tails. At the rickety yellow painted screen door frame, she knocked loudly.

"Sophia! How lovely to have you come to my house for a change!" Reina pulled open the kitchen door. The frilly curtains hanging over the four window panes of the kitchen door swung back and forth. "The kids are in the play room. Griego is showing Donna his new Game Boy. I don't think she's impressed. Come in, come in."

Sophia stepped into the extreme heat of the kitchen. The curled yellow linoleum floor was well scrubbed. The smell of baking bread hit her, reminding her how famished she was. Reina called down the hall, "Donna, your Mom is here!"

There was a silence that followed and then Donna appeared. She came toward her mother, hopping as she pulled on one of her boots. "Mom, hi. We were just finishing up some kind of computer game."

Griego rushed up behind her, "Donna, it's not some kind of game! Hey, Sophia, we went riding all over down by the school, to the river, then along the railroad tracks then under the bridges. We had a blast!"

Reina brushed back Griego's bangs with her fingers, "He's tired. I bet they both are. They had a good time though, thanks for letting them come over here. You know if there is any problem, any problem at all, just let us know and Donna is more than welcome to stay here with us. We love her company, right son?"

Griego made a sour face, "Yeah, Mom. But I really prefer to go riding. Right, Donna?" He nudged her with his shoulder. Donna smiled, "Right, Griego."

Sophia and Donna drove the few minutes down Alcon road to their farmhouse. The horses whinnied at the sight of the vehicle. Both women ran through the hard wind to the barn. In synchronizing movements, the horses were fed, stalls were mucked out and the barn light was turned off. Shonac met them at the door to run outside and relieve himself.

Sophia washed her hands in the bathroom sink to call out to Donna, "Did you two guys come back here today?"

Donna appeared to lean against the bathroom door frame, "Yeah, I know you didn't want us to, but I needed to change my shirt. I ripped it on a branch by the diversion. Hope you don't mind?" She held out her cotton plaid shirt with a tear in the sleeve. "Dad came after we were inside. Griego snuck to the door and locked it before Dad tried to open it. Of course there were no vehicles here. He did see Guaco Taco at the tie down, but Dad doesn't know anything about horses."

Drying her hands on the towel, Sophia smiled, "It's nice to know there are people here who have our backs, right? By the way, your hair is a mess. I recommend you let me redo your French braid."

The two ate their dinner quietly, thinking about the day. Sophia finally mentioned to Donna about Margaret's fall from grace and her being in the hospital. Donna's remark was, "I'm not staying with her. I agree she needs a large prison guard to watch over her. Granger won't do anything."

Sybil called just before ten o'clock that night to tell her mother of her fun day. Her voice whispered, "Mom, please come and get me early tomorrow morning. It's strange here, really strange! Got to go, bye, Mom."

Donna had fallen asleep on her own bed with the light on, covered with cats. Sophia turned off Donna's bedside light and she herself went to bed. It had been a long day.

5

Shonac licked the bottom of Sophia's barefoot. Jerking from the wet cold tongue, she pushed her barefoot back under the bed covers. At her quick movement, the dog barked. Sophia leaned up on one elbow to stare at him, "What? Is it time to get up already?" Shonac twirled in circles then stopped for a quick bark. "All right, I'm getting up now. What time is it sweet pup?" She squinted at the bedside clock, "Oh, no, it's almost nine o'clock! Thank you, Shonac, thank you!"

Showered and dressed, Sophia studied her reflection in the bathroom mirror. Her short hair was a wild mass of short brown curls. There wasn't much anyone could do with such passionate corkscrews that covered the top of her head, "A hat, today is a hat day. Wow, more gray hairs and they are more tightly curled than my plain brown. Oh, well, Granger does this to people, all people, I'm sure."

Donna and Griego were sitting across from one another at the long wooden kitchen table. They each had a blue ceramic bowl of cereal in front of them. Donna's plastic Breyer horse was standing on the table between them. Neither was talking, only slurping their cereal in large spoonfuls. Sophia walked to the kitchen counter to plug in the white kettle. Staring ahead to see out the kitchen windows, all she viewed was the unicorn blanket. She bent down and pulled the wooden stool to her, placing it on the floor in front of the sink. Opening the utility drawer in the kitchen, she took out six clothes pins to place on the counter. Standing on the wooden stool, she reached over the sink, into the window alcove and rolled up the blanket, pinning it up with the clothes pins.

Speaking to the kids over her shoulder, she said, "Thank you, both, for feeding the horses. Oh, I see Guaco Taco is eating out of the red bucket. Did he get some oats, too?"

Clearing his throat, Griego said, "Oh, I hope it is all right? Donna thought it would be rude for the other horses to be eating and Guaco standing there watching them. He just has a little bit mixed in with some alfalfa leaves. Is that o-kay?"

The kettle clicked. The water had boiled. Sophia grabbed a tea mug from the side of the cabinet, "Yes, that's fine. He's a wonderful horse. Everyone needs a treat now and again, right?"

She took her tea mug with the tea bag and hot water to the table. Sophia sat next to her daughter, "So, what do you two have planned for the day?"

Donna drank down the milk from the bottom of her ceramic bowl, to inform her mother, "We're going riding down by the river where they're building the new housing development. There are some paths down there we want to explore." She picked up her bowl and took it to the sink. Turning to Griego, she asked him, "Tell Mom about the phone call."

Griego stood tall and pushed in the kitchen chair. He took his bowl to Donna, saying, "When we came in this morning the phone was ringing. I think it's a phone. I've never seen nothing like it. That big plastic thing in the hall? Donna said it's called a rotary phone, but hey, that thing is wild. You dial by turning that round thing around with numbers. There is a curly cord to the plastic box business, wild!"

Sophia smiled, "Yes, it works when everything else fails. If the electricity goes off, we can't energize the cellphone batteries. That old phone works regardless of electricity and as you know the electricity goes off a lot around here." Sipping her tea, she asked, "Tell me about the phone call, won't you?"

Griego leaned against the side of the fridge. "This woman was calling from Mexico, somewhere, I don't know where, didn't know it. Anyway, she said her daughter Rosa was murdered two days ago or something. She was trying to contact Roberto, whoever he is, but he didn't answer his cell. She wondered if he was dead, too. Anyway, she wants you to call her back and she said if it was too expensive, to reverse the charges, whatever that means, right?"

The empty tea mug was put down on the table, "Griego, did she say how she found my phone number? I mean that old phone is limited to only a few who know the number, did she say?"

"Oh, yeah, she called a woman named Charlotte. Rosa had given her Charlotte's phone number in case something happened in Mexico that was a way to find Rosa. Hey, I wrote the number down on the notepad by the ancient phone thingy." He patted Donna on the shoulder, "I'm going to the head. Be right back. Then let's go check out the weed path by the builders."

Sophia watched as the kids saddled up and trotted out from the barn. Taking the notepad from the old phone in the hall, she went into her bedroom. Sitting on the edge of the bed, she punched in the phone number on her cellphone. It rang four times before someone answered. She couldn't tell if the voice was male or female for the static was severe.

"Hola, Hola. Quien es?" The voice spoke loudly.

Sophia answered, "Hello? This is Sophia Pino returning your phone call. Do you speak English?"

'Un momento, por favor."

A young man's voice came on, "Hello, this is Berto. Are you Sophia Pino from New Mexico?"

"Yes, I am. I am returning a phone call from a worried mother. How can I help her?" Sophia didn't want to yell, but the phone reception was terrible.

The young man answered her, "My Grandmother cannot find Roberto Mendoza. Do you know where he is or how she would be able to speak with him?"

Sophia shook her head as she told him, "No, I haven't seen Roberto for over a week not since before their trip to Mexico. Does she want me to find him for her?"

Sophia could see the young man's smile through the phone as he said, "Yes, please. If you do find him would you call us back? We are very worried and we are concerned about my Aunt Rosa's body coming home for burial. Do you know if Roberto had a funeral for her?"

Frowning, Sophia was direct, "No, I have no idea what is going on. I was visited by the sheriff a few days ago regarding your aunt's death, but I really don't know anything. Let me call you back perhaps later this evening. Would ten o'clock tonight be too late? Are you in a different time zone?"

"No, we're the same time. Yes, if you can call tonight at ten, we will be sure to be close to the phone. Thank you." He hung up.

Gathering her purse and her light jacket, Sophia pulled the front door shut and locked it. Speaking to the closed door, she said, "Well, Sophia, you are now obligated to pick up your daughter in Albuquerque, find Roberto and visit your mother in hospital. Let's not add too much more for you also teach at the university and have boarding horses to ride."

Sybil was already at the front door of Jennifer's house. When she saw her mother, she ran out and jumped in the passenger seat. Her face was flushed, "Mom, don't let me do that again, please!" Pulling the seatbelt across her chest, she clicked it in place.

Sophia waved at Jennifer's mother who stood by the door and was waving back at them. "What happened to make this so uncomfortable?"

Sybil pulled the track phone out of her pocket, "You didn't give me the charger thingy and there was no way I could tell you using their phone!"

Patting her daughter's leg, she asked, "Why couldn't you tell me from their house phone?"

Shaking her head, Sybil's face bunched into crying, "Mom, they're a certain religious group! They pushed and pushed me to join their group. Their house is all in pastel colors with some sort of fan that when it's on shows the face of their savior. They questioned if I was Christian! Mom, it was horrible. They don't have a television like ours, it has only religious channels. Their house has these pastel drawings, real drawings of their saints and saviors. Oh, Mom, it was terrible!" Tears fell as she sobbed into her shirt tail. Then she turned to her Mother, "Mom, am I a Christian? Do we believe in Christ? Oh, Mom!"

Reaching into the backseat, Sophia pulled out a box of tissues, "Here, Sweetie, blow your nose." The drive through the city took longer this Sunday morning. There appeared to be a wedding at a family's home and cars blocked the city street. Sophia had to turn around in a driveway and go back to another main street. Finally, they were cruising their way north to Fourth Street. Turning the steering wheel to go down Fourth Street from Central Avenue, Sybil took notice. "Mom, where are we going?"

Handing her daughter another tissue, Sophia pointed to a squat adobe house on the corner of the street, "There, we're going there. This is Roberto's home. The place where Rosa was murdered. We need to find him. You can stay in the car, all right?"

Sybil leaned against the passenger window, "Sure. I'm exhausted. I want to go home and sleep, Mom, please after this can I go home and sleep?"

Sophia didn't answer, but jumped out of her vehicle to walk up the narrow driveway, around an old truck to knock on the wooden door. She waited ready to knock again, but then she heard footsteps. The door slowly opened. A woman with long faded blonde hair, bright blue eyes and a cautious smile said, "Yes?"

Stepping back at the surprise to find a woman in Roberto's house, Sophia said, "Hello. I am Sophia Pino and Rosa's family has called me wanting to know if Roberto is all right. They need to speak with him and for some reason he isn't answering his cellphone. Is he inside? May I speak with him, please?"

A tall man with a pony tail appeared behind the woman in the doorway, he pushed the woman out of his way, "What do you want? I mean what the hell do you want? This poor man just lost his wife and we don't need a door to door religious fanatic bothering him! Go away!" He shoved the door to shut it.

Sophia's foot stopped the door, "Sir, I am sure you mean well, but I am here out of concern for Roberto and Rosa. I am not selling anything except kindness, which you appear to have a shortage of!" She threw her weight at the door, to push her way into the house. It was dark. The curtains were pulled closed. There was the smell of burnt food. Quickly, Sophia walked through the front living room down a hall, peering into each room. There he was. Roberto was sitting in bed with his hat on his head.

"Roberto!" Sophia stepped into the dark bedroom. She walked to the window to pull back the curtains. Sunlight blinded them both for a minute. She heard the front door shut and the house was quiet. He stared at her. He appeared to be lost in his head. She sat on the edge of the bed. Her hand felt the blankets over his feet, he had on his boots. "Roberto, que paso?"

Suddenly, he removed his hat, placing it on his lap. His purple and white striped cowboy shirt with pearl snap buttons appeared to be clean and pressed. She noticed he had on his belt buckle from the racing awards in Mexico. "Senora, they wouldn't let me leave. Peggy and Carl are my friends. They thought I should stay home and mourn for Rosa. Peggy says I must regain my balance. They wouldn't let me leave the bedroom."

Sophia walked to the bedroom door to look down the hall into the living room, "They're not here anymore. They've gone. Do you want to leave? If you're dressed I can take you somewhere. Where would you like to go?"

His boots hit the wood floor. Standing tall in his razor pleated jeans, nice shirt and with hat in hand, he said, "Please, can you take me to Senora Charlotte's? I left my truck there when the sheriff picked me up from work. They brought me home and my truck is still there. Can you take me, please, Senora?"

Turning to him, Sophia asked, "Whose truck is in the driveway then?"

"That's my neighbor's on the other side. I'm fixing his carburetor. I usually park on the street." Going to the window, he pulled the curtains closed. Then bending over the bed, he took the two pillows and shoved them under the blankets, giving the appearance of a body in the bed. He led her into their small kitchen. There was black char on the ceiling and on the windows over the sink. A pot with burnt substance in it sat on the floor in front of the stove. This room had a serious stink. Roberto jerked his chin to the kitchen table, "That's where I found her, mi Corazon. I came home." He gasped.

Sophia picked up the burned pot, "Let's put this outside in the back, shall we? It isn't good to keep it in here." Roberto opened the back door for her as she placed the pathetic pot on the back porch. "Did you find her?"

Shaking his head, Roberto sighed, "Thank goodness, no. Peggy my neighbor, the one at the door just now, she saw smoke coming out of the kitchen windows. She ran over here and found my poor Rosa. Don't know what happened." Roberto stared at his boots, "She was covered with a sheet when I arrived. The law was here and a doctor. I miss her."

They both jumped at the sharp knock on the front door. Sophia turned Roberto around to face the back door, "Come on. Let's go this way! I don't want to face Peggy or Carl again. Go. Go, go. Let's go." Roberto led the way around the small fence to the alley. They fast walked through the alley avoiding the beer cans, garbage and dog poop to Fourth Street proper. Sybil was hunkered over in the passenger seat pulling a part a tissue. Roberto stopped, "The front door isn't locked! I should lock it! What if someone goes in and steals all of Rosa's jewelry?"

Putting out her hand, Sophia said, "Here, which key is it? I'll go and lock up. You stay here with my daughter Sybil. She's in the front seat, you might get low in the back." The key in her hand, Sophia walked tall to the front door of Roberto's house. There at the door, pounding away was Carl. When he saw her, he came up to her, right up to her nose. "Where's Roberto? Peggy seriously wants him to remain in bed! His chi is all goofed up and he needs to work on his chakra."

Sophia could smell the garlic on his breath, "Excuse me, please, I am going to lock Roberto's front door. Please, let me pass."

Carl put his arms out to block her, "No, Ma'am! You tell me where Roberto is and I'll let you by, but until then no way are you going past me, Ma'am!"

A quick jerk of her knee met his groin. "No one, but no one, calls me Ma'am! No one! Now get the hell out of my way or I will hit you with my other metal knee! Move!"

Carl was bent over, gasping with his hands folded between his thighs. Sophia shoved him to kneel as she strode to the front door, locked it and walked around him to her vehicle. All Carl did was groan. Chortling to herself, Sophia muttered, "Metal knees do come in handy with assholes!"

Sybil had crawled into the back seat to be next to Roberto. He had a long string in his hand and was showing her how to make a Cat's Cradle. Sophia jumped into the driver's seat to say, "Roberto, how's your chi and your chakra?"

His whole face smiled, "You know I speak English really well after the classes, but somethings I can't figure. What are those things?"

The rearview mirrors checked, Sophia turned the van around, "I have no idea." Once back on the interstate to Calavera, she asked him, "Do you know anything about Rosa taking some herbs for her diabetes and high blood pressure?"

He patted her shoulder from his backseat, "Yes, they were herbs given to me by Senora Charlotte. I showed them to Senora Pino and she told me they were too old to give to Rosa. When I smelled them, they stank. Senora Riley told me to take them home because they had certain herbs we could buy fresh at the market."

Noticing Sybil was fast asleep with her head on Roberto's shoulder, Sophia asked him quietly, "Rosa knew not to use those herbs in that bag, right?"

Roberto stared out the window at the billowing clouds, "Yes, I told her not to take the herbs. She was going to ask Peggy to go with her to the Mercado de Yerbas and get some fresh Yerbas. We talked about it, we planned to buy herbs this coming week when I get my money."

They were quiet driving down the paved Calavera road to Charlotte's. Sophia walked with Roberto to the front door. It was quickly opened by Charlotte herself, "Roberto, oh, thank God, I was so worried! Rosa's mother has been calling and calling, she is very worried about you and about Rosa's funeral and her burial. Oh, Roberto, I am so happy to see you!" The elderly woman with the long braids grabbed hold of Roberto in a bear hug. He blushed, letting his arms fall by his side.

Then Charlotte noticed Sophia, "Hi, oh, thank you for bringing my Roberto back to me! Thank you, thank you!" Sophia got a bear hug, too. "Can you come in, Sophia, do come inside. It's cold in this wind." Not missing a heartbeat, Charlotte went on to say, "Roberto, I was worried for your truck is here. I didn't know what to do. I didn't want to call the cops and I wasn't sure where you lived or I would've taken it to you. Oh, you are a sight for sore eyes!" The woman proceeded to cry with tears running down her opaque cheeks.

Roberto took her arm and led her into her own home. Sophia quietly closed the door after them and returned to her vehicle where Sybil had fallen over asleep in the backseat. Driving to her mother's farm down the road, she noticed the truck was missing. She parked by the wrought iron gate, quietly closed her van's door and ran into the barn. Mr. Perkal almost knocked her flat as he walked quickly out of the barn. "Sophia!" He stepped to the side.

"Mr. Perkal! Hi, how nice of you to feed the horse!" Sophia caught her breath.

Mr. Perkal's voice became gruff, "No, I didn't feed Geordie. I found him."

"What? He was running around loose? Granger wouldn't let the horse out to run around. What do you mean, you found him?"

Mr. Perkal turned around to walk ahead of Sophia to the last stall in the barn. There on the ground was Geordie. He was huffing, his chest heaving. Blood ran out of his rectum and his nose. Mr. Perkal leaned on the stall door, "I wasn't sure if I should call the vet or if I should talk to your mother, but I know she is in the hospital. I didn't know what to do. I'm pleased to find you here, what should we do?"

A shriek echoed in the barn behind them. Sybil ran to the stall door, flung it open to kneel down beside the horse, "Mom! Mom, call the vet! Call Dr. Murphey! Mom, I think he's dying!" Sybil buried her face into the horse's mane, "Mom, what is happening in the world? Everything is going wrong?"

Nodding to Mr. Perkal, Sophia asked him, "Would you stay here with my daughter, please? She has had a rather difficult twenty four hours. I'm going inside to call the vet. He's an old friend and he'll probably come right away, even if it is Sunday."

Racing to the van, she pulled her keys out of the ignition. Closed the sliding door, Sybil had left open for the leaves to blow in and hurried to the back door. The house smelled empty. No one had cooked or been inside the house for a time. Knowing the vet's phone number by heart, Sophia called him. "Of course it is Sunday and we do have this emergency, but it appears Geordie is dying. Can you come?"

Mr. Perkal met Sophia at the backdoor. "I'm going to head home now. Your daughter appears to know what she's doing. She has a wet blanket and is cleaning the horse. Did you get the vet?"

The white truck, laden with drawers, doors and supplies drove up within minutes of the phone call. Dr. Murphey followed Sophia into the barn. He had his black bag and a long hose. Sybil clapped her hands when she saw him, "Yes! A hero has arrived, finally! Someone we can trust and won't kill us!"

Dr. Murphey stared at her, "My goodness, young lady, you are quite a welcoming committee." Sybil and Dr. Murphey worked on Geordie. Sophia returned to the kitchen and made phone calls. She first called A.J. to tell him about the herbs and what Roberto had told her. A.J. confirmed that was what Roberto had also told them, but the brown bag found at Rosa's home had no ingredients printed on the side. How would they know what to buy? Sophia told A.J. where Roberto was at the moment and about the strange neighbors Carl and Peggy. A.J. responded, "We did a house to house interview, but they wouldn't open their door. We knew they were in there, but they didn't come to the door."

Then she called Deputy Sheriff Cruz to be sure he could drive by the house or even knock on the door to be certain the kids at the farm house were safe and good. He scolded her for not calling him yesterday when she returned home. She plead forgetfulness and told him today she would most definitely call him when she returned home.

The last call was to Berto in Mexico. Sophia smiled as she used her mother's rotary phone that hung on the kitchen wall over the counter, "Margaret can afford a long distance call, after all she loves Roberto probably more than her own son!"

The phone rang until the answering machine picked up with a friendly request to leave a message in Spanish. Sophia left a message in English, the young man could translate and she would call them again tonight. She opened the fridge to find something she could fix everyone for lunch. A loaf of bread was in the fridge, some sliced ham, tomatoes and lettuce. The mayonnaise appeared moldy and the mustard container was empty. Taking down the cutting board, she made four sandwiches, two for the doc.

Potato chips and sandwiches were placed in three brown bags. As she rummaged through her mother's bag saving drawer, she found several bags of Granger's herbs with the logo broken. Sophia pulled one out and shoved it into her front pant pocket. Gathering a thermos of hot tea, she returned to the barn. Geordie was standing. His head was low, his nose almost touching the ground. Sybil was brushing him with a curry comb.

Dr. Murphey pulled a syringe from the horse's neck, "There you go, old boy. You have a serious case of cancerous polyps." Noticing Sophia, he explained, "We knew he has cancer, but the growths have moved to his colon and his rectum. When I looked into his mouth, the cancer is in his palate and go all the way down his esophagus. This fellow is in major pain and not well at all." He patted Geordie's neck. "Now, I know your mother will not have him put down, but his condition has worsened. No longer is it a right to keep him alive. You need to speak to her. If she won't agree to put him down, then I will be pressed to call the ASPCA. It is inhumane and cruel to keep him alive at this point."

Handing him one of the brown bags of food, Sophia frowned, "Dr. Murphey, you know she will have a fit. How long will Geordie be able to stay upright? Do you think he might, and I know this sounds cold, but do you think he might die naturally soon?"

Sybil glared at her mother, "Mom! How dare you!"

Dr. Murphey pulled a sandwich from the bag, "No, he could live for another two or three months, but he'll fall down more and more. His pain is extreme. He has internal bleeding from Cushing's disease. It's amazing he has lasted this long. He's what about forty one years old and with his Cushing's disease, this is remarkable." He sat down on a bale of hay right outside of the stall to eat his lunch, "Pour me some of that, would you?"

Sophia opened the thermos of hot tea and poured it into the cup. She had sweetened the tea with fresh honey. He smiled as he sipped it,

"There's no question now, Sophia, and this horse should be released from pain. He's been a good old boy, had a good old life and is ready for greener pastures. It's time."

They heard a truck door slam. Granger ran into the barn, "Damn, the horse is still upright! I thought he'd die when I left yesterday. What are you doing here?"

Sybil threw the black hard rubber curry comb at Granger. It hit him in the arm, "Ow! You're a nasty one, aren't you? You better watch out because I might come for you!"

Sophia loudly sighed, "Really, Granger! Really! You left Geordie here all night in pain and you did nothing?"

Throwing his hands into the air, he said, "What was I supposed to do? I'm not a vet and the horse is costing a fortune. I bet you're the vet who's charging my mother a king's ransom for the expensive medicine to keep this dumb animal alive, right?" Granger's voice turned harsh.

Dr. Murphey stood, collected his black bag, the hose and his brown bag of food. He handed the cup back to Sophia. "Guess this is my cue to depart. Yes, Granger, I'm the vet who is helping your mother keep her best friend alive. And, yes, my brother is the doctor who declared your father deceased. Perhaps it is you who should be careful." His stern face was focused on the barn's dirt floor as he departed.

"Damn, he's an ugly old man, isn't he?" Granger kicked dirt. Sybil patted Geordie. Then she pulled shut the stall door, "Mom, we're not to feed him for twenty four hours. You might let Roberto know if he comes to feed him this evening. I'm going to sit in the van."

Granger grabbed Sophia's arm, "Where do you think you're going?"

Jerking her arm from his hand, Sophia answered, "Home. I'm going home." She walked slowly to the van. Sybil was driven home to the farm house. Donna and Griego were watching cartoons on the television. They informed her that nothing unusual had happened and they were visited by Cruz who brought them each a candy bar. Sybil went to bed with a groan, "You know Donna has to return to Geoffrey's at six o'clock sharp this evening. Just saying in case you visit Grandma in the hospital, your time is limited, Mom."

Returning to the van, Sophia reached into her lunch bag. Eating her sandwich while she leaned against the van, she tried to figure out a way to tell her mother about Geordie. Patting her pant pocket, she felt her cellphone, "Yes, I better call Charlotte and let her tell Roberto about Geordie."

The Sunday visitors had filled the lower hospital parking lot. Sophia parked at the end of the upper lot where the wind blew hard and sand pelted her front windshield. Bracing against the gale, she ran through the automatic doors to the atrium of the hospital. A Pink Lady gave her Margaret's room number Two twelve.

A sign on the door stated 'bathing.' Sophia sat on a chair in the hall, watching other family members go in and out of different rooms. Most of the visitors were dressed nicely, in church clothes. Sophia sat there with her heavy clogs, old pants stained from years of love and her soft lavender pullover. She patted her head, at least she had her beret covering her wild curly hair. A nurse opened the door pulling out a trolley with a square container of water, several wash clothes and a towel. Noticing Sophia, she smiled, "Hey, she's all yours. Good luck." Sophia nodded.

Margaret was lying flat on her back. She appeared to be a frail, tiny woman. All the wrinkles on her face were darkened by her pale complexion. An I.V feed was in her boney arm with the bag of fluid hanging over the side of the hospital bed. The white hospital gown was too big for Margaret's thin body. Gnarled fingers grasped the top of the white sheet pulled up to her chin. When Margaret saw Sophia she gasped, "It's about time you showed up! No one has come to see me! No one! Not even Granger. My perfect son, the fruit of my loins, my handsome son hasn't been to see me!" Tears flowed traveling down her wrinkled cheeks to the white sheet beneath her. "I love my son, I would give my life for Granger! Why doesn't he come to see me? Is he hurt or is he sick, Sophia?"

Gulping, Sophia approached her mother, "Oh, dear, Margaret. Granger is trying to take care of Geordie. Your horse has had a bad bout of cancerous polyps. We had to call the vet, Dr. Murphey who by the way sends you his regards and hopes you get better soon."

Margaret attempted to sit up, but she was too weak to lift on her elbow, "What? What's wrong with my beautiful boy? If my horse dies then I want to die, too! What's wrong?" Her arthritic fingers clutched at the strong ligaments protruding from her neck, "I can't live, I have no purpose without Geordie! How can I live in a horse community without a horse! I'll die, I'll die."

The white plastic chair in the corner of the hospital room was pulled to the side of the bed. Sophia sat, shaking her head, she said, "Mom, or Margaret, Geordie is dying. His body is tired, petered out and filled with painful cancer. He is in terrible pain. Granger found him lying on his side in the stall with blood coming out of his nose and his rectum. Dr. Murphey believes the humane thing to do would be to put the horse down and out of his misery."

"NO! My God, kill me instead of Geordie! Kill me!" Margaret yelled at the top of her lungs. As she attempted to lift, she hit the nurse button with her elbow. Two nurses raced into the room. Margaret didn't stop screaming, "This is my daughter! She wants to kill me! Then she's going to kill my horse!" Pointing her arthritic finger at Sophia she said in a deep horrid voice, "My daughter wants to kill me!"

Sophia stood to calmly push the chair back into the corner of the hospital room. She shook her head as she walked down the hall, to the elevators. In her vehicle, Sophia slammed the door, "The world has gone totally crazy! Sybil is right!" She drove to the closest Walgreens, got out and bought herself a tall bottle of red wine. As she placed it on the passenger seat of her vehicle, she said, "This is for later. Mama needs some help." She watched the tumbleweeds roll down the hill from the factory as she punched in Charlotte's home phone number.

Charlotte answered immediately. Quietly, Sophia explained to Charlotte about Geordie and his cancer. Charlotte listened, "Roberto is still here. We're fixing dinner. He's listening on speaker phone. Sophia what can we do to help Geordie? Is there something we can do?"

Rubbing her index finger on the dashboard of the van, Sophia answered, "No, it's up to the owner. The responsible party is the owner and Margaret is the only person who can order the euthanasia."

Roberto's voice interjected, "Senora, she won't put the horse down. She says the horse was bought for her by husband and the horse is all she has left of her husband. She won't put the horse to death."

Charlotte agreed, "Your mother would rather die than see that horse put down, but you know what? Once the horse is no longer there, Margaret will forget about him. The horse is just one more reason for your mother to feel needed. You'll have Granger to fill that void now that he's home there."

Roberto asked, "Are you part owner of the horse? Isn't there someone else who is owner, too?"

Rubbing her hand along the steering wheel, Sophia had an epiphany, "Oh, yes, Granger has power of attorney. He could order it with the vet. He has declared Mom to be mentally incompetent. Maybe he would do it. What do you think?"

Clearing her throat, Charlotte answered, "He could, but you know he would blame you. He's a god in your mother's eyes. He will blame you, if you don't mind, you could try to get him to call the vet. Just prepare yourself for the blame game."

Roberto asked, "Should I go by this evening and check on the horse?"

Sophia continued to watch heavy clouds move over the hospital, putting everything in shadow, "No, Roberto. I think we should leave Granger there with the horse. Dr. Murphey said if Geordie isn't put down he could call the ASPCA, but then they would probably take all of Mom's animals away."

Charlotte's rasping voice added, "Sophia, don't worry. Roberto can go over there before dark and feed her chickens." There was some whispering and then she added, "Roberto says he wants to stay here in the guest room tonight. His house makes him sad and his neighbors are loco." There was a laugh.

Hanging up, Sophia drove back to her home. It was three thirty and she wanted to spend some time with her youngest daughter. She was tired of driving around and not getting much done. Before backing out of the parking lot, she texted Granger, telling him to visit his mother. Then she erased the text, saying to the windshield, "A fat lot of good that will do!" The vehicle was put in gear and Sophia drove home through the blowing wind.

6

The house was quiet when Sophia came into the kitchen. Donna's bedside light was on and as she walked through the hall, she noticed three of the five cats sitting on Donna's bed. "Hello?" Sophia pushed the bedroom door open, "Donna? Are you in here?"

Stepping out of the walk-in closet, Donna smiled at her mother, "Hey, how did it go with Grandma Margaret? Is she stuck in a strait jacket?"

Shaking her head, Sophia frowned, "No, and you shouldn't speak in such a way about your grandmother. She has helped us get this farm. We need to be thankful for her help."

"Mom, we shouldn't be living here, you know? You grabbed this place as soon as possible, but it is falling to pieces. Mom, the heater only works in some rooms and the plumbing is a mess. We could've moved into the city for a lot less work and probably less money!" Donna plopped down on the bed to pick up the kitten Oscar.

"Donna, we are here now. Let's make the best of it." Picking up her jeans that were on the floor next to Donna's bed, Sophia explained, "You wanted to have a horse. Now you have a horse and a good friend to go riding with and you like Griego, don't you?" She folded the jeans and placed them on the bureau.

Pouting, Donna stroked the kitten, "This place is filled with ghosts. It's crowded at night with all the ghosts roaming around. There's a small boy in front of Sybil's old bathroom that was burned alive. His clothes are black and his skin is peeling. When we see him, he stinks. Mom, this place is old and crowded!"

Sitting beside her daughter on the bed, Sophia asked, "What about the horses?"

"Yeah, well, I love the horses, but now I live with Dad. I only get to ride two days a week, well, not even that, only a day and a half. If I ride nonstop then I don't get to see you or Sybil and Sybil is my best friend in the whole world."

Hugging Donna to her, Sophia pried, "Don't you have friends at school? Your new school has smaller classes, certainly you must have made friends there?"

Shrugging her mother's arm off of her, Donna stood up to grab her backpack, "I suppose. Should I start packing to go back to Dad's now?"

Walking out of the room into the kitchen, Sophia asked Donna, "Hey, let's solve a riddle, shall we? Come on, let's have a cup of tea and some cookies."

Trailing behind her mother, Donna sat at the head of the kitchen table, "All right, Mom, what's the mystery?"

The hot water in the mugs, the tea bags soaking and cookies on a small plate, Sophia took out a notepad from her class pack. "Roberto's wife Rosa was murdered and we need to make a list of people who might have wanted her dead. You know Roberto from helping him at grandma's farm. Who does he work for and did you know his wife Rosa?" She stirred her tea.

Sybil suddenly ran to the table and grabbed a cookie, "Hey, you guys, I want to help!"

Donna smiled, "Well, let's see. Roberto works for Grandma, Charlotte and Mrs. Peters whose husband is a dentist at the Medical Center on Second Street. Mrs. Peters has two Clydesdale horses named Carl and Sirloin."

Sybil burst out laughing, "Carl and Sirloin, what's that about?"

Smiling, Donna explained, "Mrs. Peters said they are so big and fat, they look like hamburgers from Carl Juniors and a Sirloin steak. They're not to be eaten though."

Sophia wrote their names down on the notepad, "All right, did they know Rosa and what work did Roberto do for them?"

Shaking her head, Donna chewed on a cookie, "Charlotte is completely dependent on Roberto for everything and so is Grandma. Roberto cleans their houses, cares for the property, weeds the gardens, works and cares for their horses and he feeds Grandma's chickens. Mrs. Peters only has him to look after her Clydesdales, but that's a lot! They do major pooping and they're big! He has to work them in the arena, wash them down, dry them off, clean their hooves, feed them, oh, and he unloads the hay bales when they're delivered by Rusty from the Feed Store. That's a lot of major work!"

Sophia scratched her head with the end of the pencil, "All right, we have two elderly women who need his help for everything. How old is Mrs. Peters and what does her husband do on the farm?"

Shaking her head, Donna mumbled as she chewed another cookie,

"I have no idea. He's a dentist. He fixes teeth all day long and his office is in the poor side of town, so he gets people who can't afford a real dentist. I met her once, she's old. Mom, she's about your age."

Frowning at her daughter, Sophia scolded, "I'm not old. I'm only just forty years old! Grandma is old! Is Mrs. Peters as old as Grandma?"

"Nope, she's your age. Hey, guys, you want to go for a ride now?" Donna stared at the hall clock.

Sipping tea, Sybil shook her head, "No, time. Mom, its five-forty-five. You need to get Donna back to Dad's, he's already mad at us. We don't want to upset him anymore than we need to, right?"

Stretching her arm out across the kitchen table, Donna put her head down, "Mom, I hate it at Dad's. Do I have to go back? Tomorrow I have an appointment to get my braces tightened, can't I stay here and go with you?"

Putting the pencil down on the notepad, Sophia put her hand on her daughter's arm, "No, Sweetie, we have to abide by the court and the court says you can only stay with us on the weekend."

Driving to Rocoso was a time warp for Sophia. This was her route to and from anywhere else for years. It was home and then it wasn't. The sun was glowing golden in the clear gray blue sky of dusk. The wind blew harder up here on this side of the mountain rather than down in the valley. The van was parked beside Geoffrey's double cab blue truck. Donna sat staring at the front door, she didn't move from the passenger seat.

The front door was flung open and Geoffrey strode out with his little Freddy dog at his heels. Sophia rubbed Donna's back, "Let's go in and talk to him, o-kay? Come on, let's try to make the best of a bad situation."

Making an ugly face at her mother, Donna grumbled, "Mom, you always say that and it doesn't get better! I still hate this!"

Geoffrey opened the passenger door, putting his arms out for his daughter. Donna glared at him and twisted to run around his outstretched arm and into the house. Geoffrey stared at Sophia, "So, you have poisoned my daughter against me." His voice was surprisingly calm. "Sophia, I believe we need to talk."

Sophia pulled the key out of the ignition to put the ring of keys into her coat pocket. She jumped out of the van and slowly walked around to meet him. "All right, I agree. Let's go inside, it's cold out here in the wind."

Geoffrey stood still, "No, I don't believe it would be wise to go inside. You won't like it. We need to have a discussion on neutral territory where you won't pass judgement on me or the way I live."

Leaning against the side of the van, she pulled her coat tighter around her, "What do you want to discuss?"

His thin cotton shirt was buttoned at an odd angle and his brown shoes were crusted with grime. His balding head was turning red in the cold wind, but his voice remained calm, "You should know about this house and what happened when I bought it from your father."

"All right," Sophia drew circles with the toe of her clog in the dirt at her feet.

His eyes stared straight ahead, "Papa told me that he didn't want me to make a payment, not one single payment for as long as he was alive because he wanted me to have the funds to take good care of his beautiful daughter and his granddaughters who were the treasures of his life." The wind blew hard rocking the van, Geoffrey put his hand against the side of the vehicle. "His words, so help me God." His hand was lifted skyward. "Then when your father died, Margaret took over the accounts. She and Granger spoke to the accountant who knew nothing of your Father's and my arrangement. That's why there weren't any payments as long as your father was alive."

Pulling a handkerchief from her coat pocket, Sophia blew her nose, "So you say. Where did the money go that was supposed to help me and the girls? The whole time we were married you constantly spoke of how poor we were and how expensive this place cost. Where did the money go?"

Geoffrey shifted, rolling his shoulder onto the side of the van, he faced Sophia. "You won't like the answer."

Shoving the handkerchief back into her coat pocket, she turned to study his face. His pallor was gray, his blue eyes magnified in his thick lenses were bloodshot. Sophia shook her head, "It doesn't matter what I like. We aren't married anymore, remember?"

He put his hand on her shoulder, "Sophia, those days were bad times. Can't we put all that anger behind us and try to become friends again?"

Sophia stepped back, "No. Don't think so. Where did the money go that was supposed to help the girls and myself? Where is it, Geoffrey?"

Sighing, he leaned back against the van, "The money went to my mother's coffin."

Jumping away from the van, Sophia shouted, "Your mother's coffin? That monstrosity! The coffin of Italian silk with French lace pillows and coated in strips of shiny heavy metal with brass trimmings? That huge eight hundred pound coffin?"

Geoffrey walked away from her, "Yes. That coffin." Kicking small rocks out of his way, he spoke softly, "Yes, my mother's coffin. I loved my mother. She loved me regardless. When she knew her dementia was becoming worse, we went to the funeral home and she picked out her coffin. How was I to deny her?"

Sophia didn't move, but watched him, "Deny her? You could've told her you didn't have the money for such an expense. Ask her to find another one less expensive or something? Geoffrey, that money was for your daughter's college, clothes, or something! It was for your daughters!"

"Sophia, she was my mother. I was not going to deny her. How could I? I'm the one with money and she was dying." Pulling off his thick glasses in gold frames, he rubbed his eyes with his fingers, "She was my mother. She deserves to rest in a coffin of her choosing, no matter the expense." The gold frames with thick lenses were shoved back onto his face.

Coughing and gasping in shock, Sophia berated him, "What about your siblings? What did they contribute?"

Shaking his head and stumbling back to the shelter of the van from the wind, Geoffrey softly spoke, "My older brother paid for the service and the food at the church. Sophia, Stephen is in the military. He doesn't make much money. My younger brother paid for the cemetery plot. I make the most money and it was decided I could pay for the coffin, the largest expense."

Wind rolled tumbleweeds down the ravine to rest in a heap below the house. Sophia looked up at the house's front window, Donna was kneeling against the glass watching her parents. Quietly, Sophia said, "I think I should leave now. Just for you to know, Donna wants to live with us all week and all weekends. She believes that I should come inside your home and find out why, but if you won't let me in, then I suppose I should leave now. There is nothing more to be said." She sniffed in defiance.

Putting up his hand, Geoffrey pointed to the house, "Sure, come on inside. Maybe you should see your daughter's bedroom and what it would be like to have her live with you."

The two of them entered the front door. The ammonia smell of urine hit her full force. The carpet between the couch and the television console was saturated with dried dog diarrhea. Sophia turned away, she wanted to see her kitchen. This kitchen she had designed and once loved. Her breath was taken away to find the blue tile on the walls behind the counters was gone. The walls above the counters were now covered with gold and silver tiles and food, dried food splattered onto the walls. Her happy counter of decorative colored tile was now thick with gray granite stone. Her once warm kitchen filled with bright colors was dark and cold. Boxes of food and opened cans covered the stovetop. No one could possibly use the stovetop for the clutter. Her deep sterling metal sink in front of the double paned large kitchen window was filled with crusty dishes and petrified food. Some of the large black crumbs were moving. Spider webs hung low in every corner of the room.

Turning away, Sophia moved to the hall. The carpet was sticky, her shoes crunched on dried food and hard feces. She walked into Donna's room. There on a neatly made bed beside her backpack sat Donna, crying. The carpet had been vacuumed, the bureau clean and the shoes in order at the foot of her bed on the floor. "This room appears to be just fine, Geoffrey." She turned to face him.

He was leaning against the hall wall outside of Donna's room. A can of beer was in his right hand. Shaking in anger, she asked, "Can I see our old bedroom?"

His hand waved to the room down the short hall to her left. Sophia had to inch sideways around piles of books stacked in the hall outside of the bedroom. She had to shove the door open. Piles of clothes were stacked behind the door. There was no light in the room. A heavy curtain covered the one window. Reaching around the doorframe, she flipped on the overhead light. Sudden illumination revealed a bed unmade with the once white sheets now gray from lack of washing. Stale body odor of unwashed dirty clothes lifted into the air. The blankets thrown on the floor were coated with animal fur. Layers of clothes were folded on the floor behind the door, right inside keeping the door from fully opening. As she threw her weight onto the door, she asked Geoffrey, "Does your brother know of your living conditions?"

"Hell, no! Nor should he. Stephen is in the Middle East working on a top secret mission. Sophia, you leave him out of this! He has nothing to do with me or you, he has his own life now!"

Sophia squeezed around the barely open door, slowly entering the room. Rancid stale odors insulted her sense of smell. The huge walk-in closet overflowed with clothes. The clothes pole that went around the eight foot closet length was packed with apparel and then there were hotel clothes' frames laden with clothes doubly placed inside the closet, blocking the availability to get the clothes on the poles. The floor of the closet was cluttered with layers of shoes, boots, and slippers. "Geoffrey, do you wear all these clothes?"

He had remained in the hall, "Some of those are from my high school days. The ones on the poles with wheels were my father's clothes and the women's clothes on the far side of the closet belonged to my mother." His voice behind her snickered, "No, I don't wear them, but they keep me company. They're good memories." He gulped from the beer can. "You can go into my bathroom if you want?"

Donna's voice shrieked out, "Mom! No! Don't go into Dad's bathroom! It's filled with mold, bugs and the floor is sinking! Mom, I think you should go now!"

Sophia's body was uncontrollably shaking. The smell, the stench, the squalor and the hoarding was beyond her comprehension. As she backed out of the bedroom, she bumped into Geoffrey. He put his arm around her waist. Sophia slapped his hand, "Get off me, you're a pervert! Do you know that? You're a pervert!" Gasping in her anger, she called to Donna, "Get your backpack, get your stuff, we're leaving here now!"

Geoffrey put his arm out across the hall to block her, he softly spoke to her, "No. No, you're not taking my daughter. Not without a court order. Donna stays, but you can leave."

Glaring at him, Sophia whispered, "This house is filled with dirt and disgust! You are a hoarder, do you know it?" His breath reeked of beer as he bent forward to her face. She kept her words steady, "No one, but no one should live in this filth. Not even you! What do you hope to achieve by living this way? What, Geoffrey? What is your purpose for such filth? Is it pity?"

Jerking back against a pile of stacked books on the floor behind him, he snapped at her, "No! I have no one to clean for me or to pick up after me! No one! You left me! Now I live as a bachelor with no one to love me or pick up after me, that's all!"

Barking a laugh, "You left me! You deserted us! Now I see it was a good thing!" She spat at him, "No one would want to clean up this mess, Geoffrey! No one! This is the worst filth imaginable! This is beyond disgusting!" Edging her way around him as he had now sat on the pile of books, she stared at him, "You make choices in life. Choices define who we are. This choice of yours to live in this garbage dump with your poor animals is your personal character choice and this defines you!"

Sophia didn't wait to argue. She shoved around him, grabbed Donna's arm from the doorway and pulled her to her side. The two of them raced out of the house to the van. Donna jumped in, slammed the door and locked it. Sophia raced to the driver's door and as she was going to pull the door open, Geoffrey grabbed her by the arm, "No! Donna stays! I have the right to call the sheriff and have you jailed! Donna stays with me!"

Sophia let all of her emotion flow from her body. She lifted her hand and slapped his hand as hard as she possibly could. Geoffrey fell back, letting go of her as he shook his red hand. Sophia got into the van, locked the door, turned the key in the ignition to slowly back out and away from the Rocoso house. "There, let's go home."

Both of them were quiet as the van drove down the narrow Alcon road. Farmhouses were placed near the road with their pitched roofs draining onto grass patches between house and road fences. Dogs lifted their heads from their afternoon naps as the van passed by. There were horses in the open fields beyond the homes where the alfalfa fields were slowly turning yellow from cold nights and lack of sunshine. The fireplace smoke hovered close to the ground with the cold air pressing the warmth to the cold earth.

Shonac lifted his head from his slumber under the hangman's tree. He ran to meet them as Sophia parked underneath the tall cottonwood. Donna jumped out of the van to kneel down and hug the puppy, "I'm home, Shonac. I'm home and love you, love you, always! I'll never lock you in a dirty old house full of pee and poop." She hugged his neck as he licked her ear.

Boots on and barn jackets zipped up, the two worked in the barn. Donna took the key from the oat room to unlock the outbuilding beside the barn. Inside were all the saddles, bridles, halters, lead ropes and blankets as well as horse medications and special fetlock wraps. Sophia leaned in the doorway to watch Donna take down her saddle blanket, saddle and bridle. "You're going, aren't you?"

Nodding at her mother, Donna spoke softly, "Yep, you know I can't stay here. But you'll know I will be safe. Griego knows where I'll be, but I won't be with him and Reina, just for you to know." The saddle was wiped with a cleaning cloth. Donna wrapped her long hair around her hand to knot it behind her head. "You might call the dentist about my brace's appointment. Let him know I'm sick, throwing up or something and can't come in. They don't like to tighten braces on people who will throw up on them." She chuckled. "Don't worry, Mom, I'll be safe. Sybil has it all arranged."

Shaking her head, Sophia quietly held her daughter in a tight hug, "Somehow I knew Sybil already had a plan. Your sister is like that, she always has a backdoor plan ready." Kissing the top of her daughter's head, Sophia kept her hug tight, "Donna, I love you no matter what, please know this. Tomorrow afternoon you need to come home, all right? Please, please, be home by four o'clock to help me ride the equines?"

Pulling free from the tight grip, Donna agreed. "Yes, Mom, I might even be home before that, although you have classes, right?"

"Oh, sweetheart, no, my classes are Tuesday, Thursday and Friday. Tomorrow though I probably have to take care of Grandma in the morning. You know Granger isn't going to help her? Thank goodness for Roberto!" Sophia gave her daughter one more kiss on her forehead, "Do you have the track phone and the charger with you?"

"Yeah, in my backpack. Who knows who might show up and Clementine said she was going to come around four, but its way past four now, right?" Donna carried the tack for Tracy to the white pole fence of the barn. She placed it carefully to balance, ran into the farmhouse while Sophia watched Tracy come trotting up to the tie down. This horse loved Donna as much as Donna loved her. Not wanting to know which direction

Donna was riding off to, Sophia went into the house after the horse was saddled and mounted.

Sybil was in the kitchen washing pork chops in the sink, "Mom, Donna's going to be fine. Clementine called, she was called out and won't be able to ask you more questions until tomorrow morning. She said she would be here around ten and not to feed her, hah!"

Patting her pocket, Sophia remembered the brown bag she found at her mother's. Falling onto her bed, she pulled it free to study it. There were no ingredients on this paper bag. There was a number written in gold ink. It appeared to be Sanskrit for it had loops and squiggles. Closing her eyes she felt two kittens jump onto the bed and walk up her body. One sat on her chest. The other curled up under her arm. Petting the kitten on her chest, she asked him, "Where did Granger's herbs go when he went to prison? Did he give them to our mother or did he flush them down the toilet? Huh?"

The cat didn't answer. He purred and kneaded her chest. His claws went into her coat that she still had on. "Where did these women get all the herbs for their animals, huh? Oh, knowledgeable cat tell me, please?"

Striding into the room, Sybil waved a pot in the air, "Mom! There's someone banging on the front door! I am not going to answer it! Nope, not going to answer it!"

Sophia opened her eyes. The cats jumped off the bed as Sybil walked toward her mother's bed waving the pot around, "Mom! Get up! What are you doing? You have your coat on! Dinner will be ready soon. This is no time for a nap!" She turned in a huff, "I'll turn on the heater, but get up!"

Twisting her body, Sophia stood up from the bed. Her plum beret had fallen off to the other side of the bed.

Deputy Sheriff Ignacio Cruz stood tall in the doorway. "Sophia Pino, I am here to arrest you for the kidnapping of your daughter Donna. Either she is to be released to me and be returned to your ex-husband's house or you are to be detained, arrested and she is to be turned over to Children Youth and Family Services. Do you understand?" A short woman in a bright red coat peeked over his shoulder.

Standing aside, Sophia invited the tall, thin Deputy Cruz into the farmhouse. Behind him came the woman who smiled. Red lipstick matched her coat. A camera hung from a cord around her neck and a brown clipboard was in her red gloved hand. She stuck out her free hand without the glove to Sophia, "Hello. Deputy Sheriff Cruz has terrible manners."

At the sound of his name, he stopped. Abruptly he announced, "This is our Family Care Officer and this is the mother Sophia Pino. She abducted her daughter from her ex-husband's house where his daughter was to remain by law!" His emerald green eyes glanced from room to room as the three of them walked into the kitchen. Sophia smiled at his youthful face, "I understand. How nice to see you. Please come on into the kitchen. It's windy out there and dark."

The woman trotted behind. When she noticed Sybil at the stove, she lifted her camera and took a photo. The flash blinded Sybil. "Excuse me! Just who do you think you are! No one is allowed to take my picture without my approval!" The wet wooden spoon waved in Sybil's hand. "You could be a pervert or something! Give me that camera! You have no right!" The wet spoon spattered water in the air.

A red glove dropped onto the kitchen floor. Sophia bent to pick it up, "You know we have no idea who you are or why you are here?"

Taking the red glove from Sophia's hand the woman spoke softly, "I'm Helen Tafoya, the Family Care Officer. If your daughter is to be removed for any reason I am to accompany her." Nodding toward where Cruz disappeared down the long hall, she went on, "He cannot transport her without a Family Care Officer being present."

Cruz reentered the kitchen. He smiled at Sophia, "She isn't here is she? You know, Sophia, you are one smart woman. This isn't going to work! We will find her." Donna's bedside light was turned on for him to check under the bed and in the closet. Quietly, he knocked on the bathroom door. Then he turned the knob on the old cracked door and entered. Sophia could hear him pulling back the shower curtain. Entering Sophia's room, he could be heard bumping into her bed. Her room brightened with the lamp on as the closet door was pulled open and shut. Marmalade raced into the kitchen with his hackles up obviously frightened by a stranger hovering over Sophia's bed. Sophia held Shonac by the collar although the dog was wagging his tail and smiling.

Ignacio Cruz returned once more to the warm kitchen. Sybil had set the table for two and had a pot boiling on the stove. He chuckled, "Mrs. Tafoya, I believe Donna Vinder isn't here."

Helen Tafoya stood by Sybil and the old stove. "Does your mother beat you or your sister?"

Flipping the spoon quickly out of the pot of boiling water, Sybil's nostrils flared. "No! How dare you! You really are irritating."

"No, I have to ask these questions. They're here on my clipboard." The red gloves were back on the hands.

Jerking the clipboard out of the woman gloved hand, Sybil read the questions. "Does the perpetrator hit their children? Does the perpetrator lock them up against their will? Are there signs of bruising or abuse? Is the parent confrontational?"

Sybil handed the clipboard back to Helen Tafoya. "These questions are stupid and of course if you ask them in front of the said perpetrator the answer would be 'no.'"

Turning her focus back to the stove, Sybil smirked, "You must be new to this. Obviously no one has trained you regarding these questions, right?"

A bright red blush came over the woman's face. It almost matched her lipstick. "This is my third ride along. I find you to be rude and tactless, young lady. What's your name?" Sybil ignored her.

Pulling out a chair, Sophia sat down, "I have no idea where Donna is and I have not kidnapped her nor have I taken her anywhere against her will."

Waving the wooden spoon around in the air Sybil asked, "Have you guys had dinner yet? I have potatoes boiling and we have pork chops in the oven. We have enough if you're hungry." Smiling at Cruz she added, "Mom would love to see photos of your family."

Cruz shook his head, "Women! How're we men supposed to survive when we are up against you women? So, you don't know where Donna is?"

Sophia frowned, "Haven't a clue. No idea. She didn't want to stay with her dad and she didn't want to be with us. She just took off with her backpack."

Sheriff Cruz squinted his eyes at Sophia, "This won't work for the boss man, you know this, right?"

Frowning, Sophia looked up at him as he stood behind the chair she had pulled out for him, "What does that mean?"

"I have to call this into the office. Now, she'll be considered a run away and this means we call out all the troops to find her. There is no way we're going to leave a twelve year old girl to wander around in the dark on a cold October night with the possibility of being raped or worse!" He gasped for breath as he pulled his cellphone from the case at his waist.

Sybil put her spoon in the air, "Maybe we should look for a clue in her bedroom? You might find something under her pillow or in her backpack on the bed? Did you search her old backpack?" Water dripped from the spoon onto the floor as she motioned to the back bedroom.

The sheriff nodded to Sophia, "Would you allow me to search her backpack? You must be present if I search her room for a clue. I cannot search anything without your approval, that's the law."

Quickly, standing Sophia nodded at him, "Yes, please, let's go into Donna's room. Come on, let's look!"

As the sheriff moved around the table to walk in front of Sophia, she gave Sybil a shrug and shook her head at her. Sybil smiled and put down the spoon, "Go, Mom, go and help the man. I have a fast phone call to make. Leave me your cellphone!" Helen Tafoya stood with a quizzical expression. Then she asked, "May I use your bathroom?"

Sophia tossed her cellphone to Sybil, "The bathroom is this way. Its old, but it's clean." Then she hurried into Donna's room. Sheriff Cruz stood in the center of the room. He turned in a full circle and then asked Sophia, "What in this room appears to be out of place?"

Shaking her head, Sophia smiled, "How should I know? This is the room of a- soon- to- be teenager! Although, Donna is very neat. She likes everything in its place." She pointed to the bed, "Sybil mentioned her pillow. Let's look under there first." The pillow was picked up from the head of the bed. Sophia dumped the pillowcase free of the pillow. There was nothing there. Then she moved to the closet and opened the door wide. Sheriff Cruz stood behind her. She could feel his breath on her neck. Sliding the clothes from one side to the other she did notice a jacket that was new. She pulled the jacket out and laid it on the bed, "This is new. I've never seen this before." Sticking her fingers into each of the front pockets all she found was a price tag. "This jacket was very expensive, probably something her dad bought her and she didn't want to wear it." Then Sophia knelt down to check the base of the closet, but it was very dark. Her body cast a shadow on the closet floor. Turning to him, she asked, "Do you have a flashlight on your belt? I'm having a hard time seeing down here and my knees crack."

Touching her shoulder, he whispered, "Move, I'll look." He pulled a long flashlight from his leather belt. It was black metal and long. "This would make a good weapon."

Sybil appeared in the doorway still holding the dripping spoon, "Mom, its Grandma. She's upset and needs to speak to you on the cellphone. Do you want to take it or should I ask her to call back another time?" Sybil wiggled her eyebrows. Sophia stepped over Sheriff Cruz's feet as he knelt in front of the closet. Taking the phone from her daughter's hand, she said, "I better take this. My poor mother is stuck in the hospital." As she passed the bathroom she heard the toilet flush.

Holding the cellphone to her ear Sophia stared at her daughter. Sybil smiled and returned to the kitchen. Clearing her throat, Sophia said, "Margaret, what's going on? Are they treating you all right?"

Margaret screamed into the phone, "Sophia! Where's your brother! He's supposed to be here. He promised me that he would come and bring dinner! He said he would be here at five and it is going on six thirty! Sophia…" Margaret burst into tears.

"Margaret, Mom, please don't get upset. Please, calm down. Please, you know Granger. He keeps saying things and then he forgets or he doesn't do them. Maybe he's stuck in traffic or he's trying to cook you something special."

"NO! When I cooked meatloaf he told me he doesn't eat meat

anymore since he had the cancer. When I fixed a big old salad for lunch and he woke up late, he told me he doesn't have salad for breakfast. Sophia, everything I do is wrong! Now here I am in the hospital and he said he would bring dinner! I believed him! I really believed him!" Her voice softened, "Sophia, where is he?" Her voice gave out and she started crying again. "Sophia, where is my perfect boy? Did you tell him not to come because of my horse?"

Sophia was walking down the hall to the front door. Trying to figure out a way to have her mother realize her perfect son was not perfect. All of a sudden Shonac started growling and barking at her feet. Opening the front door, Sophia peered out. Shonac pushed the door open with his nose. He raced down the front path growling and barking. His aim was straight for the barn. Sybil screamed out, "There's someone in the barn!"

Sheriff Cruz shoved past Sophia as he chased out the door after Sybil who was going after Shonac. Sophia held the cellphone down to stare at the barn. Lights quickly illuminated the whole of the barnyard. There was a man leading Tracy into the center of the barn. Sybil was yelling something. Shonac was dancing around and the sheriff had his hand on his pistol. Sophia could hear her mother's voice droning on in her hand. The cellphone was returned to her ear, "Margaret, I have to go. Someone is in the barn. The sheriff is here with his gun. Bye!" She folded the cellphone and shoved it into her jean pocket.

Lights blinded her as she entered the barn. The horses were stamping their feet and shaking their heads. Tracy was tied to the center white pole in front of her stall. Don Juan Calderon had his hands up in the air in front of Sheriff Cruz who still had his hand on the butt of his pistol. Sybil was stroking Tracy's mane and speaking softly to her. Sophia walked to the men. Don Juan Calderon dropped his hand and put it out to Sophia, "How do you do? I am Juan Calderon and I'm your neighbor. I live right here, next door. I'm sorry I didn't get your name."

Sophia tilted her head to glance at Sybil who smiled at her mother. Shaking his hand, Sophia said, "Yes, how do you do? I'm Dr. Sophia Pino and I don't believe we have met before. How is it that you have my daughter's horse with you?"

Juan smiled at Officer Cruz, "Do I have to put my hands up again or can I put my hands down? I would like to inform Dr. Pino of her horse and what has happened regarding her daughter. Would this be all right?"

Officer Cruz shook his head as he stepped to the side. His hand remained on the butt of his holstered gun. "Please, I would like to hear this as well."

Sybil ducked under Tracy's neck to unlace the cinch. She peered over the saddle seat as she listened. Juan put his hand on the horse's neck and rubbed it as he spoke, "I came home late. I drive an eighteen wheeler. I had a run to Denver. Just got home and there was your horse standing in front of my door. The reins were dropped into the handle of the screen door. I knew this was your horse because on weekends I see your daughter ride this horse with my nephew Griego."

Sybil handed Juan the loose cinch under Tracy's belly. He took it to hook around the saddle horn. He continued, "I didn't know what was going on or why the horse was tied to my screen door. I had to scoot around the horse. This one tried to go through all of my pockets." His fingers went through Tracy's long mane, "In my kitchen I called Griego. He told me to look in the saddle packs that were hanging from the straps on the back of the stock saddle. I'm not one to go through other folks' stuff, so I thought I would bring the horse over here and let you guys figure out why this horse was trying to get into my house." Giving Tracy a good pat on her flank, he said, "So, here she is."

Lifting the saddle packs from the ties on the back of the saddle, Sybil handed the packs to her mother who then handed them to Officer Cruz. Sybil shrugged at them, "Don't look at me. I don't know what's going on. I'll put the horse in the stall."

Juan Calderon lifted the freed saddle from the horse's back, "Where does this go? I can put it away for you. Do you want me to take off the bridle?"

Sophia removed the saddle blanket, hugging it to her side, "Here, let me get the key." Once the key was in her hand, Juan followed her to the outbuilding. Turning to him, Sophia informed, "There is no light in here, but if you would put the saddle there on that wooden horse by the door that would be a help."

Officer Cruz trailed behind them. The heavy black flashlight lit up the whole room. The dirt floor showed all the prints of the ages and the straw in the adobe wall glowed golden. Sophia patted the place for the saddle as she placed the saddle blanket on top of it. Then taking the bridle from Juan's hand she hung it on the nail above the saddle. "There, you see, everything in its place. That's how Donna keeps things." Pushing the men forward and out the door she questioned, "Don't you think we should go into the house and see what's in her saddle pack?"

In the kitchen, Sophia noticed that Sybil had had the foresight to turn off the stove and the oven. The dishes and silverware were shoved to the side. Helen Tafoya sat at the kitchen table with a cat in her lap. "This kitty wants to come home with me. Yes, she does. Doesn't she?"

Sniffing, Sybil lifted Fergus cat from the woman's lap. "No, he doesn't. He wants to stay here and gorge on gutted mice. Bloody intestines are his favorite." Juan trailed them into the house. He cautiously stood in the doorway. Helen Tafoya smiled when she saw him, "Well, aren't you a tall drink of water? Come and sit by me, young man." She patted the chair next to her. As they sat on the chairs around the kitchen table, Sophia reached into each of the saddle packs and removed the contents. In the first pack there were pieces of candy and papers with some strange doodles. The second pack had a white envelope and it was addressed 'To Whom It May Concern.' Before Sophia could open it, Officer Cruz plucked it from Sophia's hand. The school paper had writing done in pencil. He quietly read the words.

Then he stood taking the paper with him. He made a call outside with his cellphone. Juan stared at Sophia who was staring back at him, "What was that all about? Did you get to read any of it while he had it in his hand?"

Juan shook his head, "No, he held it close to his body. All I could see was the pencil writing, no words."

Frustrated, Sophia walked to the kitchen windows. The clothes pins were still in place holding up the unicorn blanket. She could see Officer Cruz leaning against his vehicle. He was speaking into the cellphone. There was a white government car parked behind his vehicle. Shonac was sniffing around the white car. Slowly the dog lifted his leg to relieve himself on the back tire. Sybil was now outside. She ran over to the dog to kneel and pet him. Then they came in from the front door. Running into the kitchen Sybil grabbed the wooden spoon on the stove and stirred the potatoes. She pulled a match from the box on the shelf over the stove and struck it to ignite the stove under the potatoes. Then she knelt to light the oven. "Hey, I don't like greasy pork chops and the potatoes will get soggy."

Startled by Sybil's sudden appearance Helen Tafoya walked out of the farmhouse. Sophia watched her maneuver her vehicle to drive away down Alcon Road. Whispering to the window, Sophia said, "She's gone. Thank goodness, she's gone."

Stretching out his long legs under the kitchen table, Juan Calderon asked, "So, what's all this hysteria? Why is the Officer here and what's going on with the horse tied to my screen door and all the secrecy?"

Remaining at the sink to watch Officer Cruz, Sophia spoke to him over her shoulder, "Donna took off. I don't know where she went and the Officer came to get her. Donna is supposed to be with her father, my ex. Sybil knows what's going on but she won't talk to me."

Lifting his hands over his head, Juan yawned, "Pardon me, but I am totally lost here. Sybil knows where her sister is. You don't. The happy triggered Officer out there, he doesn't know either. Somehow Donna is supposed to be at her Dad's. Is she at her Dad's?" Rubbing the back of his neck, he queried further, "Who was the woman in red? I bet Donna's at her Dad's. She wouldn't put you in jeopardy, Sophia."

Sybil burst out laughing, "Damn, you just walked in and figured it all out just like that!" The spoon was slapped against her leg, "Mom, we need to keep this guy around!"

Whirling to face Sybil, Sophia grabbed the wooden spoon, "What do you mean? Why would Donna go to her father's? She doesn't want to be at her father's?"

Pointing at Juan, Sybil said, "Yes, Juan, why would someone go somewhere they should be and don't want to be?"

At this he gave her a quizzical stare. Then in his deep voice, he answered, "Because they want someone to find them there, but they don't want to be there on purpose." Rubbing his arm, he added, "Maybe Donna wants someone to find her there. Someone who hasn't been inside the house before for some reason."

Sophia gasped, "Oh, no!" She ran outside to Officer Cruz, "What did the letter say? Ignacio, please, please, tell me what the letter said, please?" He put his finger up to stop her from speaking. He was listening. Then he grunted and said, "Yes, I understand. All right, I'll stay here. But I can tell you she doesn't have any idea where her brother is." Quiet and then, "No, Margaret Pino is safe. She's in the hospital. Yes, Sophia Pino was just speaking to her. Right, right." Then he was quiet for a moment, "Yes, I have the address. Yes, I wrote it down in my notebook. Yes, sir." His cellphone off, he sighed.

Taking his free arm, Sophia asked, "Please, Officer Cruz tell me what was in the letter."

"Sophia, we need to go inside. I have some information for you and I need you to remain calm and listen. Please, let's go inside. The weather is getting cold and the horses are safe. Your daughter will be found directly. Please, let's go inside."

Taking a deep breath Sophia led the way back into the house and the kitchen. Juan was smashing the boiled potatoes with the flat of a spoon while Sybil was adding butter and milk. The smell of the pork chops filled the whole of the house. On the counter was a head of lettuce, four tomatoes and a jar of olives. A square of cheese was sliced on the cutting board. When Sybil saw her mother's stern face, she smiled, "Mom, Juan is staying for dinner!"

In a deep tone Sophia said, "How nice for him." She plopped down on a kitchen chair. Cruz smiled at Sybil, "We need to have a talk. Do you want Juan Calderon to participate or would you like this to be a private conversation? In my opinion it would be wise for him to remain. Dr. Pino, I'll need you to accompany me to your ex-husband's house. Also, I'll need you to be a witness at the hospital. Your mother will also receive a visit."

Juan lifted the pot of mashed potatoes and put it to the side of the stovetop. Sybil turned down the pork chops and they both sat at the table. Cruz took off his Officer's hat to place it beside him. "There has been another attempted murder. This took place in Calavera not far from your mother's farm. There are suspicious circumstances and there is a bulletin out for Granger."

Sybil and Sophia both gasped at the same time, "Who?" He shook his head, "At this time I am unable to release this information. I can tell you that the victim is not a member of your family." Then he took a small notepad from his brown shirt pocket, "What's Donna's last name? Is it Donna Pino or Vinder, which is it?"

Clearing her throat, Sophia said, "Donna Vinder for she is Geoffrey's daughter."

"All right, there are officers at Geoffrey Vinder's house. I can't keep calling him your ex that's getting tiresome. They did enter the house." The notepad was returned to his shirt pocket. "They did find Donna in her bedroom, in her nightgown and in her bed with her cat. At this time she is being processed by the Children Youth and Family Services Social Worker. The conditions within that house are not safe for your daughter." Shaking his head his voice took a somber tone, "As a matter of fact, the Social Worker said the house is way below acceptable health standards for a child. No one should be living in that house. The animals will be removed. Animal Control is there and Monday they will be examined by a vet. Afterwards they will be taken to a shelter. If the vet feels they are safe to be adopted they can be brought here."

Grimacing, Sophia stared at Sybil. Shaking her head Sybil said, "What? I didn't do anything?"

Officer Cruz continued, "Your daughter has requested to spend the night here with you. In the morning the Social Worker will come and inspect this house, her room and speak to you both. If she finds the house to be acceptable and if Donna wants to remain here then she will get a court order for Donna to remain with her mother and sister." He pointed to the back bedroom, "From what I saw her room is more than adequate. It's clean. It has a nice bathroom and she will be loved and cared for here."

Before Sophia could answer him, he stood and pushed in the chair, "Now, we need to go to your – no, now we need to go to Geoffrey Vinder's house and speak with the CYFD person. She will drive Donna here once Donna has packed what she needs. Then you and I will go to the hospital. You can either follow me or we can both go in the same vehicle. I will return you home after our visit at the hospital. Which would you prefer?"

Staring at the others around the table, Sophia finally answered, "Why don't I just go with you? It saves gas."

Juan's deep voice resonated in the quiet kitchen, "Why don't I stay here with Sybil and make sure she's safe. Do you guys want to eat first or would that take too much time?"

Cruz shook his head, "We need to go now. We can stop and get some fast food on the way to the hospital. I'll even buy. Sophia, I'm sorry for all of this."

Sybil stayed sitting, "We can eat when Donna gets here. I'm sure she hasn't eaten. At least not in Dad's house. Yuck!" She made a barfing noise.

Grabbing Sybil's sleeve, Sophia asked the men, "Could you give me a minute with my oldest daughter, please?" She pulled her into her bedroom and shut the door, "What is going on, Sybil? Why did you two cook up this cockeyed scheme? You do know that Geoffrey could end up in serious trouble!"

Sitting on the bed, Sybil shifted sideways to face her mother, "Mom, look, Dad was going to die in that filth. We love him and we don't want him to die. He wasn't going to clean it up or do anything about that shithole. We felt that if we did this, the police would go into his house. They'd see how disgusting it is and they would save his life. What's so terrible about that?"

Standing right in front of her, Sophia spoke sternly, "Its Geoffrey's choice as to how he wants to live. That is his choice. Now we have everyone involved in this mess. Yes, Donna may be able to live with us, but she needs to know her dad. Sybil, you stuck your nose into someone else's life and you took their power away from them, do you understand?"

Rubbing the cat that was in her lap, she pouted, "No, I thought this would be a win for everybody."

There was a soft knock on the door, Cruz called out, "Sophia, we need to get going."

Bending over, Sophia kissed Sybil on the top of her head, "We will discuss this better tomorrow. Right now everything is crazy nuts. Please, don't let Juan stay all night if I'm late. You are fifteen and you are legally old enough to be left on your own. We have had this discussion."

Dumping the cat gently on the bed, Sybil followed her mother to the door, "Yes, Mom. Yes, we have had this discussion before."

7

Officer Cruz sat in the driver's seat as he emptied the passenger seat of legal books, old wrappers and notebooks into the backseat. There was a laptop computer on a metal arm that he pushed to the side and under the dashboard. Sophia hugged her heavy coat to her chest as she sat in the front passenger's seat. The radio in the console was squawking. Cruz reached over and turned down the sound. "Ignacio, I can't leave my daughter alone in the house with a stranger. I think she either comes with us or I should stay here."

He turned to face her as he started the engine, "Don't worry. Juan won't try anything. He's family."

"What? You know him? You knew him? What was all that about in the barn?"

"Hey, I didn't know he was in your barn. I didn't know he had your horse? For all I knew he was a stranger trying to steal your horse. It wasn't until Sybil turned on the lights and I saw him that I knew who he was."

"But that…that charade afterwards, what was that all about?"

Ignacio shook his head, "That was no charade. I wanted to know where your daughter was and he appeared to know something he wasn't telling us. Family is only covered in so many ways. Kidnapping isn't considered acceptable, not by a family member anyway." He pulled out onto Alcon Road.

"All right, you two are related. How are you related?" Sophia watched Ignacio drive.

He put on his dim lights as a truck drove toward them, "Easy. Juan is my brother-in-law. His sister Reina is my wife's sister, too. Their mother had eight children and she lived to be ninety four. Grandma Calderon was at my wedding eight years ago. She only passed away about eleven months ago. Juan is the youngest and Reina is third from the oldest." He checked his rearview mirror. "Lucia Calderon is my wife. She's Lucia Calderon Cruz or LCC, hah." He chuckled at his own joke.

Sophia looked at the lights in the houses they passed, "How did Reina's husband die? If I may ask?"

Ignacio was now driving down the frontage road, "He was a trucker like Juan. One night as he was driving back from Denver he picked up a hitchhiker. The hitchhiker was an escaped prisoner with a gun. We found the truck and Reina's husband who died soon after we got him to the hospital. Later, the prisoner was picked up in Wyoming. Juan was just in high school. His goal was to become a pastry chef. Instead he took up his Uncle's trucking business once he graduated. Reina was in debt trying to pay off the truck. Juan basically saved her."

A silhouette of the Sandia Mountains filled the horizon in the night sky. Instead of turning onto the interstate, Cruz drove over it and onto a gravel road. There was a tall sign reading "Santa Rita Gravel Pit' written in red paint. Cruz drove under the sign and onto the industrial road. Rocks and stones were kicked up by the tires as he made a quick turn over a cattle guard. Off to the side of the road were four Hereford steer with their heads down chewing their cuds. Their large eyes reflected in the car lights. They didn't even blink. Sophia watched the steer disappear into the night. "How long has Juan been driving trucks?"

"Since he graduated high school He passed the license test in flying colors. So, now, I guess he's been driving for about nine years. He's twenty seven, I think."

Dust covered the front windshield as the wipers were turned on to smear the dirt across the glass. The vehicle did a fast dip and went over another cattle guard to leap onto pavement. Now they were on the main road to Rocoso proper. Sophia stared straight ahead as the car climbed the hill. "You do trust him with Sybil, then?"

"Yes. Also, his godfather is A.J. Salazar. He would be in a world of hurt if he did anything, anything at all untoward in regards to your daughters." As they came up the hill to turn onto the small road leading to Geoffrey's house they saw a large array of bright lights. The front of Geoffrey's house was lit up with different police vehicle's spotlights and an ambulance. Cruz parked on the side of the narrow side road at the top of the driveway, "Wait here, I'll be right back." His long legs took him down the sloping driveway into the open doorway of Geoffrey's home.

The driveway in front of the house was filled with all different kinds of official vehicles. Four major spotlights focused on the front of the house. People in different uniforms were milling around the front yard. Some leaned against the side of the vehicles talking. Others were walking up the hill speaking into cellphones. Sophia noticed the neighbors across the deep arroyo were sitting on chairs watching the event. Suddenly, there was a flashing of red and blue lights. Two of the inner vehicles were trying to back out and were blocked by late arriving official cars. There was laughter as a woman in a black uniform ran out to jump into her State

Police vehicle. Blue and silver reflective tape glistened as she reversed to park on the road. Two Deputy Sheriffs left the scene. One by one spotlights were turned off as voices and confusion appeared to dissipate. The crunch of feet on the gravel became louder. Clouds of dust appeared in front of the headlights from some of the cars as they emptied the front driveway disappearing into the night.

Sophia watched the front of the house. A gurney with a person on it was rolled out of the house. An I.V. sack swung back and forth as an EMT in a white coat lifted a metal rod and walked beside it. Two of the official cruisers back tires shot stones and dust into the air as they reversed freeing up a path for the ambulance. A woman and a man were holding a measuring tape alongside the outer walls of the house. Another woman held Freddy, Geoffrey's dog under her arm as she petted him. When the woman turned, Sophia noticed the dried diarrhea stuck under the poor dog's tail. A large man both in height and girth carried three cat carriers from the house, putting them in the back of his police van. The red and white writing stated it was the Animal Control official vehicle.

Watching and waiting, Sophia noticed Sheriff A.J. Salazar walking beside Cruz as they came up the hill to her. A.J. leaned forward and opened the passenger door. "Hey, Sophia, looks like the Vinders have come back with just as much excitement as seven years ago. That's Geoffrey in the gurney. He collapsed when the Social Worker was speaking with him. He has dangerously high blood pressure and his diabetes is all out of whack. The EMT's were called and they're amazed that he's still breathing." Jerking his thumb toward the ambulance, he said, "They're going to take him to the emergency room in Albuquerque. The big hospital. The one with the University of New Mexico. Evidently, Geoffrey has a doc there."

Sophia pushed the door further open and stepped out, "A.J. what is happening with my daughter? Please, tell me she's safe."

He leaned back with his butt against the front of the vehicle to cross his ankles, "She's fine. She's packing some of her things right now. Did you know how bad that house is? Have you been inside there lately?" His hands were shoved into his pant pockets.

"Mom! Mom!" Donna raced up the incline, "Mom, Mom, Dad almost died! He's really sick and he wasn't taking his medicine or insulin or anything! I told you! I told you! You should see the inside of this house! Mom, it's filthy and disgusting!" She threw herself at her mother knocking the air out of her. Sophia hugged Donna as she gasped for breath, "Oh, Sweetheart, I'm so sorry. Now, the medical people can work with Dad and help him, right?"

Sheriff Cruz put his hand on Donna's shoulder, "Young lady, you need to stay with Miss Garcia. She'll take you to your mother's farmhouse. Sybil has dinner ready for you."

A plump woman came puffing up to them, her hand was outstretched to Sophia, "Hi, I'm Bobby Garcia from the Pueblo. I'll be your daughter's social worker. Don't go into that house." Shaking her head, her long bangs fell over her eyes. She shoved her waist long hair behind her shoulder.

In a discerning frown she added, "I'm so sorry I did. Go in there, I mean. You talk about a garbage pit. I probably contracted some terrible infection from all the bacteria floating around in there. Did you know the cats were peeing all over the carpet? That poor dog is sick and pooped all over the floors? The house has bugs the size of my mule! There is more nasty food in the sink than there is sitting on the stove."

Shivering with her disgust, she continued on, "Oh, the refrigerator is dripping with liquid green mold. This one was eating food out of a can!" She put her hand on Donna's shoulder, "And a child was expected to eat in there!" Shaking her head as she put her arm around Donna, she added, "I bet you could sell the mold from that fridge in Santa Fe and make some money as some kind of healing herb or something." She took a deep breath and was going to speak again, but Cruz interrupted her.

His hand on her arm, he said, "Miss Garcia, are you going to drive Donna to her mother's farm in Alcon tonight?"

Studying his face, she answered, "Yes, if that's all right? I mean she shouldn't be left here, should she? First of all she is too young to be on her own and secondly the place is filled with disgusting stuff! You know we're going to have to call Adult Protective Services and have them tag the house as unsafe? In all the years of being a social worker I have never seen a house as decrepit and revolting…."

Sophia smiled to interject, "Please, yes, do take Donna to my farm. Do you know where it is or I guess Donna can show you?"

Bobby Garcia didn't miss a beat, "If it's all right? I will check her room at your farm and I will need to check the kitchen and the bathrooms. We don't want her going from bad to worse now do we?"

Twirling around, Donna took the woman's hand to lead her back down the driveway to her car, saying, "Oh, wait until you see my room! Oh, and the kitchen is clean. My sister has fixed us dinner. If I know her it will be good. Let's go, I'm starving!"

The two walked down the hill to get into a government vehicle. Several cars were blocking it from backing out. There was not a cloud in the sky. Bright sparkling stars of yellow gold twinkled over the crowd here at Rocoso. Sagebrush and rabbit bush were trampled underfoot as people with cameras walked around the wall outside of the house. Geoffrey's trees, roses and bushes were intertwined one into the other. There was no sense to his gardening skills. A forest of chaos struggled to survive outside of the hoarding house. Someone groaned from the back lawn. Then a voice loudly called out to watch for dog's deposits on the grass. Cameras took photos of overturned buckets, piles of cracked tiles and black garbage bags ripped open. Flashbulbs shone on trailing debris all over the yard.

Watching Sophia's face, A.J. shook his head, "That young one is a chip off the old block. Donna reminds me of you." Then his face became serious, "Did Ignacio tell you about the Peters woman?"

She glanced back at him, "What Peters woman and who is the Peters woman?"

A.J. turned to lean forward with his hands flat on the hood of the vehicle, "She's one of the women Roberto works for near your mother's farm. She was found unconscious in her horses' barn this afternoon. I'm not sure if the poor woman is still alive. Her husband Dr. Peters came home from his clinic late this afternoon and found her in the stall. The large horses had stepped on her. She was in a bad way by the time I arrived with the EMT's."

Two more vehicles backed out of Geoffrey's driveway. Dust clouds floated up in their headlights. Someone called out and A.J. waved. Then a young man in a brown uniform ran up to him, "Are we supposed to lock this place up or leave it open? Does she have the key?" He jerked his chin at Sophia.

Answering for him, Sophia said loudly, "No, I don't, but my daughter Donna does. She's in that vehicle with Miss Garcia. If you can stop her from leaving, you could get the key from Donna." She pointed to the government vehicle waiting for the other cars to leave. The young man raced to Miss Garcia's passenger door and knocked on the glass.

Officer Ignacio Cruz tapped on the top of his car, "A.J., we best get going. We're going to the hospital to see Mrs. Pino. No one has been able to find Granger Pino as of yet."

A.J. stepped away from the car, "Better let you get on with it then. Sophia, give your mother my best, she's a pistol. Hope she feels better although she is probably safer in the hospital. If she were at home who knows what might have happened to her. Be careful." As he started to walk down the hill, he turned to Sophia, "You know this house brings back all kinds of memories and none of them are good!" He waved over his shoulder as he continued to the front door.

Fresh air filled the vehicle as they drove with the windows down. The lights of Rincon lit up the valley as they descended into the village. "Hey, you want to grab some grub here? We can eat it in the car on the way to your mother's hospital?" Agreeing to fast food from the drive through, they ate quietly in the car. The smell of French fries and onions filled the cab. Sophia tried to roll down the window.

Cruz laughed, "I have to do it. Don't want you escaping do we?" Pushing a button, the window went down allowing clean air to wash away the food odors.

The tall gray building was lit with spotlights hidden in the bush framing the hospital. Automatic doors opened for them as they marched side by side to the information desk. Sophia was already to go to the elevators and find her mother, but Cruz had taken her elbow and led her to the front desk. "Where is the morgue or autopsy place, Ma'am?"

The elderly woman in a pink frock turned to punch keys into a keyboard. She read the monitor to explain, "The autopsy room is in the basement. If you get into the elevators push the S-One button. If you want to visit the morgue you need to call ahead and make an appointment." The number was written on a yellow sticky paste-it. Cruz tucked it into his shirt pocket. Then the woman leaned forward, "Sir, I know you are a police officer, but there are no guns allowed in this building. Sorry, you will have to leave it with me or in your car." Thin fingers pushed back her pink white hair from her face.

Cruz clicked his tongue, "Sophia, you wait here. I'll run out to the car. Stay here, don't go anywhere until I get back." His voice was firm with authority.

Sophia moved to the corner of the front lounge and sat on a stiff chair. The upholstered chairs appeared stained and tired. She watched him run out to the parking lot, sit and speak on his cellphone. Then he came striding through the automatic doors, "All right, let's go and find out what we can." His gun was missing from its holster.

The elevator moved slowly to the lower basement. Doors opened to a faded green linoleum floor. Empty gurneys lined the walls. There were two heavy white doors. Each shut. The first one was pushed open to reveal a startled young woman in a white coat with blood splatters on the front. "Hello? Can I help you?"

Cruz nodded, "Yes, we're looking for the M.E. who did the autopsy on Mrs. Peters, is he around?"

Her lips curled into a forced smile, "Yes, I am Dr. Silva. I did the autopsy, I was just entering my findings. Who are you and do you have an official status?" She was staring at Sophia more than Cruz.

Cruz whipped out his official I.D. and handed it to her. She read it thoroughly, "We don't usually get live people down here this time of evening. So, what can I do for you?"

A notebook was pulled from his jacket pocket. "We need to know the cause of death to Mary Peters, aged forty three who was brought in here this afternoon about four o'clock."

Dr. Silva pulled off the paper hat that covered her short hair. Her only makeup was dark eyeliner. The surgical gloves were snapped off her hands as she tapped on the keyboard in front of her. The blue light from the monitor illuminated her face and her brown eyes. "Ah, yes, Mrs. Peters. Not good, not good at all." Nodding at Sophia, she asked, "Is she allowed to hear this?"

Ignacio pushed Sophia behind him to answer, "Yes, please continue." Dr. Silva eyed Sophia as she read from the monitor on the laptop, "Mrs. Peters has Clydesdale horses who trampled her post mortem. Her body was a mass of broken bones. Pre-mortem it appears she had physical injuries when she was placed in the barnyard. There are questions regarding a wound to her chest. My boss will be giving the final assessment in the morning. Will one of your deputies be here to observe?"

Staring at the notebook in his hand, Cruz nodded, "A.J. Salazar is our boss. He's out of Rocoso office. He'll be here at nine to view the procedure. Is this the correct time for tomorrow's autopsy?"

A button was punched and the monitor went dark, "Yes. Although we have questions about poisoning. She may have been poisoned as well. There were obvious signs of poisons in her system given over time. Her teeth were discolored and her tongue was swollen. We had another case like that in here just a few days ago, another female, I believe."

Putting his hand out in a gentle motion to Dr. Silva, he thanked her. Sophia said nothing. They entered the elevator as Cruz asked, "What room is your mother in?"

Not answering, Sophia pushed the button for the second floor. Margaret was curled in a fetal position when they entered the room. Cruz flicked on the overhead lights blinding Margaret as she turned to sit upright. "What? Who's there? Granger is that you?" Her hand went over her eyes to peer out at them, "Oh, Sophia, it's only you! Who's that with you?"

Standing beside the bed, the white sheets appeared to glow in the bright light. "Mom, this is Ignacio Cruz. He's a deputy sheriff from Rocoso." Standing aside, she let Cruz nod to Margaret. "Hello, Ma'am. We're here to affirm that you are safe and in good health."

Margaret flinched at his words, "What a strange thing to say to someone who is in the hospital. Do you believe I am in danger here?"

Pulling the white plastic chair to her mother's bedside, Sophia sat down, "Mom or Margaret, you do know, Mom, that I am getting very tired of calling you Margaret when you are indeed my Mom?"

Her hand was slapped by her mother, "Go on and don't say Mom again!"

"All right, do you know a Mrs. Peters? A Mrs. Mary Peters?"

Nostrils flared at the name, "Of course I know her. She tried to take Roberto away from me! She's a selfish witch. Yes, I know her. She has two large Clydesdales and calls herself a horsewoman, but she's never sat on a horse in her life! She's a phony and a cheat! Of course I know the woman, why?"

Standing behind Sophia's chair, Cruz answered, "She's dead. She was killed and found in her barn trampled by her horses." His voice was soft barely audible.

"Good for the horses! I told Granger about her and how she tried to get Roberto to work for her full time! She would take Roberto away from me and from Charlotte! I'm not sorry she's dead. I'm glad she's not around anymore!" Margaret patted the sheet in front of her.

"Margaret," Sophia announced her mother's name clearly, "What do you know about her husband?"

Cruz nodded at Sophia as if this was going to be his next question. Margaret pushed herself to sit straighter in the bed. "He's a flirt and a cheat. He's a dentist at the homeless clinic on Second Street. There are times when he doesn't come home at night. Evidently he examines pretty woman's teeth all night long! His name is Alex. You can't miss him. Vanity drips over him what with his gray beard, moustache and curling eyebrows. I think he's Hungarian or Romanian or from over there somewhere." She wiggled her fingers toward the door, "Why?"

This time Cruz answered again, "He arrived home after being gone for over twenty four hours to find his wife in the barn. What do you know of their marriage, if I may ask?"

Gnarly arthritic fingers pushed her shoulder length hair behind her ears, she pouted, "Why? Why is that important?"

Clearing his throat, his voice remained soft, "It helps us to get a picture of her life. Since we believe she may have died from suspicious circumstances we need to know what kind of person she was and how she related to her husband."

Smirking, Margaret squinted at him, "Like on the television, you mean? Usually the first suspects are the family? Right?"

Cruz nodded. Margaret's voice took on an air of importance, "Well, I'm not sure they get along well. I mean he chases anything and everything in a skirt that has his attention. He isn't home often as I said. He drives a big black BMW. I'm sure Granger would love to have that car!" She coughed.

Sophia poured water into a pink plastic cup on the bedside table and handed it to her mother who continued, "Mary wanted to belong to the Historic Association, but they haven't lived here long enough for her to be allowed." Taking a drink of water, Margaret gave a gentle cough, "Excuse me. Mary had her hair done at a different salon than I did, but if I were you I would ask there about her. She loved to talk about her horses and her past life in New York City or San Francisco or somewhere." She handed the cup back to Sophia, "You know who would be a good person to ask would be the horse shoe fella, what's his name, Sophia?"

Impatiently Margaret shook her head, "Oh, you wouldn't know. Roberto would know." Turning her head to the side, Margaret spoke to Cruz directly, "You know my daughter doesn't like horses!" Poking at Sophia, Margaret went on about Mary Peters. "She liked to dye yarn. I'm a professional. My husband Dr. Pino and I dyed all kinds of wool, silk and cotton. We grew our own plants to use for dyes. Sophia was never interested in anything we did. She had her books and her own studies."

A nurse came into the room with a small tray. Bustling around the room to turn on the light over the bed, she flipped off the overhead light in the middle of the ceiling. Quick hands plumped up Margaret's pillow. The pink water cup was given to Margaret along with two tiny white papers with a pill in each one. "Mrs. Pino, it's time for your pills. I need to watch you swallow them." The nurse stood on one foot as she leaned against the bed. "Are these friends of yours? Visiting hours are over in five minutes."

The pills were swallowed. Margaret gloated to the nurse, "These people are asking me about the murder of my neighbor, Mrs. Mary Peters."

The nurse took the papers from Margaret's hand, "Funny that, she was my patient here just about three weeks ago. Strange she's passed. I thought she was pretty perky when she left." Then the nurse put the papers in her front scrub pocket, "Oh, you say she was murdered? Not surprised, not surprised at all." The woman pulled open the door and walked into the hall. Cruz nodded to Sophia, "I'm going to ask her some questions. Don't leave this room until I return." His voice was stern.

Leaning her head on her hand, Sophia said, "Mom, you do know that you just gave the Officer a good reason for Granger to kill Mary Peters?"

Heaving a huge sigh, Margaret glared at Sophia, "My name is Margaret! How difficult is this to remember? I did no such thing! Granger is innocent and you know it!"

"Did you flirt with Alex Peters?"

"Of course not! He's way too old for me! He's in his late seventies!"

"Margaret, you do know how old you are right? You're in your late seventies."

"Yes, but now that I'm older, I like younger men, darling girl. Women outlive men and so it's wise to marry younger men then you don't have to worry about outliving them!"

Teasing her mother, Sophia smiled, "So, he's handsome and sexy and didn't take to you?"

Sniffing, Margaret rubbed her hands together, "Yes, he's good looking. I'll give you that, daughter, but who knows where his dipstick has been!"

"His dipstick?"

"Well, he's old and he's been through many a relationship, right? He may have all kinds of diseases. Mary said he took herbs to get his dip up and he took herbs to get it down."

"Really? And where did he obtain these herbs, Margaret dearest?"

Shaking her head, Margaret gave a giggle, "Can you imagine if he had it stuck for over four hours? Isn't that what they announce on the television? Oh," and she gasped, "He's a dentist and sits on a stool all day long. What if his flag is at attention all day long?"

"Mom! Seriously?" Sophia put her hand on her mother's boney fingers, "I would think it would be exceptionally painful for the guy."

Tilting her head she studied her daughter through her eyelashes. Margaret's voice became bitter, "Would serve him right, though. He was servicing women's teeth and then he continued to service them. Poor Mary how could she stay married to him?"

Sophia frowned, "Margaret, you were married to a man who played around. Papa was a doctor with the famous phrase 'I diagnose the wives and send the husbands the bill.' Remember?"

Slapping Sophia's hand, Margaret's face hardened, "That was different, Sophia. Your father needed to be admired. He lived for the love of his patients." Her voice softened, "His popularity was important to his survival. I think it had to do with his father." She sniffed, "Your father always came home to me."

Ignacio Cruz slipped into the room, "How's it going in here?" He stood at the foot of the hospital bed.

Margaret's eyes had a twinkle, "Say, you're a man. Let me ask you a question?"

Sophia squeezed her mother's hand as a warning. Cruz appeared interested in Margaret's inquisition. "Certainly, ask away."

"Does it hurt for a man to have an, oh, you know? You know an erection for over four hours? Or when he sits down or when he tries to zip up his pants?" It was obvious she was trying not to giggle.

Cruz shook his head, "What does this have to do with anything?" His cheeks turned a soft pink.

Sophia interjected, "Margaret was telling me that Alex Peters took herbs to get it up and herbs to get it down. Mother was worried that if the herbs didn't work the man would be in pain. Especially since he's a dentist and sits on a stool all day long."

He put his hands on the side rail of the hospital bed, "Yes, it hurts. The pain would be unbelievable. I doubt seriously the man would be able to function as a dentist if he was in such a physical situation."

Almost shouting, Margaret said, "GOOD! He's a rat to fool around on his lovely wife. I bet while the poor woman was lying in the stall covered with horse manure, being trampled by giants while he had his dipstick in some woman's you know what!"

This time Ignacio Cruz burst out laughing, "Oh, dear, that may be the case. A.J. is interviewing him now. Sophia, I do believe we need to get you home to your daughters and visiting hours are over."

Pouting at him, Margaret put on her little girl face, "Oh, do you have to go? We're having so much fun!"

Sophia bent over and kissed her mother on the cheek, "I'll see what I can do about Granger. Although, Margaret, he really is a hopeless case."

Their footsteps echoed down the hospital's linoleum floor. Nurses were going from room to room telling visitors they needed to leave. The smell of pine-sol and antiseptic drifted in the air. The charge nurse sat behind the counter on the phone. Long lacquered fingernails waved to them as they passed her.

Cold air hit them as they walked to the official vehicle. A soft breeze rustled the bushes with the spotlights placed in front of them. The cement sidewalk had been swept of the blowing sand and the tarmac of the parking lot appeared to have been cleaned as well. Large tumbleweeds had rolled against the tires of vehicles parked at the outer areas. Twinkling stars glittered overhead. There was no moon and the dark sky was in contrast to Rincon's village lights. The officer's vehicle still smelled of French fries. The radio crackled. Cruz turned up the volume. They both heard A.J.'s voice calling to Cruz.

Ignacio lifted the hand piece, "Cruz here. A.J., what's up? Over."

The return response was filled w ith s tatic, b ut t he v oice and words were audible, "We found Granger. He was at a bar on Central in Albuquerque with a bunch of friends. He's well soused. Going to speak with him in the morning. Let Sophia know. Over."

Cruz responded, "Ten four."

A.J. then added, "Alex Peters is in the station. Need you here as a witness to his remarks. When are you planning on arriving or should we reschedule for early tomorrow? I have the autopsy at nine, how about eight? Over."

Cruz put the handheld piece in his lap, thinking. The he lifted it, "Eight is good. Spoke with nurse at hospital. Mary Peters was brought in three weeks ago in a case of domestic abuse although she denied it saying her horses shove her around in the stalls. She'd been taking herbs. Dr. Alex Peters took herbs. Over."

There was no response. Ignacio Cruz put the handheld piece back in the holder on the console. Sophia turned to him, "If they bought the herbs on Fourth Street? That's Meshach's store. You know the biblical man who believes the cure is all in God's natural elements. Do you think Meshach bought Granger's herbs from the old clinic?"

Wiping the cover on the dashboard clock with his index finger, Cruz said, "Sophia, you know I can't talk about this with you. You're a witness of sorts. Right now we don't know for sure what happened. Everything is in the early stages. We need more information before we start accusing folks."

The drive to the farmhouse was quiet. As he turned to park near the house's front door, Sophia noticed all the lights were on in each room. "Oh, dear, my electric bill is going to sky rocket."

Shaking his head, Cruz mumbled, "My life - years from now."

Sophia patted his shoulder, "It will be awhile yet. Show me the photos?"

The engine was turned off. His cellphone was retrieved from the leather case at his side. He flicked through his apps until he came to the photos. A young woman with long hair wrapped over her right shoulder stared out. In her arms was a bundled baby with a pink ribbon around her head. The baby was sound asleep. The next photo was of a boy about the age of three in a football uniform. Sophia touched the cellphone screen, "What team is he representing here?"

Chuckling to himself, "The Green Bay Packard team. She would kill me if we had any other team at our house."

Sophia smiled at him, "What a beautiful family! You must be very proud! Do you remember when Carol passed away in the hospital? Somehow you felt your life was over and you would never fall in love?"

The cellphone was shut and put back into his leather pouch, "Yes, I was young back then. Now I'm an old man who has fathered children with a perfect wife." He took his cellphone out to hold in his hand, "You know I'm going to call and let my wife know I'm on my way home. Are you going in now?"

Sophia waved as he drove away. She stamped her feet on the front door mat and pushed the door open. Three people were sitting on the sofa watching a DVD. Juan stood abruptly, "Hey, look who is home! How did it go?"

Sybil waved her hand over her head, calling out, "Mom, this is almost over. We're just in the good part. Hi!"

Juan followed Sybil into the kitchen. A cold pork chop and some mashed potatoes sat on a plate. She picked it up, "Oh, this is my dinner?"

"Yeah, well, we didn't know when you might return. Perhaps we should've put it in the fridge for later or tomorrow." Juan leaned against the counter to watch Sophia pull plastic wrap to cover the plate. "A woman called from Mexico. She wanted me to tell you they spoke with Roberto. Everything is going to be settled with the help of a woman called Charlotte."

Sophia kicked off her clogs. "Thank goodness. I had forgotten about the phone call." The hot water kettle was filled and turned on, "I could use a mug of tea. Did the girls tell you of all the excitement?"

A chair was pulled out and he sat down, "Yep, Donna explained everything. She's quite a storyteller. I think she's going to become an actress. I can't help but feel sorry for Geoffrey even though I've never met the man. Donna went on and on at length about the filth in the house. Sounds to me like he was seriously depressed."

Water boiled as the tea bag was placed in the blue mug. Silky cat and Fergus cat padded into the kitchen. Fergus went to his feed bowl. Silky jumped on the table to lie down, purring. Juan stroked her gray fur, "You have the most wonderful cats. Sybil tells me the plump fellow over there loves his fast food in the barn. That's what I need a barn cat."

Hot water in the mug was brought to the table. Sybil sat sideways in the chair, "Juan, thank you for keeping the girls company. I do have a question for you, though."

The deep voice had a lilt to it as he smiled, "Sure, although I bet I already know what you are going to ask. How did the horse end up at my house and how did Donna end up at her father's, right?"

Sipping the hot tea, Sophia nodded. Juan continued to pet Silky. He blew the fur off of his fingers onto the floor, "Easy. Sybil. Sybil saw us together mucking out the barn the other night. She figured we knew one another and I was someone she could trust. I guess while you were taking Donna to her father's she had concocted this elaborate plan."

The tea bag was squeezed. Sophia took it to the sink. "Certainly this was a lot to ask of a stranger?"

Fergus noticed the attention Silky was getting on the table. He leaped from the side table to the kitchen table. Silky swatted him as he leaned against her for attention. Juan rubbed Fergus' back, "Yes, it was a lot to ask, but your daughter can be extremely convincing. She told me how Donna was being abused, not in any great detail mind you, but that she was being abused." He blew Fergus' orange fur from his fingers, watching it float to the floor.

Sophia pulled Silky into her lap, "Did you drive Donna to Rocoso?"

Fergus rubbed his head against her warm mug of tea. Juan lifted him away. "No, I didn't drive Donna anywhere. That was pushing me past my limit. Griego's mother Reina drove both Griego and Donna to her father's. Reina knew where he lived. She'd picked up Donna from his house before to take Griego and Donna to the movies. No, I agreed to keep the horse and make sure someone read the note. My participation was limited to Alcon. The rest was up to Donna and Griego."

Swirling the tea in her mug, Sophia shook her head, "Wow, my girls are clever. Donna actually saved Geoffrey's life." She took another sip of hot tea, "You know at first I felt sorry for the man what with all those police cars, people going through his house, taking pictures of everything. Juan, they took photos of everything! All around his house outside and inside." Putting the mug down, she looked at him, "They even took his pets. Animal Control was there in their van. The three cats were put in carriers and the poor dog with dried poop on his bottom was taken." Sophia wiped her nose with a linen napkin from the table, "His animals are gone. They were the last of his friends."

Fergus jumped down onto the floor, lying on his side he started to clean his paws. Juan watched him, "Geoffrey still has you, doesn't he? I mean you guys are divorced, but you have children together. Doesn't that mean you are still involved in his life as a friend or as a fellow parent?"

Shaking her head, Sophia pushed her short bangs from her forehead, "You know, I don't know? He became someone I didn't know. I can't identify with a hoarder who lives in filth. It makes me ill to see him in his chosen environment. He has become someone that I can't accept. Does that make me a bad person?"

Donna ran into the kitchen, "Mom, we left you a pork chop! They were ever so good! Juan even made dessert. Did you get some lemon cream pie?"

Grabbing her daughter around the waist, Sophia pulled her into a hug, "No! Juan, you didn't offer me any of your fancy dessert!"

The refrigerator opened and a scoop of lemon cream was dumped into a beige bowl with a spoon. "Here, tell me what you think." Juan placed it in front of Sophia. She gingerly lifted the spoon with the yellow mixture to her lips. Licking it delicately, she rolled her eyes, "Oh, heaven! Wow, we have someone who knows desserts, Donna."

The twelve year old pulled free from her mother's grasp, "Juan, I want to be a pastry cook when I grow up and sell delicious foods to hungry people."

Laughing, Sophia pointed a finger at Donna, "Wait, you told me you wanted to be a veterinarian. What happened to that dream?"

"Oh, Mom!" She ran into her bedroom and shut the door. Sybil wandered into the kitchen. When she saw her mother's bowl of dessert, she asked, "Hey, can I have some more? Juan, you really need to come over more and help us with dinners."

Chuckling at Sybil, he noted the time from the hall clock, "All right, everyone is home. Everyone is safe. I am going to my house for a good night's rest. Thank you for the night of full entertainment." He waved as he walked down the hall to the front door, calling out, "Hey, don't be strangers!" They heard him turn and reenter the kitchen. "Oh, I almost forgot. My sister Reina, you know Griego's Mom? She wanted me to ask you to give her condolences to Roberto. Rosa, his wife worked with Reina at Otero Middle School. They were both cooks in the kitchen." He walked out and the door shut with a gentle thud.

Sophia turned to Sybil, "Did you know Rosa who worked in the cafeteria?"

Sybil licked her spoon, "Sure, we all did. She and Reina would sing and dance sometimes. I didn't know that Rosa was Roberto's wife though. I mean I only saw her for a split second every day for lunch and the food was horrible, yuck!"

Lights were turned off. Sophia, Donna and Sybil were all lying on Sophia's bed. The cats curled up around their legs and in their arms. The sheet over the bedroom window helped keep the room warm. The heater clicked on and forced hot air blew down from the ceiling vent. There was a feeling of peace in the quiet room. Finally, Donna asked, "Do you think Dad is all right? Maybe tomorrow we could go and visit him in the hospital?"

Stroking her daughter's long hair, Sophia reminded them, "Tomorrow morning is going to be a busy time. We have Bobby Garcia the Social Worker arriving and Clementine is going to interview us. Also, we need to ride the horses. Today was shot. Those horses need to be kept in shape for their owners. We promised to ride them at least three times a week."

Sybil lifted on her elbow, "Then I'm not going to school tomorrow?"

Leaning on the table to stand upright, Sophia smiled, "I guess not. Oh, dear, Donna's appointment with the dentist needs to be changed. Your school should be called and we need to see how Granger is doing."

The bed lifted as the girls stood. Donna shook out her long hair as she carried Biscuits cat in her arms, "I guess we should go to bed. Mom, I'm glad I'm here and not in that stinky house."

Following Donna into her bedroom, Sophia mentioned, "You know, Donna, this might have ended very badly. Your father could have been taken out of the house and put in jail. As it is, the house is going to be condemned. Where is he supposed to go when he is released from the hospital?"

Sybil pushed by her mother to give Donna a hug, "Mom, he could stay with Margaret. She loves company and Granger isn't taking care of her."

Sophia clapped her hands, "Oh! Wow! Wouldn't that be something! Geoffrey can't stand the Pino's! What if he ends up with my mother?"

Frowning, Donna put the cat on her bed, "No, Mom! Dad will not live with Margaret. What if he comes and lives with us? We could put a bed in the front room with the T.V. Dad loves watching political channels. He would stay in there all day and leave us alone?"

Sophia spoke sternly, "Bed! Everyone to bed. This isn't something we can decide right now."

Tranquility filled the adobe farmhouse. Sitting in her bed, Sophia made of list of things to do. Wally cat jumped on the bed to purr. Lifting the list, she read it to him, "Tomorrow. Donna starts living with us. This will be an extra cost. We can do this. You cats will go on a strict diet." She leaned forward and rubbed under Wally's ears. "There are the horses. Donna will be a great help with them. Donna's braces need to be tightened every other week in Albuquerque. We can plan this around my teaching."

Sitting back on her pillows, she read further on her list to the cat, "Also, from now on we need to rise very early to drive Donna to the private school." Then she remembered Donna's clothes, her books and her personal items were still in Geoffrey's filthy house. "Wally, what of Donna's things in Geoffrey's house? Does she want to bring those here? Are there bugs and mold in them?"

Putting the list on the bedside table, Sophia decided she just wouldn't deal with all of Donna's items yet. She didn't even know if Donna still had the key to the house or if she had given it to the young officer. "Wally, tomorrow morning there will be phone calls to make, people arriving with questions and family in hospital to visit." The cat rolled onto his back with his legs in the air. "Yes, you're right. It's time to sleep."

Marmalade flew onto the bed to jump on Wally. They tangled with each other and then fell asleep in a hug. Smiling at them, Sophia said, "Juan did make a good dessert. Margaret has a crush on Alex Peters." The bedside lamp was turned off as the covers were pulled over her chin. "Good night, kitties."

8

Bright sunshine illuminated the chalk blue sky. Fluffy fat clouds hovered over Sandia Mountains. Robins and barn swallows sang and swooped around the barnyard and empty stalls. The horses were all out in fields cantering in the warmth, whinnying and crowhopping. Sybil and Sophia had made cinnamon buns with white powdered sugar for topping. As they walked to the farmhouse front door a metallic-silver car pulled in to park under the hangman's tree. The old cottonwood had plenty of brown leaves still on it for shading vehicles. Coming out of the house with a huge smile was Donna. Her long hair was braided down her back and her braces sparkled in the sunlight. "Bobby, hi!"

Bobby Robertson jumped out of the car to give Donna a big hug. It was only as she started to walk to Sophia and Sybil that her limp became apparent. She put out her hand to Sophia only to open her arms in greeting to Sybil. "Hello, you beautiful women you! I can tell by the clothes you wear that you were in the barn with the horses. Also, by the odor of the boots."

Laughing, they went into the kitchen. The fresh smell of baked pastries filled the air as well as the hot sugar. "Oh, my, this house has the best food ever. I shall have to come and visit you more often, that's for sure!" Bobby sat abruptly in one of the kitchen chairs. "This is a long table. Do you have every one you know over for supper regularly and how come I wasn't invited?"

Sophia put the plate of cinnamon rolls on the table with three mugs for tea. "Bobby, would you like tea or would you prefer instant coffee? And we inherited this huge kitchen table. It came with the kitchen." She waved her arms wide to illustrate the large kitchen area. Donna had fixed herself a mug of hot cocoa and asked, "If you would like hot cocoa we have some."

Clapping her hands, Bobby answered, "So many choices, but 'yes' I would love hot cocoa. I haven't had cocoa since I was newly married and pregnant. How delightful and did you make these delicious goodies here on the plate?"

The mug in front of Bobby was removed and Donna fixed the cocoa. "No, I didn't. Mom and Sybil made them. We're going to have loads of company today and Mom is always trying to fatten up everyone. She wants them to be fatter than she is."

A wash cloth was snapped at Donna's rear, "No, I don't! I just enjoy happy people and good food appears to make people happy, that's all! Donna, really!"

The mugs of hot beverages were served when Bobby turned to the chair next to her, "Where's Sybil? She needs to be here for this intervention meeting. Can you call her?"

Not waiting for anyone to stand or walk to the bedroom door and request Sybil, Donna opened her mouth and yelled at the top of her lungs, "Sybil, get your butt in here!"

Both Sophia and Bobby were unnerved by the scream. Shaking her head, Bobby asked Donna if she had to yell to get her sister's attention. Donna nodded, "Yes, usually she just ignores me. Right, Mom?"

"No, not true at all. Donna that scream was totally unnecessary. You could've just asked her politely and she would have come." Sophia sipped her tea.

Cautiously coming out of her bedroom doorway, Sybil peered out at them, "What? Is there an emergency? Donna why are you rudely screaming at me?"

Shrugging her shoulders, her sister replied, "Hey, you are needed in here. How am I to know what you're doing in there?"

Bobby patted the kitchen chair next to her, "Come and join us, please. This meeting works better if there is an even number. Would you mind helping me out here?"

Sybil slid into the chair beside Bobby, "Hey, whatever it takes to keep my screaming sister quiet is fine with me. I miss her when she's in the garbage pit."

Lifting her carryall Bobby opened it to remove four small notepads and four mechanical pencils. She placed one of these in front of each of them. Then she took out a cooking timer and placed it in the middle of the table with the time numbers facing her. "Each one of you will be asked to write down ten ideas. I will give you the requirements when we get to them. Right now I need you to place your hands flat on the table in front of you." She put her hands on the table with her fingers stretched apart. "Now, it is important for you to touch the tips of your fingers with your neighbors. I'll touch Sophia's finger tips and Sybil you touch Donna's. Then my little finger will touch Sybil's and you two do the same."

Sophia smiled, "This is like a séance?"

"Yes, exactly." Bobby watched as the fingers were properly placed.

"Now I need for you to close your eyes. Listen to my voice and let your mind wander. Once we have finished, I will ask you to write down the ten things that were most prominent in your thoughts. The timer will be set for three minutes. Ready?"

Everyone at the table nodded. "Close your eyes. Let your mind go blank. When you think of Geoffrey what are the ten most prominent thoughts that come to mind?"

The four women were quiet. Birds sang outside. Someone was driving a tractor in the neighboring field. Shonac barked at the front of the farmhouse. Quietly, Bobby said, "Open your eyes and write. I'll set the timer."

Each of them took the mechanical pencil in front of them and wrote. Sybil wrote the fastest as Sophia appeared to take her time. When the timer beeped, Bobby asked them to lift their pencils. "All right, let's start with the oldest at the table. Oh, first let me have your pencils. Can't allow anyone to change their work."

Sophia's face turned dark as she spoke, "This was difficult for me since Geoffrey is the man I chose for a life partner and he is someone I still love. I wanted to be polite, but…"

"Sophia," Bobby interrupted her, "You aren't to give a monologue about your work first. Just read your list or we may be here all day and eat all of the cinnamon buns."

"My number one thought is how kind he can be when he isn't drinking. Number two is….."

Bobby interrupted her again, "Just read the list, Sophia. I know you are a professor at the university, but we don't need words here, we need your ideas."

The paper was lifted to Sophia's face, "He's kind, he can be arrogant, he has misused his daughters' money, he's a slob, he killed our marriage, once he was neat and clean and now he's a hoarder and lives in trash, he wants to still love me and he is filled with hate. That's all I have. There you go." She tore off the page of paper from the notepad and handed it to Bobby. "Donna, it's your turn."

Donna scowled at her paper, "I only wrote down three things. There wasn't much point in going further. I love my dad, he lives in a pigsty and he hates my mother and her family. That's it." She handed the page to Bobby who nodded to Sybil.

Sybil showed the paper to the others. It had three doodles. A garbage can with a plus sign and a man with a plus sign and a big heart. "My dad lives in a garbage can and he adopted me so he is my dad and he has a big heart. Here." She handed the page to Bobby.

The rest of the hour was spent going over the accommodations

Donna preferred and those that were able to be met. Bobby answered Sophia questions about Donna's items in Geoffrey's house. "The things in the condemned house must be cleared before they can be removed. I think some of the items the health department found were important and Sophia, we should go over those in private. Otherwise, I will return in a month's time to review the situation here once more. If it meets with my expectations then this will become Donna' permanent home. Oh, there is one more issue we need to go over." The notepads were tapped and the pencils returned. "Please write down your opinion of this farmhouse and your life here as well as your role. This is three questions. Your opinion of this farmhouse is important. How do you feel about living here and what is your role in your life here. Go."

All three of them were quickly finished. Donna read that she was not happy living way out in the sticks, but loved the horses and enjoyed working with the horses. Sophia wrote of her love of the farmhouse even though it was a lot of work with the horses and cleaning and the cost of remodeling worried her. Sybil only wrote one thing her opinion, "I hate it here." Bobby frowned at the three of them. "Have you thought of moving somewhere more compatible to everyone?"

Her question was directed to Sophia who answered, "Yes, but I have to buy this place fully before I can request the title or deed. Right now the ownership of this house is with the bank. If I move I have to get permission from my mother who holds the loan with the bank even though I am the one paying for it."

"In other words it is complicated and you can't move right now, correct?"

"Yes."

Bobby focused on the girls, "Do you understand why you have to remain here for more time?"

Both of the girls stared at their mother, "Grandma owns this place? Why?" Donna's voice was small and quiet.

"Because when I divorced your father the bank would not allow me to take out a mortgage until we had finished the divorce. The mortgage lender felt I would not be able to afford to buy property until the divorce was finalized. Grandma came to my aid and without her we might be living under a bridge with no horses or heat."

Both girls glared at her. Sybil ran into her room and slammed the door. The crack widened over the door frame as dirt fell into a pile on the floor. Donna shoved her chair back to follow Sybil into her bedroom. She gently closed the door behind her.

Reaching further into her carryall, Bobby pulled out a government paper. On it was a list of items of concern to the health department. She handed the list to Sophia who read down the items. At a gasp, she said, "Granger's packages of herbs? Really? Twenty packages of herbs? Where and why would he have those?"

Twirling the mug in front of her Bobby shook her head, "You know I asked the same thing. Your brother gave me herbs for my leg. My mother took an anti-nausea drug when she was pregnant with me and my right leg is deformed and at times painful. Granger was referred to by my doc. He gave me a brown bag like those with herbs for my painful leg. They worked and I was grateful. It was disappointing when he was imprisoned. I had become dependent on those herbs."

Staring at her in disbelief, Sophia asked, "The herbs really helped you?"

"Oh, yes. They were excellent. For the first time in my life the pain had gone away. My prayer is that soon I can get some more. Do you think your brother is going to reopen his clinic?"

The list was handed back to Bobby as Sophia studied her mechanical pencil, "Who knows? There are those who swore by his cures and there are those who accuse him of trying to kill them. I have no idea, but he is at my mother's farm if you want to call him?"

"No, I won't bother him. He has a lot on his plate what with finding a job, getting a vehicle and regaining his reputation. I'll wait and see what happens, but if you find any of his herbs in Geoffrey's that might help, let me know?"

Mugs were taken to the sink. Bobby replaced the items into her carryall and walked with Sophia to the front door. "Say good-bye to the girls for me. Personally I believe you're a great mother and you're doing just fine. Don't know how you manage to drive all over all the time, but somehow you do it. I'll give you a call in a month and set up a date, yes?"

They hugged at Bobby's government vehicle. Sophia stood under the tree to watch the horses graze. Then her attention was moved to Juan's farm where he was going around the barrels with his horse. The fluid movement was inviable. As she washed the mugs in the kitchen sink another vehicle arrived. Clementine stepped out of her brown sheriff's car. This time she was alone. Sophia met her at the door.

The two women sat at the kitchen table. Clementine sat at the kitchen table with a mug of hot tea and a warm cinnamon roll. Sophia sipped her tea for she had no need of another cinnamon roll. Clementine licked her fingers when she finished. "We have a lead on the Mrs. Mary Peters death. It may be that Rosa's death and Mrs. Peter's death are unrelated. Everything is still in early study and research." Taking the linen napkin, Clementine stuck one end in the tea and then wiped the sugar off of her fingers. "I know, I could go into the bathroom, but it is comfortable here. Isn't it?"

"Ah, a question. Yes, it is comfortable here. Although, would you mind if we walked outside and watched the horses? It is such a gorgeous day." Sophia lifted her mug to place it by the sink. Clementine did the same after she drained the mug.

At the white pole fence Clementine pointed to Teddy who was the tallest gelding, "Is he yours or is he a boarding horse?"

"He is beautiful, isn't he? Yes, he's a boarded horse, but we ride them three times a week. We get to know their quirks and understand their abilities." She turned to Clementine, "What are we supposed to do with Geoffrey? Are we to visit him in the hospital or are we allowed to go into his house? What do we do about his pets?"

Rubbing her hand along the white pole barnyard fence, Clementine frowned, "You can visit him in hospital. You cannot go into the house without the approval of the health department and I do have a contact number for you in the car. As far as his pets are concerned, well, this is the bad news. Are you ready for bad news?"

Startled, Sophia studied Clementine's face, "What? What's happened to his pets?"

"Oh, God, bad news, I hate bad news. You know I hate bad news, right?" Clementine said, "The dog is going on ten years of age. The dog is riddled with cancer. They believe the dog has cancer from all of the chemicals Geoffrey used in the house to kill mold, bugs or whatever. The chemicals found were all highly toxic. It is amazing Geoffrey doesn't have a terrible illness from those chemicals. Then the cats?"

Quietly, Sophia waited for her to continue. She did, "The cats are not in good health either. One of them, the large orange cat has inverted eyelids. Probably since birth and nothing was done about this so he had horrible infections. He is now blind in one eye and has ulcerations all around his eyes. There is no cure for this and as you can suppose, he will probably be put down. The second cat is feeble and old. She's gray and has numerous problems."

Clearing her throat, Sophia asked, "What about the third cat? There was a calico Persian cat, a female?"

"Oh, dear, oh, dear, more bad news here." Clementine turned her head toward the farmhouse, "The third cat is a petrified skeleton under his bed. She must have died ages ago and was eaten by maggots. These were found in the carpet dead as well for they had run out of food once they had eaten the cat." She wrapped her fingers around the pole fence, "The mattress in his bedroom had dead maggots in it. He must have used a spray to kill them off for he probably had maggots on him since they were found in his bed's mattress."

Turning back to watch the horses, Sophia spoke softly, "Donna knew the animals were sick. She tried to get me to steal them away and get them to a vet. I couldn't do it. I just couldn't. Geoffrey would adopt more animals, make them sick or kill them, too. Apathy is a terrible excuse, but I really didn't know what to do!"

"Geoffrey was giving them herbs. He had bags upon bags of Granger's herbs in his pantry. He was reading the directions for humans and giving the herbs to the animals mixed into the food. You knew about this, right?'

Swiftly Sophia turned, "No! I had no idea! The Social Services Worker just left here before you arrived. She showed me the list of dangerous chemicals and items in Geoffrey's house. On the list were twenty three paper bags of Granger's herbs. I had no idea! Where did Geoffrey get them? He hated Granger. He hated Granger with such a passion there was no way he would talk to Granger or ask his advice!"

"Lots of questions." Clementine's ponytail danced around her head when she shook it, "Where did Geoffrey get the bags indeed. Did he get them from your mother?"

Fast and furiously, Sophia answered again, "No! Geoffrey hated all Pino's. In the end he even hated me! Geoffrey wouldn't even say my mother's name without spitting phlegm at me. No!"

Two of the horses came cantering up to them. Sophia held out her palm to show them there was no food. Clementine rubbed Tracy's furry nose, "Where did Geoffrey get the herbs? You might suck it up and visit him with the daughters and on the sly ask him?"

Sybil came racing to them from the house, "Mom! Grandma's on the phone. She sounds hysterical! You better come and talk to her." Then her attention was taken to Clementine, "Hi! You want to come inside and have a cinnamon roll?"

Smiling, Clementine laughed, "I already had two. We were out here admiring your fine horses. Do you know that I love to ride?"

"Yes! Mom, can we saddle them up and go riding? We're supposed to ride them today, remember? Oh, and the dentist called to set another appointment for Donna's braces. Can you call them back?" Sybil let Tracy and Lucky lick her palm. "And Mom, thanks for calling the school. I did need a day off."

Pointing to the barn, Sophia agreed, "Yes, you can ride, but I would prefer to ride with you. Also, you should invite Clementine to ride with us.

Although maybe she's busy and doesn't have time today." Sophia hurried into the house. When she was in the hall picking up the phone, she called to Donna, 'Sybil wants to go riding. Do you wish to go with her?" There was no answer just a blur as Donna ran down the hall and out the door.

"Hello, Margaret? How are you today?" Sophia used her super calm voice.

There was sobbing, uncontrolled sobbing, "Sophia, sniff, Sophia, Granger called. They've taken him for questioning. He wanted me to call you and see if you could meet him at the sheriff's office in Rincon." There was the sound of Margaret blowing her nose, then, "Sophia, please keep my baby boy out of jail! Please! If it is a matter of money you can use my checkbook it's in the desk by my bed. The one on top hasn't been eaten by mice. Oh, Sophia, my poor Granger!" This was followed with uncontrolled sobbing, nose blowing and mumbling.

Finally, Sophia interrupted all of this to say, "Mom, I'll go right now. First I may call to see if he's right there. If he's left and is on his way to see you there is no point in my driving to Rincon. Do you understand?"

Sniffing, "I guess so. Please, Sophia, I know you hate your brother, but please for me help him, please!" The phone went to dial tone.

The unicorn blanket was rolled up and pinned over the kitchen window. Sophia watched the girls saddle the horses all four of them. Clementine was brushing Angel. The horse's tail was switching back and forth. Donna had saddled Sophia's horse and Sybil was cleaning Teddy's hooves with the hoof pick. Sophia flipped her cellphone open to punch in a number. At the other end, the phone rang.

A.J.'s voice came across loud and clear, "Rincon sheriff's office how can your call be directed?'

Sophia said in a pronounced nasal tone, "I need to speak with the sheriff of Rincon the one with the bad eye, please?"

His deep voice became booming, 'Sophia Pino! What is it you require and my eyeball is bad thanks to you!"

"A.J., is my brother the honorable or dishonorable Granger in your office and have you charged him with a lifetime offense?"

"No and no. Granger Pino was brought in for a confirmation on the bag that we found at Rosa's. He didn't think the bag belonged to his clinic. As for the bag found in the Peters' house, the bag is questionable. The bag at the Peters' house had no ingredients written on the sides or the bottom. This made Granger believe someone was using his seal and not his bags. He has not been charged and he was not written up in the system for his probation officer to know. He's probably on his way home." There was a silence. Sophia was watching the horses getting ready for a long ride. "Sophia, are you there?"

She turned off the light in the kitchen, "Yes, I'm here. We're taking Clementine horseback riding. Is this all right with you?"

"Sure. She's an independent Detective Inspector within a different office than ours. Certainly, if she's free to ride more power to her. Don't worry about Granger, he's a free man." There was a dial tone.

Putting the cellphone in her jean pocket, Sophia mumbled, "Everyone is hanging up on me today!" She hurried out to the hall, locked the front door behind her. Greeting the others, she mounted Lucky as the four horse riders trotted out onto the Alcon small road for a day's adventure. Sophia rubbed Lucky's neck, "Let's hope Granger is on his way to visit his mother or we are in hot water!" Ravens flew in pairs above them as the horseback riders jumped over the ditch to follow the dirt road to the diversion. Fat brown heifer cows stared at them as they passed the Romero's corral. The cows continued to chew their cuds. Feral chickens raced away to flutter and fly into the Mondragon's barnyard. Their horses cantered to the river. Donna rode beside Clementine to share stories of all the farms they passed. Sybil appeared deep in thought as she led the procession. Sophia let the soft breeze blow her short curls around her head as she watched the beauty of life unfold around her.

Water surged over the diversion barricade. Mist lifted from the high metal bridge walk over. Ducks fluttered and swam in the shallow water below the diversion. Long sleek trout of many colors swam ferociously upstream away from the metal deflector of the diversion separator. Their horses trotted below the loud tumbling water where the crossover had shallow surging water. The fork in the barricade sent river water into the large channel that later would be divided into different ditches for irrigation. The straight flow of water flowed over the metal gate to return into the river to slowly pulse through Albuquerque. In the South Valley the river water was once more diverted, leading to more ditches.

Sybil was in the lead with her horse now, high stepping carefully through the low river water. Round rocks tumbling in the fast flow could trip a horse and leave them lame. Donna and Clementine were in deep conversation ahead of Sophia who was watching the geese and ducks at the higher level of the diversion hunting for silvery minnow.

On the far side of the river the horseback riders united to ride single file up a narrow dirt road to the top of a mesa. Sophia pointed ahead to a circle of tall rocks, "Do you see those formations? This is where in old times the women would have sacred ceremony. The Pueblo is right down there. Actually, we are trespassing but the Mud Heads know us and we are respectful of ceremony days and the land."

The view was magnificent. Two other tall mesas stood separated. Clementine asked, "Who are those two standing alone over there?"

The storytelling Donna answered, "Those are the Twin War Gods, Masawei and Oyoyowei. They are the twin heroes of the land who saved the people from being killed by the giant eagle of the north."

Smiling at Donna, Clementine acknowledged her, "I can tell your mother has taught you girls all about the land and the stories of the people. How glorious. I wish my grandparents would have shared the stories of the old ones in Australia. They thought I wouldn't be interested. Maybe they were right. You two enjoy the stories, right?"

Sybil pointed, "Mom, look here comes Mr. Casaus the Land Officer. Wonder what he wants?"

A golden palomino stallion cantered to the group. The man's bandana held his long hair in place behind his ears. Brown hair streaked with gray gave away his age. Turquoise drop earrings bounced as his horse cantered. Once he was closer his age was more noticeable. "Sophia! How serendipitous to find you out here on the mesa while we are surveying." His stallion stopped beside her. "We're over there on the far side checking the coordinates for the government. Evidently Washington D. C. wants to take away some of our land. We're fighting them with all we've got!"

Sybil slowed her horse to ride beside him, sandwiching him between her and her mother. "Mr. Casaus, your son won the state basketball tournament for us! You must be really proud of him."

Turning to study her, he said, "He's got my long legs. You should be thanking him." A deep guttural laugh came out of his chest to add, "You're the one who's going to get us into the literary circle in the state competition, right?"

Blushing at his remark, Sybil trotted ahead. Sophia called to Clementine, "Say, I would like to introduce you to Detective Inspector Clementine who works on Special Cases with Sheriff A.J. Salazar."

Leaning over Sophia's horse, Clementine shook Mr. Casaus' hand gently. "Hello, it's a pleasure to meet you. Heard you mention the government trying to take your land, do you have some good lawyers?"

Chortling, he answered her, "Our Indian lawyers are the best in the country. We have had years of practice fighting Washington." Shaking his head, he added, "Years and years and years! Our guys know all the laws and how to shoot back on the politicos!"

The horses were bumping into one another as the group tried to talk. Clementine kicked her horse to catch up with the girls. Mr. Casaus pulled his horse to a stop. "Sophia, we have a problem in the pueblo and you may be someone who could help us figure out what is going on. Do you have a minute to talk or would it be better to meet at my office in the village?" His eyes appeared to hold grave concern.

Circling her horse around him, she halted Lucky to face him, "What's up? Can you tell me here?"

His deep voice became soft spoken, "There were some herbs being given to the Elders at the Senior Center in the Pueblo. The old women wanted to perk up their husbands and decided to try the herbs out on them. Some of the old men who were more anxious than willing fell ill. Two of them are still in the Indian Hospital in Albuquerque. They almost died. Luckily the old woman who gave them the herbs was careful to only try a little first. The seal on the brown paper bags is familiar. You probably know it."

"The circle in red on a gold background?"

"Yeah. I didn't want to bring in the Pueblo Police. Those guys are ruthless. They would not be kind. If I call A.J. he would notify them first."

Pursing her lips, Sophia whistled. Donna, Sybil and Clementine all turned. Pointing to Clementine, Sophia beckoned her. Sybil laughed at her mother, "Mom, what's with the whistle? Can't you just call out?"

Putting her finger to her lips, she turned. Mr. Casaus said to Sybil, "Your mother didn't want to wake up the ancients. She's trying her bird calls. They're not very good!"

Donna and Sybil shook their heads to gallop up the side of the mesa's sand dune. Clementine trotted to them. Sophia's voice was focused on Mr. Casaus, "Tell her what you just told me. She's investigating the brown bag with the gold seal problem. I'm going to catch up with the girls." Then she said, "Be kind to her, she's from Australia." Then to Clementine, "This fellow is an old time family friend who is a great trickster. Though what he has to say is dead serious. You two play nice, please." Nudging her horse, she trotted then cantered to catch up with her daughters.

The chalk blue sky now had fluffy white cumulous clouds coming toward the mesa. Below them far away was the interstate with dots traveling their way to and from Albuquerque to Santa Fe. Canyons and arroyos illustrated the wrinkles of Mother Earth while high above them a pair of ravens floated on the wind currents. The smell of pinon was strong in the air as the smoke from the pueblo's fireplaces lifted. The horses' hooves left indents in the sand as the three came to the top of the mesa. There below them was the whole of the world. High rising Sandia Mountain blocked the view to the east, but to the west one felt they could see all the way to the Pacific Ocean. Titilla Peak stood tall to the north as if pointing the way to the Sangre de Cristo Mountain Range. Santa Fe Baldy was prominent from where they were. Santa Fe Baldy hid the Truchas Mountain Range. The south sloped down to the flatlands flowing all the way to the volcanoes, all eleven of them were a line of dimples in Mother Earth. Dwarfed juniper trees and pinion trees gave shade to rabbit bush, chamisa, salt cedar and round grass.

Pointing to the southeast, Donna said, "Look there's the farm. You know, Mom, it's not terrible living here. The house is crowded that's all."

Agreeing Sybil asked, "Could we get a priest to come in and clear the house of the ghosts? It is hard to sleep at night knowing all those spirits are floating around. Sometimes they move my stuff and I can't find it."

Sophia smiled, "Oh, like your algebra homework? Or the matching socks?"

"You can make fun if you want to, Mom, but it is the truth! Donna, just you wait. After you live with us for a while they'll come after you, too."

Clementine cantered up to them, "Well, that was enlightening. Now I know all there is to know about sex life on the res. But he did give me his cellphone number, here." She put out her hand. On the back of her hand was written a phone number. "We didn't have any paper. Well, so, the bags are moving about from one area to another. They appear to have been used more or less on the same day! This is strange, don't you think?"

Taking her hand for a better look, Sybil smiled, "If you were in my algebra class you would be suspended for writing on your body. What bags and what are you guys talking about?"

Slapping her own cheek lightly, Clementine stared at Sophia, "Oh, dear, guess I put my feet in my mouth! Haven't you spoken to the girls about the bags and the herbs?"

Patting her shoulder, Sybil frowned, "Yes. Mom, had us make a list of all the people who Roberto worked for when Rosa died. You know Donna knew Rosa really well. She went over to their house sometimes when she was supposed to be at Grandma's."

This got Sophia's attention, "What? Why would Donna be at Grandma's? How did Donna end up over there?"

Tracy pushed her nose between Sophia's and Clementine's horses. Donna sat tall, "Dad didn't or couldn't pick me up from school. He asked Grandma to pick me up, but Grandma said she couldn't drive that far into town. Her poop mobile would poop out, hah!" Giggling she continued, "Roberto picked me up at the corner from the school in his truck. Sometimes Rosa was with him. She was a blast."

Confused, Sophia asked, "But did you go to Grandma's? Or did you go to Roberto's house?"

Flicking her reins back and forth across her thighs, Donna frowned, "Mom, it depended. If Dad said he would pick me up from Grandma's, she didn't want me there. She asked him to pick me up at Roberto's house. Rosa showed me how to make quesadillas and one time we made tortillas. I took them to Dad's since his food is disgusting. Dad has some of Uncle Salamander's bags in his closet. I saw them there."

Interrupting her, Clementine asked, "Did you see any of those brown bags at Rosa's home or in her kitchen?"

"Yeah, the flakey people next door, I think the woman's name is Peggy, she brought over one of the bags. She had written something down on a piece of paper in Spanish for Rosa about the herbs. Rosa speaks English, but she doesn't read English. Strange, huh?"

Sophia's horse became agitated being so close to the others and started pawing at the ground. Sophia rubbed her horse's neck, saying, "Hush, boy, hush. Say, Donna, you do know that Rosa died, right? Do you know if Peggy had more of those bags?"

"Mom, she's weird. Not Rosa, that Peggy person is beyond strange. I ignored her. Her husband has long hair in a ponytail like Clementine's. He looks like a girl! Rosa was embarrassed by them, I could tell. She called them hippies!" Turning Tracy, she contested her sister, "Let's race down to the river? Come on!"

The two women watched the two girls gallop away as dust was being kicked up behind the horses' hooves. Clementine put her hand up to shield the sun from her eyes, "Sophia, this list of suspects gets longer and longer. Do you know if A.J. spoke to these hippy people?"

Answering as her horse started to trot after the girls, "Yes, he said they wouldn't open the door. He knew they were in the house, but they refused to come to the door or speak to the law."

Shouting after her, Clementine asked Sophia, "Would you go with me to their house? Do you think they would let in two helpless women?"

Laughing wildly, Sophia called back, "I'm not sure they'd let me in! I had a confrontation with Carl and his nuts!"

As they trotted to the farmhouse, Clementine's cellphone rang. She slowed to stay behind the others to answer. Her face became serious when she finished the call. The horses were dismounted and the daughters agreed to walk the horses and brush them before feeding for the night. It was late afternoon and everyone was hungry since they skipped lunch.

In the kitchen Clementine asked if she could use Sophia's landline. Questioning her preference over the cellphone, Sophia pointed to the black plastic phone in the hall, on the table. "What's with this? Does you cellphone have a dead battery? We have charges in all sizes and shapes if you need to use one."

"No, somehow I believe my cellphone has been compromised. The last confrontation with A.J. on my cell had intermittent bleeps. It is either my cell or the sheriff's office. Need to let A.J. know, that's all."

Soup, crackers and peanut butter sandwiches were on the table by the time the girls came inside. Clementine grabbed a sandwich, thanking them for the fun day and said she had to run. Sybil slurped her soup. Donna was quiet as she ate her peanut butter sandwich and Sophia sat deep in thought. "Girls, what do you make of these brown bags popping up all over the place? Who do you think is taking or giving these bags of herbs away?"

Placing her spoon in the bowl, Sybil said, "Mom, now you sound like Clementine ending every dialogue with a question."

"No, I don't. O-kay, let's make a list. Donna, you said your Dad had bags in the closet. Rosa had a bag brought over by Peggy, but it was given to her by Roberto. Mrs. Peters had a bag and so did her husband Alex for his problem. Mr. Casaus told us the bags showed up at the Senior Center in the pueblo. Who else might have bags? Maybe my mother, huh?"

Finishing her sandwich, Donna pointed at the paper her mother was writing on, "What about we go over to Grandma's now that she's in the hospital? We could say we went to visit Salamander Granger. He's hardly home, right? Couldn't we go over there and investigate?"

Putting up her hand, Sybil reneged, "Not me. I don't want to see Granger. I don't want to have anything to do with him. He's a wart on society and probably wants to kill off the people he doesn't like on this earth. No way, Jose, I'm not going over there! No!"

Silence filled the kitchen. One of the clothes pins holding up the unicorn blanket popped off giving them a start. The blanket unfolded on the far side of the window. Donna had to turn all the way around to watch, "Mom, the ghosts agree. We should go. Let's go right now before they get all testy! I'm going to change my boots for sneakers, let's go. Sybil, you better stay here and keep everyone of these weird spirits in check." She ran into her bedroom.

Lying on her bed, Sybil waved as her mother and sister walked past her bedroom's open door through the kitchen, "Hey, guys, do you want me to fix dinner while you're gone?"

Yelling back at her, Sophia answered, "Sure, just no more pork chops. Plug in your track phone, we'll call you when we're on our way back here."

Commuter traffic slowed their drive to Calavera. Pointing to the tall cottonwood tree branches that hung over the narrow road, Donna noticed, "The trees are more and more naked as the nights get colder. What do you think we should do for Halloween? It's in two weeks and our ghosts will be getting uppity."

Sophia sighed, "Don't know. We should give out candy, but last year no one came to the house. You didn't even come with your Dad."

Donna shrugged, "The locals know the house is haunted, they won't come. Sybil and I are too old to go trick or treating, but we should do something for the ghosts. Maybe we could fix them a spiritual dinner or something? Mom, you're the research person what does someone feed spirits?"

Sophia turned into her mother's driveway. The truck was missing. The air was still. Donna ran into the barn to check on Geordie. Sophia lifted the backdoor's welcome mat to pick up the key. As she entered the kitchen she could smell the strong odor of cooking. On the counter were four of Granger's brown bags. On the stove was a pot filled with cooling water and herbs. A strainer was in the sink and a black marker was placed on the bags with a sheet of his famous red and gold sticky seals. Sniffing the pot mixture, Sophia snorted, "Nasty stuff." Lifting one of the bags, she read the ingredients and the instructions. Clearly, Granger was informative regarding his herbal medicines. The other bags had no writing on them, just the bag and the seal.

Racing into the kitchen, Donna was breathless, "Mom, oh, Mom, Geordie is down. He's down and he's not good, he's not good at all. He has green stuff coming out of his nose and stuck in his teeth. He's bad, Mom, really bad." Tears flowed from her green eyes, "Can you call Dr. Murphey? Mom, I think he's dying. It's horrible."

Picking up the pot from the stove, Sophia asked her daughter, "Does the green stuff in Geordie's mouth look like this?"

Slowly walking toward her mother, Donna stared at herbs, "No. These are stems. Those are leaves. Maybe the stems from those leaves?" Lifting her hands in the air, she asked again, "Can you call the vet?"

Dr. Murphey arrived half an hour later. Donna stayed with the horse while Sophia rummaged through her mother's bedroom and closet. By the time Dr. Murphey knocked on the kitchen door, Sophia had not found any bags at all aside from the ones in the kitchen. Following him to the barn, Sophia queried, "Have you seen Geordie already? Or did you just arrive?"

He mumbled something as he walked through the barn to Geordie's stall. The horse was standing with his head drooping to the ground. "I've called the ASPCA and they have a counselor on the way. Since you are the only member of the family here over the age of twenty one you will have to sign the agreement to put the horse down. We need to walk him out to an area where the truck can get to him to remove him from the property." Rubbing Geordie's forehead, he added, "You know the routine. You know how to do this perhaps too well."

Donna was quietly crying as she braided Geordie's tail. Dr. Murphey pulled a red bandana from his back pocket and handed it to her. "Donna, this is the kindest thing we can do for this old guy."

On the stall's dirt floor were piles of green stems. Sophia asked, "What are these things? Do you believe Granger gave these to the horse?"

Kicking the largest pile out of the stall door, Dr. Murphey said, "No. These are alfalfa stems. Nothing mysterious. I asked for Geordie to not be fed last night. Evidently someone fed him. Maybe they thought they were being kind, it doesn't matter now."

They turned when they heard a truck's door slam. Striding into the barn came Granger, "What the hell? I thought I made it perfectly clear I don't want you back here cheating my mother out of her money! Get the hell out of here, now!"

Dr. Murphey didn't move. His face remained passive. His right hand continued to stroke Geordie's forehead. Sophia put her hand up to stop Granger's anger, "That's enough, Granger. Enough anger. Enough with the accusations. Enough. We are going to put Geordie down and then you won't have to see Dr. Murphey ever again. Please, this is a difficult time. This horse deserves some respect."

A short plump woman stepped into the barn. She wore a brown cowboy hat, brown gloves, jeans and a white button down shirt. In her hand was a clipboard and a black pen. Each step was lifted high in the air as if her cowboy boots were too tight and hurt her feet. "Hello? I'm Belinda from the ASPCA. Dr. Murphey, are you here?"

Sophia pulled Granger to the side as Dr. Murphey answered, "I'm in here, in the stall. Come ahead in here."

Studying Sophia and Granger, Belinda walked carefully around them. Once she was beside Dr. Murphey, they spoke quietly as he signed the top page on her clipboard. Belinda walked around Geordie to Donna who pointed to Granger and Sophia. Belinda patted Donna on her shoulder to say something soothing and Donna nodded. Belinda hugged the clipboard to her chest as she walked out of the stall, "Hello, I need whoever has power of attorney or has legal ownership of this horse to sign the release forms. I am sorry for your loss." She held out the black pen and the clipboard.

Granger grabbed the items, "You can be sorry! I'm not sorry! That animal has eaten up most of my inheritance! Give me that! I'll gladly sign it and then get that pathetic piece of life out of here!" At the bottom of the page he put his signature in huge writing. Shaking her head, Belinda pushed the clipboard back at him, "Sir, you have signed the wrong paper. I need you to sign the last paper on my clipboard. Now I need to go and get another medical release paper from my truck. Please wait here."

"Damn!" Granger lifted each piece of paper. His signature had gone through all of the four pages over writing Dr. Murphey's signature and the diagnosis sheet. Silently, Belinda returned with fresh pages. This time only one page was given to Granger on the clipboard. "Just this one, here." She pointed to the empty line. Granger's name was written, clipboard returned to Belinda and he stormed out of the barn. Looking at Sophia, Belinda said, "Whew! He's got a temper, I wouldn't want to upset him. Thank you for your patience."

Papers in place and put into a folder with Geordie's name and address, the four of them went to the front of Margaret's farmhouse drive. Parked in front beside Sophia's van was a huge ton and a half truck. Dr. Murphey spoke to Donna, "I need you to lead Geordie around here to this gate. Then I want you to please go inside or return to the barn if you're afraid of Granger. All right, go now."

Pulling Geordie with the lead rope, Donna stared at the ground. Sophia opened the gate as she went to her daughter. Dr. Murphey stood with his black bag under his arm. Taking the rope from Donna, Sophia said, "Honey, you can lie down in the backseat of the van if you want to? Don't watch. This will be painless for Geordie, he won't feel a thing and finally he will be at peace." Sophia wiped a tear from her own cheek. Donna hugged Geordie's neck and then her mother, "O-kay, I'll be in the van. Say good-bye to him for me just before, just before….well, you know."

The ton and a half truck drove away. Geordie was released from his earthly pains and on his way to a horse cemetery. Sophia stood beside Dr. Murphey who had his arm around her shoulder as she cried, "Poor old guy, I wish he hadn't hurt these last months of his life."

Dr. Murphey closed his black bag. "I'm going now. Don't worry about the bill for this. There won't be one. This is my gift to that horse, he was more than deserving for peace." Banging on the van's window, he waved to Donna who was lying on the backseat stifling her crying. She waved back at him. Sliding the van's back door open, she confronted her mother, "I'm not going into the house with Granger here. I'm going to stay in the van." She pulled the door shut.

Dust filled the air from all the trucks. The robin's nest over Margaret's truck stared down at all the commotion. More droppings fell onto Margaret's truck cab's roof. Sophia shook her head. "You go for it, bird. You just cover that poop mobile!"

In the kitchen, Granger was sitting on the high red stool at the counter writing instructions on the brown bags. He swiveled when she came through the door, "Sophia, you do know I would never give anyone medicinal herbs without writing ingredients and instructions, right?"

"Yeah, yeah. Did you give Geordie herbs last night?" She washed her hands in the kitchen sink.

"No, why would I give medicinal herbs to a horse? I don't have any idea how to treat a horse. What gave you that idea?" He had returned to his writing. Mumbling, he added, "Why would I waste expensive herbs on a horse?"

"Geordie was fed last night. Did you give him alfalfa?" Ripping a paper towel from the roll, she wiped her face.

"No, I was told not to by dear mother. I didn't even go into the barn last night. I saw Roberto here. He took a basket load of eggs with him, but I didn't have any reason to go into the barn." He took a red and gold seal from the sheet to place on the closed bag.

Throwing the paper towel into the garbage receptacle, Sophia continued in her interrogation, "Who are those for? Who are you planning to kill off now?"

"Kill off? No one. Not one single person. Charlotte called asking for some herbs because they had helped her in the past. I bought these from the store and I have prepared them correctly for her. Don't worry, she won't die at least not by my hand." The bags were placed neatly upright on the counter. "Sophia, what's going on with my herbs? You know I couldn't have killed those people. Those weren't my herbs or my bags. That wasn't done by me. You know this, right?" Wrinkles appeared on his forehead.

Sophia was looking through her mother's mail stacked on the counter, "I don't know and that's the truth. Granger, your herbs have been found in the pueblo and almost killed two elderly men. Somehow, someone has found your stash or they took it when the clinic closed. Do you think your partners have something to do with this? Enid wasn't imprisoned until later when they found her fingerprints on the bomb stuff. Who would she have given those bags, seals and herbs to when the clinic was shut?"

He stood up and walked to her, placing his hands on her shoulders, he looked her in the eye, "I have no idea. I had nothing to do with any of these issues."

Lifting his hands from her shoulders, she scolded, "You best find out. Until you do you are the primary suspect! Come on, you must have some idea who took the bags and the herbs? Granger, come on!"

"All right, follow me. But remember, I've been in jail all this time. I'm not guilty, absolutely not!" Leading her out of the backdoor, they walked through the backyard to the warped toolshed. The fluffy clouds were now covering the sun. A soft breeze picked up threatening rain. The naked branches of the tall elm tree next to the barnyard threw strange shadows over the ground in front of the toolshed door. Turning the doorknob, the door remained stuck shut. Throwing his shoulder into the center of the warped wooden door, it barely budged. Granger stood back and kicked the door. Creaking slowly, the door swung open to become stuck onto the wooden floor of the shed. Dust motes floated all around the entry. The stale odor of old oil paint mixed with sawdust filled the room.

Waving his arms in front of his face to disperse the spider webs, Granger reached forward to flip the light switch placed on the inside wall. A dull yellow light illuminated the forgotten room. Stacked in the opposite corner of the room were Papa's oil paintings. In the center of the room was the famous Swedish woodstove Papa had proudly bought to keep him warm while painting his masterpieces. The left side of the room was filled with tools. The smaller tools were hung on pressboard while a worktable was covered with a chainsaw, a planer and other mix-matched items. Spider webs crisscrossed the room from ceiling to floor making a labyrinth of silver threads. Granger's long sleeved shirt was coated with them as he forged his way to a tall hutch filled with shallow drawers. "Come on, I've cleared a path for you. Check this out."

The tall hutch was made up of five layers of drawers that were three across. Each of these narrow drawers were long in length. As they were pulled out, Sophia took note of their holdings. The top drawers had dried flowers, herbs or leaves taped to papers with directions on how to make dyes. Margaret at one time had taken a weaving class and she and Papa had preferred to cart, comb, spin and dye their own wool for her creations. The second layer of drawers held memorabilia. Most of it was Papa's. Old photos of Papa as a boy in a sailor suit with long curls, his Navy Commander photo and a diary. Many of the second layer drawers were of children's pictures, creations or report cards. The third layer had deeper drawers. Each of the drawers was filled with herbs. Herbs on top of brown paper bags, hundreds lined each of the drawers.

The thick odor of dried herbs rafted up to Sophia, "Here we are. The clinic's herbs, then. How did they end up in here?" 181

Shaking a bag out from under the flaking leaves, Granger said, "Mom. Mom bought them from Enid. She was worried about Enid going to jail and leaving her son Alistair homeless or as an orphan." Turning the bag over, Granger pointed to his own handwriting on it, "See, I always, always wrote what was in each bag and the directions on how to use it."

Sophia took the bag from his hand, "What happened to Enid's son?"

Shoving the herbs aside as he grabbed an empty garbage bag covered with dust, he shook his head, "Mom tried to adopt him. Courts wouldn't have it. My lawyer told me Margaret tried to get Charlotte to adopt him or her son who lives in Korea, but the courts insisted he be fostered first and not locally. The poor boy disappeared into the system. Mom was heartbroken."

After a good sneeze, Sophia held the garbage open so Granger could dump the dried herbs into it. "Why was Charlotte involved in all of this?"

Slapping his hands to get the dust off of them, Granger said, "Charlotte and Roberto arrived with the truck when Enid sold the herbs to Mom Margaret. Why do we have to call her Margaret? It is so weird, strange to not call your mother Mom!"

Knotting the garbage bag, Sophia winced at the smell, "So Charlotte and Roberto were involved with the herbs as well? Do you think they could've taken some of the empty bags that had none of your writing on them?"

The black garbage bag was tossed out of the open toolshed door, Granger pulled the drawer all the way open, "Let's see what's back here." He foraged around smelly leaves and yellowed papers. "Of course, Charlotte could've taken whatever she wanted from Mom's. She had the key. Roberto had the key and it appears everyone had a key. It's a wonder there is anything left in Mom's house what with everyone having a key."

Studying Papa's paintings beside her, Sophia shook her head, "You know most of these are really good. Too bad Papa didn't try to have a showing of his work. He was a jack of all trades, huh?"

"Yeah, he was a doctor, a painter, a writer and a fornicator. Yep, he really got around." Granger snickered as he pulled at something from the back of the drawer. "Check this out, what do you suppose these are for?"

Turning her attention back to the drawers, Sophia knelt to poke at the wrapped packages. She lifted one. The yellow tape fell off to powder in the drawer. Carefully, she unrolled the brown butcher paper so fine it dissolved in her fingers. A folded white cloth revealed as the next cover. Slowly, carefully she lifted the white cloth. There in her hand was a batch of eagle feathers. Granger put his fingers around them to hold them up to the light. They unfolded to become a long, large Native American headdress. The feathers flowed from the thick leather strap in Granger's hand to the floor. They had been woven into leather strips to make a magnificent sacred piece. "Wow, who would've thought? Sophia, you do know eagle feathers are illegal to own. How did Papa get ahold of this?"

Twisting to sit, Sophia lifted out the next package. Tape fell, brown butcher paper dissolved as it was unwrapped. The white cloth was opened. "Granger, what was Papa doing with these things? Obviously, they're not legal. Look at this?"

She handed him a pair of moccasins with delicately designed beads. Inside each of the moccasins was a small animal's skull. Granger gently placed it on the bench beside the hutch where he had laid out the headdress. "Open the next one. There are five packages here. Why would Papa have these? Sophia, this is really strange!"

Letting the tape fall from the next package, Sophia said, "Granger, we don't know this was Papa's doing. Margaret may have put these here." She handed him a delicately carved peace pipe. It had been used for there was black char in the bowl and the mouthpiece had teeth marks on it. He smelled the bowl, "Or, someone else could've put these here. Charlotte or Roberto may have hidden these things in here."

"No, don't think so. Charlotte wouldn't have been able to open the door and Roberto wouldn't come in here, would he?" She handed him a large bear fetish carved from jet stone. "Mom was the one who loved all things Native American, right? She would stay at her friend's houses at the Pueblo for feast days, remember?"

More items were placed by the others on the bench, "Remember Roberto and Charlotte put my clinical herbs and bags in here seven plus years ago? They had access to this room and Roberto used the tools in here."

She looked up at him, "Supposedly. Granger, you had to sweep away the cobwebs when you came into this room. Roberto couldn't have used this room regularly or those webs wouldn't have been so thick. Maybe they put the bags and the herbs in here seven plus years ago, but no one has been in here lately." Stretching as she stood, she handed him a bowl filled with cornmeal. A small badger fetish was inside the cornmeal. "The badger is the healer in Pueblo tradition. These things were probably Papa's. You know these are probably valuable and dangerous to own. It's a good thing we found them and not some legal beagle snooping around. Maybe you could ask Mom or Margaret tonight when you visit her in the hospital."

Frowning Granger shook his head, "I'm not going to the hospital! I don't want to see her. While you were out there killing her horse, I called her. Told her you killed her horse. She's not in a good place right now."

Glaring at him, Sophia practically spit on him, "Thank you so much! You really are a bastard aren't you! Damn, Charlotte said you would accuse me!" Pointing her finger at him, she didn't let up, "Granger, you signed the paper! Dr. Murphey will show them to her, you know? He will and if he doesn't, I will!"

Carefully, he took the white cloth and wrapped the items found. "Too bad, she believes I'm her savior and can do no wrong. You're the culprit and you've been fingered, hah!" Clutching the bundle to his chest he walked out of the toolshed, saying, "You might want to close the door behind you!"

Sophia carried two of Papa's paintings as she walked out of the door, mumbling, "You really have no empathy for anyone, do you?" She stopped. "Granger, wait. Wait. Wait a moment."

"What? I'm putting this stuff in the house, what do you want now?"

"How did the bags get into the toolshed? If the toolshed is filled with cobwebs? What about the treasured Navajo baskets of Mom's? Shouldn't they be in the toolshed as well?"

Turning he stared at her, "What do you mean? The bags have been in there for seven years. The spiders spun webs during the seven years. What's strange about that?"

Sophia turned to go through the open toolshed door, "Two things.

The first being that bags were being used just this week with herbs to kill people. If these bags weren't used then where did the bags with the poisonous herbs come from? The bags with the seals on them were used to implicate you, right?"

Granger placed the wrapped items on the back porch table. "O-Kay, I'm following you. But those bags couldn't have been used because of the spider webs. No one has been in there or they would have knocked down the webs." He followed her into the toolshed. The overhead light went on for a minute then the bulb shattered and there was darkness. He pulled out his cellphone to use the flashlight from it. Sophia was gathering up the webbing, rolling it around her hand. She took it outside into the sunlight. The webs sparkled with silver highlights. "Granger, these aren't spider webs. This stuff is sold at Halloween for decoration. Look at the threading, it's some kind of synthetic material."

Holding it in his hands, Granger tried to pull on the webbing. It stretched but didn't break. 'Yep, it's plastic. Why would someone go to all the trouble to place it all over the toolshed?"

Synthetic webbing was rolled into a ball in Sophia's hand. 'We need a better flashlight or a new bulb, but I think the wiring in the light is defective. Let's get Mom's flashlight and look at the floor for footprints." Granger gathered up the white cloth bundle off the porch table to disappear into the house. He returned with a fat flashlight that had a large bulb. "We walked directly to the hutch. Our footprints will match our shoes. Over here there are work boots and someone with small feet going into the main part of the room."

Bending over, Sophia followed the strange prints, "These go then over to the hutch. Here are ladder marks where it was dragged and then placed by the light bulb where all the webbing originated." Granger followed where her finger pointed. The ladder was leaning against boxes in the opposite corner from the hutch. There was no dust on the rungs. Sophia lifted boxes to hand over to Granger. 'Let's find the box with Mom's baskets. It must be in here somewhere." Granger placed the ladder against the hutch. As Sophia handed him closed boxes he opened each one. She started opening boxes as well. 'Here, here's where they must have been." Lifting the box she showed Granger the interior. Mice had eaten the baskets and had made a large nest of dyed willow branches. Granger shook his head, 'Mice. Mom's favorite animal! Those baskets were worth a fortune! Keep looking we may find some not eaten."

After all the boxes had been opened, they gave up. There were no baskets to be found. Granger and Sophia replaced the boxes into the corner. The ladder was put back in the same location where it was found. Sophia decided to leave the roll of webbing on the floor of the toolshed.

This would inform those who had left it that they had been found out and their staged webs were useless. As they jerked the toolshed door closed, Roberto called out from the barn, "Hello? Is there someone here?"

Sophia hurried around the back wall to the barn. Roberto was cleaning out the empty stall shoveling the bloodied manure into the wheelbarrow. He lifted his hand when she walked to him, "Sophia, hi. I thought it best to clean all of this before the Senora came home. I put the eggs in the kitchen. Is Granger here?"

"Hey," Granger walked up behind Sophia, "Roberto, how's it going? Sorry to have one less horse for you to care for, but the old guy was worn out and it was his time to depart this safe haven."

Smacking him on the shoulder, Sophia frowned, "You really have no sympathy, do you? Roberto, Granger told my mother that it was my idea to put the horse down. Granger signed the papers. The poor old horse was dying slowly and it was the best for him, don't you agree?"

Pushing his hat back from his forehead, Roberto nodded, "Si, that old caballo was muerte about two years ago, but he wouldn't lie down. He really wanted to be here for the Senora. His time was now. He didn't need to suffer." He scooped up the manure and dumped it into the barrow. "Senor Granger, it is a good thing you do."

Granger leaned on the stall fence, "Roberto, you have great work boots. Are those the ones made for you because of your feet?"

Shaking his head, Roberto lifted his right foot, "No, the Senora she bought me these boots. My other boots wear out. She buy me these last year. They have good base and won't wear out soon." He dropped his foot and kicked the dirt. "The Senora is very generous." A handkerchief was pulled from his back pocket to wipe his forehead, 'You weren't here when I came. Your daughter was sitting in your van, but she didn't come outside. Do you want me to open the chicken coop now into this stall or should I leave the chickens where they are?"

Turning her back against the fence, Sophia studied Granger and then her vision moved to the toolshed door. The top of the door was clearly visible from where they were standing. Before Granger answered, Sophia asked Roberto, "Didn't you see us in the toolshed? We were right over there."

Roberto shook his head, 'No, I didn't look at the toolshed. I'm busy here. Why would I look over there?"

Granger pushed open the chicken coop gate. The chickens fluttered and then raced out into the open stall. Laughing, Roberto smiled, "Yes, it is good for them to be free and open. They'll lay eggs better. "

Roberto went back to his work. Granger tugged on Sophia's arm, "Let's go inside."

Focused on Roberto, Sophia asked him, 'Did you feed Geordie last night? Because someone did and it wasn't Granger."

Roberto turned his back to her as he raked up the stall, 'No," he said over his shoulder, "I didn't come over here last night. Senora Charlotte wanted me to help her with the Halloween things at her house. I stayed in her guest room."

In the kitchen, Sophia washed her hands. "I need to go. Donna has been waiting for me and she probably needs something to drink and go to the bathroom. Granger, do what you want with this stuff. If it buys you a Mercedes then go for it. I don't want to have it."

He smiled, "Bravo, Sis, you know I wouldn't share it with you anyway. Yes, you better go. If you see Mom tell her 'hello' from me." He didn't turn as he walked down the hall carrying his bundle into the back bedroom. She called after him, "Just remember to be careful who you show the headdress to because you could be arrested for having illegal eagle feathers in your possession."

Donna jumped out of the van when Sophia came around the corner of the outer wall. "Mom, I have to pee. Do you think I could go here? Would Granger mind?"

"I'll go with you." Sophia escorted her daughter into the house to the guest bathroom. Granger's bedroom door was shut. Donna grabbed a cold bottle of water from the fridge as they returned to the van. As Sophia drove home Donna fell asleep in the backseat. The clear skies gave way to blues and purples on the horizon of dusk.

Shonac lifted his head as they pulled in under the tall cottonwood tree. Trotting to the back door of the van, Donna jumped down to give him a hug. "Sweet pup, we're not putting you down."

Sybil opened the front door, "Well, finally, I thought you guys got lost. Clementine returned. She came back with Mr. Casaus. There's been a development. She wants you to call her."

Donna stormed by her, hitting Sybil's shoulder, 'Don't ask about the horse! Don't ask about Geordie!"

Twirling around, Sybil grabbed Donna's arm, "What's with you?"

Sniffing with tears in her eyes, Donna explained to Sybil about Geordie's departure from the farm. The two girls hugged one another as Sophia went inside to the black plastic phone in the hall. She punched in Clementine's cellphone number. All she heard was a recording. Sophia left a message. Her cellphone was put on the charger in her bedroom. Returning to the kitchen, Sophia made dinner. It was eaten quietly for the three of them appeared to be lost in thought. While washing the dishes, Sybil stood on the stool and let down the unicorn blanket over the kitchen window.

Sophia mentioned, "Tomorrow is going to be a crazy day. Everyone needs to be up an hour earlier. We leave here to take Sybil to the Middle School forty five minutes early. Then drive Donna to her private school in Albuquerque. After you are dropped off, Donna, I drive to UNM branch to teach classes in the morning. In the afternoon, I teach here at the Elementary School. Then, Sybil, I pick you up from Middle School and we will pick up Donna in Albuquerque. Got it?"

Sybil shook her head. "Mom, that's crazy. What am I going to do at school for an hour before the bell?"

Donna stared at her mother, "I get picked up late? That's not gonna work. They want all students picked up by three thirty. If you won't be at my school until almost four o'clock, you better get me first!"

Sighing, Sophia hugged her daughters, "We'll figure it out. This will work. Tomorrow is a trial run. I'll talk to the schools. Now, everyone to bed."

Shonac went under the kitchen table. The cats found perspective beds. Sophia locked the doors and turned out the lights. In her bedroom she noticed the blue light flashing on her cellphone. The caller I.D. read Clementine had called and left a message. There was another voice mail from her mother. Changed into her pajamas, Sophia returned Clementine's call.

'Sophia, Mr. Casaus' mother-in-law finally spoke to him about the herbs. He translated for me. Evidently they were given to her by a doctor. She didn't remember the doctor's name, but he handed her the bag two weeks ago. Since they are having a social dance this weekend, she thought she would take the herbs now. That's all I've got, right?"

Sophia put her cold feet under the covers, "Did she remember the name of the doctor?"

There was a silence and then Clementine said, "No. She doesn't speak English very well. Someone recommended this doctor to her. The cousin drove her in his truck to see the doctor. The cousin is back in Arizona and doesn't have a phone." There was a pause, "The only thing the old woman remembered was the man smelled like garlic. That's it, not much, huh?"

Marmalade cat jumped on Sophia's lap. She stroked his fur as she asked, "This means it wasn't Granger because he was in jail. Listen, I'm exhausted. We had to put my mother's horse down today. Granger called Mom and told her it was my idea, but the horse was dying a horrible death from cancer." Two more cats jumped on her bed, Sophia continued, "Granger and I found bags in Mom's toolshed. There are some questions there. Can I talk to you about this tomorrow afternoon? Right now, I'm spent."

Acknowledging exhaustion, Clementine signed off. The cellphone was put back on the charger, the diary was left closed on the bedside table. Sophia turned off the light, hugged the cats and fell asleep.

9

The alarm clock screamed to shock Sophia awake. Five forty in the morning. It was grabbed and turned off in one movement. Standing in front of her window to stretch, she pulled back the sheet. Darkness confronted her. Cats scattered off the bed, down the hall and into the kitchen. Donna screamed from her bed. Sybil's bedroom door slammed shut. Sophia hurried to be first in the bathroom. Sophia banged on the bedroom doors as she placed bowls, cereal boxes and spoons on the long kitchen table. Breakfast was eaten in a hurry. Sophia's professional pull-along was shoved into the back of the van with her thermos of tea. In the kitchen she found Sybil shouting at Donna, "I have to go first because my school is closer than yours so I get picked up first! What's so hard to understand?" Donna pouted as she threw her backpack over her shoulder, 'I should be first and you can go last! I'm the youngest!"

Sybil lifted her heavy backpack from the kitchen table. It was obvious of the weight. Sophia pulled it away, "What's in here that weighs so much? You only need two books, your sack lunch and where's your jacket?"

Grabbing it back, Sybil spoke harshly, "I don't need a jacket and, yes, it is heavy! I have heavy textbooks!"

Sophia unzipped the backpack to pull out two textbooks, a book on Dracula and another fat book on the Myths of Ireland. 'Well, now you have something to read while you wait for first bell, huh?" She zipped it closed. The canvas blue backpack was thrown over Sybil's shoulder, "No privacy in this house! Mom, you have no right to invade my space!" She ran to the van's front passenger seat and slammed the door. The van shook.

In the backseat, Donna fell over as they drove through the narrow farmland road. The Middle School was started by a long standing New Mexico Territorial family. The descendant of Don Mariano S. Otero believed in education. Buying acres of land in the center of the largest population of farmers outside of Rincon, the Middle School was named after him. The Otero family was proud and certain the history of New Mexico should be known to all the farmers and their offspring to honor the long trials and history of Mexico's importance to the land. Don Otero had French relatives who had turned over the earth east of the Sangre de Cristo Mountains when France sold the area to the United States. His grandfather from Mexico bought land after the Treaty of Guadalupe in 1848. When Mexico ceded its northern lands to the United States as a Territory, the United States recognized the Mexican farmers as whites so they were able to vote in the Compromise of 1850. On January 6th, 1912 the mixed cultures of French, Mexicans, and Spanish conquistadores became a state within the U.S.A. The immigrants became White Citizens filled with pride, able to vote. This small Middle School touted the wisdom of Don Mariano S. Otero's ancestry with honor.

The narrow paved road became dirt as the farms on either side had ditches feeding the acreage of alfalfa fields. New Mexico is famous for the channels and ditches. Montgomery Pike wrote in his diary of New Mexico as having as many complicated waterways as Egypt.

The early morning sun was barely rising over the Sandia Mountain. Dark clouds were floating over the western sky slowly turning the world a pastel pink. The goats in the shed next to the road were lying on the warm ground. Turning down the bumpy dirt road into the Middle School's paved entry, Sophia explained, "Donna, I'm going to run and tell the principal about Sybil being dropped off early. Wait here, I'll be right back." Donna did not respond. She appeared to be sound asleep on the backseat with her horse backpack used as a pillow. The van was parked behind a high metal fence with a narrow opening to the main school entry area.

Sybil and Sophia ran up the three cement steps through the heavy metal doors into the silent school. A guard was leaning against the far wall opposite the doors drinking from a thermos of what smelled of coffee. He nodded to them, not moving. Hurrying down the shiny linoleum floor Sophia and Sybil entered the office. Three women turned to stare at them. All three of them held mugs of steaming coffee. Melissa the secretary stared at them, "Sophia, Sybil, what are you doing here now? The school is still closed, legally that is. This is way too early for Sybil to be dropped off."

Sophia explained. A clipboard was handed to her, "You need to fill out all of this paperwork to assure that we are not responsible for her being here at this time without supervision. Please fill out these five pages."

Flustered, Sophia took the clipboard, "I can't do this right now! I have to get Donna to her school and I have minutes to drive into Albuquerque."

The vice principal walked up to the counter. Her short hair was neatly curled behind her ears. The white blouse ironed and her black pants creased to perfection. Her smile had turned to a pinched frown of bright pink lipstick. She pointed to the clipboard with her dangerously long bright pink lacquered fingernails, "If you don't fill out these pages you will need to take her with you. These papers validate that we are not responsible for her while she is here prior to the school being open. We are not insured to cover her while she is here, are you?" Her fingernails tapped loudly on the clipboard, "If you can't read and sign these now, then you need to bring her back and fill out the information." She shook her head, allowing her curls to bounce, "Otherwise she will be here illegally. If you take her with you she will be marked absent. We love Sybil and her flute playing, she's the star of our concerts."

Melissa smiled at Sybil, "Hey, you didn't know that we talk about you behind your back, huh?" She pointed a pen at Sophia, "Please fill this out now? Sybil is one of our best students!"

Taking the pen from the secretary, Sophia sat down on the plastic chairs for waiting parents, "All right. I'll do this right now." Sybil dropped her backpack and in a huff sat next to her mother, "I told you this wasn't going to be simple." Ignoring her, Sophia read the questions, signed the forms and returned the clipboard. "There you go, have a nice day." She waved to them and with her other hand she gave Sybil a one side hug, "You enjoy your day, Sweetheart. We'll figure this out."

Sunlight broke through the high peaks of the mountains. Long shadows appeared drawn on the parking lot's paved area. Sophia jumped into the driver's seat. "Well, one down and one to go." Donna had moved to the front passenger seat, "Mom, that's an awful thing to say about us kids." As Sophia put on her seatbelt, Donna whispered, "We're going to be late. We won't make it in time. If I'm late three days in a row I get suspended. Dad will be totally pissed."

Tightening her jaw, Sophia turned to Donna, "Think good thoughts, daughter dear. We will get there when we get there." They drove out of the farmland to the main road and then onto the freeway. There were lines of cars from Santa Fe struggling to hurry through the traffic jam. Stuck behind two eighteen wheelers, Sophia thought of Don Juan Cabazon and his early morning drives from Albuquerque to El Paso. Finally, they were off the freeway and onto the side streets. Every twenty feet there was a city signal light. Most of the ones Sophia came to were red lights. The medians were planted with flowering chamisa. The yellow pollen a poison to insects and found to be horribly allergic to most people. Though cheap to buy, easy to plant and grow the chamisa was not a good choice.

At a main street where Sophia needed to turn there were detour signs for a water main had broken. Donna groaned with her head in her hands, "Mom, this isn't going to go over well with the tough principal. She won't stand for my being late. She hates people who are tardy! Mom, go. Go! Go!"

Finally finding a street not blocked in this busy city of Albuquerque, there were the flashing yellow lights notifying drivers of a school crossing. As the van entered, the yellow lights went off. "NO!" Donna slammed her hand down hard on her backpack. "This is horrible!"

The School had four parked school buses. They were small standing next to one another at an angle to the left of the school. The tall brown brick building was newly finished two years ago. Advertisements prided the institution as a school for those students who did not do well in large classrooms. They offered private tutoring for a cost after school. The U.S.A. flag waved right before the entryway on a tall pole. Everything was concrete. The parking lot, the steps to the school and the back area for sports. Everything was clean and sterile. The rest of the small parking lot was empty. The area had large arrows designating entrance and exit in loud form. There were no students outside.

Donna jumped down from the van, slamming the door. "Mom, the principal will be upset with us." Sophia tightly held her daughter's hand as they walked up the cement incline to the school. The solid metal door was covered with wood paneling. Sophia grabbed the door handle to pull the door open, but it was locked. A camera with a speaker was above the door. "State your name and purpose of your visit." Donna squeezed her mother's hand to point to the camera.

"Dr. Pino with my daughter Donna Vinder. We are late and she needs to be in class." The door clicked open. Grinding her teeth, Sophia pulled the heavy door towards her and Donna. "I don't like this, Donna. This is similar to the prison where Uncle Granger was incarcerated."

Donna jerked her Mother's hand forward, "Come on. We have to go inside now." The carpeted floor was a soft beige material. The hall smelled of cinnamon. Donna led Sophia to a carved wooden door. There was a bell beside it and a camera above it. The bronze plaque beside the high door handle stated 'Principal.' Donna pushed the bell.

The door clicked to slowly open. Muttering under her breath, Sophia said, "This is like Granger's prison." Sophia shook her head as Donna led her mother into the room smelling of lavender and lemons. Donna brought her to a dark wooden desk. Behind the highly polished desk sat a stern woman with thick glasses. Donna stared at the floor as she introduced Sophia. "Mom, this is Mrs. Monterey. She's the headmaster of this school."

The woman stood. She was large in girth, tall in height and formidable in character. "How do you do? I don't believe I've had the pleasure. Mrs. Vinder is it?" Her wide hand stretched out to Sophia. There were rings on every finger. A large diamond on her ring finger of left hand flashed from the overhead lighting.

Standing tall, Sophia grasped the woman's hand firmly. "No, actually. My name is Dr. Pino. Donna's father and I are divorced. Her father is in the hospital and she is living with me now."

Inhaling through her nose the woman's nostrils flared. "Oh, yes, he spoke of you quite often. You have the brother who is in prison. Is this correct?" The dark red lipstick smeared across her lips was absorbed to flow upward through her wrinkles. The woman's hair was pulled back in a tight French roll. The skin around her hairline reflected the dye used to keep her hair dark brown with no highlights. Her suit was a heavy cloth with a herringbone design. The white silk blouse was accessorized with a pearl necklace of three strings layered. The top of her desk was cleared of all papers. The only item seen on the polished wood was an open laptop with a bowl of chocolate candies on the far left edge. The anglepoise arm of the desk lamp was pulled over the open laptop. A green glass covered the oblong bulb.

Sophia quietly informed Mrs. Monterey of her brother's status, "No. He's no longer in prison. He is living at my mother's farm at the moment. I must apologize for Donna's tardiness, but today it could not be helped." Sophia was about to continue, but she was interrupted.

"There are no excuses allowed in this school. One is expected to do their best or they are to go elsewhere. We will not accept excuses and we will not accept tardiness. I'm sure Donna has explained this to you?" The woman's tight face revealed wrinkles of age. The well placed red smile was a grimace of professionalism more than one of empathy.

Sophia put her arm around Donna's shoulders, 'Yes, Donna did explain. There is another issue you need to be aware of for after school I cannot pick up Donna until three forty five this afternoon. Is this a possibility?"

The woman leaned forward with her plump hands spread out on the desk. Her rigid face remained tight with control, "No. This is not acceptable. All students are to be picked up and removed from this institution by three thirty. No later. Any child left here after that time will have their child taken to Children Youth and Family Division. That is our rule. We never waver. Never. Not for any reason or excuse."

Then the large woman spoke directly to Donna, "You had best go directly to class, Miss Vinder. Please, go now." A button was pushed under the desk. The door behind Sophia clicked open. Donna ran out of the room.

Sophia stood firm. "Excuses are not allowed? What if these are not excuses, but facts? The fact is that I am unable…"

The woman abruptly sat. Her pearls bounced on her pronounced bust, "No. There is no further discussion. You can abide by our rules or you can remove your daughter from her enrollment here at my institution.

I do believe you should leave now. Certainly you have somewhere else to be." The door clicked open.

The air was cold when Sophia walked out of the private school. Now she understood why Geoffrey liked the school. It fit his regime. His need to have everything done precisely his way. Donna must have been living in hell at his house. Sophia started the van and let the heater run. Staring at Donna's school, she shook her head, "Learning is to be pleasant and interesting not a ruthless controlled demand."

Classes at the university went well. Sophia finished entering the roster list on her computer in her cubicle. She called Clementine to ask about Donna being taken to CYFD if she was late. Clementine gave her Bobby's phone number at Children Youth and Family Services. Sophia called Bobby. The bubbly woman's voice became stern when she finally understood what Sophia was asking, "Yes. Mrs. Monterey could bring Donna here and she would serve a complaint against you. If I could, I would pick up Donna, poor kid, she's had a rough time of it what with her Dad and all, but I can't pick her up. It's against regulations." Bobby took a drink and then added, 'If it is humanely possible get Sybil second and pick up Donna first. Sybil strikes me as flexible. The only other solution would be to pull Donna and put her in the Public School system, but you said she doesn't do well at Public?"

Trying to be patient with Bobby's news, Sophia asked, "Where is Mrs. Monterey from? Is she military?"

"Oh!" Bobby laughed, "She should be a drill sergeant don't you think? No, her husband ran the state penitentiary somewhere back east. He was fired for stealing funds. Her family is from a wealthy political family, I don't remember who. Be careful with her, she's ruthless. We have had seven children in here thanks to her and she pressed charges to have them removed from their homes and put in Foster Care. Luckily Judge Salazar refused."

"Wow," Sophia sighed, "She's not someone who is flexible then?"

"Absolutely not." Bobby spoke firmly, "In my honest opinion Donna has had enough trauma in her life. As a social worker I would recommend that now she is living with you, have her go to a school closer to where you live or where Sybil goes to school. She needs stability but not imprisonment."

Sophia smiled, "Thank you, Bobby! Thank you, so much! Geoffrey felt the school was good because of the expense of it. Donna was so frightened this morning. I don't like to see her afraid to go to school. Thank you, Bobby!" They ended the call on a good note.

Speaking to the computer in front of her, she said, "This is where I need a partner to help me. Damn. The buses don't go to Alcon from Sybil's school."

The clock reminded Sophia of her time limit. She drove to the Alcon Elementary School for Story and Writing Classes. The third and fourth grade teachers had her come once a week to tell a story to the students, leaving off the ending. The students then were excited with the stories ending in high suspense to write their own ending in their notebooks. Their work was graded and this helped their interest in being literate and creative. Sophia loved these young students and always appreciated their teachers' input. Today, Sophia felt overwhelmed. When the bell rang ending her last class, Sophia didn't even stop to speak with the teacher, she ran out of the building to the old van.

It was two thirty and she had to pick up Donna no later than three thirty. Driving to the Otero Middle School she ran into the building to ask Melissa if Sybil could be excused early from her art class. She would only miss the last thirty minutes of art. The vice principal met her in the hall, "This isn't going to work, Dr. Pino. Sybil needs to have stability. She's of an age where she needs a routine that works. Please, figure out how to make this work so it is best for her, not you." Smiling, she put her hand on Sophia's shoulder. "If you need to talk, please, call me and we will figure out a way for this to work best for Sybil, o-kay?"

Melissa called Sybil's art classroom. Sophia signed Sybil out and waited in the hall. The guard was leaning against the far wall across from the girls' bathroom. He was studying his cellphone. As Sophia was about to ask him if he actually walked up and down the halls, Sybil hurried to meet her mother, "Did you sign me out?" They hurried to the van. The Dracula book was held in Sybil's hand as she quietly read while Sophia drove.

A tractor was slowly making its way down Otero road to the paved road. Once on the paved road, she drove onto the interstate. The three lanes were down to two lanes due to an accident. The off ramp where Sophia needed to exit the interstate had another accident. A truck had hit an elderly woman's Saab. Two police cars were blocking traffic with their lights flashing. Sophia shook her head, "This isn't going to work, you know? Somehow this isn't going to work, not at all."

The water main had been fixed as Sophia drove the van down the wet street. Flashing yellow school lights slowed all traffic. Sophia studied the front of the tall brick school. There was a line of cars parked outside of the school. This institution rated a police officer who was guiding traffic. Realizing she was on the wrong side of the street in order to be in line with parental cars, Sophia drove on to the next street. In someone's driveway she turned around and headed back to the school. Parking behind a metallic silver Jaguar with white leather seats and a sunroof, Sophia prayed Donna wouldn't be in trouble. Glancing in the rearview mirror she watched a tall red Mercedes Benz SUV pull behind her.

Dracula's book was put down on the floor of the van. Sybil studied the car in front of the van and then stared at the tall red Mercedes behind them. She patted the dashboard, "Good old van, you have taken us places those other cars would never dream of going. You be dirty, you be happy and you be ours!"

Sophia laughed, "You tell it like it is, girl!" She patted the dashboard as well. Then they both saw Donna standing next to a serious man.

Quickly, Sybil leapt out of the van to race up to Donna and gave her a big hug. The male teacher immediately separated them with his thick hands. Sophia watched as the male teacher pointed his finger at Sybil speaking with his chin down and his eyes critical. Sybil stood with her hands on her hips to listen. Sophia watched Sybil as her foot started to tap on the cement sidewalk. "Oh, no, this isn't going to be good." Sophia started to unhooked her seatbelt, but stopped to watch. Sybil grabbed Donna's backpack and flung it at the man's lower abdomen. He bent over double as the pack hit him. His hands were between his thighs. Sybil shouted something that turned heads. Quickly, the two daughters walked to the van. Glaring at the Mercedes behind them, Sybil slid open the back door for her sister and then she jumped in behind her.

Sophia started the engine. "What was that all about? Dare I ask?" She glanced in the rearview mirror to see Donna's reflection. Donna was smiling, "I think I've been expelled, thanks to my pushy sister."

In a huff Sybil loudly explained, "That turd! He told me Donna had to stand there until our vehicle reached her. There was no allowing for students to be rushing about and getting run over by careless parents. I told him that you were not careless and he was an idiot! Then I hit him!" She jumped up and down in her seat to finally put on her seatbelt. Hugging Donna, she turned to watch the school disappear through the rear window, "Idiot! What a fool! Donna, is he one of your teachers?"

"Yeah, he's my math teacher. He slaps our desks with a ruler if we get the wrong answer. His wife just had a baby and she's divorcing him. He's in a real bad mood all the time." Donna leaned sideways into her sister, "Thanks. I really hated that school. I hope Dad won't be too angry."

Twisting in her seat, Sybil asked, "Aren't you getting good grades here? I thought you liked it and you were getting good grades?"

Frowning, Donna answered, "No, not really. You have to get an A in every class. You have to! You have to do the work over and over and over again until you get an A, even if it takes you all of your life! Yeah, I got

A's, but I hardly ever advanced into the next class. I couldn't sleep or eat or do anything! We aren't allowed to have friends because then we might cheat off their work."

Twisting the backpack's straps, she stared at her mother in the rearview mirror, "Every Monday the classroom's announcement system orders us to not be friendly with the other students. We're told we are the best we can be and we can all be winners if we give it our best. No excuses are allowed, blah, blah, blah." Then she poked Sophia's shoulder, "Mom, now what? Now where do I go to school?"

Sophia shook her head. "I have no idea. We have entered a new interplanetary universe. This is a life in progress." The cellphone on the console chirped. At the red light, Sophia picked it up. "Oh, dear, it's your school, Donna." The city signal light turned green. "I better call them when we get home. No ice cream today, folks, this driver is tired out." The cellphone chirped again.

Sybil reached forward from the backseat to grab it and answer her Mom's cellphone, "Hello?" Sophia tried to grab it from her, but Sybil was too fast. She watched Sybil smile, "Grandma or Margaret? How are you? Donna just got expelled from her school! Yeah, ain't that great? What?" She turned to Sophia, "Grandma hung up on me. Evidently, she only wanted to speak to you and I'm a brat, huh."

Putting on the turn signal for Rincon, Sophia decided to visit her mother in the hospital. "You do know we need to visit your father, girls? He's been in the hospital now for a day or so and he has no other family here. Let's go and see if he needs anything and be nice to him."

Giggling Donna said, "Yeah, we could take him a bag of garbage and some cat pee from the kitty litter box in his house."

Sybil shrugged, "What would we take him? He's diabetic so he can't eat chocolate or candy. He doesn't like cut flowers and he's on special medication for high blood pressure. What would he like?"

Sophia made a U-turn and drove back into the University. "You go and visit him while I go to my cubicle and do some work, how about that?"

The girls kicked the back of her driver's seat, "No, you have to come. You're the one with the money, Mom!"

The University Hospital Parking was hell. There was a parking structure of four levels. Each level was filled. Even some of the cars had parked in the loading and unloading spaces. Three blocks away from the hospital Sophia found a place to park the old van. There was a meter that took only quarters and thankfully the girls had plenty of quarters that they used in the machines at the schools. The midafternoon sun brought a strong breeze blowing white plastic bags across the roads. Bare trees waved in the wind. A string of cars waited at the signal light to turn onto the main street.

Arm in arm, the three walked into the sliding glass doors of the University Hospital. The elderly woman in a pink coat at the information desk gave them Geoffrey's room number, but explained that the girls had to be older than twelve to visit. Sophia assured her they were all over the age of twelve. The elevator dinged and opened as three women exited. The moving carriage smelled of perfume. On the third floor, Geoffrey's room was quickly found by the clever daughters. Sophia stood outside, "You two go on in and hug your Dad. I'm staying out here. There is no reason for me to upset him. You go ahead."

She leaned against the green wall. Nurses hurried past her. Some asked if she was lost. Suddenly the door opened and Geoffrey stood there with the two girls on either side of him. "Mom, we got Dad upright. He almost fell over twice. His butt crack shows when he stands up!"

Holding the back of his gown closed with his right hand, he growled at Sophia, 'So, you've been busy. You got Donna expelled from her school! You've managed to continue killing people with your brother." His red face appeared naked without his thick lensed glasses. The blue eyes were horribly bloodshot. Spitting words came from his chapped scabbed lips, "What's this about you having an affair with your neighbor who barrel races?"

Leaning towards her, his body fell. The girls grabbed him to hold him tightly to stand. Spit flew from his mouth, "Sophia! Where the hell am I supposed to live now? Huh! Where the hell am I supposed to live! Where are my clothes, my things, my pets and my life! What have you done to me?" Shaking radically, his arms around the girls, he added, "You have killed me!" Tears fell down his pale cheeks.

Standing at an angle ready to run, Sophia shook her head, "Geoffrey, I haven't done anything to you. You have done this to yourself." Her purse strap was pulled up on her shoulder as she kept her hands around it, "I didn't call anyone about your house or your life choices. I had nothing to do with your poor decisions. This is all on you, Mister!"

Her lips pressed together, Sophia turned and walked hurriedly down the hall. She stood at the elevator and pushed the down button. A person in scrubs walked out of the elevator to hear Sophia say, 'I have nothing to say to that man. Nothing." She got into the elevator as the doors closed. Downstairs Sophia bought three bottles of water, three candy bars and a magazine. She sat with her full package in the front entry waiting room and read the magazine. Half an hour later the girls arrived. Sybil was the first to approach her, "Mom, what's with you? All he wanted was some information."

Standing, Sophia handed Donna the bag with their things in it. "No, he didn't. He wanted to accuse me of being a failure as a mother. I'm not in the mood. Let's go and be verbally attacked by Margaret. Then we're going home." They walked out into a stronger wind. Donna took Sophia's hand, "Mom, if anything this was all my fault. Dad would've died if we hadn't done what we did, right?"

Squeezing her daughter's fingers, Sophia quietly answered, "I don't know, dear, I really don't know. What happened, happened and now everyone has to make new choices. Hopefully, they will be good choices." Leaves in clusters blew into the street from the back of a small house's backyard. Sybil caught up to them as she drank her water, "Doesn't Dad have a younger brother somewhere? I know Stephen is in the Navy somewhere overseas. But can't Dad stay with his younger brother and start over?"

Donna twisted the cap off of her water bottle, "Yeah, he can't live with us, can he? I mean he'd just junk up our house, right? Dad doesn't like horses, he hates them and he told me so! He wouldn't buy me my horse backpack until I refused to go to school."

In the van with the seatbelts fastened, Sophia thought out loud, "I did consider having Geoffrey come and live with us until he found his way. But that would be like being married all over again and I just can't do that, not again. We're free and now we can make our own choices." Then she added, "Within reason of course, only within reason and within our budget." All she heard was the sound of candy bars being chewed.

The drive to Rincon was easy. The back roads were taken as the interstate at five o'clock to six o'clock is a rat race. Driving through the quiet streets out of Albuquerque was relaxing. The daughters talked quietly in the back seat as Sophia studied the farms, the fields, the animals and the high flying cranes. This hospital on the hill had tumbleweeds smashed against the west side. Sophia chose to park on the east side by the side entrance. Racing through the parking lot they went through the front rotating doors. They stopped at the gift store to buy Margaret a Get Well card, a small handful of pink carnations that smelled like wax and some chocolate in a golden wrapper.

Margaret's visit went as expected. She cried and screamed about Geordie being put down and her not being there to say goodbye. Then she interrogated Donna about the school and why she was expelled. This information appeared to please Margaret to no end. "Good, you don't need to go to some hoity totty school. You're a real person not some phony snob. Come here, give you're Margaret a hug." Cautiously Donna allowed herself to be embraced. Sybil stepped back with her hands in the air. Sophia asked Margaret, "Do you know what happened to Granger's herbs when he went to prison? Have you stashed some of his herbs somewhere or given them to someone else? Be honest, Margaret, please, be honest!"

Margaret fell back on her pillows, "Now, why would I do such a thing?" Her gnarly fingers pushed her bangs off her forehead, "It was Katrina. Granger's lesbian girlfriend came back after his last court hearing and she demanded to take Granger's herbs, bags, jars and even his seals with her. She's a lesbian, you know? The girls know about lesbians, right?" She nodded to Donna and Sybil who were staring out the hospital room window.

"Margaret, Katrina was long gone by the time you were in your accident. You gave Katrina money to disappear. She was far away from all of us when Granger went to court or you were in the accident." Sophia sat in the white chair by the bed.

Shaking her head, Margaret was adamant, "No, Sophia, that woman or lesbian, you can't call her a woman can you? She was greedy. She was nasty. She came back to my home and she demanded Granger's things! Even his toothbrush! She took almost all of his stuff!"

Sybil turned from the window to look at her grandmother, "How could she do that? You were in the hospital. Uncle Granger was in jail. There was no one at your house. How did she get in? How did she take his stuff and how did you know all about this?"

Sophia watched Sybil's grownup attitude and then she turned her attention to Margaret, "Yes, how did you know this?"

Straightening the folded sheet covering her chest, Margaret smiled, "Charlotte told me. Charlotte had the key to my home. She said Katrina was threatening to break the windows to get inside and so Charlotte let her inside to get Granger's things."

This time Donna asked in her twelve year old voice, "Why would Charlotte let someone she didn't know into your home? That's just crazy, Grandma."

Sophia stood, "Margaret, I think we should go. This has been a very busy day and you must be tired. I'm sorry about Geordie, but now he isn't in pain. Granger will be told to visit you."

Slowly walking to the end of her Grandmother's hospital bed, Donna said, "Granger signed the papers to put Geordie down, Grandma. Mom was there to help him with the vet. Dr. Murphey said if you didn't put Geordie down he would call the Animal Protection people and have you put in jail." Then she patted Margaret's feet under the sheets, "I'll miss Geordie, too."

The drive home was quiet. Donna fell asleep in the backseat. Sybil read her book. Sophia was pleasantly surprised at the quiet weather outside. Shonac ran to the van when she parked. Donna hugged him as Sybil ran into the house shouting, "I'll fix a celebratory dinner!" Sophia sat in the driver's seat watching the horses graze. It was only seven o'clock and the sun hovered high over the western horizon. Stepping out of the van, she spoke to Donna, "Say, you fancy a ride before dinner? Those horses are supposed to be ridden three times a week. I could do with a pleasant ride, how about you?"

"Yes!" Donna hugged Sophia, "What am I going to do about school?"

"Honey, I don't know. I honestly don't know right now. I'm going to change. I'll call the school to find out what they want, but right now we are floating between schools. Let's enjoy our time of freedom, shall we?"

Running to the front door, Donna called out, "Yes! Freedom!"

The school counselor answered Sophia's call. "Dr. Pino, is it?"

"Yes, it is Dr. Pino. How can I help you?"

"We regret to inform you that your daughter Donna Vinder is no longer enrolled in our institution. Please accept our empathy because of your decision."

Sophia's voice became professional, "I shall accept your empathy. Thank you, very much. I can't believe it took me this long to dis-enroll her." She hung up quickly before her mood changed.

The horses brushed and saddled, Sophia and Donna trotted down Alcon Road to the clear ditch. As they jumped the final ditch turnout, a voice called out to them. Juan cantered up behind them on his sorrel barrel racing horse. "Hey, want some company? You guys are home late."

Smiling at him, Sophia said, "Ah, yes, the ears and eyes thing. We have family in the hospital and had to visit them after school."

Trotting, his deep voice carried, "There are more cranes by the river. This means the weather is going to turn cold. Donna, don't you barrel race on your Tracy horse?"

Slowing Tracy down to be even with his horse, Donna agreed, "Yeah, I'd love to barrel race her, but I don't know the rules and I don't have any barrels."

Patting Tracy on the rump, Juan said, "Problem solved. Come over this Saturday on Tracy and we'll put her through her paces. Oh, watch out for that hole. The gophers are going under and there are holes all over the place."

Cantering at a fast pace, the three of them raced around the gopher hill up to the top hill overlooking the reservation. Sophia studied the squat adobe houses that were way below them. Smoke rose out of most of the chimneys. There was a drumming practice going on and the sound echoed up to them. Juan circled his horse around Sophia's, "There is news of herbs hurting the locals. Do they have anything to do with you?"

"No." Sophia studied Juan's face. His dark brown eyes showed concern. His hair fell over his forehead and just to the collar of his blue chambray shirt. Swallowing, she continued, "I was asked about the herbs since my brother used to prescribe herbs to heal the sick. He's just out of prison, if you must know and he had nothing to do with this."

Kicking her horse, she galloped up the hill and down the other side to the diversion channel. Fast flowing water churned into the channel going to the main ditch. River water flowed straight through the diversion and back into the river bed. There standing in the shallow water was a flock of long legged white cranes. The deep throated purring warned of danger. Sophia pulled her horse to the side, trotting away from the flock. Juan and his horse were soon behind her, "Sophia, I wasn't accusing you of anything. I was just asking."

Donna trotted Tracy right between them. "Juan, I'm not in school anymore. Can I come over tomorrow and you could show me how to barrel race then?"

A deep long laugh came from Juan, "No, Donna! I have to work to live and tomorrow I work. Why aren't you in school tomorrow? Are you on a holiday I've never heard of?"

Donna pushed her long hair behind her shoulders, "No, I've been expelled. My mother can't get me to school on time and they don't allow tardy students in the school." She glared at Sophia.

Changing the direction of her horse, Sophia added, "Yes, this is all my fault. You see Donna's ex-school was paid for by my ex-husband and that school is in Albuquerque in the northeast heights. This driver here," And she pointed to her chest, "Yes, this driver here couldn't manage driving from Rincon to Albuquerque's northeast heights at Superwoman speeds! The school fired me and expelled Donna."

Licking his lips, Juan clapped his hands, "Bravo! This appears to work well for both of you. Where's the classy Sybil? Is she the one cooking dinner?"

Donna's smile filled her whole face, "Yes, I'm so glad I don't have to go back to that school! The principal is evil and the teachers are all getting divorced!"

In a softer voice, Sophia explained, "Sybil is fixing us a celebratory dinner. If you interested, you're invited?"

His reins were pulled tight as he backed his horse out of their close proximity, "No, sorry, I can't. I have a date with a nine year old. My son and I are going to Pizza Hut for dinner tonight, but some other time I would be pleased to join."

Donna explained to Juan all about her miserable experience at the expensive school. Sophia trailed behind watching the clouds. A large flock of geese flew overhead to the west. Slowly, the sun fell onto the horizon. Pastel colors decorated the October evening sky. Patting her horse's neck, she quietly whispered, "I am tired. This has been a strange day and I'm tired."

Juan cantered with them to Alcon Road. Turning in the saddle, he questioned, "Why don't you women come over to my house about eight? I'll fix us an excellent desert? How about it?"

Sophia and Donna stood the horses at the tie down. Donna insisted on walking, brushing and feeding the horses in order for Sophia to call Clementine. First Sophia walked to the chicken coop to throw feed at her strange collection of hens and her rooster Faust. The eggs in her hands, she stepped out of the coop. Clementine's vehicle drove into the farm. As her window rolled down, she called to Sophia, "Hey, how about a hug? I heard from your oldest that you've had a rough day! How about it?"

The two woman hugged as Sophia explained about Donna's school ordeal. Clementine smiled, "You know there are some really good Charter Schools around here. They have small classes and a bus. There's a Charter School called Los Vecinos and its right next to the store." She pointed down Alcon road," Right over there. They are fussy about the students they take, so be aware they may or may not take her. It might be wise to get her transcripts first before approaching them. What do you think?"

Noticing Clementine, Donna ran to her waving the horse brush in her hand, "Hey, you want to help me? You like horses, right?"

Clementine took the brush from Donna's hand, "Sure. Let me help. Your sister invited me for dinner. Do you think I should stay?"

Jumping up and down, Donna clapped, "Yes! Oh, yes, and I have to tell you about my school, well, it isn't my school anymore. Come on!"

The eggs were carefully held in Sophia's hands as she entered the kitchen. "I guess you invited Clementine for dinner, huh, Sybil?" She pulled the egg cartoon from the fridge and placed the five eggs in it. "You know you could've asked me first, right?"

Sybil clapped white flour from her hands, "Mom, you weren't here. You were out riding with what's her face?" She put a coated white finger to her nose, "Huh? My sister, right? Clementine has some important questions for you and she's at the end of her shift. What could it hurt for her to stay for dinner, huh?"

Sophia chuckled, "Do you know that when we are around Clementine we only ask questions? I think that's weird."

Sybil dunked the sliced eggplant into the flour mixture then tossed the slices into the hot frying pan with oil. "Dinner's going to be good. The chicken should be ready in twenty minutes, the eggplant just right and I'm reheating last night's rice. Yummy."

The bread box was opened to find it was empty. Sophia pulled out the large bowl. Yeast, warm water, sugar and three eggs were all blended together. Two cups of flour added and then covered with a clean dish towel to stand on the warm stove. The wooden spoon was placed in a bread pan as Sophia turned to Sybil, "You do know how serious this is about Donna being expelled from school? This will take effort and work to get her into another. She now has a reputation for being tardy and all because Geoffrey is in the hospital."

Dancing in circles around her mother, Sybil smiled, "Well, yeah. I mean now she's living with us. We're the real deal. She needs to be in the real world not hidden away with those school people who believed they are perfect and are too afraid to be stupid or dumb."

"What? What do you mean by stupid and dumb, young lady?"

"Well, we know that Donna doesn't like school as a matter of fact she absolutely loathes it. If she's in a smaller school the teachers might try harder for her to like it, that's all. Don't get all testy, Mom." She went back to frying her eggplant.

The dinner conversation was mostly about Donna's school and the Charter School. Donna seemed eager to try the Charter School. Sybil was anxious for Donna to go to the Charter School for she could walk to it and Sybil wouldn't be compromised at her school. Sophia listened. After dinner the girls went into Sybil's room and shut the door. Clementine insisted on helping to wash and dry the dishes.

"Sophia, there is something you need to appreciate about the United States and Geoffrey. You do know there are laws that protect citizens, right?"

Handing a dripping plate to Clementine, Sophia smiled, "Well, let's see. Geoffrey lives in the United States. He is a citizen. What are you trying to tell me?"

"I checked with Adult Protective Services. They have a wellness check they do on elderly people who live questionably perhaps in garbage or in a hazardous environment." The wiped plate was stacked on top of the other clean, dried plates. "It appears if Geoffrey wishes to live in filth, but it is not true garbage. It is his inalienable right to live as such. The problem arose with Donna living with him. She is underage and she has chosen to not live in filth. Geoffrey is an adult, right?"

Another wet plate was handed to Clementine as Sophia asked, "Therefore Geoffrey can stay in his house?"

"Ah, yes, but there is a catch." Clementine pulled her long blonde hair back from her face to wrap it around her fingers and knot it behind her head. "He is now a suspect in a murder inquiry. A suspect in several murder inquiries as a matter of fact. Did you know that Geoffrey had brown bags, several sheets of Granger's seals and a large box of herbs?"

Shaking the soap suds from her fingers, Sophia turned to stare at Clementine, "Geoffrey?" Then she noticed Donna had come into the kitchen and was foraging in the cookie jar for her favorite type of cookie. "Sweetie, did you know your father had Granger's bags, herbs and special red and gold seals?"

A chocolate chip cookie with icing was held in Donna's hand half way to her mouth, "Yep, Grandma insisted he buy them. She was wanting to adopt Alistair."

"What? Alistair? Henker and Enid's son? Why would she want to adopt him? She thought they were all Nazis and were from some dark family who immigrated here."

Shrugging her shoulders, Donna ran back into Sybil's room. Clementine asked, "All right, now I am out of the loop. Who are Henker and Enid and what does Alistair have to do with all of this?"

Hot water was added to the wash sink as Sophia explained, "Henker was Granger's partner in the Health Clinic. Henker has a degree in Chinese Medicine and was the only one who could actually give out prescription herbs. Granger has his certificate in acupuncture, but not in Chinese Medicine. They worked as a team. Henker had no interest at all in herbs, he was interested in the cures available through meditation, shock therapy and holistic types of stuff. Enid is Henker's wife."

Two more dishes were wiped dry and added to the stack set aside in front of Clementine, "So who's Alistair?"

"Alistair was there four year old son, who is now about eleven or twelve. When both of his parents were taken into custody and put in prisons, he was put in foster care. Evidently, my dear mother Margaret wished to adopt him as some sort of reparation."

The last of the washing up was done. Clementine draped the dish towel over the handle of the fridge. "Where is Alistair now?"

Shaking her head, Sophia cleaned the bottom of the kitchen sink with her hand, "Who knows? Although, I bet Charlotte would know. Charlotte was involved with many of the clinic's things. Margaret was too weak to be involved because she was still in the hospital when the clinic was ordered to close and be emptied."

Sybil came into the kitchen, "Mom, Donna dropped cookie crumbs all over my bed and she's bragging about not having to go to school now. Is this true?" The cookie jar was opened and she took out two cookies. "I don't want to go out trick or treating this Halloween if it's all the same to you. Besides I volunteered to be on the decorating committee for the gym dance."

Clementine pulled out a kitchen chair and sat down to watch the mother and daughter in conversation. Sophia dried her hands on the dish towel, "You volunteered for something? I'm impressed and Yes, your sister does have to go to school. We're just trying to figure out where. Who's helping with the decorating of the gym? You're art teacher?"

Both cookies had been eaten. Sybil's long curly hair was in her face as she stared at the kitchen floor, "Mom, you make me sound like a Grinch. Yes, I volunteered, besides Robby will be there, too. He dared me to join and he's a turd face."

"Oh, wow, a turd face, huh? Who's the adult helping out with the decorating?"

"Oh, you know people from the community. I think Charlotte will be there. She loves stringing up the webs with some type of glue she designed with her late husband. He liked to build things and make things. Her back room is full of all kinds of neat stuff for decorations." Sybil grabbed another cookie, "Besides her I think Mr. Flores will be there, too. He has the Art Store in Rincon and the school is buying some supplies from him."

Leaning against the kitchen counter, Sophia plied her daughter, "Charlotte makes webs, huh? Are they silver and have sticky stuff all over them?"

"Yeah, something like that. She's really cool. Well, I'm going to finish my English report. Night, guys." Sybil walked into her bedroom and slammed the door. Dirt fell from the crack over the dirt frame to the floor. The pile was getting larger.

Clementine watched Sophia's facial expression. "You are certainly curious about Charlotte's webs, huh?"

The kettle was flipped on beside Sophia, "It's just a thought. Say, would Geoffrey be able to return to his home soon? Tomorrow in fact? Would that be possible?"

Clementine was handed a mug and a teabag. The honey jar and two lemons were cut and put on a plate in the center of the table. Clementine dropped her teabag into her mug, 'Now, I do believe he can. The investigative team has gone through his house. He will be required to have it cleaned. Adult Protective Services has a cleaning crew that can come in and clean up the worst of it for no cost. But they will be monitoring the condition of the house once he is living in it."

Sophia pulled her cellphone from her pants pocket. "Would it be all right if I gave him a quick call since it is almost eight and they shut off the phones in the hospital at eight?"

"Sure, the man who will be monitoring him is named Mr. Ferguson. He will be attending the cleaning crew the first time they come. You might let him know to be prepared the crew will arrive in hazmat suits and gloves with masks. The place is mighty bad."

Sophia walked into the long hallway between the kitchen and the back rooms to call Geoffrey. He picked up the phone at the first ring. Sophia cautiously spoke, "Geoffrey, it's me Sophia. Don't hang up, please." He hung up. She dialed again and waited. It rang four times and finally he picked up, "What do you want? You've done enough damage to my life!"

"Listen, please, just listen. You will be able to return to your home. Adult Protective Services will have a cleaning crew come into your home and clean it. This is free of charge. You can return as early as tomorrow if you're well enough to be released and I can drive you home, if you want me to."

"What? I can't hear you! Did you say I can return to my home? My clothes, my place of existence are there for me? You aren't going to throw me out so I can live under a bridge in Albuquerque?" His voice became gruff.

"Geoffrey, you can be polite and allow me to drive you home or you can take a taxi. Either way you can go home. Good night." This time she hung up on him.

Clementine was pouring the hot water into the mugs when Sophia returned to the kitchen. "What did he say? Is he pleased?"

Sophia shook her head, "He's a bastard. He's angry and pissed and always has a burr under his girth and won't be nice if it kills him."

"Oh, sit down and drink your tea. You'll feel better." Clementine put the kettle back on the counter. "Now, tell me about Charlotte and the web interest?"

The hot mug of tea was twirled in Sophia's hand, "Granger and I went into the toolshed at Margaret's just to check things out. The door at the back sticks and Granger had to kick it open. Once inside there were spider webs crisscrossed from ceiling to filthy floor. Both of us believed the webs were spiders' webs. Although they were thick and silvery. We found Mom's old hutch where she put her most valuable items." She took a sip of the hot tea after blowing on it.

Continuing, she went on to say, "In the hutch were Granger bags, herbs and again pages and pages of the famous clinic seal. There was the thought that they had been there for all the years Granger was imprisoned, but then once we were leaving the toolshed, I noticed the sparkling of the webs and the sticky matter. We both believed the webs had been strung to give the appearance of age that no one had been inside the toolshed for ages." She pulled out the teabag from the mug, "It was the false image of the webs to show no one had entered for the length of time it would take many spiders to weave all those many webs."

Holding her mug of tea up to blow on it, Clementine asked, "You think Charlotte who makes these webs was responsible for the webs in the toolshed?"

"It would be a great coincidence, wouldn't it? Roberto works for Charlotte. Charlotte knew Mary Peters. Charlotte has Roberto staying with her because he is uncomfortable staying in the house where Rosa died." She poured some honey into her mug, "This would be a horrible accusation if it were true. Charlotte is Mom's best friend in the whole world."

Standing, Clementine walked to Donna's back bedroom and knocked on the door, "Donna, can you come into the kitchen for some tea and a conversation with your Mom and me?"

The bedroom door quickly opened. Donna was in her horse pajamas with her long hair loose to her lower back. Her bare feet padded into the kitchen ahead of Clementine, "Sure, if I can have another cookie or two."

A soft laugh from Clementine to say, "I thought you were full from dinner. Now you want more dessert?"

"Well, yeah, I'm a growing girl, you know?" Donna sat at the kitchen table next to her Mom. "What's up?"

Four cookies were placed on a plate in front of Donna by Clementine who sat down opposite the two of them. "Who brought the bags to your Dad's house? You said Margaret wanted your Dad to buy them, but she was in the hospital. So who brought the bags to your father's and why?"

Donna studied the cookies, "These aren't my favorites, but I'll eat them anyway. Roberto and Charlotte brought the bags in Roberto's truck. Margaret or Grandma called Dad the night before begging, really begging for Dad to buy the stuff. Dad had refused. He said the Pino's were a bunch of killers and he didn't want anything to do with them." Donna shoved a cookie into her mouth. The two women watched her chew.

Then Donna stood to get a mug and poured milk into it. "I don't need tea." She sat back down next to her Mom. "So, Grandma started crying I guess. Dad is a real sucker for women who cry. He agreed to buy the stuff but only for twenty dollars. Grandma wanted him to pay a hundred! A hundred dollars for a bunch of junk!" She sipped her mug of milk. "He was red in the face. He poured himself a plastic cup full of booze and guzzled it down while he was talking to her! She went on and on and on until he snapped at her. He said forty dollars was all, if she wanted more than that she could go to the Judge and ask him. Then he slammed down the phone."

Clementine studied Donna's face, "When did they bring the stuff to your Dad's house? Were you there?"

"Oh, yeah, I was there and I was expected to help. I mean it wasn't heavy or anything, but this had nothing to do with me. I don't even like Uncle Salamander slime bucket!"

The investigative detective sat back in her chair, "Uncle Salamander slime bucket is your name for Granger?"

"Yeah, he makes us sick. Especially Sybil. She practically throws up when she's around him."

"All right, what did you unload and who was in charge of accepting the money?"

"That's simple. Charlotte knocked on the door. It was after dinner. Dad took me out to dinner because all he had was slime in the fridge. We went to Twisters. I was about to go into my room and do my homework because at the old school you have to have an A in every subject and do the work over and over again until you have an A. So I was walking down the hall to my bedroom when there was a knock on the door." Donna swallowed some more milk.

"Dad wasn't going to answer it. He was in the bathroom. He has bathroom issues. I answered the door, holding onto Freddy Dad's dog." She took another sip of milk. 'It was Charlotte. Behind her was Roberto with a box. Charlotte told me that Dad wanted this stuff and where should they put it and would I bring in the two bags that were on the seat in the truck and where was my father anyways."

Clementine got up to get Donna another cookie. She put it on the plate in front of Donna who appreciated the gesture, "These are my favorites. Well, Dad finally came out of the bathroom. They stood in the middle of the kitchen staring at all the stuff Dad has piled on top of everything. The sink was filled with dirty dishes and cockroaches because he won't wash dishes, he puts them in the dishwasher and the dishwasher hose leaks. So the sink gets fuller and fuller."

Donna chewed her cookie and the women tried not to stare. Finally, she went on, "Charlotte asked Dads if he had a cleaning lady. That wasn't good. Immediately he got angry. You know, his favorite emotion. Anyways they placed the stuff on the kitchen table on top of all the other stuff and Charlotte asked Dads for the forty dollars. She had been told by Grandma to collect or else." Donna stood up and pushed in her chair, "That's it. That's all. I'm going to bed. Mom, do I have to get up with you guys in the morning or can I sleep in?"

Sophia hugged her Donna as she stood next to her, "You have to come with us. You're not old enough to stay home alone, not yet. Besides we're going to check out a Charter School right over here by us. What do you think?"

Shaking her head, Donna frowned, "I think I know everything I need to know. I don't need any more school. I'm done with it. I'm going to bed." She flung her long hair behind her shoulder, "Good night, Clementine. Hope you find who's killing everybody. See you in the morning, Mom." Donna's thick glasses were pushed up her nose as she stomped off to her bedroom.

Clementine finished her tea, "Well, that was certainly enlightening. Wonder what your mother knows about all of this? Do you think you could give her a quick call?"

The hall clock chimed eight. "No, the phones are turned off and she won't use a cellphone. I can ask her in the morning. This is strange though that Roberto is involved in this with Charlotte, don't you think?"

Silence filled the kitchen as Sophia looked at Clementine. Finally, Clementine put her tea mug on the table to ask, "Hey, you have something you want to tell me. Your expression is giving you away. Tell me and then you won't have to worry about telling me, right?"

Grinning, Sophia noticed her tea mug was empty, "There is something nagging at me. Nestor Casaus was here on our multi-cultural barrel racing day. He mentioned something that has been stuck in the back of my thoughts. Perhaps it's nothing or perhaps it's something, but maybe you could think on it for a change?"

"Sure, toss it over here." Clementine put her hands out as if to catch a baseball.

Sophia shook her head, "There is no way I want to get anyone in trouble or give a false lead, you understand?" She moved the mug to the center of the table.

Nodding, Clementine clinked her mug with Sophia's, "Go ahead, spill it!"

"Nestor is a strange man who has strange ideas and not everything he says can be taken seriously, right? He took me into the barn and told me that the herbal supplements at the Pueblo were actually outdated Viagra." Sophia frowned as she watched Clementine who nodded, "Yes, we know that already."

Leaning back in her kitchen chair, Sophia shook her head, "He said the herbal supplements were given to the woman at the Pueblo by a cleaning woman who worked for a doctor. Did you know this as well?"

Clementine put her elbows on the table to lift her mug, "Now, what? A doctor, an M.D. gave the herbal supplements to his cleaning lady who in turn gave them to a woman who lives in the Pueblo for her husband? She must have given this woman a huge bag if six men were sick."

Smiling at the thought, Sophia went on, "Yes, a lot of problems with the men, but my thoughts were of the cleaning lady or cleaning woman. Charlotte had a cleaning woman, right? And wasn't she also once working at the Otero School?" Sophia put her hand flat on the table.

Shaking her head, Clementine smiled, "Why would a woman who has been widowed for over twenty years need Viagra? Why would she keep the stuff? Personally, I can't see Charlotte getting it on with anyone can you?"

Mugs were picked up by Sophia who took them to the sink, "This is why I hesitated to say anything."

Clementine stood up, "I've get to go home. Tomorrow I have early duty. Thank you for the evening and the information. This may be wrapped up sooner than we had hoped. I need to share this information with A.J." She lifted her jacket from the back of the kitchen chair, "Oh, listen Ignacio asked if you would go with him tomorrow to speak with Dr. Peters about his wife. Would you be available?"

The two women walked to the front door, Sophia nodded as she stood to open it, "Certainly, although why does he need me there? He can call me and set up a time if he wants, but why does he want me there?"

"It's important to have a witness with a sheriff when he interviews someone. We are seriously short staffed or didn't you know? Maybe he feels since you and your mother knew Mary, you would help Dr. Peters feel more comfortable. Ask Ignacio when he calls, all right?"

The night sky was clear. The bright yellow moon was three quarters full. Stars lit up the sky. Cold air brought the smell of burning fireplace pine close to the ground. The horses lifted their heads in the stall as the women walked to Clementine's vehicle. The quiet of the country brought an element of peace. Off in the distance they heard the train rattle away down the tracks. Alcon's farming community was tucked in for the night. Don Juan Calderon's farmhouse was dark. Clementine gave Sophia a hug, "You have a good night. I hope whoever is responsible doesn't try to kill anyone else. The one thing I can't get my brain around is why would someone offer the outdated Viagra to the Pueblo Senior Center and openly give them to people. If this person was not respectable why would they take the bags of herbs?"

Clementine drove off down Alcon Road. Sophia stood outside

listening. A barn owl hooted off toward the Dominquez farm. The water in the irrigation ditch gurgled as it quietly flowed west. She walked down to the barn to rub Teddy's nose, "Hey, big fellow, you have a good night."

Suddenly the lights turned on at Juan's small home. Turning as she heard her name called, Sophia watched as Juan raced to the white pole fence, his long legs straddled the fence. He jumped down and hurriedly walked to her. "Hey, I'm home late from dinner with my nephew. Do you want to come over for desert or are the girls already in bed?"

Smacking her forehead with the palm of her hand, Sophia shook her head, "Damn, I forgot. Sorry. The girls are getting ready for bed. Let me ask them. Can you wait here for a moment?"

"Of course, no worries. I'm a patient person when it comes to women."

Sophia was not going to ask about the comment. Inside the kitchen, she called out, "Juan has dessert ready for us. Does anyone want to go next door for a late dessert especially since tomorrow is up in the air?"

No sooner had she finished her question when Donna stood in front of her fully clothed with her hair braided around her head. "Yes, I'm good. I love dessert, let's go!"

Sybil stood outside her bedroom door with her hair tangled, but she had on her jeans, an old shirt and her slippers. "Yes, I'm good. He's gorgeous and I'm ready for dessert since Donna ate all the cookies!"

The three followed Juan over the white pole fence rather than walking down the driveway to the road and then up his driveway to his small home. As they walked into the kitchen, all three noticed how small his home was. The kitchen was the size of Sybil's bedroom. The old counter was of worn green linoleum. There were cloth curtains hanging from small rods under the counters instead of cupboard doors. His old white porcelain sink was chipped around the edges and a tin percolator stood on the counter next to a two burner stove with an oven. The green and white linoleum floor was scuffed and worn from the bedroom through the kitchen to the only door going outside. In the corner of the kitchen under a narrow bay window was a round table. An oil cloth covered the round table. It, too, was worn, the yellow flowers had faded and the green stems were barely noticeable.

"Pull out a chair. I'll get some plates, have a seat. Have a seat. There are four chairs, the fourth is in this corner. Don't worry, there's room for everyone." Juan lifted a weathered reed cane chair from the corner and placed it in front of the round table as he pulled it out into the tiny kitchen. "Here, see, we can all fit."

Sybil quickly sat down with a big smile, "Yes, Juan, this is quite cozy. Do you live here alone?" She stressed her pleasure at being in his house.

"Hah! Yes, there is no way two people would fit in this house.

Sophia, do you want a tour?" He waved his hand toward the door opposite of her. "This is my bedroom. There is my bed. The twin bed is extra-long for these long legs. This is my grandfather's armoire, I hang my clothes, my horse and my extra money in there." His brown eyes sparkled, "That is if I had any money to hang." Donna bumped into him as he turned to point to a smaller room behind him, "This teeny tiny room is the bathroom. Small enough for just the necessaries if one of you ladies should need it."

Putting her hand on his arm, Donna asked, "Where is the dessert?"

"Ah, yes, the famous desert. Let's go back into the kitchen, shall we, Madame?"

Donna and Sophia walked behind him to find Sybil staring into the three foot tall refrigerator. "This doesn't hold much, does it?" She pointed to the items inside.

"Sit, sit, Miss Sybil. Sit." Juan gently gestured with his index finger to the chairs. White china plates were placed at all four settings with large serving spoons. Juan knelt to remove a large platter from the bottom shelf of the fridge. "This is a mousse with a flambé icing. Lean back and be amazed." Striking a match on his jean leg, the flame was placed near the mousse now sitting in the center of the table. It burst into orange and red flames. Gasping, Donna said, "Wow! Can we eat it when the fire is going?"

They watched as the flames slowly died out. A large serving knife appeared magically in Juan's hand as he cut the beautifully shaped mousse. "This is cast from one of my grandmother's collections. If you will please notice the cast is of a large fish with wings." Small pieces were placed on each plate. "This is very potent, eat it slowly. If you would like seconds, just ask."

Each of the large spoons held tiny bits of the delight. Sophia rolled her eyes as she tasted the mousse, "Oh, my, this is dark butterscotch with a hint of mint, right?"

Juan turned to Sybil, "What do you believe is in this?" She licked her lips, "Anise? I think it tastes like licorice." Shaking her head, Donna smiled, "I need another piece if I'm going to give my account." He sliced another small piece for her. "Now, what?" She smiled, "Yes, I agree. It's chocolate butterscotch and licorice with mint."

He laughed, "No. You three were all way off. Although, I'm pleased you enjoyed it. This is vanilla cocoa with rum, thus the flaming dessert. Although, I ran out of rum and put some mint liquor on top."

Sybil blushed, "Anyway, this is to die for. Can we take some home for breakfast tomorrow?"

Suddenly, there were three loud bangs on the kitchen door. Juan jumped, "Oh, that's my older sister. Just give me a moment. Please, enjoy more if you wish?" Before he was able to get close to the door, it opened. A short, plump woman stormed into the room. "Juan! Juan! I think we're in trouble!" The woman quickly stopped with her hand to her mouth as she noticed the three sitting at his table. "Oh, opps! I'm sorry, I didn't know you had company! Oh, Juan!"

She burst into tears. Pulling his vacated chair from the table he shoved it toward the woman, "Here, sit down, Maria Elena. These are my neighbors. They're friends." His hand on her shoulder, he knelt down beside her, "It will be all right. It will."

The woman sniffed, "Hi, I'm Maria Elena - Juan's sister. I apologize for coming to your party. Maybe I should go now." Juan kept his hand on her shoulder, holding her down. "No, we're all fine here. Would you like some dessert? I made your favorite the vanilla cocoa mousse."

The woman ran her short stubby fingers through her closely cropped hair. Gray highlighted her dark black curls. Juan cut a large piece for his sister. "Now, tell us what has you so upset, Maria Elena, and how we can help you." He gave her his spoon.

First she tasted the mousse and then with a big smile she laughed, "You're right, this is good. Mine is better though." She swallowed another spoonful. "The job at Otero School was supposed to be mine when those pushy women gave it to Rosa. That job was mine! I'm a good cook! I was going to make tacos, chimichangas and enchiladas for the students. You know, real meals? Instead they hired Rosa to save money. She took a cut in pay to put out pre-made sandwiches all soggy and moldy for the students."

She looked at Sophia who agreed with her, "That is just wrong. Sybil goes to Otero and she repeatedly wants to take her own lunch for the school's is nasty, right Sybil?"

She turned to her daughter who nodded, "Yep. That stuff isn't fit for pigs. So what happened? Isn't Rosa dead and now you can have the job?"

Shocked, Sophia smacked Sybil's arm, "Young lady, do not be disrespectful of the deceased!"

Maria Elena continued, "Yes, this is very sad. Charlotte and Mary Peters who both have money and both are volunteers want to put someone else as cook! She wants to push me out again! What do those women have against me? I'm a good cook! I serve food the kids eat and I can save the school money by not having all those kids toss their lunches in the garbage!"

Juan's knees popped as he stood upright, "Maria Elena, this is fixable. We just need to speak to Charlotte and Mary Peters. I'm sure they will understand. Did they say why they want to hire someone else?"

Rapidly shaking her head, Maria Elena's face turned red as tears fell, "Yes, they believe it isn't good to have so many Calderon working at the school. They feel this doesn't look good."

Turning in her chair, Sophia asked, "Too many Calderon? How many of your family work at the school?"

Before Maria Elena was able to answer, Sybil said, "There are six. Mom, there's the janitor, the gardener, the receptionist, the math tutor, the hall guard and the counselor. That's all right?"

Shaking her finger at Sybil, Maria Elena smiled, "Do you know them? Aren't they all great people? Yes, they're my family." She pointed to Juan, "They're our family. What would be wrong if I became cook? I'm a good cook, right, Juan?" An alarm went off in the bedroom. Juan quickly disappeared.

Sophia glanced at her watch, "Girls, we need to go home. It is late and these two need to have a talk." She stood to walk to the door. Juan returned. As Sophia herded her two daughters out the door, Juan handed her a small container with the mousse, "Here. Glad you enjoyed it. Tomorrow I'm out of town, but when I get back perhaps we can talk?"

Back in the farmhouse, the girls ran to their rooms. Sophia locked the doors, turned off the lights and set the alarm clock. Cats slept on the beds as Shonac snored under the kitchen table.

9

Birdsong woke Sophia before the alarm clock rang. Cats were sitting in the window seat behind the sheet used for a curtain. Biscuits was making strange singing noises and Oscar was purring loudly. Sophia stood, stretched and pulled back the sheet. High on the cottonwood tree outside her bedroom window sang a red breasted robin. Knocking on the window, Sophia called to it, "You need to fly south, little bird. It's going to get cold here and you won't do well. Fly way south, fly, little bird."

"Mom, you're weird." Sybil leaned against her mother's bedroom doorframe. "By the way, just for you to know, hey, you know? I'm not your secretary, the phone rang a while ago. It was Dad." Flipping her hair around her as she walked away down the hall, "You might give him a call. He wants a ride home. Right now!"

Everyone dressed, fed and in the old van driving south to Rincon. Donna mumbled in the backseat as she tried to comb her hair with her fingers. Sybil was anxiously watching a flock of cranes flying south overhead. Tumbleweeds continued to bash into the cars on the narrow road. At the school's drop off there was the long line of cars. Sybil jumped out and raced to the school, leaving the passenger door open. Donna jumped out of the backseat and into the front passenger seat, "Hey, Mom, can we stop and get some doughnuts on the way to get Dad?"

Sophia watched the cars move slowly forward. Finally, she put on her blinker and moved with caution around the parked cars from the school's pavement to the dirt road. "No, you had breakfast. You don't need anything more."

"But Dad would like some doughnuts, right?"

"Well, he just might, but he is a diabetic and he shouldn't be eating doughnuts, right?" They both laughed.

The drive into Albuquerque's UNM Hospital was a trial. There were cars backed up to get off the freeway and once they were on the side street they were met with a long line of orange barrels limiting the street to one lane for turning, one lane for going straight and for the store entrances. Sophia was quiet as she reconnoitered around barrels and other frustrated drivers. Donna pointed out a parking place in the high rise parking structure. It was on the third level. The elevator down to the main floor smelled of cigarette smoke and stale cheese. Finally, out in the open air they had to walk across another tarmac to enter the building. Inside it was shiny clean, smelling of lemon and bleach.

When they walked into his room, Geoffrey was standing by the hospital bedroom window. He had packed a clear plastic bag with hospital toothpaste, soap and lotions. His wrinkled shirt still had stains and his brown khaki pants were covered with brown spots and what appeared to be mustard on the left thigh leg. His brown shoes were hidden by the long pant legs, but the smell was obvious. The odor of cat urine filled the room. His expensive leather hat was placed flat on the bed, the stains on it were also obvious. Sophia looked straight at Geoffrey, "Are you able to leave now or do you still need to be discharged?"

Both Donna and Sophia stood in the doorway not wishing to enter the room. Geoffrey pointed, "You have to sign me out and the nurse will come in with the papers. You go and Donna can stay with me."

Donna wrinkled her nose, "Nope, I think I'm going with Mom." They walked down the hall to the nurses' station. Donna skipped to keep up with her mother's fast walk, "Mom, we have to buy Dads some new clothes. He stinks and we can't have him in our van. We can't, unless we get him something different to wear, Mom, please!" Donna held on to her mother's hand. "Mom, Dads stinks!"

Sophia continued staring straight ahead. At the nurses' station she gave her name, Geoffrey's name and was then handed a clipboard with papers. She looked up at the nurse who was standing waiting for her to finish, Sophia shook her head, "I'm not his wife nor am I responsible for his health or care. This is incorrect." She handed the clipboard back to the nurse.

Donna's foot kicked the base of the counter, "Mom, we need to get Dad some new clothes! Please!"

The nurse read the top sheet of paper, "Ma'am, we can only go by what the patient tells us. He has to be released by a next of kin and he stated that you were his wife. Otherwise we have to find someone who can legally sign off on him." Sophia said nothing. The nurse read further down the page, "Also, he cannot live alone, he needs care. Someone needs to monitor his high blood pressure and his diabetic medications. Evidently, he was not doing this when he lived by himself and thus the reason he was brought in to us."

Sophia's nose began to run. She forged in her purse for a tissue. Donna faced the nurse, "I'm his daughter. I'm twelve and I'll sign him out, but I won't live with him, he stinks something awful."

Studying Donna, the nurse smiled, "Yes, we noticed his clothes. Do you live with your father? Could you take his blood pressure and make sure he takes his medication? You seem like a mature young lady."

Donna shook her head, loose hair flew around her face, "Nope. Not anymore! I don't live with him, won't live with him and nope I won't take his blood pressure. Besides he threw the machine across the room and it smashed against the wall into pieces. Then he hit the dog and yelled at me. Nope, don't live with him." Donna walked away to sit in one of the raspberry colored plastic chairs lined against the hospital hall wall.

"Well, we certainly learned of her opinion." The nurse held the clipboard to Sophia again, "Is there someone who could visit? A visiting nurse could be ordered by the doctor. Do you want me to page him for you?"

The clipboard was placed in Sophia's hand once again, "Yes, please, let's get the doctor here. He needs to know what will happen when Geoffrey leaves. Please, yes, call the doctor."

The smell arrived before he did. Geoffrey came to stand beside Sophia, "What do we need the doc for? Just sign the papers and let's go. What's the problem here? Sophia, with you there is always a problem!"

The nurse spoke before Sophia, "She's not your legal wife, Sir. She is not legally responsible for you and when you leave here you will be living alone. Someone needs to check your vitals until your next appointment. We want to keep you alive."

"Bullshit! Sophia only wants to cause problems! That's what she does! She tried to take away my home and now she's trying to take away my life! Damn, you, Sophia!" He slapped the counter hard making everyone turn to stare at him.

"Sir, I must ask you to return to your room. We will be with you shortly. Sir, please go back to your room." The nurse waved to a tall orderly who came to Geoffrey's side. The orderly took Geoffrey by the elbow, "Mr. Vinder, let me walk with you back to your room. It's best if you don't upset yourself with your high blood pressure. Come on, I'll walk with you."

Geoffrey jerked away, "I'm perfectly capable of walking myself to the room, thank you!" He stormed off down the hall.

The orderly turned back to the nurse, "He must have some other clothes or shoes. Those are not healthy. Don't we have some clothes in the lost and found we can give him? Those are seriously not healthy for him or for anyone."

A box was pulled from under the far corner of the counter. The orderly rummaged through it to find a baggy pair of sweat pants and a matching top. "These have been washed and these are clean. Would you mind if I had your husband change into these?"

Sophia scrunched her face, "He's not my husband. Yes, please have him change. I'm driving him home in my van and I don't want it to stink. Please, if you can, have him change."

Cautiously, the orderly walked over to Donna, "Do you want to give these a test smell, make sure they're all right?"

First Donna put her hand on the pants and rubbed them, "They're soft." Then she sniffed, "They smell like lemon. Yes, they pass the smell test. Good luck with my Dad." As the orderly walked down the hall to Geoffrey's room, a tall man with a thick head of white hair came striding to the nurses' station. "Becky, what's the problem here?"

"Doc, this is Sophia Vinder. She says she is not Geoffrey Vinder's wife and she does not live with him. He lives alone. How should we discharge him and would it be possible for him to have a visiting nurse come to the house to check his vitals?"

The tall man put out his hand to Sophia, "Hello, I'm Geoffrey's doctor. Dr. White and I'm afraid with the rules of Adult Protective Services behind this, someone who is a relative or someone who is a legal representative must sign him out. Also, we can get a visiting nurse to come each day and check up on him, but a legal representative has to be here to discharge him. Unless you waiver this misinformation, which is illegal, but which we can ignore, if you do wish to sign him out?"

The clipboard was placed on the counter between Sophia and the nurse, "Excuse me, did you say it would be illegal for me to sign him out, but you would look the other way and let me sign him out?"

Taking his reading glasses from his pocket, he picked up the clipboard, "This isn't unusual. We have some immigrants who visit us here and we have the social worker or someone sign them out. We can't keep people in here indefinitely, we need the beds." He pointed to a line at the bottom of pink paper sheet, "Here, sign here and I'll sign my name under it. I believe you will take Geoffrey to his home and not kidnap him. Give me a minute to call his Medicare provider to find out about the visiting nurse issue. Sign here, right here." He tapped the pen on the line.

Sophia signed the pink paper and Dr. White signed his name under hers. He took the phone from the nurse behind the counter as she dialed the Medicare number from his chart. The orderly arrived at the group with Geoffrey's clothes in a sealed plastic bag. "Do you want these or should I throw them out?"

Quickly, Donna walked to him, "Throw them out. They're disgusting!"

He smiled at her, "I need to ask your mother. Mr. Vinder may want these and they are in a sealed bag. What do you think, Ma'am?"

First Sophia studied the bag and then she looked at the orderly, "Yes, we better take them with us and secondly I am not a Ma'am. My name is Dr. Pino or Sophia Pino, but not Ma'am nor am I Mrs. Vinder." The orderly smiled as he handed the bag to Sophia. She dropped it on the floor by her feet.

Dr. White hung up the phone, "This is the plan. When you leave here you are to call this phone number." He handed her a sticky note. "The nurse is a man called Kevin Ortiz and he will meet you at Geoffrey's house. He's in Rincon right now doing a house call. Once, you drop off Geoffrey, you may leave. Kevin will take over from there. He needs to get a feel for the house and see what kind of medical assistance Geoffrey Vinder may need." He stared at the plastic bag at Sophia's feet, "Does this meet with your approval?"

Nodding at him, Sophia agreed. The nurse lifted the pink page marking an 'x' for Sophia to sign the following three forms. Dr. White signed his name under hers. Then he pulled his medical card from his shirt pocket, "This is my phone number and my cell. If you have any further questions, please call me. After hours, you will get my answering service, but they are good at finding me." He turned and walked down a different hallway.

The orderly led Sophia and Donna back to Geoffrey's room. He was trying to clean his shoes in the small bathroom. When they entered, he quickly wiped the tops of his leather shoes with a paper towel. "Thought I'd give these a quick cleaning." His face was red and flushed, "Are we ready to go now? Or are we going to have more problems?"

The orderly patted the hospital bed, "Mr. Vinder, I need you to sit here for a moment while I take your blood pressure and check your oxygen level. Then you are a free man."

The plastic bag was set in Geoffrey's lap as the orderly pushed him in a wheelchair down the hall. Sophia and Donna followed. Once outside, Sophia hurriedly walked to the parking structure. A man smoking a cigarette and a young woman were sitting on the concrete floor of the parking area. He had his hand around her shoulders. When they saw Sophia the young woman stood up, "Excuse me, do you have any extra change, please?"

Sophia shook her head and hurried to her old van. As she jumped into the driver's seat, she pulled out her cellphone and called Kevin Ortiz. He answered immediately to ask for directions to Geoffrey's house. Sophia noticed there had been a call from Granger earlier. She flipped her cellphone shut and shoved it back into her pant pocket. As she drove to the front of the hospital there was a smiling and waving Donna with her Dad at the hospital's doors. The orderly held tightly to the wheelchair handles as they moved beside the van. Wind blew debris into the open forum. Donna gave her father the choice as to where he wanted to sit in the van. Geoffrey insisted on sitting in the backseat. Donna was pleased.

The drive out of town was done in silence. When Sophia glanced in the rearview mirror, she saw Geoffrey's head forward on his chest. He was sound asleep. Poking Donna, she nodded to the backseat. Donna quietly giggled, "Poor Dad, he doesn't sleep well away from home."

At the Rocoso house they parked next to a tall white van with the words, Medicare Nurse. When the old van came to a stop, Geoffrey woke up and snorted. Donna jumped from the van to slide open the back door for her father. Geoffrey stared at the house, then he stared at his clothes. "Where did I get these?"

Answering quickly as she watched Kevin walk from his van to hers, Sophia answered, "They were given to you at the hospital, Geoffrey. They look good on you and they're clean. No smell."

Kevin walked around to meet Geoffrey who slowly stepped down from the backseat. "Hello, Mr. Vinder, I presume? I'm Kevin Ortiz and I'm here to help you while you stay in your own home. How's that?"

Both feet on the ground now, Geoffrey glared at the man through his thick smudged glasses, "Are you a Mexican? I won't have a damn Mexican in my house!"

"No, Sir, I'm New Mexico through and through. My mother is from the East Coast and she's a Green Bay Packer's fan. No worries. No Mexican here." He helped Geoffrey keep his balance as they walked to the house. Sophia called to him, "Do you need us to stay or do you have this now? I've got a meeting to get to and can't really stay."

Before Geoffrey opened his mouth, Kevin called back to her at the front door, "No, we're fine. You go ahead. I have your cell number because you called me. Go to your meeting. We'll be fine."

The plastic bag was carried to Kevin by Donna, "Here, Dad may want this. We don't want it." She pinched her nose.

Both Sophia and Donna laughed with joy as they drove down the hill away from Rocoso. Sophia rolled the window down, "Thank God for Kevin! He appears to know how to handle ornery old farts like your father!"

The twelve year old clapped her hands, "Oh, thank you, thank you, thank you! I don't have to go back there ever again! Thank you!" Her window rolled down, she called to the world, "Thank you, Universe, Thank you for my freedom!" Her blue framed glasses were pushed up the arch of her nose.

Warning her, Sophia said, "Donna, if Geoffrey cleans up his act he may try to get you back with him. Don't put the cart before the horse just yet." Donna's smile glistened with her metal braces to ask, "O-kay, now Mom where to? Should we celebrate with a good lunch or how about a doughnut?"

A stern motherly frown turned to Donna, "No, neither. We're going to the Charter School and meet the people there to find out how we can get you enrolled. If this works, you can walk to school. You won't have to get up at dawn and run around with us. You can meet someone who becomes your friend and walk with them to school. How's that?"

Silence. Clementine's directions were excellent. Sophia drove behind the Mom and Pop store in Alcon and there was the sign; Los Vecinos Escuela. The school was tall of white cement block. The solar panels on the roof appeared to be new. The heavy metal doors were painted Virgin Mary blue. Rose bushes were planted all along the wall and under the thick glass windows. Donna raced ahead to get the door for her mother. She stopped and stared above the door. There were no cameras, no sound box and the door opened easily as Donna pulled.

The hallway was of white linoleum. The walls were painted a Navajo White. The sound tiles in the ceiling were a soft beige. There was a corkboard outside a metal door stating this was the front office. Donna held the door for Sophia. A tall Navajo woman stood behind the counter. She had a phone in her hand as if she was about to dial a call. Long brown hair to below the woman's waist was pushed back behind her shoulders as she put the phone down, she smiled, "Hi, how can I help you?"

Sophia walked to the high counter, "Hi, I'm Dr. Pino and I would like to enroll my daughter in your school, but first I need to know about your school, right?" Sophia laughed, "Maybe I should have said the last part first."

The woman pointed to Donna, "Is this the student in question? She looks all right to me. Let me get the principal and you can ask her about the school. We do pick and choose, just for you to know." A metal device was lifted in her hand, but before pushing the fat button at the bottom of the device, the woman said, 'My name is Tracy Yazzie, by the way. You can call me, Tracy."

Donna gently elbowed her mother, "Like my horse!" Ten minutes went by and finally a woman came through the doors who was the principal. When Sophia turned she gasped, "Catherine? Catherine from my Western Civilization class, is that you?"

The woman's face lit up, "Yes, Dr. Pino! What a surprise! Are you visiting our school? I had no idea you were coming today although my teachers do have outsiders come in as speakers! How fun to see you here where I work!"

The two women hugged. Donna stepped back. The secretary laughed as she nodded to Donna, "Who would guess these two know one another?" It was decided after filling out numerous pages and filling out a medical report that Donna would start school there the next day. As they walked to the van, Donna frowned, "Mom, you only got me into this school because she's your student. Now you have to give her an A or she will expel me."

Unlocking the van doors, Sophia stared at Donna, "I don't think so, Missy. You need to work hard and do well and then you will be in her good graces. If you fool around because you think she's wanting a good grade, think again."

Pouting as she shoved on her seatbelt, Donna asked, "Can we go for food now, I'm hungry."

"Yes, we can go home for food. You can fix peanut butter and jelly sandwiches with potato chips. I've got some phone calls to make. We don't eat out, it's too expensive for us. Besides we have good food at home."

As they walked in the door, the phone in the hall started to ring. Sophia hurried to answer it. Shonac practically knocked her down trying to get outside. Donna didn't come inside immediately.

"Hello?" Sophia stood in the kitchen doorway. Staring out the kitchen windows she watched her daughter stroke Tracy horse's nose.

"Sophia, this is Ignacio. Would it be all right if I swing by and pick you up in about an hour? If you are free? I need someone to come with me to Dr. Peters' home. It isn't good for me to ask him questions by myself and you have met him, I suppose?"

"Ignacio, there is a problem. Donna is home and she isn't old enough to stay by herself. If we go, she'll need to come with us. Is this appropriate? We're just home. We took Geoffrey home from the hospital. He's with the visiting nurse now. If it is all right for Donna to come, she could be with Dr. Peters' horses?" Fergus cat was rubbing against Sophia's legs, purring. Silky was lying on the kitchen table cleaning her paws.

Bread was cut from the freshly baked loaf and peanut butter and jelly placed on the table. The bag of chips was ripped open and stood up right next to the bread board. Sophia called Donna into the house. She watched as Donna dragged her feet to the front door. Shonac was racing around her barking. Once in the kitchen, Sophia made Donna wash her hands. "You know, you might meet some really neat people at this school? Don't pass judgement on it until you try it. Come and eat, we're going with Ignacio to the Peters' after lunch."

Donna's face perked up, "We're going to see the Clydesdales? How cool is that?" Peanut butter was spread on her homemade bread slice, "Mom, it's just all of this is going to be new. I have to meet new people, make new friends and have new teachers. To be honest, Mom, I'm tired of it."

"Well, I'll tell you what, my lovely tired twelve year old. After we drop off Sybil in the morning I'll go with you to your new school. It will be after first bell, but I can go with you to meet your homeroom teacher. This may give you a chance to feel safer. What do you think?"

Chips were grabbed and shoved into her face as Donna mumbled, "That would be great, Mom. Don't you have classes tomorrow?"

"Yes, but you're my daughter and your safety is important first. I can call the university and they can put a note up on the door to have my students work on their presentations in the library tomorrow. We can hang at your new school, how's that?"

Tears filled Donna's eyes, "Mom, you're the best. I was scared, really, really scared!"

Shonac started barking at the front door. Then he growled a low and fierce noise. Sophia hurried to him, "That's probably Ignacio." She held Shonac by the collar as she opened the front door. Ignacio had his hands up, "Whoa, a killer dog. I promise I'm harmless unless you're a perp and then I'll attack!" He laughed a deep guttural laugh. Shonac wagged his tail in recognition.

Sitting at the kitchen table all three had a lunch of homemade bread with the peanut butter and jelly. Sophia's cellphone chirped as they were taking the plates to the sink. "It's Granger, I had better take this. Donna, can you wash up, quickly, Sweetie? We have to go soon." She walked into her bedroom and sat on the side of the bed. "Granger, what's up?"

"Where the hell have you been?" His voice was terse.

"We picked up Geoffrey and took him home to his visiting nurse. Geoffrey's back home in Rocoso. Otherwise, Geoffrey would be living with you. I couldn't answer my cell because we were speaking with the doctor and checking him out. What's going on over where you are?"

There was a loud squawking noise on Granger's end. He yelled into the cellphone, "I found my Mercedes! It's only eleven thousand! I found it, mine, my original Mercedes! I need you to call Mom and see if you can't get me the money. It's my old one. I'd know it anywhere! It's here, Sophia. It's here in Albuquerque!"

The cellphone was snapped shut. Sophia stood, shoved the cellphone into her pant pocket and went into the kitchen. Ignacio and Donna had cleaned the kitchen table and washed the dishes. "Beautiful! You two work well as a team. Shall we go?"

Taking Sophia's arm, Donna asked, "Who was that, Mom? Was it Dad?"

"No, Sweetie, it was nobody. Get your jacket because we may be out late and the sky is getting darker with heavy clouds. We're going to have to pick your sister up at three o'clock. It's going on twelve thirty now, so we best be prepared. Also, you'll be out with the big guys, those big old horses, maybe you want to slide on your boots?"

It was agreed. They would go with Ignacio in his brown sheriff's cruiser. "Sybil will get a kick out of being picked up in a sheriff's car, huh?" Donna giggled in the backseat. "Mom, this car smells like Dad's house."

Ignacio shook his head, "Miss Donna, I pick up all kinds of strange characters and they have to sit in the backseat. Sorry, it should've been wiped off before you got inside. Sorry."

The wind began to blow as they drove down into the valley. Tumbleweeds kept coming at them. Tree branches waved back and forth overhead as they drove through Calavera. The small roads appeared to be deserted in the middle of the day. A large UPS truck pulled out of the County Store almost backing into them. Ignacio put on his sheriff's car lights for a few seconds as the UPS driver waved and hurried ahead. Dogs behind fences barked at the large UPS truck. A man riding a Quarter horse held fast to his cowboy hat as he trotted down a side ditch road. Ignacio cautiously drove down the narrow Calavera road, but instead of turning into Margaret's farm, he drove straight through to the dead end. As they passed Charlotte's small farm, they saw Roberto out in her orchard sawing down a dead tree limb. His hat had blown off. Saw dust was billowing into his face as he worked the metal saw back and forth.

Dr. Peters's farm was at the very end. A high ditch bank loomed over the farmhouse. A warped wooden fence surrounded his property. Drying green fields appeared fallow in the cold October weather. A sloping tin roof reflected the sunlight as the sun darted in and out between clouds. Under the open barn's roof two huge horses were milling around. They would stop and stare at the field behind the gate as if they were ready to run and play. A large expensive vehicle was parked sideways beside the house. This structure was adobe brown with a painted sloping tin roof of azure blue and a porch with a brick floor. Hanging chili ristras dangled from the vigas protruding out from the porch roof. Ignacio stopped his car next to the side door away from the horses, "Damn, those are giant horses!"

As they got out of the vehicle, a tall gentleman met then at the door. His brown eyes were bloodshot. He wore a leather vest over an ironed white shirt that was tucked into dark jeans. Polished black boots with round toes were a stark contrast to the concept of living on a farm. His thick white hair had a prep school cut. Sadness enveloped his ashen gray face. Dr. Peters attempted a smile when he saw Donna, "Hi! The guys need to go out into the field. I don't know how to open the gate! Roberto usually does this, but he has chosen not to work for me anymore. I'm looking for good help. Donna, would you let the horses out? Do you know how to open that fancy gate of Maisy's?"

Donna didn't answer, she ran to the barn. Sophia laughed, "Those big guys are beautiful. How I bet they miss your wife."

The two men shook hands as Dr. Peters invited them into his home. He had a roaring fire in a Taos fireplace. There was a plate of biscochitos on the short coffee table in front of a green leather couch. Two comfortable easy chairs faced the fireplace. They were set at an angle to view the fire. A pitcher of iced tea and four tall glasses sat next to the cookies. A sprig of sage stuck out of a Pueblo pot on the fireplace hearth. The tall man waved to the seats. "Please, please, take a seat. Is there anything else I can get for you?"

Sophia and Ignacio sat next to each other on the wood framed couch. Dr. Peters moved to where he found comfort in what was noticeably his own easy chair. A large Airedale dog slapped his tail against the brick floor. Dr. Peters waved his hand at the dog, "He's my great protector. Although he's older than I am and I'm pretty old."

Ignacio pulled a notebook from his shirt pocket and a ballpoint pen. "Would it be all right if we asked you some questions?" A cellphone taken from a leather holster on his belt was placed on the coffee table. "We need to record this conversation. Is this all right with you? Standard procedure now a days. These devices come in handy, keep life simple."

Dr. Peters nodded, "All right, nothing to hide and everything to gain." He lifted the plate of cookies. He offered one to Sophia, saying "Sure, but first you have to try my wife's cookies. Maisy makes special cookies for the old church gatherings." Sophia took a cookie and handed one to Ignacio who placed it on his knee.

"Can you tell me about your wife? We need to know her habits and her personality if we are to understand why someone would want to harm her." Ignacio put the notebook on the knee opposite the cookie. Sophia ate hers.

Dr. Peters rubbed his hands, "I'm not sure what you need to know. Where to begin?"

Clearing her throat, Sophia took a drink of the iced tea, "You call your wife Maisy is there a reason for this? It's a wonderful name."

He gave Sophia a crooked smile, "Certainly, we can begin there. Maisy's mother was named Mary, too. When she was born, my wife not her mother, they gave her the nickname of Maisy. This avoided confusion as to who was whom. When we moved here Maisy felt she would have her friends call her Mary since her mother has passed and she could be Mary. She loved it here."

Smiling, Sophia said, "I had a student named Maisy my first year of teaching. She was wonderful gal. What did your Maisy do during her day? Did she go riding or have a hobby?"

"Oh, yes! Charlotte and my wife both loved arts and crafts. Although Charlotte is much more of an artist than my wife. They worked on several projects together for the Community Center. Maisy was more of a craft person. She liked to make collages and work with the children or the seniors. Charlotte had the tools and the creative spunk. The two of them were a real scream when they got together." Leaning forward he put his hands on his cheeks. "Sorry, I'm trying to keep it together here."

Ignacio asked, "What kind of crafts did they do?"

Remembering appeared to help him to relax, "The latest project was making posters for a talent show. All ages were invited to participate. This is going to happen the day after Halloween. It's still a ways off yet. Two weeks or three weeks something like that. They drew these crazy posters, printed them out here on my old printer and were going to put them up the weekend next. My copier is part of my old printer, but something happened with the ink and they had to finish at Charlotte's house."

Searching the room, Ignacio lifted his cookie and took a bite, "Yummy, good cookie! Oh, dear, I have toddlers and sound like cookie monster." Smiling at Dr. Peters he asked, "Your wife and Charlotte worked together. Did they ever work on dyes or plants for healing or for projects? How did they meet?"

Dr. Peters stared into the fire, "I keep thinking she's going to walk into the room. She could answer your questions so much better than I. Maisy and Charlotte met at the Otero Middle School. Maisy was approached by a Mr. O'Brian concerning Maisy's publications on natural dyes of the southwest. Maisy dabbled in dyes and different types of woven cloth. How different dyes work on different types of fabrics such as cotton versus wool." A deep sigh escaped from his chest, "This seems like yesterday. Charlotte was at the Otero Middle School putting together a type of glue for the spider's webs the students were going to use for last year's Halloween party. They became instant best friends." He shook his head, "Maybe not best friends, but friends."

Sophia put her glass of iced tea on the coaster in front of her, "What do you mean by just friends?"

Dr. Peters jerked to stare at her, "Oh, I forgot you were here. Well, Charlotte has a manner about her. She's from the East Coast as well. Charlotte likes to delegate authoritarian style. This didn't go over well with Maisy. There was a point when Maisy had to ask Charlotte to call here before she would arrive to storm into the house demanding something. Charlotte would show up when Maisy was in the shower or I was getting dressed. We had to put a stop to that. There is a reason for doors." Pointing to the front door, he added, “That was when Maisy and I decided to start locking the doors all the time even if she had just come in from the barn.”

Interrupting him, Ignacio interjected, “Charlotte felt she could do what she wanted? Come and go? Did she continue to try and enter your home after you locked the doors?”

Smiling, Dr. Peters answered, “Oh, yes. She would bang and bang away, yelling and screaming at the windows. She could see us, but we wouldn't open the door. This set off a troublesome time. Charlotte tried to have Mr. O'Brian block Maisy from doing school activities. Finally, he ordered them into his classroom and all three had a talk. After Mr. O'Brian's mediation everyone appeared to be polite to one another. Charlotte was just here last week. They were working on the Halloween party supplies in Maisy's office. From what I heard, they were having a good old time stuffing bags and printing labels.”

Ignacio lifted his cellphone from the coffee table, “Sir, would you be kind enough to show me your wife's printer and copier?”

The two men stood up and walked down a brick hallway. Sophia went over to the dog to pet him. “You poor old guy, you've had a hard time now with your Mom gone.” The dog's tail slapped the brick floor and then he put his head down and went to sleep. “Or maybe not.” Sophia followed the sounds of the men's voices into a small side room at the end of the hall. The tall windows looked out to the east overlooking the barnyard and beyond to the farming valley. Sophia watched as Donna put a halter on one of the large horses and then in one movement Donna pulled herself up onto the horse's wide back. She rode bareback with her fingers intertwined in the horse's mane. They trotted around the large field.

Dr. Peters stopped speaking to look out the window, “Sophia, your daughter is amazing. Do you know Roberto put in this fail safe latch on the field gate it has a safety mechanism and there is no way I could figure it out. I must have been out there for an hour trying to open the damn gate!”

Ignacio's voice was soft as he asked, “What happened between you and Roberto? Why isn't he working here for you anymore?”

Shrugging his shoulders, Dr. Peters turned to face him, “Do you know, I have no idea, none. It was the day after Maisy was found here.” Sniffing he added, “I still can't believe she's gone. My God, how I miss her. She was my life, my rock, my grounding rod.” Ignacio put his hand on the doctor's shoulder. “I'm so sorry.” The tall man gathered himself, “It was after I called the Sheriff A.J. Salazar. Roberto left me a note on the kitchen table. The note was succinct. It said, ‘I can no longer work for you.’ Signed Roberto and the date and time.”

Watching his face, Sophia said, “That doesn't sound like Roberto at all. He wouldn't put the time and date. That's so not him. He's a warm man, someone who would want to help. I might ask him about that if I see him at my mother's."

Shaking his head, Dr. Peters spoke firmly, "Yes, I really want to know what his purpose was in doing this to me, to us. He knew I couldn't find anyone right away and I'm not familiar with the horses at all. They were Maisy's pets, her loves. Why would he be so cruel?"

Lifting the old printer, Ignacio asked Dr. Peters, "Can I take this with me? I would like to check out the ink and see if it matches some other items we found."

"Sure, you can have it. I was going to throw the damn thing out." Dr. Peters's voice was now becoming angry. Sophia put her hand on his arm, "I know you're angry. I don't blame you, not at all. Why did Maisy take herbs? Was there a reason for her to want herbs?"

Suddenly he sat down in the office chair behind him, "She thought I was playing around on her. She thought she was fat and her diabetes was back. It wasn't and she wasn't. I loved her with all of my heart, my being. I worked at the Dental Clinic during the day and at night I worked at the Sanctuary Hall to help immigrants with their teeth. Sometimes I slept there if it was too late to drive home and I was too tired. I loved her, I always came home to her." He put his head in his hands.

The printer was put back on the table, Ignacio flipped open his notebook, "Evidently, the neighbors believed you were playing the field. They said they saw you with different women in town. Is this true?"

Staring up at Ignacio, Dr. Peters frowned, "No. Those are flat out lies! I was never in town with strange women. I would go into town with my dental tech Karen, but we were in town to buy supplies. She's married and has three boys. There was nothing untoward with us. It was business. Many times I gave money to help out the immigrants to get toothbrushes or medicine for their kids, but I never, ever, never was with another woman. Maisy was my love, my wife, my life and I would never be unfaithful to her. She knew me. She knew this."

Leaning against the cold adobe wall in the small room, Sophia asked, "Where would Maisy get these herbs she was taking? Do you know who gave them to her?"

He stood up, filling the room with his tall stature, "No! I have no idea! Who would give a beautiful woman herbs for her weight when she was perfect? Who? It had to have been someone she trusted! Maisy wasn't stupid! She wouldn't take herbs or drugs from just anyone!" He shoved his way out of the small room, "I can't stand it! I can't stand what has happened to her! I want my wife back!" His fist pounded the adobe wall as he walked down the hall to the living room.

Ignacio carried the printer to the front door as Sophia held it open for him. She watched as he placed it on the hood of the vehicle, opened the car's back door and shoved it onto the backseat. Sophia went back into the living room. Dr. Peters was poking the fire with a poker, "I'm sorry to be angry. I miss my wife. This house and this life feels empty without her here. God, how I miss her! I should never have been gone so much!" He jerked his chin to the wall, "What the hell am I going to do with those horses? I don't ride! I don't even like horses!" Tears fell from his eyes as he poked at the fire.

Sophia picked up the plate of cookies and carried it into the large kitchen. The cupboards were of natural wood with carvings of birds, beavers, foxes and cats. The counters were butcher block, well-oiled and clean. The double stainless steel sink glistened from the overhead light above the window. There on the counter were three bags. Each brown paper bag had Granger's red and gold seal. None of them had been opened. Sophia turned when she heard Ignacio's voice in the living room. She hurried to him, "There are three bags in the kitchen of herbs. Dr. Peters, where did those come from? I thought the sheriff took all the herbs that were here."

They walked into the kitchen. Dr. Peters lifted the bags and handed them to Ignacio, "I found these in her car. She has the station wagon in the garage. Most people don't notice the garage because it is on the far side of the house. When I was going to move her car, it's the blue station wagon Ford, I dropped the keys. These were under the front seat. Well under the front seat, I had to struggle to get them out. I was going to show them to you, but somehow I forgot."

Ignacio quickly set the bags back down on the counter. He pulled a clear plastic bag from his back pocket and dropped each bag into a separate plastic bag. "We can check these out at the office. Thanks, Sophia."

Dark clouds gave the house a shadowy feeling. Sophia checked the clock over the oven, "Oh, dear, we have to go. I need to pick up Sybil from school in forty five minutes!"

Dr. Peters walked with them to the barn where they found Donna brushing the large beasts. "Mom, can I stay here and feed these guys? They are so lonely and they need to have their hooves cleaned. They're a mess."

"No, Sweetie, we have to go. You have school tomorrow and we have a list of things we still need to get once Ignacio gets us home. Right now we need to leave to pick up your sister." Sophia rubbed the nose of the horse closest to her.

"But, Mom." Donna whined.

"Nope, don't you dare try to blackmail me, Young Lady, we have to go. Please put the horse brush away and say goodbye to these guys." Her attention was turned to Dr. Peters now, "Would it be all right if we came by this weekend to visit your horses?"

"Certainly, just give me a call first. Although Charlotte said she's found someone who might want to buy them. Someone who lives in Santa Fe and shows these types of horses. Yes, call first and see if I'm here. That'd be great." He took the horse brush from Donna's hand. "You better go. We don't want to anger your Mom."

Ignacio drove slowly forward down Dr. Peters' driveway. Then he stopped put the vehicle in reverse and backed up to where Dr. Peters was standing by the barn gate. He rolled down the window, "Yes, did we forget something?"

The tall man leaned forward to the car's window, "I just remembered Maisy has a whole drawer full of those brown bags. Did you want to take them all? I don't have a purpose for them and they certainly won't do anyone any good if I just throw them out." He stood to point to the house, "They have that crazy seal with them. Charlotte and Maisy were printing dates on the bottom of each bag. Come, I'll show you."

Donna jumped out of the backseat of the car, "Can I feed the horses? They need special grain and it's in the green bag by the oat room. Can I feed them, please?" She half turned to the barn, "Mrs. Peters showed me how to feed them when I stayed with Grandma Margaret. Please, Mom, please?"

Dr. Peters nodded to Sophia, "I'm sorry. I just remembered those stupid bags. Is it all right for Donna to…." Sophia was now walking around the vehicle.

Laughing, Sophia patted Donna on the shoulder, "Sure, go on, Sweetie. Feed the large beasts their special grub."

Ignacio slammed the driver's door as he walked to the house. "Why were your wife and Charlotte putting dates on the bottom of the bags?" He hurried to catch up with Dr. Peters' long strides as they walked into the house. Leaves from the tall Mulberry tree in the yard were blowing down the front hall. Sophia stopped, "Dr. Peters, Sir, do you have someone to help you with the housecleaning? Is there someone who comes?"

He turned to her, "That's another funny story. The woman who cleaned the house came about in a circular way." Ignacio glared at Sophia, "We need to hurry this along, please."

Dr. Peters ignored him. "There was a woman who was to be working at the Otero School cafeteria. She was all set up for the job. They needed a good cook and believe me this woman can cook. Well, evidently another woman was hired and our cleaning woman was bumped. This woman was a widow, had no other job prospects and is destitute." He stared up at the hall's ceiling, "Sweet Maisy hired her to clean house here. We really didn't need a cleaning woman. This is a small home just for the two of us. No kids, no guests, just us living here. After Maisy died the cleaning woman, I forgot her name." He stepped back and thought for a moment, "Oh, yes, Maria Elena was her name. She called to say she now has her dream job and won't be coming back here." Another sigh escaped him, "She deserted me as well."

Clearing his throat, Ignacio pointed to the room at the end of the hall. The three of them were back in the small office room. Sophia knew if she put out her arms she would be able to touch both sides of the office walls on each side. The doctor's deep voice asked her to step into the hall because he needed to open the drawer to Maisy's desk. She moved down the hall to lean against a tall wooden door. The door opened with her weight pressing on it. She was able to overhear the conversation as she stepped into the room.

Dr. Peters' deep voice carried as he told Ignacio, "Maisy and Charlotte usually decorated for the Halloween parties at the schools. I do believe they were going to put strange items in each bag and give them out at the door as the students entered the gym. My lovely wife was not able to have children. She made up for this love of kids by being involved in all their activities here in the valley."

Sophia slowly moved into the large room as she studied the oil paintings hanging on the walls. This room was obviously Dr. Peters' office. His large desk was topped with green leather. An old fashioned phone stood on the right side of the desk. A hovering oil painting of an elderly woman in a soft blue dress with a lace collar stared across the room. The painting was a portrait of a dignified stern woman, although it was almost a photograph for the detail was precise. Books were stuffed in the floor-to-ceiling bookcases. Framed diplomas hung next to the large window to the right of the desk.

Sophia walked to the left side of the heavy desk to read the book titles. People's personal choices were always fascinating. Next to his desk at arm level were four books on dental implants. Her hip hit the side of the desk as she bent to read the titles. Something fell over on the desk. Turning she noticed the old fashioned earpiece of the phone had come off its frame. The dial tone was loud. Quickly, she placed it back on the prong holder. Next to the ancient phone was another book open with pictures of plants. Quickly looking over her shoulder for the men were no longer in conversation, she checked the title on the cover. "A Pantheon of Painless Poisonous Plants, by M. Peters." Quietly, Sophia muttered, "An alliteration. Cute and deadly."

Ignacio's voice came from the hall, "Let us know if you think of anything else. Here's my card if you remember something and the main number to the sheriff's office is here at the top."

He stepped back to notice Sophia in the office. She shook her head and put her index finger to her lips. Ignacio crinkled the plastic bags in his hand, "I bet Sophia's outside with Donna. They both love horses. Thank you for these. We'll check them out and if there is anything further, I'll call." The two men walked down the hall to the front door. Sophia started to leave, pulling the office door shut. Then she changed her mind and hurried to the desk. Pulling out her cellphone she took photos of the plant books on the desk, also, the page the book was opened to with the photograph of plants.

She heard Donna's voice ask for a glass of water. The two men and Donna were in the kitchen. Sophia closed the office door to peek into another room that had a narrow door. It was the bathroom. Stepping inside, she bent over and flushed the toilet. Dr. Peters' heavy footsteps came down the brick hallway. "Sophia, are you back here? Donna's ready to go."

Opening the bathroom door, Sophia wiped her wet hands on her pant leg, "Sorry, I found the bathroom as I was in need. Didn't mean to be a problem." His large hand opened to welcome her down the hall. Smiling at him, she almost curtsied. In the kitchen she found Ignacio and Donna staring out the window. Donna turned to her, "Mom, could we buy one of Maisy's horses? They are so beautiful."

"No, and that's absolute. Those guys would eat us out of house and farm. They belong together, too. Haven't those two been together since they were colts?" Sophia turned to Dr. Peters. He shrugged, "I have no idea. I have no interest in equines."

Ignacio pointed to something out the window, "That's quite a garden you have back there. Are those herbs or weeds?" Sophia moved to stand next to him. The plants illustrated in the book she found on his desk were those growing in the middle of the back garden. Dr. Peters laughed, "That garden was Maisy's. She loved exotic things such as the horses. Many of those herbs were ordered on-line or her older sister sent them to her. Her sister is a leading herb scientist in Connecticut. They were experimenting with different herbs. On Sunday evenings they would call each other and share their findings." He walked to the front door, "Don't want to keep you. I know you want to get your daughter from school. Children don't like to be kept waiting."

Donna made a nasty face, "How would you know what we kids like or don't like?" Dr. Peters bent to speak directly to the twelve year old, "Young lady, I work with kids from countries all around the globe. One thing they have taught me is to be polite, punctual and prompt in my prognosis. Polite being the operative word, do you understand?"

Pouting, she stared at his polished boots, "Yes, Sir."

Sophia took Donna's arm, "Yes, thank you for your hospitality. Again, we are sorry about your wife. Thank you." Jerking her arm away from her mother's grasp, Donna ran to the car and jumped into the backseat. Ignacio tipped his wide brimmed brown hat as Dr. Peters shut the front door behind them. Driving down the driveway once more, Ignacio glanced in the rearview mirror at Donna. "You know I was going to ask that question myself. Sad they couldn't have children though."

Twisting in the front passenger seat, Sophia answered, "You didn't have to be rude, Donna."

Donna growled, "He doesn't like horses. I don't like him. He's a jerk." Under his breath, Ignacio agreed, "Yes, I believe you are correct young lady. O-kay, Sophia what did you find in the office or on the desk?"

"When we get to the Community Market can we stop? You need to see the photos I took." She lifted her butt in the air to pull out her cellphone from her pant pocket. Ignacio shook his head, "Sophia that's illegal. It's called entrapment. We can't use those photos in a court of law nor are they able to be part of our investigation. You're not an official investigator and you got those without his permission."

Straightening in the seat, she flipped to the photos on her cellphone. "These pictures of herbs in the book on his desk are the same plants that are in the back garden. Maisy published the book. She knew all about poisons and probably he does as well."

"Sophia, plenty of people have books on poisonous plants. We live in the southwest where there are poisonous plants all over. Look there, that's Datura. It will kill you if you eat too much of it. Although in Italy during the renaissance women chewed on the plant for beauty, right? You know this? Right now we don't have any proof just conjecture." His voice became extremely terse, "Anyway, Sophia, you're not part of this investigation. You need to butt out of this. It could be dangerous if you find out who the actual killer is and they know you know they know, or something like that." The Community Store was ahead, Ignacio asked, "Do you still want to stop?"

"No, let's go get Sybil. She will be upset and we're already fifteen minutes late. Let's just go get in the parking line for pickup." Fireplace smoke hovered close to the ground as they turned onto the dirt road to the school.

Cars and trucks lined the school's pickup area. Donna spoke softly, "You know, Mom, Sybil won't know we're here because we're in

Ignacio's car. Maybe I should get out and find her?" Donna jumped out of the backseat, slammed the door to disappear in the mass of milling students.

The ignition was turned off as Ignacio shook his head, "I don't want to view the photos you took, but do you think you could be staring at them and perhaps I could glance over and notice them?"

The cellphone slowly turned on with a flip of her thumb. Sophia ever so casually scrolled through the photos. Ignacio stretched his neck to see them. At the last photo, Sophia enlarged it and pointed the purplish blue flowers. "These are Foxglove and can be used for high blood pressure. This guy with the darker blue color is bittersweet. It slowly paralyzes the nervous system. Chaparral is another one. Here, this one is used for a natural remedy in curing cancer, but it can be deadly. The one plant growing on the outside ring of the back garden is arnica. The floppy yellow flowering plant. It can cause, let me see…" Sophia lifted the cellphone closer to her face to read, "Can cause paralysis of the heart and skeletal muscles. There you go. What do you think of those fancy herbs?"

"You photographed all of these while we were in the tiny office room? Or when we were in the kitchen?" Teenagers walked by the sheriff's cruiser pointing and laughing. Ignacio nodded to some of them as they waved.

Sophia hesitated to answer as she watched girls smacking a group of boys on the arms. "Both. You moved from the small room to the kitchen." She flipped her cellphone shut, "So, let's think. Dr. Peters has the brown paper bags. He has the clinic's old seals. He has deadly herbs in his back garden growing ever so gleefully. Do you think he wanted to get rid of his wife? She couldn't have children?"

Ignacio sat back in the driver's seat, "No, that's not a good reason to do in the love of your life. They'd been married for over thirty some years. No, there's something else. We can't accuse him of anything. We don't know where those herbs came from or who had access. Charlotte worked with his wife. Charlotte was the one who took the bags and Granger's clinic seals to Maisy. There are too many people who are suspects. Including you, by the way."

She jumped, "Me? Why me? I have no reason to murder Rosa or Mrs. Maisy Peters. How can I be a suspect?"

Ignacio frowned as he studied her reaction, "That's just it. Who has a reason to kill anyone? If he killed his wife and Roberto decided to stay away, who would look after his place? His horses? Who? He needs Roberto. Charlotte loves Roberto. She wouldn't want to hurt him by killing his wife Rosa. Then there's Granger. He was in prison and he supposedly doesn't know any of these people. Why him?" Ignacio pointed out the window, "Here come the girls. Sybil doesn't appear to be pleased about this vehicle." Turning to the backseat, he shoved the copier to the side on the backseat. "Also, Sophia, why would anyone want to poison the elders in the Pueblo? Why them?" He waved at Sybil who had a very unpleasant facial expression.

Sophia opened her door to stand and give Sybil a hug, "Ignacio has been giving us a tour of the valley. He offered to pick you up." Noticing a folded white paper in Sybil's hand, she asked, "What's that?"

The paper was shoved at Sophia, "It's the layout for the Halloween party. Charlotte brought us each one. It's like a map. We choose the area we want to decorate and we're responsible for decorating it. Mom, we're supposed to bring supplies so I need to go by the store. Oh, hi, Ignacio. I thought you were arresting Mom. Too bad, huh?" She sat in the backseat next to Donna who had pushed the printer all the way over to the other door. A noticeable pout was on Sybil's face as she pointed to the printer, "What's that thing?"

Patting it, Donna said, 'It's a printer. Ignacio needs this thing for some sort of investigation."

Bending over Donna, Sybil asked, "Where are the connection cords? Did you get the connection cords? It won't work if you don't have the right cords to fit the machine, but you know this right?" The backdoor of the vehicle was slammed. "I mean, duh, computer cords won't work on this old thing." She mumbled.

Turning down the dirt road toward Alcon, Ignacio smiled, "Damn, opps, sorry girls, I completely forgot. I bet we have some cords that will fit at the office. We have nerdy guys there who have everything." His hand slapped the steering wheel, "I should know these things. Dr. Peters was intimidating, don't you think? He seemed to think he was better than we are. What did you think?"

Before Sophia could answer, Donna piped up from the backseat, "Yeah, he's a jerk. Sybil, this guy Dr. Peters may be a dentist but he doesn't like horses and he certainly didn't like his wife!"

Tilting the rearview mirror, Ignacio studied Donna's face, "Why do you say he didn't like his wife?"

Sybil put her arm around Donna's shoulders, "Yeah, smart sister of mine, why didn't he like his wife?"

Donna shoved Sybil's arm off her shoulder, "Well, for one thing he hasn't fed the horses since she died. They were starving. If he loved his wife, he would love her things and take care of them. Roberto hasn't been around and he was desperate for his help. The horses' hooves were packed with filth and they had no water."

Leaning back from the front seat, Sophia questioned, "And the second reason he didn't like his wife?"

"Well, her station wagon. The doors were all open in her station wagon. There were leaves blowing into it. The front windshield is filthy. It didn't look like anyone has driven it at all. I think it doesn't even work. The hood is up and there are leaves and old rags in the engine. I was trying to find an old rag to wipe down halters and the lead ropes in case I had enough time to take them for a walk." Sybil lifted Donna's long braid from her shoulder, "What else?"

Her braid was jerked from her sister's hand. "He said he couldn't figure out how to open the gate. Duh. He's really dumb. All you have to do is lift the latch. It ain't rocket science. Also, her scarf was trampled in the manure. It's still there. I was going to bring it into the house, but then I thought the horses might like to have it there to remember her by." Donna elbowed Sybil in the ribs, "Don't mess with my hair! I don't fiddle with yours!" Quickly, her attention turned back to her mother, "Oh, and I don't think Roberto stopped coming to help him, I really believe that he fired Roberto. There is no way Roberto would leave horses in such a mess! Roberto has a bleeding heart when it comes to horses. He loves them and would do anything for them, really, Mom, he would. He'd sneak over there for free and take care of them!"

A large tumbleweed rolled to slam and splinter all over the front of the sheriff's car. It covered the front windshield. Ignacio turned on the windshield wipers to remove the debris, "So, you believe Roberto was fired, huh?"

Donna pulled her hair braid over her shoulder away from Sybil, "Yeah. Roberto wouldn't ever leave a horse to be in that sorry condition. He wouldn't. That barn is a mess and the horses didn't have any water. They sucked up that liquid silver with gusto."

Tilting her head back, Sophia smiled at Donna, "Liquid silver, huh?" Sybil put her hand over her mouth and nose, "Unlike your boots that stink of manure. You and Dad know how to stink up a vehicle!" She received another elbow in the ribs. The Alcon road was peaceful. Kids were walking down the road on their way home from the school. The older kids held hands with the younger siblings as dogs ran to the edge of the fence barking and charging them. Suddenly, Donna yelled, "There's Griego! Look, there he is!" Ignacio slowed to roll down the back window on Donna's side of the car. She called to him, "Griego, you want to go riding later?" He bent down to stare into the vehicle, "Donna? Were you arrested? What're you doing in this car?"

Donna put her hand on the window, "Hey, do you want to go riding later? We can talk?"

"Nope, I have homework and stuff. My Mom needs me to help her. Hey, I heard you're coming to my school. The Charter School behind the store, right?" His long brown bangs blew over his eyes. Donna smiled, "Yep, I'm going to be there tomorrow. See you then, gotta go." Griego lifted his hand as Ignacio drove down the road to pull into Sophia's farm. The girls grabbed their things to crawl out of the backseat. Sophia thanked Ignacio for the ride and the fascinating afternoon. He backed up and drove away.

"Wow, what a day!" Sophia walked into the kitchen. She leaned against the counter to read the gym's map and list of items Sybil needed for the Halloween Party decorations. It was quite a list. "Sybil, are some of the other kids bringing these things or are you responsible for all of this?"

"No, Mom, let me change out of these pants. They're too tight. I need new pants, Mom." The bedroom door slammed. Dirt fell from the crack above the doorframe. Donna had gone into her own room, leaving her door open. She was lying on her bed with four of the cats. Her eyes were closed. Sophia took the list to her own bedroom. Kicking off her sneakers, she sat and then fell back onto the bed. Shonac was outside barking at the kids walking down the road.

Soon Sybil came into Sophia's room to lie down next to her. "I only have to provide the things with the star next to them. I think they're six things. Tomorrow we're going to vote on where all the games are going to be in the gym and where the guys will dance. We're not having a live band, too much money. We're getting a D. J. I think she's Jeff's mother. She's cool."

Folding the paper, Sophia handed it back to Sybil. "You like Jeff. Is he going to help decorate, too?"

"Who knows with guys? They say one thing and they mean another. Who knows? I'm going to get a cookie, you want one?"

"No, I have to get up or I'll fall asleep. Would you do two loads of laundry while I take Donna to the store in Rocoso for her school supplies? She's starting tomorrow at the Charter School. I think she's excited. We better go before we are too tired to move. Please, do a load or two of laundry or we won't have any clean underwear tomorrow."

Fergus cat padded into the bedroom. As he was about to leap on the bed, Sybil grabbed him, "Come on, Tubs, let's get a snack and do laundry." She hugged him to her.

10

Sybil was dropped off at her Middle School with very little drama. The sky was a soft chalky blue with fluffy white clouds covering the mountains on the eastern horizon. Fat geese had arrived to peck away at the dried ground in pastures with grazing horses and cows. The arrival of geese and cranes meant the weather further north was too cold for them to stay, they had traveled to warmer climes down here. Sophia parked her old van in the parking lot. There were only three other cars in the large lot behind the school. Donna held her horse backpack tightly in her hand as they walked into the building. Catherine was standing at the counter talking to Secretary Tracy as they entered the office. She quickly turned her attention to Donna, "Would you like to start with your home room being art or math?"

The twelve year old quickly answered, "Math. I really like math." Sophia knelt to be at eyelevel with Donna, "Math? Seriously, math?"

Donna had a big smile on her face, "Yes, math. Mom, Griego has shown me how important math is and I want math to be my homeroom, o-kay?"

Shaking her head, Catherine asked Donna one more time in a different way, "Griego has math fourth period, but he has art for homeroom. Now, let's rethink this, which would you prefer for homeroom?"

Wrinkling her nose, Donna looked up at Catherine, "Well, in that case, how about art? Mom says I'm really good at art, taking photographs and drawing horses."

"Then art it shall be." Catherine turned her attention to Sophia, "Are you staying for the first day or are you going to the university? I already received a call that you asked the students in our class to work on their presentations for next week. That's why I'm standing here and not sitting in your class."

Putting her hand on Donna's shoulder, Sophia answered, "Yes, I thought I would sit in and observe your profession for a change. No judgement though, absolutely no judgement here. Is it all right with you if I do this?"

Lifting a batch of books from the counter, Catherine started to walk ahead of them. "Follow me." The school had eight rooms with four grades. The classrooms were small as were the number of students in each room. The art room had nine students. The teacher Miss Cole was a formidable artist in her own style with her work on one of the walls. The pastel she had done of a cowboy leaning against a fencepost was very life like. It appeared he could walk right off the wall and have a conversation with the kids. Griego was busy at work on a collage using yarn, pieces of wood and some sand. When he saw Donna he jumped up and went to her, "Come sit over here by me. We can work together at the same table." Donna didn't hesitate. Then she turned to Sophia, "Mom, I think I'm fine. Why don't you go ahead and do your stuff." She ran to sit beside Griego.

Catherine followed Donna to her chair, "Miss Donna, these are your books for the day. I've put you in with Mr. Griego and he can show you where to go after each class. Is this all right?"

"Yes, Ma'am. Thank you, Ma'am." Donna pushed the books to the side of the table. Catherine bent over to speak to Donna, saying privately to her, "You can call me Ms. Catherine. Don't call me Ma'am, please." Donna's face turned red as she watched her mother smile at the other side of the room, "Yes, Ms. Catherine. My Mom doesn't like Ma'am either."

Outside of the Charter School Sophia sat in the van to watch a fat cow rub her backside against an upright cottonwood tree stump. "I guess I should visit my mother and then head to work." The van started, was put into gear and Sophia drove off to the small hospital at the base of a hill outside of Rincon. Fluffy clouds had gathered over the Sandia Mountains. Flocks of white cranes flew overhead. Layers after layer of cranes called out in the crisp blue sky. Sophia smiled, remembering her mother's quote, "When a person is blessed with flying cranes overhead, it is a suggestion to cultivate one's resilience in life. Hah!"

Large signs were being put up notifying the general public of the balloon fiesta coming next weekend to central New Mexico. As Sophia drove through Rincon proper she noticed the out of state license plates parked beside the sidewalks. The Ristro Café served breakfast with lots of green, red and Christmas chili. It was packed with people standing outside on the sidewalk waiting for tables. Driving west, Sophia saw the highway department working on the bridge going over the Rio Grande. Whenever there was a tourist event in this area the highway department had to come out and tear up the roads placing miles of orange barrels to confuse locals and tourists.

At the hospital Sophia found a nice parking place away from the tumbleweed collection. She stopped at the gift shop to buy her mother some chocolate and life savers. As she entered the room she almost bumped into a short man with a bald head who was right on the other side of the door. Shocked at the thought of almost hitting him, Sophia blurted out, "Excuse me! I didn't mean to hit you!"

The man stepped aside, "No, it's all right. I do this all the time, you'd think I'd learn wouldn't you? Come in, please, come in."

Margaret sat upright in the bed. Her face was flushed and her hands were twisting the sheet in front of her. "Dr. Sawyer, this is my daughter Sophia Pino. She's a doctor of philosophy not a real doctor."

He put out his hand, "I'm impressed. I tried to get a PhD, but could never handle the heavy load. We were just talking about your mother's health. She was upset by what we've found. Perhaps you could speak about her concern."

Sophia moved to stand next to her mother's hospital bed. "What is the issue?"

Not waiting for Dr. Sawyer to say anything, Margaret blurted out, "They found a lump on my breast! A lump! It wasn't there before and now it's there! A lump!" Margaret grabbed Sophia's wrist..

Carefully removing Margaret's finger tight grip from her wrist, Sophia held onto her mother's gnarly fingers. Sophia said, "Mom, there are lumps and there are lumps. Now Dr. Sawyer explain to us what you believe is the problem with my Mother's lump?"

Squeezing Sophia's hand with all of her weak might, Margaret interrupted again, "Sophia, call me Margaret!"

Dr. Sawyer watched the two women with a smile on his face, "Margaret, your daughter is correct. There are lumps and there are lumps. Some are malignant and some are benign. All we need to do is a biopsy. If it is malignant, we have it removed and can go from there. We can find out if it is cancer or just a benign lump."

Margaret's body started shaking, tears fell from her face, "Cancer? No one said anything about cancer?"

Sophia pulled the white plastic chair closer to the hospital bed. She sat down still holding her mother's hand, "Margaret, listen to me. Many people and especially women get lumps. They can be anything and sometimes they are cancer and sometimes not. No one will know what it is until they do a biopsy. The doctor needs your permission and understanding to do the biopsy. This is what he's saying."

"Call Granger!" Margaret's free hand hit the gray princess phone on the bedside table. Severe panic screamed out in her voice, "Call Granger!" The handheld device dropped with a clunk to the floor. A loud dial tone filled the air. Dr. Sawyer hurried to pick up the phone and place it back on the cradle.

Twisting her body in a strange manner, Margaret desperately

grabbed the phone. Before she was able to dial, Sophia nodded to a man entering the room behind the doctor, "Granger? Come in, you're right in time!"

"What?" Granger gently pushed the door all the way open to stand next to Dr. Sawyer. He held a large brown bag. "Why is everyone staring at me?"

Twisting back to the front, Margaret gasped, "Granger! Oh, Granger, they say I have cancer! They want to remove my breasts!" Gnarly fingers grabbed at her sagging chest, "Oh, Granger, I have cancer!" Margaret folded in on herself. A small frail woman sobbing with her dry hair flying around her forehead, "Oh, Granger, I want to die." Her shoulders heaved in despair. Granger glanced at Sophia with a nasty smile.

Dr. Sawyer put his hand on his chest, "Margaret Pino, as I live and breathe I never said you do have cancer. Please, you two talk to her and let me know what you choose. I'll be at the nurses' station writing charts." The hospital door softly closed as he left the room.

Margaret's hand flung wildly, "Granger, come here. Son, come here." Granger put the bag on the bed next to her. He didn't take her hand, "Margaret, I'm sorry I've not come to visit you. I was searching for my Mercedes." His serious tone turned gleeful, "I found it! Mom, I found it!" His face glowed, "Mom, or Margaret, I found it and she's only ninety-nine thousand dollars! Margaret, I need the money! Please, can I have the money? Please! I beg of you!" His clasped hands were held in prayer in front of his chest.

Both of the women stared at him. Finally, Sophia spoke, "Granger, your mother is upset regarding the lump on her breast. I don't think your Mercedes is an issue right now, not right at this moment."

The twisted sheet in Margaret's hands was used to wipe her nose and the tears from her cheeks. Hysteria had subsided into a strange calm. "That's nice, dear. I'm glad you found your Mercedes. But right now I am worried about my lump." Margaret patted the bedsheet in front of her chest.

Hands to hips, his flushed face confronted them, "Look, I'm sorry about your damn lump, Mom. But I found my Mercedes! Someone else could buy it while we're standing here talking about a stupid lump." His weight shifted from foot to food, "I need to get my car back right now! Right Now! This minute before it disappears again or the price goes up!" He stopped to sniff the air, "What is that nasty smell? Do I smell stink?" His large brown eyes bored into his mother's frightened face.

Banging open the room door, a nurse charged into the hospital room, "Excuse me, Miss Margaret, but we had emergency at the end of the hall. I'm here now to clean you up." Suddenly she noticed Sophia and Granger standing beside the bed. "I'm sorry. I didn't know she had visitors. Would you two mind excusing us for a few minutes?" She held the door open. Her hand in a sweeping gesture for them to depart the room.

Granger shook his head, "Ew, how gross. Margaret, you messed in the bed?"

The nurse received one of Granger's warm pathetic smiles as he hurried out into the hall ahead of Sophia. The brown bag was back in his hand. The nurse whispered to Sophia, "She's on the bedpan. She would rather die than mess her bed!"

Brother and Sister walked to the end of the hall where there were two tall plate glass windows. A couch was placed underneath them with a coffee table in front of it laden with worn well-thumbed magazines. Pointing to the brown bag in his hand, Sophia asked, "What do you have in there? Herbs?"

Granger raised his eyebrow, "If you wish. Here, go ahead and look. There are a type of herbs in here, but not what you're thinking. Here, look?" He shoved the bag at her. She pushed the magazines aside to sit on the coffee table. Gingerly, she took the bag from him. Opening it carefully, she pulled out a box of English toffee wrapped with a pink silk ribbon. A white envelope with 'Mother" printed on it was stuck under the pink ribbon. Laughing, Sophia handed him the box, "She won't like this! Not at all. You better fix it if you want her to buy you a Mercedes."

"What? What's wrong with this? Mom loves English toffee. She would kill for this box of toffee after the yucky food she's eating in here. There's nothing wrong with a box of English toffee to win her heart, right?"

"Sure, here's the bag. Surprise her. You're right. She'll love this. Here put it back in the bag."

The box back in the brown bag, Granger sniffed, "What's all this about her lump? All they do is a biopsy and if it's benign, which it probably is, she's fine. Why is she birthing a bovine?"

Leaning back on her arms, Sophia noticed his cellphone in his khaki pant pocket by his knee. "Granger, when you were told you had prostate cancer, how did you feel? Were you elated or scared?" She patted the coffee table top beside her, "Sit and tell me about your experience."

Instead of sitting, he picked up a magazine to scan through it, "I was terrified. My cancer was a sure thing. At first I didn't believe the prison doc. I mean, come on, I was sure they did all kinds of practice surgeries on us guys. You know, we're the perfect guinea pigs for the medical profession. We're sitting ducks like guys in the military where could we go to say no?"

Plucking the magazine from his hand, Sophia placed it on the stack of others beside her, "So, you were scared? What changed your mind to go ahead with the surgery knowing what you know now?"

His leg swung over the coffee table as he sat on the couch. The plastic cover creaked with his weight. "They showed me the blood test. My white blood count was high and my red count was nil. Then there was the ultrasound. The pictures were done with me right there, no way could they forge those. And yes, it hurt to pee. So, I was convinced I had prostate cancer. No doubt in my mind."

She turned to see his expressions, "What did you think of the doc who did the surgery? Before and after the big event?"

"Hell, I just wanted the cancer gone, out of my body! I was furious that cancer had found me of all people! Papa didn't have prostate cancer. Why me? Hey, get this horrible cancer out of me, get it gone! That's what I thought." He shivered remembering.

Sophia patted his knee, "After the surgery, then what?"

He set the brown bag beside him on the orange plastic couch. "Well, I knew there would be pain afterwards. I mean they were digging into one of my most precious parts. A place where pain is super awful!" His fingers pushed back his bangs from his forehead, "I mean the word pain doesn't even come close to what I was going through. My brain felt fire, my groin felt burned with acid. I slept because there was no other way to comprehend my condition. I wanted to die. Seriously, I wanted to die rather than feel such excruciating torment."

The bag was pushed aside as Sophia twisted to sit next to him on the couch, "What did the doc say? Didn't they give you something for the pain?"

His eyebrows lifted, "Seriously? They don't give opioids to prisoners! What do you think? No, they gave me aspirin and then when I didn't stop screaming they tried ibuprofen. I kept right on screaming until the orderly gave me a shot that knocked me out. I must have slept for four days, out cold. Slowly, I learned to shut up and suck up the pain or else they would knock me out."

Sophia watched the nurse walk up the hall to them, "Your mother's all clean and ready for company. Please, don't make a big deal out of the bedpan. I was busy and your poor mother was stuck. She is very embarrassed by this. Anyway, she's ready if you want to see her now." The nurse scurried away to a room with a light on over the door.

Sophia stood, "Well, here we go. Granger, is your cancer gone now? Did you have to have chemo afterwards?"

Slowly, he stood to pick up the brown bag, "Yes, I had chemo. Strong doses for eight months then another test. No sign of the cancer. They continued the chemo for another four months and then pills for a year. As of a month prior to my release, there is no cancer in my body. I still need to go in for tests every so often to be sure I'm clear." He stepped over the coffee table to stand beside Sophia, "Mom though, no, she doesn't have cancer. Can't see it."

As they entered the hospital room, Margaret's hand waved to the corner of the room, "Sophia, get me my purse. It's in the closet over there. The tall gray thing is a closet, get my purse." Margaret's gnarled arthritic finger pointed to the steel upright cabinet in the corner of the room. Sophia didn't move, "No, I'm not getting your purse. You'll give Granger the money and then you won't have anything to live on, Margaret. This is all the money you have in the whole world and even more."

Jerking the metal door open, Granger lifted his mother's purse that hung on a hook inside. "Here, Margaret, here you go." He carefully handed the leather purse to his mother. A checkbook in a green leather case was found. Digging further she extracted a fountain pen. "How much for your car, dear?" She stroked the back of his hand with her fingers. The room suddenly became dark with a cloud moving in front of the sun. Sophia glanced out the window. Sandia Mountain was purple black in the shadow of the cloud. Wind blew dust devils around the parking lot.

Standing tall while glaring at Margaret, he said, "I'll need one hundred thousand dollars. This includes the tax." His chest filled with pride.

Margaret flipped shut the rectangular pages in her checkbook. "I can't make it for that much, Sweetie. This check will bounce. We'll both be in jail." The check book was returned to her purse. "How much did you say you needed again?"

In the dim light of the room, Granger stared at his mother, "Margaret, do I need to say everything twice?" He stepped back, leaned over to stare at her in the face, "One hundred thousand dollars and this includes tax." Margaret gasped, "For a car? Just to get around? Can't you use my truck?" Tears welled up in her eyes.

Quietly, Sophia lifted the white plastic chair to its place by the window. She nodded to Granger as she watched her mother put the pen to her mouth, "Margaret, I have to go teach. You two have fun." Pointing her finger at Granger, she said, "I'll talk to you later, huh?"

She stopped at the nurses' station. Dr. Sawyer looked up as she paused in front of him, "Dr. Sawyer, may I ask how you found the lump on my mother's breast? Can we talk?"

They stood in an empty conference room. "Your mother is very weak as I'm sure you noticed. There was concern about her not eating the food served to her. She needs food if her bones are going to mend. Her cracked pelvis is such that the only way it will mend is if she eats a balanced diet, takes her calcium, does her physical therapy and gets plenty of rest."

Sophia nodded. "This was explained when they brought her in with her first doctor. Yes, but how did…"

He put his hand up, "Let me explain something to you. This information may not be new, but it is important. Evidently, your mother believes she is fat. She refuses to gain any weight or weigh anything at all in order to be pleasing to your brother. Now, wait, wait a moment, I know what you're going to say. This is what she's told the ward nurse and she has expressed this to me."

Turning away from him in confusion, Sophia said, "This is sick. This is seriously sick. Granger isn't interested in her that way. What is she promoting by saying such a thing?"

Dr. Sawyer followed her to the end of the long room. They stood staring out the large window facing the hill covered with rabbit bush, chamisa and stunted juniper. "Your mother refuses to eat. She has lost four more pounds since she has been in here. Soon we will have to force feed her or put her on a strict regime with consequences. The amount of protein she needs cannot be given only by an I.V."

"All right, I accept that, but she'll hate you forever. Still, you haven't answered my question, how did you find the lump?"

One of the large conference chairs was pulled out and the Doctor sat down. "She was unable to wash herself yesterday. She can barely do the physical therapy. The ward nurse called me. I asked to have an aid wash your mother." He stared at the table as he traced an outline of a coffee cup stain on the wood with his index finger, "Your mother wouldn't have it. Eventually the aid allowed her to wash her upper body. The aid found the lump and it is an impressive lump."

Leaning forward with her hands on the conference table, Sophia asked, "But why wouldn't my mother have mentioned the lump or found the lump? How is this a new thing to discuss? Certainly my mother was aware of it?"

Pursing his lips, he glanced at Sophia, "Evidently, not. She was shocked that I would ask her if she had checked her body. Her reply was most succinct, "I do not stare at my body! That's obscene!' If I had been standing any closer I think she would have slapped my face." He watched Sophia's reaction.

"What do you recommend we do now? I bet you want to do the biopsy, right?"

Something in his jacket pocket beeped. He ignored it and spoke directly to Sophia, "Yes, I believe in a biopsy. There are those who think it best to just remove the whole breast and be done with it. Myself, I'm a slow and steady type of fellow. Let's be cautious. This could be nothing at all and then there would be no reason to cut. After all your mother is not a spring chicken and a major surgery in her frail condition would not be advised anyway." He coughed, than added, "There are choices and not all of them are radical. Seriously, I believe your mother doesn't have cancer but has a natural benign growth. These do happen in older women." He pulled out his prescription pad and wrote down a phone number, "Here's my phone number. This one up here is the office phone. My office is on the first floor here in the hospital. Give me a call if you want to talk further, but right now your brother has power of attorney and he is the only one who can make this decision."

Sophia ran to the old van. A hard wind had picked up blowing more tumbleweeds across her path as she quietly drove to the university. She was early for her second class, but there were always things she could do. Two of her students were sitting waiting for her in the faculty office. She called them back to her cubicle. Her day passed without confusion. No word from Granger. Between the second and last class, Sophia was tempted to call him on the cellphone, but she thought better of it. There was enough going on in her life right now. At least Sybil had done all the laundry the night before while she and Donna shopped for school items.

Her last class ended with good humor and many of the students showed their appreciation for her style. This class would be a lovely experience. Returning to her cubicle, she entered the roster of students in all the classes onto her computer. Curiosity got the best of her though as she pulled out her cellphone. Before she could press Granger's number, it rang. "Hello?"

"Dr. Pino, this is Mr. Goldfarb your father's attorney. I thought it best to call you and ask your opinion on something your mother is trying to do with the stocks your father entrusted to her. You mother is only able to sell these stocks with my approval. It was stated in his will if you remember?" His deep legal voice was confident and firm.

"Ah, yes, Mr. Goldfarb, how are you? We haven't seen each other for some time."

Mr. Goldfarb cleared his throat, "Sophia, I wish this was a social call, but it isn't. Your mother called asking to sell all of the stocks your father entrusted to her through me. Evidently, she needs to buy a Mercedes for your brother. If she sells all of her stock, she will no longer have dividends to live off of. Do I make myself clear?" His elderly voice was becoming raspy.

"Yes, loud and clear. No, I do not believe Granger needs a Mercedes. An old truck would be fine for him. He's just out of jail."

“Thank you, I always value a second opinion. I shall pass this on to your dear mother.” The last of his sentence dripped with sarcasm. “Your mother will blame you of course for Granger’s disappointment, but I believe you can handle her.” Dial tone.

Sophia stared at the cellphone, “Well, that was quick an easy.” Books were loaded in her pull along as she glanced out the window to check the weather. Dark purple clouds had moved over the mountain and into the valley. They hung low giving the afternoon sky a feeling of doom. The faculty secretary stopped Sophia as she was leaving to hand her four printed papers. “Your students asked if you would e-mail them to let them know what you thought of their outlines.”

Taking them, Sophia thanked her. Thunder rumbled overhead as rain clouds threatened as she drove to Otero Middle School. Sybil was huddled within a circle of her school chums when Sophia arrived to pick her up from Middle School. The girls appeared to be studying something and were oblivious to parents waiting. Sophia honked the horn with a gentle tap. All the girls turned to stare at the lineup of cars. Suddenly, Sybil noticed the old van. She raised her hand, lifted her backpack from her feet and ran to her mother. “Hi, Mom, this Halloween Party is going to be something. If we can make money by selling tickets. It will only take two hundred and eight people to buy tickets and then my school band can go to Washington and play for the President. Isn’t that something?”

Slamming the passenger door, Sybil kept talking, “Two hundred and eight tickets, that’s not too many, right? We could get all the Sheriffs to buy one and all the people at Donna’s school. I could go up and down Alcon Road and sell tickets, right, Mom?” She snapped her seatbelt. “So how’s the murdering going?”

A serious face confronted Sybil, “Murder isn’t funny. As far as I know no one else has been killed. But then I’m not part of the investigation. I’m a regular citizen.”

Sybil hugged her backpack, “You’re in a solemn mood. What’s going on?”

Putting on the blinker, Sophia drove from the school tarmac to the dirt road, “Oh, nothing. Granger wants to buy back his old Mercedes for thousands and thousands of dollars. Margaret has a lump on her breast and I haven’t eaten anything since this morning and that was only a piece of toast.”

“Oh, that’s all, huh? Let’s get Donna and get food. I’m starving.”

“Your sister is walking home with Griego. She was put in most of his classes if not all of them. When I left her this morning she was in heaven. We'll get a report this evening. Yes, let's go get food." Sophia turned her head to watch for traffic as she drove onto the main road to Rincon.

Six tacos, three packaged enchiladas that came with four sopapillas were wrapped in aluminum foil and placed in the white bag held in Sybil's lap. The Ristro café had filled their order in only fifteen minutes. Chalk blue was the color of the sky now that the strong wind had blown the rain clouds far to the southwest. Fluffy white clouds blanketed the eastern horizon. Two ravens flew in a synchronized motion over the road to Alcon. Mr. Owen's chickens were out wandering in the road as they drove by Griego's small house. Reina waved to them with her free hand. A clothespin was in her mouth and a basket of wet clothes at her feet. Her clothesline was decorated with Griego's jeans, t-shirts and one of her house dresses. Freddy Chacon was out on his tractor disking his long narrow field. Later, he would laser level it for better irrigation. Turning into the farmhouse driveway, Shonac ran from the barn to meet the van. Ignition off, Sybil jumped out of the van to race into the house, to the kitchen.

Donna and Griego stepped out of the barn. Both wore cowboy boots, had on black felt hats and pleased expressions. Sophia grabbed her purse, threw the strap over her shoulder as she walked to the two horseback riders. "Hey, how're you two doing?"

Leaping into the air, Donna landed to dip and jump again, "We're fine, Mom! Griego is in all of my classes, but P.E. He has an extra math class since he's an expert in figures. The only elective I could take was P.E. It's all right, though, because this spring the P.E. class is going to have a rodeo." Griego thrust his fist into the air, "Yeah! A rodeo!"

Donna punched him in the shoulder, "Yeah, and you're not going to participate. This means some of us actually will have a chance to win something."

Sybil skipped up to them from the house, "Well, dinner is ready! I'm a fast cooker and the food will be excellent." Then she noticed Griego standing behind Donna, "Oh, Griego, are you going to eat with us?" He shook his head. He was his Uncle Juan Calderon's nephew, tall, slightly built with the same benevolent attitude, the same warmth in his smile. "Nope, have to go home and help Mom. She's busy today with the chores. So, I get to cook dinner and clean the kitchen. Yippee!" He frowned.

Sophia and Sybil returned to the kitchen. The rich smell from the beef tacos and the simmering enchiladas Sybil had placed on a cookie sheet in the oven, brought out Sophia's hunger. She watched from the kitchen window as Griego trotted out of the barn on Guaco. Donna waved at him with a horse brush in her hand. Minutes later, Donna arrived to wash her hands and help with the setting of the table. As they finished the delicious meal, Donna raised her fork in a salute, "This meal has not been interrupted or infringed upon by any outside person or peoples. Hurrah, for the first time in several days!"

Swallowing the last of her honey soaked sopapilla, Sybil chorused, "Absolutely! At last, the three of us have eaten in peace and quiet. A salubrious gastrointestinal delight for which we can joyously croon a carol to marvel with elation. How's them apples?"

Clapping at the incredible word use, Sophia cheered, "Bravo! Now to do the dishes!"

Her hand up in the air, Sybil deferred, "Not me! I have algebra to study and then cut orange paper pumpkins for the Halloween party decorations. Mr. O'Brian seriously wants to make this the best decorated event of the year."

Plates were stacked beside the kitchen sink as Donna ran hot water, "Mom, I'll wash. You can dry. Then I have to do some catchup work in English. My teacher is Miss Casaus from the rez. She said no matter what language you speak it is important to know it to the best of your ability. We're going to learn some Keres words, too. First, we have to know how to spell the words in English and how to use them in a sentence and then to know what they are called in grammar. We didn't do any of this stuff at the private school. Just spelling and I worsened at it."

Glasses were carried to the kitchen sink in Sophia's hands, "You didn't worsen at it. You didn't do well in spelling. Sounds to me you will learn how to spell the words by learning their purpose much faster. We can go over your words once the dishes are done, how about that?"

"Sounds good." Donna filled the sink with warm water. Dishwashing soap was added and stirred for bubbles. Sybil arrived to fold the linen napkins at the end of the table, "Mom, did you sign the release paper for me? I need to work after school next week on the decorations in the gym? Mr. O'Brian is a stickler for parent permission forms." She lifted her backpack from the kitchen chair, "You know you might want to meet him. He's going to be strapped for help this year because Mrs. Peters was a person who was big on using the spiders' webs and the batik dyes for the haunted house we put up behind the gym. Mom, maybe you could help out?" A side pocket from the backpack was opened. A folded piece of paper was placed on the table beside the green linen napkins. "Here's the form, please, sign it for me? Tonight, please?"

Dishtowel held in midair, Sophia stared at Sybil, "Mr. O'Brian worked with Mrs. Peters? Wait. Now I remember. Last year, they had huge spider webs strung from the ceiling of the haunted house to the floor, right?"

"Yeah, so what? He still needs help this year. Mom, you're tall and you could help. What's so important about spider webs? All the schools use them, but Mrs. Peters had this stuff she made with Charlotte that really sticks. I mean it sticks to your clothes, your hair and it's seriously scary."

"Sybil, what else does Mr. O'Brian do? What does he do with dyes?" Sophia's interest was now piqued.

The backpack unzipped to pull out a fat algebra book and a three ring binder. "He showed us in science class how Mrs. Peters used dyes to make batik stuff. She twists a cloth, scrunches it with a rubber band and dips the puckered part into different colored dyes she's made from plants. In science class we boiled the plants, drained off the plant stuff and dipped cloth into the color liquid junk. It's really cool. People did this to their clothes in the seventies. Did you wear batik clothes in the seventies, Mom, or were you still a baby?"

Slapping the dishtowel against the chair beside Sybil, Sophia smirked, "No, I wasn't a baby and 'yes' I did wear batik when I was pregnant with you! Remember you were born in the seventies, stinker!"

Algebra book hugged to her chest, Sybil took a pencil from the clear plastic holder, "I better get busy. The gym is going to be beautiful and frightening. I hope Donna can come and maybe even Griego. I'm going into my room, bye!" Her bedroom door slammed shut behind her. Dirt fell from the wall above, adding to the pile on the floor. The evening ended peacefully.

Sophia's diary completed for the day. The bedside lamp was turned off as cats curled on the bed around Sophia. Petting Silky and then Marmalade who was beside her chest, Sophia let her body relax. "This has been an extremely busy day. A good day for once. May tomorrow be peaceful? Good night, kitties."

11

Robin birdsong pierced the air. Then the phone rang in the hall. Sophia stretched as she watched the numerous cats race into the kitchen. Someone was using the electric can opener. "The girls are up. Although, I bet that's Donna who's excited about her school for once."

A soft knock on the bedroom door brought Donna into Sophia's bedroom. Sophia had finished tying her shoes when she looked up at her daughter, "What's up, Sweetheart?"

"It's Grandma. She needs to speak with you. She's desperate. I didn't know grandma had cancer? Why didn't you tell me?" Donna leaned against the doorframe. "She's sounds sad and small, Mom. You better talk to her."

Sophia followed Donna into the hall. Sybil was sitting at the kitchen table. A bowl of oatmeal was steaming in front of her. Pointing to the bowl with her spoon, she asked, "Mom, you want some? I can make you a bowl? You need to eat more food!" Sophia nodded, "Yes, please. I have to teach today and need to be in my best form. Please, oatmeal sounds just right." She picked up the phone, "Hello, Margaret? How can I help you?"

Sybil turned on the water kettle to make her mother's breakfast. Donna ran out the door to feed the horses. Sophia smiled, "Margaret, I'm just fine. I have the most wonderful daughters on the planet. So, now what? You need me to bring you some items from your farmhouse? Yes, let me get a paper and pencil." Six things were written down before Sophia reminded her mother, "I teach today, Mom. You know this, right? I won't be able to get these things to you until after four o'clock. Why don't you have Granger bring you these things? He's living in your house."

Sybil made a face at her mother, then whispered, "Mom, we won't have time to go to the hospital today. We have the Halloween meeting after school. Granger will have to get Grandma's stuff."

Griego knocked on the door as Sophia and Sybil were about to open it. Quickly stepping back, he asked, "Hey, I'm here for Donna? We better head to the school if we don't want to be late."

Sybil's fifteen year old laugh echoed through the farmhouse, "She's in the barn, of course. She has her stuff ready. I like your school. Wish I could go to it?"

Sophia's motherly voice said, "No! You're finishing up Middle School at Otero and then high school. Griego's school isn't ready for you, not yet." Warm air hit them as they got into the old van. Ducks circled Diego Ortiz's field full of irrigation water. Pointing at them, Sybil asked, "Don't we irrigate later? After Juan?" Then she dropped her backpack onto the floorboard at her feet, "He could come over for dinner and fix us dessert?"

Turning her head to watch Donna and Griego run down Alcon Road, Sophia chortled, "Wouldn't you like that? No, tonight you both have homework."

Sybil was dropped off in front of her middle school to forge along with the other students. The long drive to UNM was tedious for there were two accidents on the off ramp. Sophia had to follow the frontage road to the next exit and double back. Suddenly, she spoke to the street sign above UNM, "Wonder how Geoffrey is doing? Hope he's cleaning his home, poor guy." She parked in the lower parking lot. Grabbing her pull-along, she hurried into her cubicle. Four post-it notes were stuck on her computer monitor. "A fire drill in half an hour? This should be interesting right in the middle of a lecture!"

Lights were flicked on in the large hall. Several students were already seated. Sophia placed her notecards on the podium beside the computer. She shoved in her thumb drive and placed her books on the table beside the podium. No sooner was the sign-in sheet returned to her when the fire alarm rang. The high pitched scream was deafening. Hands over ears, students slowly walked out of the large room into the hall and out of the double doors to the center open garden. Hundreds of people stood around waiting for the obnoxious sound to cease. Acting dean Alice walked around the horde of people, counting professors who had their hands in the air. Suddenly, there was silence. Clapping her hands as she stood on a cement flower wall, Principal Alice called out, "Please, return to your regular classes!"

Milling back into the lecture room, students were quietly upset. Sophia stood at the front before her podium, "Welcome back to class. Now that our morning has been rudely interrupted by screaming banshees, I believe we should all retreat to the library where you can work on your presentations for next week. I will be there to advise and appreciate what you find. Let's go."

Catherine caught up with Sophia as they entered the library. "Dr. Pino, your daughter Donna is delightful. She's quite the storyteller. Mr. Davis is excited to have her in his drama class next year. He heard her telling everyone about the ghosts in her bedroom. She reminds me of you when you share history stories in class."

Smiling, Sophia admitted, "Yes, people who know both of us speak of how alike we are. Although, I'm not sure. I think I'm taller!" Classes moved smoothly as Sophia finished her day of teaching. The drive to Sybil's school was uneventful. When she parked in the parental line-up to retrieve the students, Sybil ran out to her, "Mom, come inside and meet Mr. O'Brian. He wants to talk to you about the party and maybe you could offer some ideas to help?" Studying the cars behind her in the line-up, Sophia said, "I can't leave the van here. I better go and park in the parking lot. Wait for me, I'll meet you inside."

The art room smelled of wet paint and glue. Mr. O'Brian and Sybil were sitting in a circle with other students and another teacher. Charlotte was at the white board writing a list with a diagram. "We will have the dunking for apples here at the front of the gym. There will be towels and a spoon. We can't have anyone actually dunk their heads in the water bucket because this would spread germs. We are going to do what we did last year, use the colander spoon." Charlotte drew a bucket by a square representing a door. She turned to notice Sophia standing by the door. "Sophia! Come in, come in. We're putting together our plans. Come join us!"

Nodding, Sophia quietly sat down on an empty chair next to Sybil who smiled. Charlotte continued with her drawing on the white board, "Now, here we will have the ball throw unless you guys think it is too juvenile. What do you think?" Students raised their hands and joined in open discussion. Sophia was impressed with the thoughtfulness of the young people. Mr. O'Brian appeared to urge them to add their ideas and rarely put in his own. Finally, the brain storming was finished. Everyone stood to gather their things. Mr. O'Brian put out his hand to Sophia, "Dr. Pino, I presume? How nice to finally meet you."

Their conversation remained on the decorations for the Halloween party. Sophia did ask him about his use of herbs and dyes, but he preferred to ignore her questions sticking to the party plans. Once outside, Sybil was excited, "Mom, what if our class makes enough money for us to go to Washington D.C.?" Sophia stopped to stare back at the school, "What is it about Mr. O'Brian that makes me nervous? Sybil, he didn't, no, he wouldn't answer my questions. What's with that? There is something about the man that makes me concerned."

Sybil stuck her arm into her mother's, "He's fine. He's a man. They're all strange. Even you said that men are strange. Don't worry about him. Let's go home. I'm tired and it is only Wednesday!"

A plastic container was pulled out of Sybil's backpack. "Damn, I'm starving! We had a stupid fire drill this morning. Thought my brain was going to ooze out of my ear holes." Sybil munched on her rolled tortilla filled with cheese.

Turning onto the dirt road from the school, Sophia smiled, "Yes, we had a fire drill at the university as well. I wonder if they have them at all the schools at the same time on the same day."

Her mouth full of food, Sybil agreed, "Yep, I bet they do. Why don't they have Billy Joel sing his song instead of the high pitched noise they try to fry our brains with on the intercom?"

"You mean 'I Didn't Start the Fire' by Bill Joel?" Sophia pulled tissue from the box in the backseat to hand to Sybil. "You know that's a great idea. If we all agreed to Billy Joel and his famous song then we wouldn't have nervous breakdowns, destroy brain cells and be in a much better humor after a fire drill."

"Yeah, I vote for Billy Joel." Sybil put her hand into her backpack to pull out a brown paper bag with the grocery's name on it. "Oh, Mr. O'Brian gave me this to give to you to give to the sheriff. I guess he didn't want to get involved with the law or something."

Pointing to the mid-console, Sophia asked, "What is it? What's in the bag?"

Sybil wiped her mouth, "Rosa the Cook's stuff. Evidently Mr. O'Brian has lockers in his classroom, at the back. He lets people who work at the school keep their stuff there. There's nowhere else for them to have a lockup. He forgot to give it to someone and he thought you'd know who should have it. Want a carrot?" She pointed a cut piece of carrot at her mother.

"No, thank you. Are the lockers locked?" Sophia watched two men unload a fat hog from the back of a truck at Freddy Chacon's farm.

"Duh! Of course lockers are locked. That's why they're called lockers. Mom, you're not real bright for a PhD are you? Anyway, she kept her stuff there and he forgot to give it back."

"Did you look in the bag? What's in there?" Sophia turned into their farmhouse to park under the hangman's tree. The chalk blue sky echoed the cold breeze that blew down from the mountains. Leaves cluttered the driveway as they danced along the ground with the cold air. Sybil handed her mother the brown bag with Rosa's name neatly printed in black on the front of it.

The backpack was held against Sybil's chest as she dropped down to the ground from the van. "No, I don't look at other people's stuff. Besides it's none of my business." Sybil pointed to Juan and Donna who were both in the barn area. "What are those guys doing here?"

Sophia turned off the ignition in the old van, "Well, your sister lives here and Don Juan Calderon apparently is giving her some discussion. Let's go find out shall we?"

The door slammed hard shaking the whole of the van as Sybil said, "No! I'm going inside and rest. I'm exhausted!" Shonac followed her into the house as the door slammed behind them. Sophia shook her head, "That girl really knows how to make noise and slam doors."

Juan met her half way to the barn, "Would it be all right if I showed Donna how to barrel race? She's shown an interest in it and her small Quarter horse with a fine butt would be excellent at going round the barrels. Would it be all right? I have some free time."

Sophia smiled at him, "All right. You sound as anxious to do this as she probably is. Fine, yes, I think it would be great. I'll just go inside and change into my farm clothes." Juan stepped back to study her, "You look mighty fine for a professional woman."

Sophia shook her head as she went into the house. Sybil was lying on her bed with the Dracula book held it in both hands. Sophia changed into her old jeans, a cotton work shirt and her heavy socks for her boots. Staring at her reflection in the mirror, she noticed her short hair was tight with her natural curls going in every direction. "Tough! This is who I am, live with it." Her fingers tried to comb her thick curls down, but they bounced right up again. Sophia went outside.

Juan and Donna were rolling the old oil barrels out from behind the tack outbuilding. The barrels were rusted, shedding powdered red-brown steel and smelled awful. Running in front of the barrel Juan was rolling, Sophia put her hand out to stop him, "Juan, these are foul. Don't use these. Don't we have better barrels somewhere?"

"No. These are fine. We're just using them as markers for her horse to ride around. They're no big deal. We aren't going to be professionally recording this. They're fine, no worry." He rolled the barrel around her. Donna ran back behind the outbuilding to get another barrel. "We need three, Mom. Don't worry, I won't run into them or anything. We won't get hurt." She hurried the barrel into the dirt then dragged it into the arena. Sophia shook her head, "I never thought she'd get hurt, now I wonder?"

"Hey! You!" A horse galloped into the farm. It was Mr. Nestor Casaus on his golden palomino stallion. "Hey, I need to speak to you, lady!" The stallion came to a sliding stop in front of the barn's tie down. Mr. Casaus tossed his reins over the tie down as he jumped to the ground. "Sophia, I have something serious to say to you and it is highly confidential. Do you keep secrets or are you a loud mouth Gringa lady who tells everything she knows to everybody?" His face was stern. His eyes were laughing. Sophia shook her head, "What? What is it that is so vital you almost ran me down with your wild horse there?"

He took her arm and led her deep into the open barn enclosure. "Remember I told you about those herbs the women were giving their fine upstanding husbands?"

"Yes, like you, Mr. Fine Upstanding Husband?" Sophia leaned against the stall's poles. He smiled, "We found out where they came from and they're not from your brother at all. They're from another doctor who has a cleaning woman who took the supplement herbs for her family or friends. This cleaning lady borrowed some of the bags to help her sister-in-law who's married to my cousin who works in Santa Fe. What do you think about that?"

Sophia scratched her head, "What do I think about what? You haven't told me anything."

"The herbs weren't herbs. They were old expired Viagra tablets." He grinned. His large white teeth smiled at her. "Your brother is fine. He's not going back to prison. You're not going to prison. I'm not going to prison and we can all dance at the next feast day, how about that?"

Donna ran into the barn. She stopped when she noticed Mr. Casaus standing smack dab in front of her mother, "Oh, sorry. I didn't know you had company."

Mr. Casaus leaned over to face Donna to sternly ask, "What? Are you calling this crazy old savage company?"

Donna's face blushed. His tone was severe. Quickly glancing at her mother, Donna raced out of the barn to Juan. The arena gate was open. Mr. Casaus' stallion was standing in the middle of the arena staring at Tracy who was making whinnying noises. Sophia admonished Mr. Casaus, "You're stallion is flirting with my daughter's mare. There was no need for you to be angry with my daughter." Sophia walked to the side of the arena. Juan cantered into the driveway with his barrel racing horse. A shiny breastplate on the horse's chest read 'Smokey.' Easy flowing strides took Smokey around the barrels. Juan stopped to help Donna onto Tracy and with instruction he let her canter around the barrels.

"Easy! Go easy! Canter her slowly. Take your time. Let her feel the flow and the pattern of the barrels. She'll get it. Give her rein and let her make her own pace." He called to Donna as she joyously moved around the barrels. Mr. Casaus was not to be outdone. He took his horse's reins, jumped into the saddle to follow Donna. At first Donna didn't notice. She was having a wonderful time. Her long braid bounced on her back as her horse Tracy cantered round and round the upright barrels. When she heard Mr. Nestor Casaus behind her, she pulled to the side and let him canter around her. Mr. Casaus laughed as he cantered out of the arena and out of the farm's driveway down Alcon Road.

"Good, he's gone. I didn't like him anyway." A woman's voice spoke right beside Sophia. Clementine's freckled face smiled, "Hi. I thought I'd watch before saying anything. Mr. Casaus has a chip on his shoulder as big as Australia, don't you think?" She nodded to Alcon Road, "He's a smart one on his steed of gold, but his manners need work. Although, I can't blame him for his land was taken from him. We have the same with our Natives down under."

Sophia gave her a hug as Clementine added, "See, I didn't end my sentence with a question then, right?"

They both laughed as they watched Juan and Donna on their horses go round the barrels. Then Juan pulled a stop watch from his pocket. He trotted over to the women, "Hi, Clementine. Nice to see you. We're going to time Donna and Tracy now to see how well they make those barrels fly by."

A bright red blush came over Clementine's face as Juan patted her arm, "You want to time her or should I?" Clementine shook her head, "You do it. I don't know what's going on except we're having a multicultural event here today. We've had Mr. Casaus, you guys and this Aussie. I love this farm." The sound of a truck pulled in behind them. All three turned to watch Roberto climb out of his blue painted truck. The driver's door slammed shut to bounce open almost hitting Roberto in the arm. Waving at them, he took the door and slowly shut it to remain closed. "Hola, como te va? Estoy aqui por las cosas de Rosa. Estamos hacienda un espectaculo de caballos?"

Clapping her hands, Clementine answered him, "Si` ! Un expectaculo de caballos y carreras de barril. Si` por que no?"

Juan burst out laughing, "Wow! An Aussie who speaks Spanish, who'd have thunk it? I'm impressed." Juan shook hands with Roberto who was studying Donna going around the barrels on her horse. Roberto pointed to Donna, "She's your hija, correct? She's got a good seat. I bet she'd be good at jumping, too. Hey, Mr. Juan, isn't she going slow for barrels?"

"Yeah, well, she just started. She's just got these barrels figured out and we're going to time her now, but I want her to go slowly so she won't get hurt or scared. Slow and steady, correcto, verdad?"

Roberto walked into the barn. He waved to Sophia, "Which horse is yours? Do you think I could ride?"

Proudly, Sophia introduced Roberto to the horses. "This is Teddy. He's a boarded horse. This is Lucky. He's my horse or I share him with Sybil. This is Angel and he's a boarding horse as well. Then here was

River Shore. He was boarded, but the owners have him for the month. They're showing him in Texas."

Roberto was rubbing Lucky's furry nose. "I'll take him. He likes me and we'll get going." Sophia brought him the saddle blanket, saddle, bridle and a bucket of oats. Roberto pushed away the oats, "No Bueno ahora, despues." Three mounted horses trotted and then cantered around the rusty oil barrels. Donna smiled gleefully as Juan and Roberto followed her around the barrels. Sophia sat on the pole fence to watch. Clementine beside her stood to watch, then asked, "Is Teddy available?"

Perched on the corral's white pole fence, Sophia waved and cheered the riders on as they flew around the barrels. Tracy appeared to come alive in the competition with her tail straight out and her ears forward as she raced around the barrels. Roberto disappeared into the tool shed, leaving Lucky at the tie down. After a lot of banging around he returned with a make shift jump. He put it together in the center of the arena. Motioning to Donna, he led her on Tracy over the low jump.

Geese flew overhead honking their way to the river. Suddenly, Sophia realized the sun was sitting on the very edge of the foothills. It was time to call for the horse lessons to end. Jumping from the fence, she called out to the group, "I best get inside and fix dinner. This has been an absolutely magnificent afternoon. Thank you for coming!"

Clementine pulled the saddle off of her horse. "Hey, I came prepared. Ristro has the most incredible enchiladas and I brought a huge box into the kitchen. Sybil is going to show me how to make sopapillas."

The kitchen was warm from the cooking by the time the men came inside. The delicious aroma of hot chili mixed with the refried beans on the stove top. Donna remained outside to have a quiet word with her best friend, her horse Tracy. Don Juan washed his hands at the kitchen sink. As he dried them on the kitchen towel, he mentioned he had dessert at his house and he'd be right back. They were to wait before putting the food on the table. Sybil was expertly dropping the squares of dough into the wok her mother used to heat the sunflower oil for sopapillas. Clementine stood beside the hot stove with pinchers in one hand and with the other hand she was spooning hot oil over the dough squares quickly. The dough rose in the hot oil to become cooked dough pillows as the oil was spooned over. Once they were browned, she lifted the cooked pillows out with pinchers to place them on a papered plate. Sophia stirred the refried beans heating on the back burner of the old stove.

Roberto sat at the kitchen table with the brown bag from the grocery store in front of him. Somberly, he took out each item one by one. In front of him was Rosa's lipstick, a nail file, some pens and pencils, a small notebook and a stack of papers. His solemn face reflected his sadness. Clementine pulled the last of the sopapillas from the hot oil. "Roberto, what have you there? Did you find Rosa's million dollars?" She smiled at him.

"No, lo siento. I miss my beautiful Rosa." The pens and pencils were dropped back into the bag. "I thought there would be something in here to say how she died." Shaking his head, he added, "There's nothing. Nothing, nada." Clementine sat in a chair opposite him. "What did you find?"

He gently placed the stack of papers in front of her, "I need the contract she signed with the school to show she worked. The insurance needed the paper. It's in there somewhere." His fingers flicked the papers toward Clementine.

Taking the papers, Clementine thumbed through them to ask, "Is it o-kay if I look?" He nodded. Then, slowly, Clementine reverently took each piece of paper and read it. One by one she placed the papers one on top of the other in front of Roberto. Finally, in the middle of the stack, she pulled out one particular paper. "Here, this is her contract. She wasn't getting paid very much money. Did you know how much she was paid?" The paper was placed in front of Roberto who sighed, "No, she wouldn't talk about her money. I knew she wasn't buying herself very many things. She was very careful with money. Is this what the insurance company wants?"

Donna spoke quickly as she placed the filled cat bowls on the small table in the corner of the kitchen. All five cats were eagerly waiting for dinner. "Roberto, thank you for showing me how to jump Tracy horse. She loved jumping. I don't think she's eager to race around those yucky barrels. You taught me a lot!"

Smiling at her, Roberto nodded, "You did good, hijita, you should be proud. My daughter had no interest in the horses. She was more interested in fancy things. But still I loved her."

Fergus was picked up after he scarfed down his food and was ready to eat all the other cats' dinners. Donna held him close to her chest, "Where is your daughter now? Does she visit you?"

Clementine gave Donna a wincing stare. Roberto answered, "She died about four years ago. I thought she was safe here, but she was killed. Now she is with God."

Donna knelt down next to Roberto, holding Fergus out to him. Roberto took the fat cat from her young hands as he embraced the furry critter to his chest. Donna's forehead furrowed as she quietly said, "No, I don't think your daughter is with God. She's with His horses. If she knows how much you love horses, she's with His horses. I bet she may even come back as a horse for you to train. You know my horse Tracy is four years old and she listened to everything you told her."

Sophia and Clementine stared at one another from across the kitchen. Silence filled the air until Roberto put the cat down on the floor. He leaned over and gave Donna a one sided hug with tears in his eyes. "Do you think I could come back and work with you and your Tracy horse again?"

Not thinking of anything else but the love of the horse, Donna put her arms around him laughing, "Of course! We would love it! Hey, you can even show me how to make more jumps!" Wiping the tears from his eyes, Roberto turned to Clementine, "This country is filled with good people." Sophia handed Roberto a hot sopapilla, "Here, try this and tell us what you think?"

He smiled, "I don't know about cooking, Rosa was the cook." He took a bite after dripping a load of honey inside of it. "Bueno, good food. This is really good." He finished the sopapilla. Then to Sophia he said, "Your mother Margaret is a woman who knows her own mind. Her horse is thankfully with Dios. This is good for the horse. I'm not sure about Margaret for she cries and cries."

Gasping, Sophia ran to the hall land phone. She punched in the numbers to her mother's hospital room, "Margaret, how are you?" She turned to speak quietly to her mother. After hanging up, she entered the kitchen with a big smile. "Granger is with Margaret. Finally, he remembered to bring her some food. Although I do believe he is desperately trying to get money for his Mercedes!"

A white piece of paper with many signatures at the bottom was handed to Roberto. Clementine pointed to the top print on the page, "This is what they want. Roberto, where are you going to live now? Are you going home to Fourth Street or are you going to stay with Charlotte?" Clementine rubbed her arm where the oil had burned her. Roberto frowned at the paper, "I can't go back. Fourth Street is no longer a home. It needed Rosa. My Rosa died in there. I can't go back."

Sophia handed Clementine some ointment for her burn, "Roberto, what is the arrangement you have with Charlotte?" The ointment was rubbed onto the burn.

"She says I can stay in her guest house as long as I take care of her horse and her dog and her. She's very nice. Everyone I take care of lives there in Calavera. My life is better there. I can't go back." His eyes filled with tears. Clementine put her hand on his arm, "Roberto, I have an offer for you. What if we clean up the house on Fourth Street? You need to go with me and we can take some of Rosa's things to the church, some things to sell and some things we could send to her family in Mexico. You get what you need out of the house and I will rent it from you? You can pay the mortgage you owe and I would have my own home to live in? What do you think?"

His shoulders shook as he cried, "My Rosa died in there! She lost her life in that house! You want to live in there? No one wants to live in there!"

Quickly, he started to walk out of the kitchen down the hall and outside. At the front door he was met by Juan. The two men walked outside to stand talking by Roberto's old truck. Sophia watched from the kitchen window as the two men embraced. Roberto smiled, shook Juan's hand and got into his truck. Juan came into the kitchen. "That's one sad hombre. He dearly loved his wife. I hope when I fall in love that I am so fortunate." He held out a covered bowl. "Here, this is surprise. It goes into the fridge to remain cool until after dinner." He pulled open the refrigerator and placed his delight on a shelf. Closing the door, he spoke to Clementine, "Roberto is going to think over what you offered. He was surprised you wanted to live there with Rosa's spirit. Give him time, maybe a week or two. He'll come round if you offer to have the house blessed by a priest. The mortgage payment will be due the end of the month. Give him time, he's still in shock."

The delicious dinner was eaten with gusto. Everyone helped with the washing up except for Donna and Juan who went outside to check on the horses. When they returned dessert was shared. "Juan, anytime you want to come visit me at Roberto's old house please bring dessert! Wow, you have a real knack for excellent pastries and desserts!"

A big smile came across his tanned face, "My goal was to be a chef. I attended three years of Cuisine College here at UNM, but then my older brother passed and I had to fill his shoes in the eighteen wheeler world. At least I can keep one hand in cooking while the other holds the steering wheel. Thanks for the compliment!"

Watching his face, Clementine asked, "What happened to your brother? If I may ask?"

Juan spooned out custard to the now empty bowls in front of the females. "Mitch was actually my brother-in-law. He was married to my older sister Maria Elena, but he was part of the family since I was seven so I think of him as a brother. He was a big burley guy who drove his huge eighteen wheeler all over the southwest. His one fault was he liked to drink and argue at truck stops. Specifically truck stops where he could argue with other truckers about roads, conditions, weights of freight and such." Juan sat down to lick the spoon, "One night late after a heavy rainstorm he pushed this heavy guy from Arkansas. They were yelling, red faced, damn mad about what someone had said and a knife came out."

Sybil held her breath. Donna leaned forward. Clementine shook her head as Sophia watched her daughters' faces. Quickly, Juan apologized, "I didn't mean to offend by swearing, sorry."

"Go on!" Sybil put her hand flat on the table top. "Please, go on, what happened next?"

Juan's solemn face studied the spoon in front of him, "The ending of this story isn't good. Mitch was certain he was invincible and the other guy was a fighter, real aggressive. They tumbled to the floor. Other truckers were trying to pull the two of them apart, but then the fighting stopped. The cop said the knife should have stopped the fight cold. Mitch should've walked away and counted his blessings, but he didn't. He had to prove he was right with might, using his fists. The other guy had to defend himself. Death by self-defense. Mitch was gutted by the guy. His work overalls cut and that was that. Don't think I need to say more."

Collecting the empty bowls, Sophia took Juan's spoon from his hand, "So you were expected to carry on? If you were in university why would your family want you to follow in Mitch's eighteen wheeler life?"

He stood up and stretched, "It was simple. Mitch's wife, my sister Maria Elena or M.E. as he called her, needed someone to pay their mortgage, buy her food, help with the expenses. I'm the youngest Calderon and the eighteen wheeler was being bought, money still owed, so there I went. Duty called and off I followed in Mitch's eighteen wheeler." Shaking his head, he added, "There are times it freaks me out driving that huge truck. At night there is a feeling that Mitch is in the cab with me. Spooky strange times with rain falling and wind blowing. It is as if he wants his eighteen wheeler back and he's trying to get me out. Weird feeling, huh?"

Clementine reached down to lift Marmalade into her lap. "This cat is light and fluffy. Would you consider giving him to me, Donna?"

"No." Donna rubbed Marmalade's head, "All these cats are related and they all have to stay here to protect us from spooky ghosts. You'll have to get your own cat or you have your own cat right?"

Marmalade was taken over by Donna, "You have a cat!"

Sophia put the bowls in the sink as the hot water was turned on to fill it. "Juan, your sister was the one who worked in the cafeteria at Otero School, right?"

"Yes," he turned to the hall, "listen I'm about done irrigating. I need to go and check the turnout and make sure the water is still flowing evenly. I better go. I can get the bowl later. Thanks for dinner!" He waved as he turned to disappear down the long hall to the front door.

Sophia pulled her cellphone from her pocket as the dessert dishes were being washed. "I have to go to Margaret's to pack her a suitcase. Will you be safe here if I leave?"

Clementine closed the dish cupboard, "Sophia, I have to go home. These two probably have lots and lots of homework to do. Since Sybil is fifteen, she's old enough to kid-sit her sister. I'd better go. Thank you for the most wonderful afternoon and dinner!"

In stereo Donna and Sybil both answered, "Yes! We'll be fine!" Sophia stepped back, "All right, but no television. No, not, nunca, nyet to television. You both have homework. Please, please, do your homework. I should be home by ten o'clock."

Sybil turned off the hot water as it filled the kitchen sink. "You do know that you are irrigating in about an hour, right? Do you want Donna and me to irrigate with Juan?"

Startled Sophia gasped, "Oh, scat! Damn, I forgot! I promised my mother I would pack her a suitcase for her surgery tomorrow." Sophia walked to the kitchen door and looked at the hall clock. "Is that correct? It's already seven thirty? I won't make it to my mother's and to the hospital by eight! Oh, damn!" Sophia's boot stomped on the wooden floor.

Clementine put up her hand, "You know what? If Granger is with your mother right now and you need to irrigate. Why don't you call Granger and ask him to make an excuse for you or tell your mother the truth?"

Donna, Sybil and Clementine all stared at Sophia who was tapping her foot on the wooden floor in consternation. "Yes, I'll call Margaret. She won't understand, but then she's already angry at me for putting her horse down."

The October sun hung just above the horizon. The smell of freshly cut alfalfa filled the air. A soft breeze blew cold from the northeast. Cackling crows sat in the old dead Mountain Ash tree by Mr. Maldonado's truck. Dry earth sucked up the delicious moisture flowing from the pulsating ditch turnout. Don Juan and Sybil waded through the irrigation water in the far field. Both wore knee-high irrigating boots. Shonac raced through the water to Sophia as she climbed over the white pole fence to jump into the field. Shonac danced in the water as she bent to pet him. "Hi, fellow, are you having fun yet?" His long tongue hung from his wide mouth. His large brown caramel eyes smiled at her. Laughing at his excitement, she asked, "Let's go out together, how about that?" His whole rear end wiggled with his long tail as he raced beside her into the field.

Don Juan Calderon smiled when he saw Sophia wade toward the lower pasture. She had left her boots in the barn on the soft sand and was now barefoot. Her jeans were rolled up to her knees. Sybil was kicking up water to make small rainbows in the sunlight's last hour. Waving at her, Don Juan called out, "Hey, old lady, are you willing to get wet? Your daughter over here has me soaked!" Shonac ran ahead of Sophia. Water flew up behind him. Joyously, Shonac shook his whole body right next to Sybil. The lovely cool water flowed over the dry fields. Wild ducks and plump white egrets waded in the water under the tall elm trees on the east side of the field.

Two of the fields were flooded as the sun slowly disappeared over the orange horizon. Now the front alfalfa field was about a third wet. Water slowly trickled its way toward the front gate. Juan leaned against the barn pole fence to watch the water lapping gracefully to flow over the berms. "This field will be done in about an hour. Do you want me to call the Vialpando's and let them know? They can open their turnout and catch the flow before we shut down the check." Sophia nodded to him as she studied Sybil's bucket full of snails. "How many did you save this time?"

Sybil lifted a fat snail, "This guy is Hector. He's going to be my first pick to toss into the chickens." Sophia reached over and flicked on the barn light. For a moment they were blinded by the bright florescent beams. Blinking, Sybil counted, "There are about fifty-three. They keep moving, but the hens don't care. They just gobble them up."

Juan shut his cellphone, "Mr. Vialpando is going out now to open his turnout." Pointing to Sybil's bucket he asked, "Really? You saved the lives of these guys and all you're going to do is feed them to the chickens?" Sybil's thumb was held in Juan's large hand, "Why are the tips of your fingers blue?"

"I don't know, maybe from my marker." Sybil pulled her thumb away from him, "Wow, you didn't know that hens love snails? Snails are full of protein and good for the hens and their eggs. Come on, I'll show you how they snap these suckers right up."

He followed her out of the bright barn lights to the chicken coop. "How do they get the snail out of the shell?" Juan turned on his cellphone flashlight.

"Hah, watch. They peck right through the shell and gobble up the goodies." Sybil opened the latch on the coop. Hens ran to her as she dumped the bucket over with the snails falling on the ground. A whirlwind of feathers raced about pecking away at the slithering delicacies. Sophia laughed, "This is Sybil's special time with the chickens. Otherwise she won't get near the coop."

Agreeing with her mother, Sybil shouted over the hens, "Yep, these birds stink and I don't want to smell at school!" Juan called out, "It's ten forty at night and it is dark and quiet. Who's going outside with me to help the ghosts shut the ditch turnout?"

12

Sophia waved to Sybil as she raced into Otero School. Friday was Sophia's day. A time for her to be by herself for herself. Sophia smiled and waved at the school crossing guard. Wild geese populated the dry alfalfa fields along Calavera road as she drove to Margaret's farmhouse. In her mother's bedroom closet she found the small raspberry suitcase. Once open it smelled of lavender. Sophia found her mother's cotton nightgowns in the drawer. As she was folding them over her mother's slippers, she heard a loud banging on the kitchen door. Sophia hurried down the hall to the kitchen.

Roberto's voice was screaming, "Ayudame! Ayudame! Se esta muriendo, rapido! Ayudame!" His fist was slamming against the glass panes in the backdoor. Sophia yelled at him as she moved to the door, "Entren! Entren! Cual es el problema?"

Her hand pulled open the door before he could bang on it again, "Cual es el problema? Que paso?"

Roberto's face was red with fury, "La Senora Charlotte ha sido envenenada!"

Sophia grabbed his arm as he waved it around his chest, "Roberto, calma se, hable en ingles, por favor! Cual es el problema?"

Words spewed out of his mouth, "She's been poisoned! Senora Charlotte has been poisoned! She's dying, come, come quick!"

Sophia pulled him into the kitchen, "Now, please, calm down. I just saw Charlotte at the school when I dropped off Sybil. She's fine. What do you mean about poison?"

Fearful emotion flowed from his nervous chatter, "No, no! I was feeding her horse. Her dog Sparky was at my side. We went into the kitchen to warm up mush for old horse, I found her. She was on her knees in front of counter. Her head in her hands. She was sobbing and she fell over. She's not breathing! She eat something that kill her! Come, come, rapido!"

Her cellphone taken from her pant pocket, she called A.J. Salazar, "We need help. We need help right now. Roberto is here at my mother's and he says Charlotte has been poisoned. I don't know how to help her! Can you send an ambulance?" Keys to the backdoor were stuffed in Sophia's pocket as she ran outside to follow Roberto down the short road to Charlotte's. Driving by them was Dr. Peters in his fancy BMW SUV. Sophia ran to the driver's door and knocked on his window. He rolled it down, "What's up? You both appear worried."

Her hand on the window, Sophia asked, "We believe Charlotte has been poisoned. Roberto said she doesn't appear to be breathing. I called for an ambulance, but it will take them time to get here. Can you help us? Please, can you help save Charlotte?"

His solemn voice took charge, "Yes, let me get my black bag and I'll be there directly. Go to her, get her to lie down. She needs to have her digestion slowed. This means she needs to be resting supine. I'll be right there."

Roberto was already in Charlotte's kitchen when Sophia raced through the door. Charlotte had fallen onto her side. She was frozen in the fetal position. Sophia knelt beside her, "Roberto, can you lift her? Can you carry her to her bed? The doctor said she needs to be lying down on her back, quietly resting. Can you carry her?"

His strong arms lifted her up as if she weighed nothing. As he walked down the hall in front of Sophia, he tapped open each of the semi-open doors with his foot to peek inside. They passed the library, the bathroom, the guest room and the second to last room on the right was her bedroom. Situated under a wide narrow window was a pine branch bedframe. It was stained a golden yellow. The sturdy bedframe was king size with an earthen colored afghan quilt. Roberto placed Charlotte as if she were a human sized doll onto the bed. Her legs straightened and her head fell back with her arms by her side. Sophia sat on the opposite side of the bed to feel for a pulse.

"Hello? Where are you?" Dr. Peters' heavy footfall came down the hall. Roberto met him at the bedroom door. Dr. Peters knelt beside the bed with his stethoscope. He unbuttoned her plaid cotton shirt of yellow and pink to listen to her heartbeat. "She's still alive. Barely." He gave his attention to Sophia, "Did you get a strong pulse?"

"No, I can barely feel it. What do we do? How can we help her?" Sophia patted Charlotte's arm.

"There are two choices." His deep voice was strong in the quiet room. The walls were paneled with honey mahogany. The floor was sealed flagstone. He took two containers from his black bag. "We can use ground charcoal. This has been found to absorb the poison and is less intrusive than this." He held up a brown bottle with a black lid, "Ipecac will cause her to vomit the poison, but if the poison is burning or chemical the vomit can be worse than the poisoning."

Sophia glanced at Roberto who was white faced staring at Charlotte. She pointed to the bottle, "Ipecac was what my father used on the rez. How do we get the charcoal down her throat and into her stomach?"

"We will need warm water. Lots of warm water and I have a tube. We can push the charcoal down her throat with the tube and warm water. I've never done this before, I'm not sure actually how to do this with charcoal." Roberto shook his head and pointed to the brown bottle.

Sophia's voice was shaky, "All right. I agree. Let's try the Ipecac. Do we need to put it in a glass or how do we get it down her throat?"

Dr. Peters didn't say anything. He lifted Charlotte to sit upright bracing her against his body. He knelt behind her on the bed with his bent knee. The brown bottle was handed to Sophia who unscrewed the black lid. Taking the bottle from her hand, Dr. Peters tilted Charlotte's head back. His free hand opened her mouth. The clear yellow liquid was poured into her mouth. His large hand rubbed her throat and she swallowed. He pointed to Roberto, "You better bring that wastebasket over here. We're going to need it. Let's hope this works. I'm not sure how old this ipecac is, but we need to pray this works!"

Charlotte started to cough. Her eyes opened to go wide and then her mouth. Vomit spewed forth as she coughed. The liquid flew into the wastebasket held in Roberto's hand. He knelt by the bed to hold the wastebasket closer to her. She continued to cough and vomit. A voice called out from the front of the house, "Hello? Anyone here? We're the EMT's for assistance?"

Sophia ran out of Charlotte's front door. She guided two men into the large bedroom. Dr. Peters smiled when he saw their white coats. "Hi, we're trying to get her to vomit out the poison. She appears to be awake now at least."

The two young men came to his aid. One of them listened to Charlotte's heartbeat. The other hurried out to the ambulance to bring in the gurney. Sophia helped him route it through the hall and through the narrow doorway. Dr. Peters was standing away from the bed as the EMT who had remained was asking Charlotte questions. She kept shaking her head. Roberto stood beside Dr. Peters glowing. Suddenly, Charlotte started to cough again. Roberto quickly held the wastebasket near her. Nothing came up this time.

Dr. Peters patted Roberto on the back, "Good man, you saved her life!" He put his hand out for the wastebasket, "Let's give this to the EMT guys. They can have their doc examine what she had in her stomach. I think we need to let them do their duty. Let's go in the other room." He jerked his chin toward the door.

Charlotte was gently lifted onto the gurney. They had her sitting up in case she aspirated in route to the emergency room. It was decided Dr. Peters would ride with her in the ambulance since he was a doctor of sorts. No one had confessed that he was a dentist, only that he was a doctor. Roberto chose to drive his truck behind the ambulance to the hospital and he would return Dr. Peters to his vehicle at Charlotte's farm. Roberto was staying in the guest house at Charlotte's anyway. This would not be an inconvenience for him.

Quietly, Sophia walked to her mother's. The key from her pocket unlocked the backdoor, she returned to the bedroom. The list was still on the bed beside the raspberry suitcase. Relief flooded over her as she sat in her mother's rocking chair. Picking up the elderly cat, she said, "Wow. That was certainly exciting! I pray Charlotte survives this and lives to tell what poisoned her." The backdoor slammed shut. Granger's smile lit up his whole face as he entered Margaret's bedroom. "I have my Mercedes! Sophia, I got it!" Twirling around the room in a very unfashionable male move, he kissed the top of Sophia's head, "The headdress and the other stuff we found was a gold mine! I sold it to a man in Old Town who was more than willing to give me almost all needed for my car! My lovely car!"

The elderly cat was gingerly placed on the bed. Sophia walked around him to go into the kitchen. "I need a drink of water." She mumbled as she opened the fridge.

Granger danced behind her into the kitchen, "Sophia, we can have a martini or a margarita now. We're good. I have my car back, finally." His sister took the tall white plastic pitcher from the top shelf of the overly filled refrigerator. Sophia poured herself a glass of cold water.

Slapping the kitchen's thick adobe wall that separated it from the hall, Granger continued, "You wouldn't believe me if I told you how I got the money! None of it came from Mom!" Then he mumbled, "And I know you wouldn't want half of what I got."

The empty glass was placed in the sink next to other dirty dishes, "Granger, you need to do the dishes. Mom has a dishwasher, if it wouldn't be too much work to just put them in there and turn it on, right?" Sophia pointed to the dishwasher stored under the kitchen counter.

Frowning, he followed her back into the bedroom. "I will. I was waiting until there were enough dirty dishes to wash. There's only a bowl, two spoons and my coffee mug. I don't want to waste water. This is New Mexico after all. The land of drought and dry."

Toothbrush, toothpaste, six pairs of clean white underwear, along with pairs of navy blue socks and Margaret's hair brush and comb were neatly placed in the compact raspberry suitcase. "Come on, did you seriously make enough money to buy your Mercedes with the stuff we found in the tool shed? I find this hard to believe?"

Granger rubbed his hand on his khaki pants, "Let's see. The headdress was ninety thousand dollars! Can you believe it! Wow! Ninety thousand!" He leapt into the air to try and touch the dusty ceiling in the bedroom. "You were right, who would've thought? Evidently this guy seriously wanted one and had found them almost impossible to buy since the government is such a stickler about feathers!"

Sophia picked out three magazines her mother wanted to read and a book from the bedside table. "Ninety thousand dollars is a lot of dinero, Granger, but not enough for your mighty Mercedes. How did you make up the rest of the funds needed?" She swept mouse poop off of her mother's bed quilt.

He leaned against the bureau by the door, "All right, let me tick these off for you." A receipt was pulled from his khaki pant pocket, "The beaded moccasins were fifteen hundred. The peace pipe was huge bucks after the man made a phone call to New York, he gave me six thousand dollars for it, although I know the guy in New York was willing to sell the New York Island for that piece." The paper was turned over, "The jet bear fetish was something used in ceremony in the Mid-West. That brought another phone call and he smiled at the answer. I smiled, too, when he said two thousand for that. The cornmeal bowl and the small badger weren't worth much, he threw in two hundred for those and the animal skull was worth fifty bucks."

The raspberry suitcase was closed and a red leather belt tied around the middle. Sophia lifted it to her side, "Granger, I don't have a calculator, but I'd say you were about ten or eleven thousand dollars short. What did you do to make up the difference? Did you steal from Mom? Did you go through all of those drawers you're leaning against? Huh?" She turned to stare at him with her anger showing her red face.

Slowly, he folded the paper to shove it back into his pant pocket. "No. No, I didn't steal anything from her. If you remember when we bought her the truck or the poop-mobile as you guys call it, I put it in my name since Mom doesn't believe women should own anything. I traded in the poop-mobile."

The suitcase fell from Sophia's hand to land hard on the brick floor, "What? You did WHAT?"

Granger's grin was offset by his shrug, "Yeah, I took it to the carwash place. You know the place where all the ex-cons wash cars? It took three car washes to get all that poop off and they really had to scrape."

He walked over to her and lifted the suitcase, "I can carry this to your old van and you can see my Mercedes." His grinning made Sophia cringe as he said with a smirk, "How about them apples?"

Fists were clenched. "What is Mom supposed to drive now, huh? You just took away her freedom, do you know this? Do you care?" Instead of slugging him, she slapped his shoulder, "You really are a jerk!"

"Hell, no! Mom shouldn't drive anyway. She can't even get into the truck. The truck is too high off the ground and she can't get her walker in and out of the truck by herself. The woman is a menace on the road. She can't see over the dashboard or the steering wheel!" He walked ahead of her down the dark hall to the back door, "I just saved us the grief of having to tell her she can't drive anymore. The truck is gone. Now the point is mute. She can't drive something she doesn't have, right?"

Sophia studied Granger's backside as she walked behind him. "You know you're someone who should be poisoned. Not Mom. I can't believe you would be so blazon to do this to your own mother."

Beside the old yellow van was his Mercedes. Beige leather seats, gold rims and leather steering wheel cover. Waxed, washed, glowing to appear new it was almost obscene next to the old van. Sophia grabbed the raspberry suitcase and put it on the van's passenger seat. She walked around her van to get into the driver's seat. Granger followed her like a puppy, "Well, what do you think? Gorgeous, right?" His face glowed as he continued to stare at the Mercedes.

Sophia backed out, drove around the Mercedes to barely miss the back bumper of the Mercedes. As she braked, she lifted her hand to give Granger the Espanola salute. "Fucker, eat this!" Smiling, she headed out to the hospital. Her jaw was set as she glared at the tumbleweeds smacking into the van. The hospital parking lot was full. There were no available spaces anywhere near the entrance. At the back wall filled with tumbleweeds, Sophia stopped in the middle of the parking lot to stare straight ahead at the rolling tumbleweeds. The air was dry and filled with dust. Sitting in the van, Sophia put her head down on the steering wheel. "Damn. First the horse is put down and now her truck is gone. Slowly, slowly, Granger is getting his way. Poor Mom." A car honked behind her. She turned to wave and noticed a truck pulling out of a parking place in front of her. The van was finally parked, far from the entrance, but at least safe.

Wind blew dirt against her as she leaned into it. The front-entrance automatic doors weren't working. The side door was slightly open. Sophia slid into the building. Ammonia and lemon odors filled her senses. A line of people stood in front of the elevator doors. Sophia helped an elderly man push his wife's wheelchair into the deep elevator. They got off on the same floor. Nurses flitted from room to room as visitors milled around in the hall. Just as Sophia was about to enter her mother's room, a new nurse ran up to her. "Dr. Pino? Dr. Pino, right?" The woman held her hand up to stop Sophia.

"Yes. I'm Dr. Pino." Sophia sighed as she hugged the compact suitcase to her chest.

"Your mother isn't in there anymore. We had to move her to another ward. She's on the third floor now. Room 312 at the end of the hall. Ask at the desk regarding her condition. They'll tell you what happened." The young nurse waved to disappear into another room.

One floor up and at the nurse's desk, a woman with short gray hair in tight curls around her head, smiled at Sophia. "Hi, yes, Dr. Pino, we had an issue with Miss Margaret. She pulled out her catheter and tried to get out of her bed to dress. She is terrified her son will no longer come to see her if she couldn't get her stockbroker to sell all her stocks and bonds. We found her on the floor in tears. Her arm was bleeding from the removal of the I.V. catheter and we needed to sedate her." Leaning forward to speak quietly, "This is the psychiatric wing. We are keeping her sedated and watched." Then the woman pointed with her short fingers, "Down there, room 312. Try not to upset her. We have an orderly with her right now and she will be on a fifteen minute watch." The woman gave a sincere smile of warmth, "Good luck, Sweetie."

Sucking in air, Sophia realized she still had on her barn boots. The leather soles echoed as she went down the hall. Cautiously, she pushed open the hospital door. Margaret was sitting up in a cheerful mood. Next to her was a tall black man in an extremely white medical coat. His goatee and mustache were neatly trimmed. Large brown eyes greeted her as he stood to put out his hand, "Hello," his voice was superficially calm. "My name is George Tasker. If you need anything, I'll be right outside." Eagerly he departed the room.

Margaret's small body was enveloped in the white sheets of the hospital bed. "Sophia, don't be angry. I did a bad thing and now they're scolding me. George is a fine young man. He's taking good care of me." She nodded to the vacant chair beside the bed, "Come sit down. Did you get what I needed?" Her voice was frail, almost a whisper.

"Margaret, what's going on with you? Why would you let Granger upset you? He's a manipulator, you know this, right?" Sophia sat on the empty chair. Her farm boots parked under the hospital bed holding her frail mother.

Shaking her boney hands forward, Margaret reached for the raspberry suitcase. "No, Sophia, no. Now I know you hate your brother. You always hated him. Now isn't the time to be angry at me or at him. He was in prison." She choked and coughed. George entered the room within seconds of her choking. "Miss Margaret, here let me get you some water." He placed a plastic straw into a yellow plastic cup and handed it to her. "Here you go, take a good long drink."

George nodded to Sophia, "Why don't we let her drink the water and we can talk outside?"

Not moving, Sophia stared at him, "No. I don't think so. I'm staying right here and finishing this conversation with my mother who is known as Miss Margaret."

George took the yellow plastic cup from Margaret's hand. "All right, but I must warn you to not upset this fine woman."

Sophia placed the raspberry suitcase on her mother's bed. Her mother hardly filled any space in the narrow bed. Slowly, she sat up and delicately unhooked the belt of the small case to open it. Sophia put her hand on her mother's blue hand, "Mom, everything you asked for is in here. Now, George, perhaps it would be best if you stayed for this conversation since I have no knowledge of psychiatry or how to proceed with this information." Sophia pointed to Margaret, "My mother needs to know this information and the only way for her to know it is for me to tell her, right?"

George stood tall against the side rail of the hospital bed. His tall presence appeared to hover over Margaret as if protecting her from Sophia. "If it must be said then say it, but remember we're dealing with a fragile soul here." He put his hand on Margaret's shoulder. Margaret delicately patted his large brown hand.

Sophia studied her mother. This frail woman was no more than skin covering bones. The fat fingers her mother used to knead bread, lead horses, milk cows or shovel while irrigating could hardly hold the plastic yellow cup. Wrinkles creased Margaret's face, her hands, her arms, her whole being. Yet, this woman could tear apart the strongest of wills if she was tested to do so with her words. Sophia stood from the chair reaching to take out her mother's favorite white cotton nightgown with blue flowers out of the suitcase. "Margaret, here I believe this will help you relax." Quickly, Margaret grabbed it. "George, wait until you see me in this. It's quite stylish, you know?" She giggled.

Toothbrush, toothpaste, hair brush and comb were all neatly placed on the hospital table next to her mother's bed helped by George. "Margaret, this is serious and I need you to believe what I am about to say. This should bring you peace."

Hugging the nightgown to her frail chest, Margaret smiled, "Say what's on your mind, Sophia." Then she turned to George, "You know she always believes what she says. Somehow, she convinces herself that her stories are her truth."

Slippers were held in Sophia's hand, "Margaret, Granger did buy his Mercedes. He didn't need your help after all. We went into the toolshed and found some old things of Papa's and he was able to sell those and buy his Mercedes."

Clapping her hands, Margaret screeched, "Yes! Oh, George, my son Granger is a saint! When he was misplaced in prison I had to sell his Mercedes to pay for his legal fees. I got him out!" Pink cheeks glowed in delight, "I did! I did it all by myself!" Waving her index finger at her daughter, she explained, "Sophia wasn't interested, but I got him out! Now he's found his Mercedes the one with the gold rims and leather seats and the coffee cup holder between the front seats!" Tears fell from Margaret's eyes, "Oh, thank God! Now Granger will love me." Suddenly, Margaret's body started to shake uncontrollably.

George pressed the down button on the automatic control for the hospital bed. He nodded to Sophia, "I think this is about all the excitement she can take right now. Perhaps it would be best if you leave now!"

Her purse tucked under her arm, Sophia was more than pleased to leave. As she walked down the hall, she heard a woman screaming and then a bedpan flew into the hall in front of her. Sidestepping it, she hurried to the elevator. Outside the sun was barely touching the western horizon. A flock of black birds flew close to the ground to settle all around the chamisa bushes on the hill beside the parking lot. Sophia fluffed up her short curls with her fingers as she sat in the old van. "Now home to quietly ride a horse. Granger can tell her about the truck. I've had enough excitement for one day. Come on, van. Let's go home."

An ambulance passed her going the opposite direction when she turned onto Alcon Road. Mr. Vialpando was getting his mail while his wife waved to Sophia from the front step of their farmhouse. A huge alfalfa truck was being unloaded at Mr. Perez's barn. Three hefty men were throwing the bales over to his four sons to stack.

Pulling in to park under the hangman's tree, Shonac raced from the south side of the house to Sophia. His wagging tail and a wide smile were quite a welcome. Sophia tacked up Lucky to canter up Alcon road. She walked her horse around the Charter School's playground and up onto the high ditch road. There they trotted and jumped a fallen tree trunk. Sophia pushed Lucky to a full gallop up onto the mesa above the Pueblo. Fluffy white clouds billowed across the sky high above the V formation of sand cranes that purred loudly to one another as they flew to the Rio Grande. Sophia pulled Lucky to a halt. Staring across the open valley was a glorious sight. Rabbit bush dotted the plains with yellow flowers. Short purple asters waved in the breeze. Smoke rose from the fireplaces below in the Pueblo giving out an aroma of burnt pine. A jackrabbit hopped from one bush in front of her to disappear into a hole by a large chamisa bush. Rubbing Lucky's mane, Sophia whispered, "Isn't life grand? From up here we can almost see the whole world." Lucky shook his head jangling the chains on his bit. His tail swatted her leg. She urged him to walk to the top of the mesa as two ravens coasted on the winds up above them.

The silence was broken by her name being called. "Sophia!" She turned in the saddle to watch two men approach. Mr. Nestor Casaus waved as his golden palomino kicked up dust behind his hoofs. The two halted one on each side of her. "Hey, don't you know this is private land? You need a permit to get up here! You're seriously trespassing!" He pulled his straw hat from his head to reveal his bald head on top and two long thin braids tucked into his pant belt.

"So, shoot me!" Sophia stuck out her hand to the other man. "Hi, I'm Sophia Pino. We live down there in the civilian world, but come here to the spirit world to find solace."

Gently taking her hand to touch palms only briefly, he smiled, "Yes, I know who you are. My second nephew speaks of you daughter Donna all the time. He thinks he's in love with her horse." His face blushed a deep purple. "Also, my second brother-in-law by marriage Juan lives next door to you." His hand rested on his thigh as he continued, "My elder sister-in-law M. E. visited your brother in jail every week. He gave her herbs to help with her compressed vertebrae in her neck. So, yeah, I know who you are. Huh?"

Lucky snorted before she could answer and took off at a fast canter. Sophia waved as they hurried down the mountain back to the stream. "Lucky, you know how to make an exit! Good old boy!" She pulled him into a trot as they forded the stream. On the other side, she patted his neck. They jumped the dead and down tree trunk as they walked through the school's playground and home. Sophia gave him some extra oats, patted the other horses in their stalls since the fields were still too wet for them to graze. It was now time to pick up Sybil from school

The van was parked in line with the other parents who were waiting to pick up Otero School students. The group of girls moved as if in a herd to the sidewalk. Slowly glancing up, Sybil saw her Mom and ran to the van. "Hey, Mom, can we go to the balloon festival tomorrow? Saturday a lot of the kids are going to see the balloons take off at dawn. Want to go?"

"No, thank you." The van pulled back onto the main road as Sophia explained, "Saturday is our day of rest and there is no way I'm getting up at dawn to watch a bunch of idiots fill balloons with climate killing gas and fly above the earth when we can do this on horseback with no air pollution!"

"Oh, o-kay, just thought I'd ask. Damn, didn't meant to upset the teapot." Sybil rolled down her window. "Besides I want to sleep late, too."

In the farmhouse that night they spoke of Donna's new school and Griego's volcano. Sybil shared her excitement about the Halloween party in two weeks. The volunteers were mostly students. She elaborated on Mr. O'Brian and what a great guy he is and how he showed them how to do batik and mix dyes. "Mom, did you know that you can dye any type of porous material?"

Donna broke into the conversation, "Hey, I was telling Mom about Griego's volcano that erupted all over the science room. Even the ceiling was coated with bubbling baking soda. He used Minto's, baking powder and coke. That volcano didn't stand a chance! Whoosh! All of us were covered in sludge."

Smirking Sybil laughed, "So, he had to stay and clean it up, right? Bet you loved that?" Suddenly Sybil jerked, "Don't kick me under the table. We have rules in this house, young lady!" Leaving her chair, she ran into her bedroom, slammed the door and shouted, "Leave me alone!" Donna and Sophia watched dirt fall from the doorframe to the floor's pile. Donna stuck out her tongue at the door. Sophia picked up on the conversation regarding the volcano. "Did Griego have to clean up the mess?"

Donna smiled, "I really like this Charter School, Mom. The principal came in with buckets of water, sponges and dry clothes and told the whole class to clean the mess. She said the project was for class and the class would clean." She picked up Marmalade from the floor to put him in her lap. As she patted him, she continued, "We had that room sparkling within minutes. It was as much fun as the explosion. Yep, I really like the school, Marms!" The cat received a kiss on the top of his head.

After homework had been completed this left the weekend free for the family of three. As Donna decided tonight would be her turn to fix dinner, Sophia and Sybil went outside to feed the horses, collect the eggs and check the gates. They were returning to the house when Juan came racing to the tall pole fence. He jumped over it in one bound to catch up with them before they were able to stamp their boots at the front door. "Hey, do you think I could bring dessert if I come for dinner tonight? It gets a bit lonely over at my house on a Friday evening." The two women stared at him. He shrugged his shoulders, "What? Am I being too forward?"

Sybil laughed, "It depends on what you're bringing for dessert. Warning though, Donna is fixing dinner tonight. It could be more than interesting." Sophia gave Sybil a stern glare and then said to Juan, "Certainly, you are invited to dinner whether you have a dessert of not. Please, come." Then under her breath, she added, "Just no tea."

At dinner, Juan verbally illustrated the trips he had taken the week before while driving to Denver and then Austin to deliver home goods for Sears and J.C. Penny's. "The traffic in Denver is insane. They talk about Albuquerque having bad drivers, but in Denver no one uses the rearview mirror. People drive right in front of you without a thought. Accidents everywhere."

Sophia lifted the bowl of whipped chocolate mousse. "This was very good. Donna, your chicken dish was exceptional. Glad you're here to cook for us. Juan, this chocolate mousse was divine. Really, you need to visit us more often or perhaps we could keep up a dinner date every month?"

He shook his head, "I don't know how long I can keep you women happy with sweets." Then he turned to Sybil, "What kinds of dyes is Mr. O'Brian using? Because, you know, some of the dyes can make you sick? Are you wearing gloves and masks when you cook up these dyes or what do you do?" Everyone turned to study Sybil's blue fingertips. Defensively she rubbed her fingers with the linen napkin. "I think this is from my markers. Mr. O'Brian wouldn't do anything to jeopardize us or himself. Usually we wear gloves although lately he ran out of them. His wife is a nurse at the dental clinic. She's the one who provides us with the latex gloves."

Taking the napkin from her hand, Sophia asked her, "What types of dyes are you making? What kinds of plants does he use?"

"Mom, I don't know! Don't ask me! I'm just a student and do what I'm told to do. Get off my case!" Pushing back her chair, she ran into her bedroom and slammed the door. Dirt fell from the ever widening crack over her doorframe.

Juan stared, "Damn. That doorframe is going to fall one of these days. Why does she need to slam the door?"

On cue, the house phone rang in the hall. Sophia took her plate to the sink and then walked to answer it. "Clementine? How nice to hear from you? Why aren't you calling me on my cellphone?"

Donna and Juan carried the remaining dishes and glasses to the sink. Juan waved at her to show he and Donna were going outside to shut down the irrigation turnout. Sophia hung up the house phone to stare at it. "Well, I'm supposed to back away. Evidently, this is none of my business. Huh?" The dishes were washed as Sophia waited for Sybil to come and help dry them. Sybil did not return from her bedroom. Noisily Donna came back into the house. She was jumping up and down with Shonac. "Hey, Mom, Juan said he can come and help in two weeks with the irrigating. If you want him to? He had fun." Shonac was called into Donna's room and the door was quietly closed.

Sophia brought her pull along to the kitchen table. She pulled out a large bulk of class papers and began reading. There was a soft tap at the kitchen window. Sophia turned to check the time on the hall clock. It was quarter to eleven. Late. Very late for visitors. At the front door stood Clementine. "I wanted to come by and speak with you in person since our phone conversation felt strained. Can I come in or is it too late?" Clementine was dressed in loose fitting jeans, a white cotton shirt and sandals. Her hair was pulled back in a side ponytail. "Can I come in, Sophia? Please?"

At the kitchen table the two women sat with tea mugs and a plate of freshly baked cookies. Clementine started the word flow, "Look, I know you want to find out who poisoned Rosa and Mary Peters, but this is a police matter. You could get yourself in a world of hurt if you confront the killer or ask the wrong questions to the wrong person. I care about you and the girls. But you know this, right?"

Shaking her head, Sophia grinned, "Yes, I care about the health and wellbeing of myself and my girls. I haven't intentionally put any of us in harm's way, have I?"

The tea mug was twirled in Clementine's hand, "No, but we did find out that Mr. Casaus and the Pueblo people were not poisoned by herbs. Somehow one of the BIA docs had an old prescription for Viagra. He was one of those people who believe the expiration date on the bottom of the bottle is bogus. He ground down the pills and put them in a different bottle. The women of the rez were complaining their men were being and I quote here 'less sexy.' Can you think of anything worse to say about your mate?"

Sophia's eyes grew wide, 'Seriously! They complained about their men? Oh, dear, I bet this is going to cause all kinds of trouble! Why were the women taking this stuff?"

Clementine shrugged her shoulders, "Who knows. The doctor is on the verge of retiring and this will help him move along. I don't think anyone is going to sue anyone, but this was a serious mistake on his part. As a doctor he should be above suspicion. This isn't for you to know, o-kay?"

"Would he have been the same doctor who was giving Dr. Peters medication for his sexual problem? Mom said Dr. Peters was taking herbs to get it up and down, this sounds as if the two could be related?"

"Nope, not related at all. Sophia, this is for us to research, not you. Your place is to be here with your wonderful daughters and to take care of your terrific horses." She sipped her hot tea, "Also, your busy mother. Of course you love her dearly, right?"

The front door slammed and footsteps came down the hall. Clementine turned to see who had arrived. Sophia stood all of her defenses were on red alert. Granger bumped into the doorframe as he walked into the kitchen. "Damn, that hurt! Hey, look who's here? Miss Clementine the mother's helper. How are you doing, Miss Clementine?"

Sophia stopped Granger from moving farther into the room, "Granger, are you drunk? What are you doing here?"

He pointed to a chair, "Can I at least sit down? No, I'm not drunk. Tired, Yes, I am extremely tired. I have been going for over twenty four hours and feel like a machine. I did get here though in my magnificent Mercedes."

Clementine pulled out the chair next to her, "Here, sit. Why have you been going for over twenty four hours?"

Leaning his elbows on the table with his head held in his left hand, he related his story, "I was minding my own business searching for a job when a cop pulled me over in my Mercedes. My emotions were through the roof when I saw the red and blue lights behind me. I pulled over and my heart was racing. I thought I was going to have a heart attack. He made me park my wonderful Mercedes in a store parking lot. I think it was in Albertson's by the main Calavera Road." He rubbed his eyes and pushed back his bangs.

Patting his shoulder, Clementine asked, "Why? Why were you pulled over? It wasn't one of us. It wasn't a sheriff was it?"

He leaned back in the chair to stretch out his legs under the long table. "No, it wasn't one of your lot. This was a State Trooper. Did you know they have cameras in the Albertson's parking lot? They have these tall tall poles and at the top are cameras that record everything within that parking lot and the three stores beyond. I thought that was clever." Yawning he pointed to the mugs on the table. "Sophia gives everyone tea. You know I think I'd like a stiff drink, but if that won't happen how about a mug of tea? Huh?"

The kettle was turned on and Sophia sat down again, "Granger enough with the suspense. What was going on with you and the State Trooper?"

"Sophia, it was the headdress. Guy Thompson was the fellow who bought it. They caught him with it red handed at a show in Santa Fe. He wore it to this show in some kind of Native American costume. He was drunk and bragging about it. There were folks there who took an exception to his loud attempt to be cool. They called the State Bureau of something or other. He was arrested. This was tonight about nine o'clock, by the way."

The kettle shut off. Sophia fixed Granger his favorite licorice tea. The mug was placed in front of him. As he took a cookie, he smiled, "They had me in handcuffs. Do you know the whole time I was in prison for over six years, no, no, it was six years and seven months and three days, I was never in handcuffs?"

Shaking her head, Clementine mumbled, "Amazing. You had to do something totally illegal to be handcuffed. Go on, then what?"

"The room they put me in was small. Smaller than that haunted bathroom of yours, Sophia. The walls were white, stark white. Enough to make you want to scream. They have this policy where they leave some poor schmuck, the schmuck being me, in there for hours. This makes a person want to get out as fast as possible by the time someone actually come into the room to question you. Although, I was ready to choke the guy when he finally showed."

Sipping the tea he gave a thumbs up to Sophia. "They wanted to know where I found the headdress. Was I a thief? Did I steal it? Where did it come from? You know the routine?" He turned to Clementine, "Those police don't fool around. They grilled me. When I said that I didn't know where it came from or where my father found it, they left the room. Again, I was alone in the stark white room with no windows, no mirrors, nothing but some kind of skylight about twenty feet up in the air."

Sophia pushed the plate of cookies closer to Granger, "What did you tell them? Did you say your sister Sophia bought it illegally and she's to blame?"

He jumped forward in his chair, "No! Hell No! Sophia, come on! I wouldn't implicate you unless I was charged. Right?"

Clementine looked at her watch, "Granger, can you get to the point? Sophia has papers to grade and I've get to go home. Hurry this along, huh?"

"All right." He munched on a cookie, "The end result, I was there all night. Not sleeping. When I asked them if they would follow me to my mother's farmhouse I was sure we could find the paperwork regarding the headdress. We drove to my Mercedes, which was fine by the way, and then drove to Mom's." He swallowed. "In Papa's bureau where Mom has kept everything of Papa's, in the bottom drawer, there was the receipt. Well, it wasn't a receipt. It was a letter from a man in Oklahoma whose mother was saved by Papa. The man sent Papa the headdress with a grateful letter. He had made Papa a chief of his clan. There it was in black and white."

Turning in her chair, Clementine shook her head, "Yes, but you didn't have ownership to sell it. The headdress belonged to your Papa and thus when he died, the ownership would go to your mother. You are still in a heap of big trouble Chief Granger. Are you the chief, now?"

"Ah-hah, that's what you think, huh? No, Ma'am. I showed them the legal letter Mom signed making me full ownership of everything hers after Papa's death. Mr. Goldfarb put up a battle over the letter. I didn't get full ownership of her stock, but all of her things and Papa's things in that house belong to me now. There. It was mine by proxy and thus I was able to sell it."

All this time, Sophia had been reading students' presentation reports. Every now and then she had made marks in green pen. Suddenly, she slapped her left hand flat on the table, "Clementine, did you know that Mr. O'Brian, Sybil's science teacher is having them make dyes from plants? Sybil's fingers are dyed blue. Do you think this is safe for her to do? What if the dyes are poisonous?"

Clementine stood up and stretched, "Sophia, we do know about Mr. O'Brian and his dyes, his work with the Halloween decorations and his relationship to Mary Peters and to Rosa. You should not worry about him, not at all. Also, the students will no longer be making dyed batik clothe. They have enough and there are no more plants in his lab. Why would her fingers be blue if Mr. O'Brian's wife was bringing in latex gloves?"

The green pen was placed on top of the stack of papers, "I don't know. One would think the kids would want to be safe, but maybe some of them figured the gloves were uncomfortable and just took them off?"

Granger set his mug on the table, "That was excellent tea, Sophia. Yes, latex gloves can make some people's hand break out in a rash. They itch like crazy if they have an allergic reaction to latex. Maybe that's why Sybil took them off." He put his hands up in front of him, "I can't wear latex. The gloves we used in the clinic were specially infused with baby powder to protect our skin."

Clementine pulled the rubber band from her side ponytail to let her hair fall to her shoulders. "All right, troops, it is time for me to head home. Please, Sophia and Granger, stay away from this case. We are doing the leg work. We have found numerous issues to pursue and by the way Charlotte is home now. Roberto came and got her from the Emergency room. Dr. Peters did indeed save her life with the ipecac solution. Bravo, to you Sophia. Quick thinking on your part! Tell Granger all about it, o-kay?" She wiggled her fingers as she turned to walk down the long hall to the front door. Sophia raced after her, "Should I ask Sybil about the gloves or should I let it go? Clementine, I'm scared for my mother. I don't want anyone else in Calavera to die from poisoning and Granger is innocent."

Reaching over, Clementine gave Sophia a hug. "Be safe, all right, just be safe, please?"

In the kitchen, Granger had his head in the refrigerator, "You do know I am starving, right? What do you have that I can eat?" He pulled out a covered tray wrapped in aluminum foil.

Back in her kitchen chair, Sophia shook her head, "You won't like that. It's left over roasted chicken. There is a head of lettuce and some cheese, but the cheese is fermented. Why don't you go home and fix yourself some of your quinoa and marinated soy chunks?"

He leaned against the closed door of the refrigerator, "You know I might do that unless you have some chocolate or something safe?"

"Hey, you wanted a drink. Yet you say you won't touch alcohol. What's that all about? And you were found in a bar on Central?"

"No, I don't drink. I didn't have anything to drink that night either. I just pretended because I was tired. That drinking bit is for show. Do you have chocolate?"

"No. I don't have any chocolate. What are you doing here anyway?" Sophia took her empty mug to the sink.

He sat down in the kitchen chair. "I've got a job. I just came from Milaca's store. An appointment to find out how much I actually knew about herbs and I helped him with inventory." He traced a circle on the table, 'He was impressed. I wanted to share my good news with someone. You were it."

Back at the table, Sophia pointed the green pen at him, "Bravo, Granger. Now go home and leave me to my work. You can tell Mom all about it in the morning when you visit her. She's now on the third floor of the hospital in room 312. The third floor is for mental patients. She has a drop dead handsome black man taking care of her. She's charmed all the way down to her socks."

Standing, he shoved the kitchen chair back to the table, "I bet she's pleased as punch. He's probably her new best friend." Rubbing his hands together, he said, "You know I don't think I will see her tomorrow. I have to show up for work at ten when his store opens and I don't want to be mentally confused." He walked down the hall and shut the front door quietly.

The presentation papers were finished. Sophia wrote in her diary with all five cats sitting on her bed watching her. She turned off the bedside lamp and said, "Good night."

13

A quiet purring erupted from Sophia's bedside clock. Slowly, she opened her eyes, reached out her hand and shut off the alarm. None of the cats moved. The room was cold, but the bed was delightfully cozy and warm. Shoving her feet under Biscuits' heavy weight, he leapt off the bed with three of the others. Silky remained next to her. "Silky, girlfriend, we have to get up and run around. Come on, I know you're old, but come on."

Sophia called both girls into the kitchen for scrambled eggs and bacon. Today, she wanted everyone to have a good breakfast in case lunch was missed. Griego met Donna at the mailboxes to walk with her to their Charter School. Sybil was dropped off at Otero Middle School. She had her nose in her Dracula book as she walked up the three cement steps into the school. Sophia drove onto the interstate following the surge of vehicles ahead of her. The sky was a chalk blue. Three large hot air balloons floated high above the city. The northern sky was filled with numerous hot air balloons in a colorful array. UNM parking was filled, but the lower lot had only four vehicles in it. Sophia parked next to an old VW bus. Her yellow van looked spiffy next to the old bus.

The lecture hall was full as the students were excited about getting their presentation outlines. Sophia called student groups up to her and handed back the outlines. Some had questions for her, but most were excited to get started. The class ended soon after the papers were returned for the following week the presentations were to begin and students needed to do their research as a group.

Sophia sat in the empty lecture hall for the remaining time in case anyone needed help. At the allotted time, she flipped off the lecture hall lights and went to her next class. The smaller room was overflowing! Students were standing against the wall for there weren't enough chairs at the tables. Excusing herself after passing around the sign-in sheet, she ran to the office. Melissa the secretary found a room with twenty more chairs for the students.

The whole class moved into a different building with windows all along one side of the room. Students joked and laughed at how large the room was compared to the one they left behind. A microphone was placed on the podium, which Sophia found to be dampening to her style. She turned it off to walk up and down the aisles of tables and chairs to speak loudly. There was a great repartee between her and the students. Many of them were taking this class for the second time. The previous professor had only given assignments with no discussions or lectures. As the class was wrapping up, Melissa entered from the back door of the room to wave a small piece of paper at Sophia who laughed asking the students if they minded leaving five minutes early. Everyone clapped.

The note handed to Sophia stated that her mother had gone in for the biopsy and she was now in the recovery room. They needed a member of her immediate family there right away. There was no further information. There was no phone number. Sophia spoke with the Dean Dr. Reyes who recommended they put a notice on the door of her next class. "It is best if you go. Life is fragile and this appears to be something serious or they wouldn't have asked you to come right away. Go, Dr. Pino, and let us know how things are with your mother."

There was no wind as Sophia drove all the way to Rincon. The road up the hill was basically empty of cars. Sophia checked her watch. It was only twelve- forty- five. Hopefully, there were no problems concerning her mother and she would be able to pick up Sybil. Sybil constantly complained about Sophia being late in retrieving her from school. The hospital loomed large in front of her as she found a parking place near the front entrance. There was a Mercedes there, but it was metallic blue, definitely not Granger's.

There was only one elevator working and it went up to the second floor and stopped. When it didn't move up or down, Sophia got out to ask if there was an elevator to the third floor working. The harried nurse stared at her, "I know nothing about elevators. I've been stuck here for ten hours and have two more to go. If you want to use the stairs, they're over there. Help yourself." The nurse raced away to answer a beeping light over a door.

Sophia took the stairs to enter the third floor. Her mother's room was right across from the stairwell. Standing, staring at the empty bed, Sophia remembered her mother was in the Recovery room in a different part of the hospital. She hurried down the stairs to the first floor. At the Information Station the Pink Lady pointed to the long hall going north, "Follow the blue tape on the floor. It will take you to the Recovery Room waiting room. There is a black phone there. Pick it up and ask for information about your mother. They shall help you. Just follow the blue tape on the floor."

Lifting her leather purse strap onto her shoulder, Sophia followed the blue tape. It wound around the hospital corridors and finally she came to the end. A small room with two people sitting in it who were watching the television. A cooking program showed how to make shish-kabobs outside in a barbecue. Sophia picked up the black phone headpiece and waited. Pointing to the quiet of the phone, she said, "This reminds me of the prison." The man and wife got up and left the room. Sophia laughed. Finally, a woman's voice came onto the line, "Hello, can I help you? Who are you waiting for?"

"I was given a message to come immediately from work regarding Mrs. Margaret Pino. Is there a problem? I'm her daughter, Dr. Sophia Pino."

"One moment please." Dial tone.

Sophia hung up the phone. The orange plastic chairs were well worn. The man on the cooking show was sitting at a table chewing on his shish-kabobs. Sophia realized she was hungry. After fifteen minutes, a tall man came into the room. "Are you Dr. Sophia Pino?"

She stood and put out her hand, "Yes, I'm Dr. Pino. What is going on with my mother?"

He didn't take her hand, but sat down on one of the orange plastic chairs. "I've got to sit. I've been standing for a long time, most of my life, I think. We asked you to come because of a situation." He rubbed his bald head and then studied his hands, "We warned your brother Granger Pino of the dangers of Margaret having a general anesthesia. Your mother is frail, undernourished and has numerous issues with congenital heart failure, congenital kidney failure and intestinal issues." He leaned forward to put his elbows on his knees. "She's weak. Terribly weak. Margaret asked Granger his opinion for we felt your mother was capable of making her own decisions and she didn't need anyone's help in signing for or against this biopsy surgery."

The stethoscope around his neck was pulled off for him to fiddle with in his large hands, "We warned Granger about how part of her body might shut down if she had a full anesthesia. We had warned Margaret about this first, but she said she would do whatever Granger wanted." The stethoscope was placed around his neck, "I don't understand why your mother insisted on doing whatever Granger wanted her to do. Your mother is a smart woman, but you know her better than I do."

Sophia moved to sit straight across from him, "Doctor, I don't even know your name or who you are or what you have to do with my mother. Could you start there?"

He studied her face, "I'm sorry, wow, I must be really tired. Yes, I'm Dr. Carrow and I'm the anesthesiologist who was with your mother in the operating room. Basically, I'm the one responsible for keeping your mother alive and in good condition." His eyes were now staring down at his brown leather shoes, "Your mother has asthma, did you know?"

"Yes, I put the information on her chart. Why, what's happened?" Sophia now was leaning forward trying to get his attention from his shoes.

"Yes, we knew. It was or is in her chart. The biopsy was done. We sent off the tissue. It doesn't take long to get the results probably by tomorrow morning, but none of us believe she has cancer. Someone put a bug in her ear that she has cancer. This was enough to push her into having this general anesthesia. Personally, I would have recommended doing a simple syringe test of tissue, but then I'm not family." Now he was staring at her.

Shaking her head, Sophia frowned, "I had no knowledge of any of this. No one asked me my opinion of her getting a biopsy. The last time we spoke of this subject my mother was screaming that I was trying to kill her and her horse."

His attention piqued, he asked, "Did you? Did you kill her horse?"

Not wanting to go into great detail, Sophia flatly answered, "Yes. I did. I killed her horse. I had no intention of killing my mother. I certainly will leave that goal up to you here in the hospital." Her words were sharp and focused.

He leaned back quickly, "Ouch, and well shot. Yes, if anyone would kill her it would probably be us or your brother. Have you spoken with your brother? We have tried to call him on his cellphone, but it goes directly to voice mail."

The leather purse was placed on a neighboring orange chair beside Sophia. "He's at work. He probably turned his phone off. Aren't you supposed to have a family member here when you do a surgery or at least have a contact person prior to going into surgery?" Her stern voice amplified her displeasure at the turn of events. "Also, I was under the impression she had a regular doctor, a Dr. Lenton?"

The beeper in his pocket made a dull thumping. He ignored it. "We did. He still is her doctor, however, I am responsible for your mother's anesthesia. Your brother Granger signed a paper stating that he would be here, be present for her in pre-op and he would remain in here, in the waiting room until the surgery was completed. We believed he was here. No one told us he didn't show."

A package of gum was pulled out of Sophia's purse. She offered a piece to the doctor who took one. She unrolled the paper from the gum and stuck it in her mouth. The doctor noticed the cooking program on the television, "That is just cruel. People sit in here all day and night and they have a cooking show to remind them how hungry they are! That's cruel."

Chewing her gum, Sophia asked, "Why did you go ahead with the surgery if there was no one here to represent her family?"

The gum paper was folded and refolded in the doctor's hand, "Her main doctor felt we should go ahead. We thought Granger would arrive eventually. Also, your mother was adamant the surgery proceed. She signed an agreement for the surgery to commence. She's an intelligent woman. She is in full mental capacity and aware of her surroundings. The paper was signed. The deed was done. Now, here we are."

Sophia studied his solemn face, "Yes, here we are. I have no idea where we are. What's going on with my mother? Tell me."

Dr. Carrow shook his head, "She won't wake up. We can't get her awake. We need someone to sign for an MRI to find out what is going on with her internal organs. She isn't waking up. Every now and then she winces as if she is in extreme pain. It's my job to have her wake up and get going full steam ahead." He stared straight ahead. His forehead wrinkled in concern, "Mrs. Margaret Pino will not regain consciousness. Her heartbeat is slow. Her pulse is slow. Her BP is low. We don't know if there is internal bleeding or if she has an infection that is spreading. We need to do an MRI immediately, that's where we're at."

Standing, Sophia took her purse and shoved it under her arm, "Fine, let's go and get this done. Where do I sign and how fast can this be done?"

Dr. Carrow didn't stand. He bent forward with his arms resting on his legs, "You can't sign for this. It has to be Granger. She put his name down as her personal legal advocate. We contacted you because we couldn't get a hold of Granger. He has power of attorney. Can you bring Granger here?"

Sophia didn't answer. The blue tape was followed to the front information desk. Walking out into the billowing cold wind, she heard the honking of the geese overhead. In the van, Sophia called Granger on her cellphone. It went to voice mail. She called A.J. He answered immediately, "Sophia, how are you? Did Clementine scare you?"

"A.J., I need you to go to Malakai's Herbal Store on Second Street and arrest my brother Granger. He's trying to kill my mother. Can you get him for me and bring him to the Rincon Hospital outside of town?"

"No. I cannot. You know better than to ask me. What's going on?" His voice was calm and steady.

Tears fell from Sophia's eyes as she related her mother's dilemma. When she finished A.J. told her most emphatically that she must be the one to retrieve Granger and bring him in to be the responsible party for his mother. Sophia slid the cellphone into her pant pocket. It was now one-forty. She had less than an hour to get Granger and get to the Otero Middle

School. “No time like the present.” She mumbled as she backed up the van and drove into Albuquerque. The store was hidden behind a Fix-It Shop. Sophia missed the turn the first time and had to go to the next street and turn around. She stormed through the incense filled store to find Granger. Malakai was ringing someone up at the cash register.

Sophia walked up and down the aisles, but found no one else. Finally, the customer left. At the cash register, she confronted Malakai. “Do you know where Granger Pino is?”

The tall black man with dreadlocks stared at her. He said nothing. Sophia took a deep breath, “Malakai, I am Sophia Pino, Granger’s sister. His mother is in trouble at the hospital and I need to speak with him. Would he be here? Do you know if he’s here?”

The tall man had emerald green eyes. He continued to stare at her until finally, his deep voice asked, “Your Granger’s sister? Right?”

The hard wind rattled the front windows. Sophia leaned against the counter, “Yes, I’m Granger’s sister.” Her voice was almost shrill, “Do you know where he is?”

Ever so slowly the man shook his head. Dreadlocks floated around his head. His large hand picked up a two-way radio. His fat thumb pushed down on a button, “Granger, your sister is here. Can you come up front?” There was no answer only static. Taking a deep breath, Sophia turned to walk down an aisle toward the back of the store. Malakai’s voice resonated as he called into the two-way radio. No one answered him. Jars were picked off shelves. Labels were read as Sophia listened for a response on the radio. Minutes went by and then she checked her watch. Slowly, she inched her way back to the counter. Malakai was reading a newspaper on herbal supplements. “Excuse me, is Granger here?”

He glanced at her. “He isn’t here. If he didn’t come from the back room, he isn’t here.”

Sophia put her hands on the cool glass countertop, “Did Granger check in with you this morning?”

The newspaper was folded. “No. I don’t think so. I can’t imagine why Granger would check in with me. Was he supposed to check in with me this morning?”

Flustered, she put her purse down on the counter, “Malakai, I need you to be straight with me. You’re a smart man. You’re not stupid and you know very well who Granger is and that he is working for you. He was supposed to start today. Now, is he here or isn’t he? His mother may be dying in the hospital. I need him to come with me to the hospital. Is he here or not?”

Concerned, Malakai placed the folded paper on the counter next to her purse. “He was here. He told me about his mother’s surgery and

I told him to go and take care of it. He could start tomorrow. I was just messing with you." His lips turned up into a large smile revealing crooked front teeth stained brown. "There is the blessing that if you really are his sister, you don't look anything like him." His large hands flattened the newspaper in front of him. Chuckling, he shook his head, "Granger said you weren't a doctor."

The purse was pulled up to her chest, "Malakai, my brother isn't at the hospital. He isn't answering his cellphone. Are you sure he isn't hiding in the back somewhere?"

His smile turned into a frown, "Granger left here. He drove off in his fancy classy Mercedes. He was bragging about it. He told me directly that he was going to the hospital to be with his mother. That's all I know so help me God."

Turning on her heel, she walked out of the strong herbal odors of the store. Standing next to her van, she stopped. "Where the hell is he? Where would he go?" She jumped into her van. Fat cumulus clouds floated overhead. A flock of fat geese flew right over the store. She studied the cars parked along the street. None of them were Granger's. The cellphone was pulled from her pant pocket as she noted the time. It was now two ten. She had twenty minutes to get to Sybil's school if she wasn't going to be late. Margaret's landline was punched into her cellphone. It rang five times. Sophia was about to hang up when Granger answered, "What? Sophia, what do you want?"

"Granger, it is you!" Sophia gulped air in relief.

"Yeah, so what? You called this number who were you expecting to answer? The dead horse or the dead dog or the almost dead cat? What do you want?" His voice was tense.

"I'm at Malakai's store. I came to get you. Mom is in serious trouble at the hospital. They need you there to sign a consent for her to have an emergency MRI. Mom didn't wake up from the general anesthesia. You were supposed to be there for her!" Sophia checked the rearview mirror. A man in a large truck was backing up directly into her van. She hit the horn.

Granger said something she couldn't hear because of the car horn. The man in the truck was jumping out and running up to her window. Sophia yelled into the cellphone, "Granger, get your ass to the hospital or you will be tried for murder. Get your ass over there now!"

The elderly man with a gray grizzled beard knocked on her window. Sophia rolled it down. He spoke with a cigarette dangling from his lips. The nasty smoke came into the van. "Ma'am, you need to move your van. I gotta get outta here and you're blocking my way." He hunched his stained brown jacket up over his shoulders. Then he spit on the ground. Sophia smiled at him, "All right, I'm leaving now." The van was maneuvered around his big old truck to go out the back alley and out onto the main road.

At Otero Middle School Sophia was early. Smiling at her luck, she parked fourth behind the first car. Sybil would wonder how this was possible. Finally, the bell rang and the students poured out of all the doors. Sybil was with her group. When she studied the line of parked cars, she opened her mouth, clapped her hands and pointed to her friends. Sophia waved. Sybil ran and jumped into the passenger seat. "Amazing Grace, you got here early. I don't believe it! Is this going to be your new thing now, Mom?"

Sophia explained to Sybil about Margaret and the surgery. At the ice cream shop, Sybil asked her what had happened to Granger, "Why wasn't he there at the hospital if he took the day off? This was his first day of work and he took it off for his mother and then he didn't even show up? How's that even possible?"

Licking her cone, Sophia then wiped her chin, "Who knows? Granger probably won't have a job now. I think I blew it for him by going to the store. The place reeks of herbal incense. If they burned the same incense every day it could be nice, but it appears to be a whole conglomerate of incense. Heavy odor and smell."

Sybil stirred her ice cream in the paper bowl, "Did Granger go to the hospital?"

Sophia watched as Sybil turned her thick ice cream into chocolate-mint mush, "I have no idea. Evidently, I am not one who should be concerned. This arrangement is between Granger and Margaret. I was not asked nor was I given permission to save her life. The two of them kept me completely out of the loop."

"Mom, what does it mean when someone won't wake up from a surgery? What happens to them?" Sybil now was licking soupy ice cream from the small pink spoon.

Customers filled the ice cream parlor. A teenager bumped Sophia's elbow. He quickly turned to apologize. She nodded to him and then looked at Sybil, "There could be numerous issues. Margaret has always had a serious reaction to pain medication. Even aspirin makes her sleepy. It's my opinion and what do I know? I believe Margaret had an extreme reaction to the anesthesia. She'll wake up in her own time as usual. Somehow, she does things her way. For some reason I'm not worried about her. Granger worries me. What he might do to her is a serious concern, but somehow Margaret will wake up and be fine."

Licking the inside of the ice cream's paper bowl, Sybil smiled, "Oh, well, then let's go home and find out how Donna's day went at school." The pink spoon was placed in the empty paper cup. "You know I really love my sister and I'm glad she's living with us. Takes a lot of pressure off of me!" Smiling, Sybil tossed the paper cup into the trash receptacle by the door. The bag with the container of peppermint ice cream for Donna was firmly held in Sybil's hand.

Wind hit them full on when they stepped outside the shop. Trees whipped around and around flinging broken branches onto the tops of cars. Trash and plastic bags blew wildly in the whirlwind dust devils as they ran to the old van. The one signal light going out of Rincon was swinging back and forth from its long metal arm. A man passed them with six pigs in the back of his truck. They were squealing with their tails twisted. Dirt pelted the right side of the old van. Sybil put her jacket against the passenger window to keep the sound down as the pummeling dirt drummed on her window. Sophia turned on the windshield wipers to remove the dead leaves and twigs hitting front on with the tumbleweeds blasting against the grill. A Mourning Dove was trying to fly against the wind current, but appeared to be going backwards.

"Mom, look out!" Sybil grabbed at the front dashboard. A large branch blew in front of them as they turned to go down Alcon Road. The branch didn't stop, but did a summersault to the opposite side of the road. It came to rest against the Montoya's wooden fence post. His six Heifers ran over to munch on it. Sophia put her hand on Sybil's arm, "I saw it. Don't worry. Wasn't that wild?" The ditch running through the Ayala's farm was muddy from irrigating yesterday. His two huge hogs were waddling in the mud. Instead of being black and hairy, they were brown with mud. The sun had dried the mud on their backs to have a metallic sheen. His herd of sheep were all hunkered down, sleeping close to the earth for warmth.

Sophia turned into their drive and suddenly a large branch from the hangman's cottonwood tree broke loose to crash to the ground directly in front of them. It splintered in pieces. Bark flew all over just missing the van. "Damn, I'm not parking anywhere near a tree." Sophia turned the steering wheel to park beside the far side of the barn.

The horses were running wild in the field. Their backs were muddy from rolling. Jumping down from the van, Sophia saw Donna in the barn holding her arm at an angle. "Sybil, go and check on the house. I'm going to talk to Donna in the barn." As Donna walked to her mother tears fell from her large eyes. Donna's glasses were in her right hand as her left hand was cradling her right elbow. "Mom! Mom, I took Tracy out for a short ride. A nasty branch fell down from an elm tree by the old school and hit me hard. Right here. My arm really- really- really- really- really hurts. Feel this?"

Sophia knelt down in front of her daughter. Gingerly she put her hand around the right elbow. There was a sharp bone close to the skin where there shouldn't be. "Get in the van, Sweetie. Just get in and sit down. Where's Tracy? Is she in her stall or is she still waiting to be dressed down?"

"She's in her stall. I got her tack put away, but then my elbow started hurting big time. Mom, what do you think is wrong?" More tears fell.

"Honey, I don't know. But this isn't something we can ignore. Let's go to the Urgent Care in Rincon. Do you have to go to the bathroom or anything? Do you want a drink of water before we go?"

"No, I just want my elbow to stop hurting." Donna stood beside the front passenger door. Sophia opened it for her and clicked the seatbelt around her. "Honey, I'm going to tell Sybil that we're going, all right? Stay here and I'll be right back."

The traffic had increased as it was now after four o'clock. The workers from the drywall factory were lined up to go through the red light at the private exit. Sophia had to wait for all of their cars to drive through and then there was the Amtrak train. All the railroad lights were lit and the crossing bars were down. Finally, in Rincon they had a break from the heavy traffic. Driving up the hill, Sophia thought of Margaret. "You know this is a good thing for us to come here. Not a good thing you hurt yourself though, but now you can visit your Grandmother, huh?"

Donna groaned, "No, I don't think so. She'll want to take a chainsaw and cut my arm off. Let's not see her, Mom, please!" Donna shut her eyes and leaned her head back against the headrest. There were two parking placed by the Urgent Care Entrance. Sophia clicked her tongue, "Oh, dear, this place appears to be packed. Maybe everyone is getting slammed by tree branches."

Inside there were several empty chairs. Donna sat down by the door. Sophia walked to the sign-in sheet at the counter. "Excuse me, but I do believe my daughter has a broken arm. Are you doing this by triage or is this first come first serve?" The young man in purple scrubs stood to lean forward. His head out the reception window he studied Donna. Sophia motioned to Donna who was crying and rocking back and forth with her elbow cradled in her hand. "No, we can see her now. Most of these people are waiting for family to pick them up. As for the parking, everyone parks over here even if they don't come into Urgent Care. Bring her back through this door."

Sophia and Donna followed the young man in purple scrubs to an empty examining room. Once sitting down in front of the young man, Donna appeared to come round. She smiled at him and told him it really hurt. After taking her blood pressure and her other vitals, he told them a doctor would be right in. Sophia laughed after he shut the door behind himself, "They all say that. A doctor will be right in and after four hours the cleaning lady comes in to tell you the doctors have gone home for the evening."

Donna kicked her mother, "Mom, have some faith!" Sophia pulled out a pair of purple latex gloves. She blew up the glove and tied it off, "Here, Donna, let me show you how to milk a cow." As she held the glove to grasp one of the fingers, the door opened and a middle aged woman entered the room. "Hello? I'm Dr. Martinez. I understand you hurt your elbow." She turned to notice Sophia, "Ah-hah, I caught you purple handed. Are you going to milk the cow?" Sophia laughed, "Oh, you know this trick?"

After the x-rays were taken and the elbow discussed, Donna was put in a cast. "The tuberosity of the radius had a clean break. The cast is to make sure the bone or the radius heals fully in this one particular area. Donna was lucky it didn't break the elbow neck. Tell me how this happened? This is a strange place to have a break." Dr. Martinez watched the casting tech put the fiberglass material around Donna's arm.

Donna was cautiously watching the wet rolls of fiberglass go round her arm. "I was riding my horse Tracy. We were trotting down by the river. There is an old elm tree, we call it the Grandpa tree. It doesn't have any leaves anymore. The wind came at us in a whirlwind and caught this big old branch. I was watching where we were going because there were big branches on the ground and this big old branch fell. It whapped me right here! At that same time, Tracy jumped over a tree trunk that was down in our path. We decided to canter home." Donna's nose started to run. Sophia handed her a tissue. Donna blew her nose to continue, "Once we were in the barn, I took the saddle, saddle blanket and the bridle off of Tracy. As I was carrying the stuff into the tack room, my elbow made a popping noise."

The casting tech plugged in a blow dryer. Once he turned it on, no one could hear anything but the blow dryer. When he finished he took the sheet off of Donna's lap, rolled it up and threw it in the receptacle. Donna shook her head, "Now, it really hurts. No, it throbs. Will this stop?" Her glasses were askew on her nose. She grimaced at the doctor. Her braces shone from the overhead lights. The casting tech returned. This time he had a pole with a strap. "Here, you need to use this until the fiberglass is dried. You can probably take this metal stick off tonight by the time you're going to bed. Don't wear this to school. This is only temporary to be sure the fiberglass dries and doesn't rub off on your clothes." A fat strap of canvas was wrapped around her wrist. The other end of the strap was attached to the metal stick with a flat surface at the end. He put this part against her ribs. "Now, don't move this until tonight. If you need help for some reason, ask. Don't let this cast rub against anything for at least four hours. Got it?" His white hairnet held back his long brown bangs. He had on faded blue scrubs, clear gloves and a large smile.

Blushing, Donna agreed. Dr. Martinez walked with them to the exit of the casting room. "I'm not going to give her any medication. The break didn't puncture the skin and I'm thinking you probably have some Children's Ibuprofen at home. You can give her two once your home and perhaps tonight before she goes to bed. It would be wise to lie on your back tonight with a pillow holding your elbow up above your heart. This will keep the swelling down."

Sophia pushed Donna's long hair back. Her braid had come unraveled and her hair was in her face and down her back. "Should Donna go to school tomorrow? But I'm not sure if she should stay home?"

Dr. Martinez bent over to ask Donna, "Do you want to go to school tomorrow? You know what, I will leave this up to you. If you elbow continues to hurt, you can stay home. You have my permission." Standing straight, she pulled a prescription pad from her white jacket's pocket. "Let me write a permission slip for her to miss school. If she needs it - you have it."

Sophia clicked Donna's seatbelt around her. "You do know you smell of horse, don't you?" The drive home to the farmhouse was quiet. Donna pushed her thick lensed glasses up her nose. "Mom, really!"

Donna sat on her bed with a sad expression on her face. Sophia sat next to her. "Honey, your arm will heal. It just takes time." Brushing back Donna's long hair from her face, Sophia asked her, "How would you like some bangs? Your hair is always in your face and with your glasses, we can hardly see you under there."

A big smile grew across the girl's face, "Yes! Mom, would you cut me some bangs? I think I want to be someone different now that I'm here with you guys. Would you?"

"Certainly, come on into the bathroom. Let's see what we can do." Donna followed her mother into the small compact bathroom. Sophia placed the toilet seat down and sat on it. Leaning forward she pulled out a large round tin from the bottom of a multiple use bookcase wedged between the sink and the wall, next to the edge of the toilet. The round tin had a painting in acrylic of a large fish. Donna watched as her mother traced the fish with her index finger. "Papa painted this for my mother when I was about your age. He loved to cook and his greatest achievement was always salmon. Here feel how the paint lifts off the top of the tin."

Donna ran her finger along the lining of the fish and then the horizontal wavy lines that made up the waves of water. "Why did he make this for her?"

"Margaret had long hair when I was small. She pulled it back in a tight bun at the back of her neck. Her eyes were pulled wide since her hair was thick and tightly held. She used a lot of bobby pins and he made this tin for her to keep her hair items inside of it."

Donna stepped over her mother's feet to perch on the edge of the old porcelain tub. Sophia placed the tin in her daughter's lap, "I remember when I was just a bit younger than you when we received a phone call right as we were about to eat dinner. It was a school night. Papa sat at the head of the table with his back to the main kitchen. The phone rang and he shook his head. Being the only doctor for about one hundred miles who still made house calls, the phone was always ringing."

Sophia carefully pulled the lip off of the tin. Inside were various hair devices. Bobby pins, catches, two silver hair combs and a lot of rubber bands. At the bottom of the tin was a pair of scissors. One edge was sharp and flat the other edge had tiny teeth like a precise comb. Next to the scissors was a steel comb with very fine teeth. Sophia pulled these two items out of the tin.

"Our kitchen was small. Not like ours here at the farm. Against the far wall in the corner in the darkest part of the kitchen was the stove. It was gas. Gas was the only kind of stove Papa would cook on, it had the quality of being able to control heat. Next to the stove was a counter. Under the counter were four drawers filled with cooking tools. Next to the counter were the sinks. We had two large stainless steel sinks, cutting edge of the time." Sophia took a cup from beside the small porcelain sink in their bathroom and filled it with water. She dipped the comb into the water to part Donna's hair. Combing the long hair over her face.

Under the sink were all the things we needed for cleaning and for making butter. The board and the drip runner. Next to that was another counter and then the dishwasher.

Donna put her hand up, "A dishwasher? You had a dishwasher back in the dark ages?"

Laughing, Sophia shook her head, "No, I'm wrong. You're right. No dishwasher. I was the dishwasher, hah! We had a washing machine. Oh, what a delight. Before Papa bought the washing machine we had to wash our clothes outside in the washer barrel. It was a large metal barrel in an outbuilding. It had a stopper in the bottom. We kept it in an open room with a drain in the center of the floor that flowed out to the ground west of the building. We would fill the metal washer barrel with a hose or boiling water carried from the house. The washer barrel would be filled with water and washing flakes of detergent. I was the one who turned the handle round and round to make the flakes dissolve in the water. Once the water was all bubbly we would put in the clothes. Usually we washed the delicate underwear and bras first. Socks and the guys' t-shirts. It was a big washer barrel. I would turn the handle round and round while Margaret would poke the clothes down with a clean wooden pole. Once we felt the clothes had churned enough, Margaret would open the drain stopper and the water would flow out. Then we would put the clothes through the ringer. This was attached to the top of the washer barrel."

"Mom, I know about washer barrels. We studied them at the expensive school. Don't go into all the detail. I thought you were going to tell me about the phone call, right?"

"Oh, yes, well after the clothes were put through the ringers we would hang them on the clothesline. The pants were put onto stretchers and hung on the line. This way they had creases in the legs and I wouldn't have to iron them. Margaret had me iron everything from sheets to Papa's boxer shorts!"

"O-kay, Mom. I got it. The washing machine was a terrific invention. Now what about the phone call?"

"Well, Margaret put the phone down on the counter that was between the main kitchen and the dining area. She turned to Papa and told him he had better take the phone call. It was serious. Papa sat at the table ready to serve all of us. He was holding the long French knife in one hand, it was straight up in the air in his hand. In the other hand he held the meat forked prongs. A long instrument with two prongs on it. He looked like he was going to skewer Mom."

Sophia wet her daughter's long hair and then carefully stood over her to cut her hair straight across by her nose. Then she quickly grabbed a towel and wrapped it around her daughter's neck and across her lap. She had her hold the towel up to catch the cut hair. "When Papa put the phone down, he nodded to me. To tell me we were going out. I was his nurse. He bought a nurse hat for me and I would carry his black bag with the nurse hat pinned to my braids. We went into his make shift office in another outbuilding and he gathered things to put in his large black bag. Then he took a roll of surgical things in a linen wrap that was inside a sterile box. He had an autoclave in this room where he would sterilize his own instruments for surgery."

"Mom, don't cut my hair too short!"

Sophia reached over to the makeshift bookcase to hand Donna a small mirror. "Here, look. Anyway, we drove in the truck down our bumpy road to Manzanita, a small town to the north of where we lived. When we arrived there was no one there. Papa honked the horn. A long legged man came running up to the truck from the field. There were three dogs sleeping on the long portal. They didn't even bark, but came up to us with tails wagging. As if they hadn't seen another human in years. The man said something to Papa, I was interested in the dogs."

Trimmed hair had fallen all over the floor by Donna's boots as Sophia continued her story. "Papa told me to follow him into their kitchen. He told me to clear all the stuff of the long kitchen table and put it on the counter. He would be back with a patient. The table needed to be cleaned and to keep his black bag at the end of the cleared off table. He had his stethoscope already around his neck." Sophia sat back down on the closed toilet seat to study her hair trimming ability. Smiling, Donna's bangs were combed flat and trimmed a little more as she spoke, "I worked hard to get all the papers on the table in order and placed stacked on the counter. The salt and pepper shaker and the cooking things were moved. Then when I went to the sink to clean it off, there was no faucet. They used the well pump outside to get water and carry it into the house. I ran outside with a cloth and soon had the table sparkling." Sophia lifted the small mirror to show Donna how her bangs looked. Donna put her hand on the mirror, "Please, keep telling, I'm worried about the man."

"A thin woman with a haggard expression trudged into the kitchen. She smiled at me when she noticed the kitchen table. Suddenly, she ran out of the kitchen to go down a brick floored hall. She returned with a beautiful hand sewn quilt and a sparkling white sheet. I helped her place these items on the hard wooden table. The woman didn't speak to me, she just nodded and pointed. The loud sound of men's boots on the wooden floor were heard coming from the front of the house. Six men were carrying the removed front door horizontally with a man lying on top of it. He appeared to be asleep. Papa was walking beside the man, pounding on his chest. One of Papa's hands was flat on the man's chest while his other hand was hitting it hard. A tall man was bent over as he pinched the sleeping man's nose and was breathing off and on into the sleeping man's mouth. Everyone was in a hurry. Papa grabbed a corner of the quilt and pulled it and the sheet off of the table onto the floor. The front door was placed on the wooden table." Sophia leaned back to ask, "Donna do you want to check your bangs and see if I cut them too short or if they should be shorter?"

"Mom, finish the story! Sit still and leave the scissors alone. Tell me what happened." Donna reached for her glasses on the bathroom sink.

The painted tin was put back on the side of the bathtub. "Well, not too much is known to me after that. Papa told the woman and myself to leave the room. The wife took my hand and we sat outside on the front porch. There was a couch and some chairs out there. I sat down and she sat next to me. Soon they carried out one of the younger men. Evidently, he had fainted. They laid him in a sort of sitting position in one of the chairs. Finally, I asked the woman if I could use their bathroom. She nodded to the far side of the house. I sat in the outhouse for a long time reading a Popeye Comic book that had been left there."

Sophia took the hair brush and started brushing Donna's long hair. "Once, I realized I had been in the outhouse perhaps too long, I went back to the porch. The woman was carting freshly shorn sheep's wool. She showed me how to comb the thick clumps of wool and then she went inside and came out with a spinning wheel."

Donna grabbed the brush in her mother's hand, 'Did the man die or did he live?"

"Papa came out soon after we had spun the wool. As he was rolling up his sleeves, we noticed his shirt was covered with blood. An ambulance arrived and everyone ran around, taking the man now on a gurney into the ambulance. Evidently Papa had saved the man's life. He had a clot going into his heart and if Papa hadn't done the surgery right then and there on the kitchen table, the man would've died."

"Well, Papa really was a hero. Good thing he answered the phone and didn't blow it off."

Sophia wrapped the towel around Donna's face after taking her glasses and lightly patted the cut hair from her forehead and lips. "Now, check out my beauty parlor tricks and see if this is all right?" The glasses were returned to Donna's nose.

Standing on her tip-toes Donna stared at her reflection in the mirror. "I look different don't I? Do I look older or younger?"

"You appear to be gorgeous. Now why don't we check this fiberglass cast and see if it's dry. I can wrap another towel with plastic wrap around it and you can take a shower or would a bath be better?"

They both touched the fiberglass on Donna's arm. Frowning Donna answered, "I want to take a shower because I've got hair all over me. If I sit in the tub it will float all around. Can you help get my clothes off?"

Sophia left Donna in the warm shower with her elbow wrapped in a plastic bag sticking out of the shower curtain to avoid any possible chance of it getting wet. Thunder roared overhead as Sophia stepped outside to shake the hair trimming towel. Shonac was sitting under the cottonwood tree closer to the house. His tail thumped the dirt as he watched her. The green towel was placed on the clothesline and stuck firmly in place with clothespins. Sophia knelt down next to Shonac and scratched his ears. 'How you doing, little fellow? You don't care for thunder, do you? Do you want to come inside and be safe with us crazy women, huh?"

The front door opened. Sybil stood in the open doorway. Her image in silhouette as she spoke, "Uncle Salamander is on the phone. His honor is waspish and is in need to hear your voice. He is not welcome over here, please, don't let him come over here!" Sybil's voice became louder and louder. Finally, she added, "Granger wanted me to tell you directly that she isn't dead yet, whatever that means?" Rain drops began to fall around the woman and the dog. They both raced into the house. Sophia stood in front of the hall phone, "Did you hang up? The phone is on the cradle? Sybil?"

Waving her arms in the air Sybil grimaced, "No. I wanted to hang up, but I didn't. He's on your cellphone there on the kitchen table. He didn't call on that one." She slid on her stocking feet back into her room and slammed the door. Dirt fell on the already well placed pile.

"Granger, what's up? What's the worry?" Sophia heard the shower water turn off in the bathroom. She knocked on Sybil's door and waved to her, mouthing 'Go help you sister in the bathroom.' Again, Sybil slid on her stocking feet out of her room and to the small bathroom. Sophia walked into her bedroom with the cellphone. After listening for a time, she snapped shut her phone. "Nope, not going over there tonight. No, thank you." A hard rain hammered down on the tin roof. The strong wind blew twigs and dirt hard against her bedroom window,.

Hot left overs were placed on the kitchen table as the three sat around it in silence. Sybil was eating and working on an algebra problem. A large language arts book sat in front of Donna and Sophia graded papers from the pile in front of her. Shonac was under the kitchen table snoring. Sybil interrupted the silence, "Mom, what's happening tomorrow? Are you going to deal with Granger and Margaret or could you come by the school sixth period and help us with the decorations?"

A paper was flipped over in front of Sophia, "First thing in the morning, after dropping you off, I plan to visit Margaret in the hospital. Granger said she has come back and is conscious although she's in a lot of pain."

A long yellow pencil was stuck up Donna's fiberglass cast at the wrist. She was trying to scratch inside the cast. Donna flipped her long hair braid behind her shoulder, "Will Margaret take her pain meds? Remember how she refused after the car accident?"

A motherly hand pulled the yellow pencil out of the cast, "Don't do that. If you stab yourself with the sharp end and it gets infected you'll be in a world of hurt. As for Margaret I have no idea. Granger was disappointed Margaret regained consciousness."

The algebra problem completed, Sybil said under her breath, "Granger is weird." At ten o'clock it was decided everyone should go to bed. The language arts assignment had been read and the story outlined with help and Sophia knew she had the rest of the weekend to finish grading papers. The rain fell all night long. Cats slept soundly on different beds and Shonac was quite comfortable under the kitchen table.

14

Friday. Sybil was pleased with the homework she was able to complete the night before although she was still worried about her Friday test. Donna had set off bright and early with Griego explaining to him how she broke her arm. Sophia stopped at the grocery store on her way home from dropping off Sybil at school to buy basic staples at the T & D Grocery. They didn't have a wide selection, but without much walking she was able to find what she needed. Twice her cellphone chirped, but she wanted to get home before having to make phone calls. The food was put away. Shonac was eager to play as Sophia carried the heavy sack of chicken feed into the coop to pour into the four feeders. She took the water holder out to the barn to scrub, wash, fill and return. Her hens did enjoy fresh clean water.

Shonac followed her into the kitchen as the hall phone began to ring. Sybil quickly washed her hands, took the dish towel and while she dried her hands she held the big plastic phone against her shoulder and ear. "Hello?" Quickly she threw the dish towel onto the kitchen table. "Geoffrey, wait a minute. You're speaking so fast I can't understand what you're saying. Slow down. Now what is going on with Margaret and why did the doctor call you?"

Shonac rolled over on his back for a tummy rub. Sybil bent down and rubbed his ears. His tummy was full of burrs and dried alfalfa. "Geoffrey, all right, I understood that part. But why is there such an emergency and did they say if they had found Granger?" Suddenly, Sophia took the phone from her shoulder and placed it in the cradle. Speaking directly to the dog, Sophia said, "Shonac, I seriously don't need anyone yelling at me and criticizing my mother this early in the day." Her cellphone was pulled from her pant pocket. Three calls from Granger and two from the hospital. "So much for a pleasant day of horseback riding and cleaning the house. I better get to the hospital. No use in trying to converse with too many people who have different ideas all at the same time." A large bowl was pulled out from the lower kitchen cupboard. Hot water from the sink mixed with dried yeast. Two eggs, a pouring of oil, sugar and a couple of cupfuls of sugar were mixed in with the dissolved yeast. A dish cloth covered the concoction as it was placed on the stovetop. "Shonac, you're in charge of kneading the dough until my return." His tail thumped on the wood floor.

Sophia changed into her nice clothes and sneakers. Shonac was given a fat puppy cookie and the cats received a bowl of dry food newly bought at the grocery store. The lights were turned off. The doors locked as Sophia stepped out to walk to her old van. Standing on the other side of the door Juan was inches from her face. "I was going to knock, but then miraculously here you are!" He smiled.

"Yes, here I am. There is an emergency at the hospital with my mother and I have to go. Is there something you need or I can do for you? Like get you into your spaceship and fly to another dimension?" Sophia grimaced at his happy smile.

His strong hands held her shoulders, "Whatever is going on at the hospital it will still be there regardless of how fast you drive there. Don't panic. Your mother has doctors, nurses and all kinds of grief to give them all, at least if what Donna was telling me is true?"

Sophia relaxed her shoulders, "Oh, yes. Margaret can upset the calmest of folks. You're right, I need to slow down. Now, Juan, what can I help you with this morning?" Sophia walked slowly to the van.

Juan came in step beside her. "I will be driving up north. Today I may make it to Denver if the weather holds and then tomorrow will be on my way to Cheyenne, Wyoming. I was hoping you would hold onto this letter for me just in case something strange happens along the way."

He held out a business size white envelope. "It is nothing serious. I just like to leave instructions on how much to feed my horse and where I hide the keys to the house and the truck. Simple things like that. Usually, I leave these with my sister but she is busy now. A job she wanted may be falling into her lap. So, would you put this in your van or in your purse or somewhere safe, just not the chicken coop? This puts my mind at ease if something were to happen."

Sophia stared at the white envelope. "Really? There isn't anyone else you could leave this with in your whole large family? Someone who knows you better than we do since we just barely met?"

Juan put his hands up and danced away from her, "I have to leave right now. Right as soon as you take this envelope. Then I'm gone, I'm outta here, I'm riding the highway to the byway up north to Wyoming. There's no time." Sophia reached out and grabbed it from his hand, "All right, but you better come back in one piece. I have enough to do with all those horses in my barn. So, come back and fix us a dessert and tell us some great stories."

He saluted her, "Yes, Ma'am. Oh, yes, Dr. Pino. Bye!" He ran to

Alcon Road into his driveway where Sophia heard him rev the engine of his eighteen wheeler. The white envelope was shoved into her leather purse. Shaking her head, she mumbled, "There is enough to do without asking for more." She ruffled Shonac's ears as he had followed her outside.

The sky was a glorious blue with only a few fat white clouds floating overhead. Flocks of geese and a huge population of cranes flew overhead as she drove south to Rincon. Mr. Vialpando was talking to a young man who was carrying heavy sacks of grain and putting them in Mr. Vialpando's truck. Sophia waved as he turned and noticed her van. All the signal lights she came to miraculously turned green. At the hospital parking lot there were several open spaces for her to park. The tumbleweeds were stacked in a tall pile near the dumpster at the west side of the hospital building.

As she walked through the parking lot she noticed the Mercedes with the gold radials and leather seats. Granger was already here. At the elevators, Sophia held the door for an elderly couple who were smiling and bragging about their first great-grandchild new born that morning. They had photos to share on the cellphone and were anxious to tell Sophia all about the birth. Finally, on the third floor, Sophia stepped out to find Granger, Dr. Peters, Charlotte and an unknown doctor all huddled around the far side of the nurses' station. Dr. Peters noticed Sophia first and walked over to her. "Hey, glad you could make it. Don't let Granger try to pull you into his way of thinking. He's a warped individual, but I bet you already know this." He took her elbow in his hand and led her to the group.

Charlotte was dotting her eyes with a tissue. Granger's face was bright red and he was grinding his teeth. The doctor had drawn a diagram on a flat white sheet of paper. Granger introduced Sophia to him, "This is my sister. Sis, this is Dr. Lenton. He's a specialist who delves in intestinal stuff. Consider yourselves introduced." Charlotte sniffed and walked away to the large windows. Dr. Peters pushed his way between Sophia and Granger. "Sophia, your mother has a complication with her intestinal track. Evidently she has had this problem for some time. It's all related to her anorexia and her inability to keep food down or eat a balanced diet. I'll let Dr. Lenton explain."

The doctor looked up at Sophia. He had one brown eye and one green eye. He was younger than she expected. A red pen was in his hand, "This is where the issue is regarding your mother's knot or kink. She has a prolapsed small intestine. This is extremely painful and not an easy fix. Last night your mother collapsed on the floor in the hospital room's bathroom. At least George was there to help her into the bed. She passed out in pain. We now have her severely sedated. I was explaining the surgery to repair this damage and the prognosis to these fine people who were called in when we couldn't find you or your brother."

Sophia whirled around, "Granger, where were you? Why couldn't these people get a hold of you?"

Granger put out his hand almost touching her, "Hey, I have a right to a life, don't I? I'm no longer in jail. I have the right to be free, go out with friends or go to work or to just not answer the phone. I'm not a prisoner anymore, right?" He smirked at her. Sophia lifted her hand to slap him, but he caught her wrist, "Now, now, little sister. Let's not have all this hostility in a place of ill repose."

Charlotte hurried over to Sophia to put her hand around her waist. "Come on, let's walk and talk. Stay away from him. Come on, Sophia, come with me."

Sophia allowed herself to be pulled into the hall. Charlotte's soft voice was calming, "Come on, Granger's helpless."

"What's going on with Mom? What does the doctor say?" Sophia stared at Charlotte. Staring up into Sophia's face, Charlotte answered, "The surgery for the biopsy evidently did something to your Mom's intestines or maybe she had this problem before, but never said anything and tried to fix the pain herself. Granger said your Mom has a shelf filled with laxatives and constipating pills. Maybe for this exact problem, we don't really know."

Sophia turned to the chairs and sat down, "Mom has always had issues with her stomach. Papa would make her eat and she would want to be thin so she would take laxatives and then when she had diarrhea she would take chalk. Mom was always embarrassed with her bodily functions."

Charlotte sat next to her, watching Granger pace back and forth in front of the nurse's station. "Well, I wasn't aware of this happening. At least not with humans, but with horses if they don't eat for a long time and then suddenly eat too much the intestine collapses in on itself and this is extremely painful. If the intestine isn't repaired and stays folded inside itself, it can grow that way and then there are serious problems, really, really, bad problems."

Sophia took Charlotte's hands in hers, "Say, you never did tell me who poisoned you the other day when Roberto came and got me. Who or what happened?"

Shaking her head, Charlotte frowned, "It was a fluke. I thought the herbs in the small bag I picked up from school were for tea and they were for dyes. Yes, a stupid mistake that could've killed me. Thankfully you and Roberto had Dr. Peters on hand to save me. It was stupid and here I thought I was an expert. Not again, nope, not again. I think from now on I will buy my herbal tea from the grocery store in a box. But about Margaret, your mother is too weak to undergo surgery and she is in horrible pain."

Granger's boots echoed as he walked to them. Shoving Sophia to the side, he sat down next to her on the same chair. His deep voice was soft as he spoke directly to her, "The only thing we can do right now is keep her comfortable. Dr. Lenton is going to call a friend of his who is an intestinal specialist at Harvard. Right now our mother is blissfully out cold with some strong painkillers. Let's leave her that way, huh?"

Charlotte stood up to be directly in front of Sophia. "Yes, your brother the doctor over here has given his diagnosis."

Quickly, Sophia stood up next to Charlotte, 'What do you mean, my brother the doctor?"

"Charlotte!" Granger's voice was harsh and loud, "There's no call for your attitude here. Leave us alone to discuss this! I think it would be wise for you and the dentist to go home! Don't you?"

Sophia stepped on Granger's foot. "I think you need to explain yourself, Granger, before you start ordering people around. You're not a doctor at least not a medical doctor and you have no authority here!" She walked beside Charlotte to the nurses' station. Dr. Lenton was on the phone and Dr. Peters was standing at the large plate glass windows staring out at the billowing tumbleweeds outside. Sophia and Charlotte came to stand beside him. He turned, "So, I guess your brother the all-knowing, all wise medical doctor has informed you of his choice?"

Charlotte placed her hand on Dr. Peter's shoulder, "No, Granger has ordered you and me to go home, to leave. I haven't had a chance to explain to Sophia what he wanted to do." Dr. Peters looked over his shoulder to see Granger still sitting on the chair with his cellphone in his hand. "Sophia, Granger believes the best thing for you mother is to keep her comfortable and let her pass away using painkillers to basically euthanize her. He doesn't say such in so many words, but this is the main idea. Dr. Lenton is wanting to do some more tests or to have a specialist come in who has more knowledge of your mother's situation. But he, the good Dr. Lenton - who really is a medical doctor, doesn't believe your mother would survive any kind of surgery."

Charlotte interrupted, "Right, he feels Margaret would live for many years, but under constant care. She would need to be monitored and be in a special facility. She wouldn't be able to return to the farm. Her sad farm is dying around her anyway and there she was in so much pain." Sadness showed in her face. Dark clouds covered the sun to darken the hospital's hall.

Staring at their reflection in the window's thick glass, Sophia sighed, "We all thought she was in pain from the truck accident. We didn't know she was having painful intestinal problems, too. Mom never spoke of her own issues, everything was always about Granger or Papa, when he was alive."

Dr. Peters put his hands in his jacket pockets, "I didn't really know your mother. She was Maisy's friend. Your brother feels there isn't much point wasting money on a nursing care facility and he believes she would hate it. Have you spoken to Margaret about the possibility?"

"Oh, no, Mom says she would rather be shot than be put in a nursing home. She hates the idea. Ever since she was a child she wanted to live on a farm with animals. Slowly, her animals have been dying. Now she's too weak to have horses or go riding. She has her chickens, but Roberto is the one who cares for them. She wouldn't want to be in a nursing home, no." Sophia shook her head.

Dr. Lenton walked up to them. "That was my friend from Harvard. He agrees that Margaret should be able to live for several more years if she's in a care facility. She's too weak to be on her own at home and her condition could quickly become fatal, but with care she would be able to live several more years. She will always be in pain, that won't disappear, but her pain would be monitored and watched."

Granger's voice broke through the thoughtful group, "She won't stand for it! Sophia, you know she won't stand for it! I recommend she be placed on strong amounts of pain medications and keep her here in the hospital. She won't go into a nursing facility, Sophia, you know this!" He turned and stormed off to the elevators.

Driving rain pummeled the old van as Sophia and Sybil parked beside the barn. They raced into the warm kitchen to find Donna munching on a cookie in front of the sink. "Mom, something terrible happened today at school."

"What? What happened?"

Donna tried to brush her long hair with her fingers, 'While we were in Language Arts with Miss Casaus the secretary Tracy came in and took Griego out of the classroom. He didn't come back. I'm not sure he's coming back to school. When she was speaking to him quietly, we all watched, his face turned red. I thought he was going to cry. They went down the hall and we couldn't tell what had happened."

Sophia turned on her headlights. The blowing dirt was thick, blocking out the light from the sun. "What do you think happened? Do you think something happened to his mother?"

Shaking her head, Donna answered, "I don't know. You might call her. But earlier he was in a real happy mood. His aunt Maria Elena thinks she's got Rosa's old job. She had wanted the job before, but the people gave it to Rosa instead. Now this woman has the job she always wanted. Griego said his aunt really needed this or else she was going to starve. Everyone in their family was sad when Rosa took the job away from his aunt." Gathering up Donna's coat off the kitchen table. She handed it to her daughter, "Come on, we need to go into town for supplies."

Sophia honked her horn. A man in a ton and half truck pulled right smack in front of her. He rolled down his window and stuck his hand out to wave. Sophia slowed down as they drove through town. A man was herding his Guernsey cows down Main Street. He shrugged and waved at the people. Sophia watched him as he waved his hat at two of the cows who were trying to go into the gas station. "I guess they got out somehow. Maybe the wind knocked a branch that knocked down the fence and the cows got out and now they are taking a tour of the town." Sophia burst out laughing.

"You're sick, Mom." Donna leaned her head against the passenger door window. There was a short siren and then two sheriff's cars approached. They parked on the side of the street and four brown uniformed people were out helping the man herd his cows out of the town. Sophia smiled, "Only in Rincon!" As they turned in to the small grocery store, Sophia asked Donna, "What did you mean when you said Griego's aunt really wanted the job that Rosa took? Do you mean the job in the Otero Middle School Cafeteria?"

"Yes. Yes. That's what I was saying. Come on, Mom, get with the program! Yes, Griego's aunt is a widow. Her husband died and she had no income. She's younger than Griego's mom Reina and she needed this job. I guess Juan Calderon is the youngest and his oldest brother is in his sixties. This aunt applied for the cafeteria job and was excited to get it, but then Rosa showed up. Peggy somebody or other is head of the cafeteria and Rosa moved next door to her. Peggy gave the job to Rosa and Griego's aunt was stuck." Donna sniffed, "Mom, my elbow really hurts."

"O-kay, when we get home I'll get you something for the pain. Let's not worry about school tomorrow until tomorrow comes. If you still have a lot of pain, you better stay home." The long straight road ahead of them was dotted with tall cottonwood trees. Their bare branches flailed about with twigs flying. Black birds held tightly to the lower branches. "Who did you walk home with today?" Sophia turned to Donna.

Smiling, Donna said, "Now I have two new friends. Lindy Vialpando is in my math class and Millie DeGrazia is in my homeroom class. They both live on our road. Lindy lives with her grandparents and they irrigate after us. Millie lives behind the old post office at the end of our road. Griego would walk all three of us girls home. He's such a gentleman, I hope he's all right."

The van parked by the barn. The horses were eating in their stalls. Sybil was in the kitchen making a simple lasagna with fresh cornbread. "Mom, don't hate me, I'm just the messenger. Grandma's doctor called. He needs you to come to the hospital. Granger called, he needs you to come to the hospital. Clementine called and she said she'd meet you at the hospital. Griego's mother called and she wants you to call her back ASAP." Stirring the cornbread mixture, Sybil added, "I need a raise if I'm going to be answering all these calls. By the way, your cellphone was by the barn. I guess you dropped it when you were putting Donna in the van to go to the hospital. I still need a raise."

Donna leaned against the back of her sister, "I broke my elbow! It hurts and I'm starving." Sybil opened the freezer at the top of the fridge. "Here, eat this." She handed her the small container of peppermint ice cream. Quickly, Sophia pulled it from her hand, "No! This is for dessert. It is too close to dinner to have this now. Also, Donna, let me give you something for your pain. Come on, sit down." Two cookies and an ibuprofen were given to Donna. Sophia stood in front of her to watch her eat and drink. "When am I supposed to go to the hospital? You know I was just there? I have been driving back and forth and now I am tired. Didn't anyone say what it is they wanted?"

Shrugging her shoulders, Sybil poured the cornbread mixture into a bread pan, "Nope. But then I'm not the one they needed to speak to. That was you. Why don't you just call them and find out? Dinner will be ready in half an hour anyway. Ask Clementine to come here. We have enough. Call them?"

Sophia fell onto her bed with the cellphone in her hand. She could hear the girls talking in the kitchen about the Urgent Care and the casting. Closing her eyes, she felt she needed to speak to a friend first. She called Clementine. Then she felt two of the kittens jump onto the bed. Marmalade rubbed against her hand and Biscuits fell over against her right leg. "Hi, you guys. I'm tired. You want to drive me to the hospital? Huh?"

Her cellphone chirped. Sophia answered. "Granger, hi. I'm just home from the hospital. Donna broke her radius while riding Tracy. We're just home. I'm tired. Please, do I have to drive to the hospital right now?" Sophia stroked the cats as she listened. "All right, I'll be there first thing in the morning. This is good news that Mom is awake and she's eating and drinking. Why did you want me there and why do I have to be there first thing tomorrow?" Finally, she shut her cellphone.

The house phone rang in the hall. Jumping up from the bed, Sophia ran to answer it. "Hello?" Sophia waved to Donna. Donna stood up from the kitchen chair and came close to her Mom. Sophia put the phone on speaker, 'Sophia, I hate to bother you, but there's been an accident north of Denver. Juan was driving his eighteen wheeler and someone pulled in front of him. They're having a blizzard up there. His truck went off the edge of an escarpment. The police and rescue are still trying to get him out. This happened this morning. Please, ask Donna if she could get Griego's assignments from school for him? We're in Denver now at my sister's house. Would Donna do this, you think?"

Rapidly Donna nodded her head. Sophia said, "Reina, yes! Donna will get his assignments. Do you want me to call you back or do you want to call us? Our prayers are with you and with Juan. Please, let him be all right!" She hung up once Reina promised she would call once they heard something.

Standing, leaning against the door frame, Sophia combed her short curls with her fingers. She dialed Clementine. "Hey, you want some really good food? Sybil's making her special simple lasagna and cornbread for dinner. I can't drive back into Rincon. I've been there twice today or actually three times and I just want to stay home. Do you want to come here?"

Sophia kicked off her shoes. Her old sweatshirt was pulled on and her sweatpants. Walking barefoot into the kitchen, she let Sybil know that Clementine was on her way and would arrive in about thirty minutes. Sybil was sitting in a kitchen chair next to the oven. "Mabel isn't happy with this wind. She keeps shutting off. I've had to relight her twice already."

Donna wandered into the kitchen, "Mom, can you help me change? I want to get into my pajamas and then if it is all right, can I call Dad?" She turned to wander back into her bedroom. Sophia followed her, "Sure, honey. Here let me help you get comfortable. Most certainly you should call your Dad and let him know what happened. He may be confused, but he's not the enemy."

Donna held her Mom's cellphone in her hand as she fell back onto her bed. Sophia shoved a pillow under Donna's hurt elbow. Sophia waved as she quietly backed out of the room, closed Donna's bedroom door and went into the kitchen. The cornbread smelled delicious as did the lasagna. Lights flashed outside. Sophia ran out to greet Clementine. "Hey, park over here by the van. The big tree is dropping branches." Sophia waved her arms. There was a pile of tree branches already formed under the cottonwood tree. Clementine got out of her car to hug Sophia, 'Wow, I didn't think I would make it. The roads are full of debris and accidents. People drive into one another without looking. I thought Australian drivers were bad, but here it is insane! I could use a strong mug of hot tea!"

Inside the cozy home, tea mugs were filled and the table set. Donna was in the kitchen smiling. "Hi, Clementine. Guess what? Dads going to come by Saturday and take me shopping. I broke my arm, look?" She lifted her fiberglass cast up in the air. It was dry and hard. The metal stick left in her bedroom. Sybil gave Clementine a wave as she flipped the bread pan over onto a long plate. Clementine was impressed with the cast. She told Sybil, 'I don't know what you're cooking, but the smell of it is making me hungry!"

At dinner, Donna explained to Clementine about Juan's accident and Griego being taken out of class. Smiling at her, Clementine added, "Yes, we've been in communication with the highway and rescue people up north. We have been following Juan or Don Juan Calderon as you guys call him. He's a person of interest down here." Buttering the hot cornbread slice on her plate, Clementine added, "We are busy right now trying to figure out how to keep traffic flowing what with the balloons coming this weekend. It's going to be crazy!"

Sybil spoke about the two balloonists who had come to her school. They offered rides to the students, but the principal wouldn't allow anyone to go up in the balloons without parent permission slips. None were given out to the kids. Sybil expounded on the loud sounds of the fans and the heaters blowing air into the balloons. Mr. O'Brian talked about the movie 'Around the World in Eighty Days' and how the hot air balloons had developed. After dinner, Sybil spooned the peppermint ice cream into a bowl for Donna. The two girls ran into Donna's room to eat the ice cream and talk. Clementine and Sophia were left to do the cleanup in the kitchen. The old house creaked and moaned with the changing currents of the wind outside.

Clementine offered to wash this time. "Sophia, I didn't want to say anything in front of the girls, but we have solved our murder by poisoning mystery. The ending may be more than awful." The faucet water frothed the detergent bubbles in the sink.

Sophia turned to study Clementine, "What do you mean? Who is the person behind the poisoning?"

Dishes were dunked into the hot sink water. "Griego's uncle Juan felt he was the responsible male for the whole of the family when his father died. By the way, what does Don Juan Calderon mean?"

Leaning against the counter, Sophia frowned, "No. Not Juan." Then she added, "Oh, Don Juan Calderon is an old children's story about Sir John Cooking Pot. But what are you saying?"

A dish was lifted and scrubbed, Clementine shook her head. "Juan felt he needed to help his family regardless of the cost. Evidently, his sister, his older sister is a widow, her husband worked. He was never given social security or any kind of retirement. When he died two years ago, the belief was Maria Elena would have the job at the Otero Middle School

Cafeteria." The dish was placed in Sophia's hand for her to dry. "Rosa showed up the week before the job was to be handed over to Maria Elena. Peggy Crowley is the supervisor for the cafeteria. Peggy and her husband Carl were selling the house and Roberto and Rosa are buying the house. Rosa was given the job over Maria Elena. Rosa needed to work to pay the mortgage payments to Peggy and her husband. This worked out well for all concerned around Peggy." Another clean wet plate was handed to Sophia.

"Maria Elena was left out of the loop. She had no income, no job and now no other place to find work. Mary Peters knew her from the times Maria Elena had helped at the school's parties. Mary Peters hired Maria Elena to come and help her clean her house two days a week out of sympathy. Mary Peters had stacks of your brother's bags in her tiny office."

Sophia put up her hand, "Wait, wait. How did Maria Elena get the herbs? Where did the poisonous herbs come from? Not Granger?"

Staring at the bubbles in the kitchen sink, Clementine sighed, "Oh, Sophia, this is a tangled web of trouble. Mrs. Peters or Mary Peters has an herb garden. When Maria Elena came to work for her she showed the herbs to Maria Elena, explaining how deadly they were." Clementine used the back of her hand to push her hair away from her face, "Mary Peters grew wonderful plants for dyes, her herbs. She grew Western Water Hemlock, Lupine, Larkspur Blue, Rhubarb and Blue Periwinkle. The deadliest I found was Datura in pod form. All of these are terrible poisons if ingested. Some cause delirious reactions. Others cause exhaustion. I don't know all of the different types of reactions, but these are not good plants to have just growing around the house."

The dried plates were set into the cupboard. Sophia turned, "Maria Elena plucked the poisons from the garden? Wouldn't Mary notice? Mary wasn't stupid certainly she would know if she was being poisoned if she grew these plants, right?"

Agreeing with her, Clementine added, "Mary Peters didn't die from poisoning. She was stabbed. She was slowly being poisoned as well, but that wasn't what killed her. Dr. Peters is being held without bail right at this moment. Mary Peters was slowly being poisoned with anthrax. According to the M.E. office, she had been ingesting anthrax for some time. It was found in her hair, her teeth, her skin cells, well throughout her body. Her death, her sudden death was caused from a stabbing to the heart."

The towel was held in mid-air, Sophia stared at Clementine, "You mean her kind and loving husband was trying to kill her as well as someone else?"

Clementine let the bubbly water out of the sink by pulling up the stopper. "Yes. We don't believe he stabbed her though. He wasn't anywhere around when she was stabbed. We believe the person who stabbed her was Juan. We found the knife buried in the horse muck in the barn. There were no obvious fingerprints on it, until it was taken to the special services lab in Dallas. They found Juan's fingerprints on the side of the blade."

A kitchen chair was pulled out and Sophia quickly sat down, "Our Juan? Our Juan killed Mary Peters? I find this hard to believe?"

Clementine plugged in the hot water kettle and turned it on. She sat facing Sophia, "Yes, I agree. Also, the herbs that killed Rosa were done by his hand. We found the bag of herbs. Many of them are the ones I mentioned earlier. The bag had been emptied into the tea Rosa was drinking. Rosa believed the tea would help her with her diabetes and her high blood pressure. Evidently, Rosa was not in good health by any means." Clementine took the rubber band from her wrist. Her long blonde hair was combed with her fingers and pulled back into a ponytail. She fastened it with the rubber band.

"Roberto came to take care of the Peters' horses as he did every day. Mary Elena handed him the bag of herbs telling him that the good doctor felt these would help his wife with her medical issues. She told him how much to use and how often, knowing full well how toxic the herbs were. These two worked together to get their goal."

The kettle turned off. Sophia stood, took two mugs, a bowl of different types of teas, the milk jug and the honey jar and put all on the table. "I can't believe this. Reina isn't involved is she? Griego's mother?"

"As far as we know, no."

Sophia stared at Clementine, "Do you know how helpful he was here to us? He helped us find Donna when she disappeared. He helped us with the horses, the irrigation and with wonderful desserts. This is hard to take in right now."

Quietly, Sybil walked into the kitchen, "Mom, I couldn't help but overhear what you guys were talking about. Donna's asleep. She's wiped out." Sybil pulled out a chair and sat next to her mother, facing Clementine. "Is it true about Juan? I really liked him."

Clementine put her hand on the table, "Sybil, it is hard to know anyone, truly know a person. We had our suspicions, but until we had proof I was like you. I couldn't believe it. Juan wanted what was best for his family. He wanted it at any cost to anyone else. This is a frightening reality. He was or is willing to do whatever it takes to help his family."

Clementine finished her mug of tea. "Yes, I had best get home to bed myself with my cat. I wanted to come and tell you before you heard anything through the grapevine. Truth is best coming from the source."

Sophia smiled, "Clementine, you stopped ending sentences with a question. How fun. Now I think I miss it." The two women walked out to Clementine's car. Sophia gave her a hug, "Be safe going home. The wind has died down some, but the other drivers are what are dangerous."

The house was quiet when Sophia walked into her bedroom. She had locked the doors, brought in Shonac and turned off the lights. The thermostat by the gas stove was low. She left it. In her room there were only two cats on her bed. Sophia pulled off her shoes, realizing she was exhausted. After brushing her teeth, she checked up on Donna. The casted arm remained on the pillow. Two cats were sleeping between her legs. The wind had finally stopped to let the small farm be at peace tonight.

A loud knock on the front door frame startled both of them. Marmalade was put down as Donna raced to the door. Sophia plugged in the kettle on the kitchen counter. She peered out the kitchen window. There were no vehicles parked beside the van. Donna walked into the kitchen leading a very serious Juan and his solemn sister Maria Elena. Both had serious expressions on their faces. "Sophia," Juan spoke first. "We need to discuss something with you privately. Do you think this would be possible?" He pulled out a kitchen chair and nodded for his older sister to sit. Pulling off her jacket, she placed it on the back of the chair and sat down. Donna reached down to lift Marmalade from the floor. Hugging him to her chest, she kissed him and walked to her room softly closing the door behind her.

Sophia leaned against the kitchen counter with the kettle heating up behind her. "What is all this about?" Juan sat in the chair next to his sister. "We thought it would be best if you heard this information directly from us and not from someone else. We wouldn't want you to get the wrong impression." The kettle clicked off. Sophia turned to ask over her shoulder, "Would any of you like some tea?" Maria Elena reached behind her to pull out a paper bag. "Here, we brought you some tea. It's in one of your family's familiar bags. You could use this?" Sophia pulled tea bags from a box in the cupboard in front of her, "No, we can save that. Let's have some Earl Grey for a change. Herbal tea is so over rated, don't you think?"

Maria Elena quickly rolled up the bag and stuck it behind her shoes and under the kitchen chair. Sophia reached out to her, "Oh, no, please, let me keep it for another day? Please, I didn't mean to be rude. It's just the time is late and you both appear solemn so English tea is probably the best for right now." She stood with her hand outstretched to Maria Elena who was shaking her head, "No, no, that's all right. I can take it home for later or if you go over to Juan's, he can serve it to you. Don't worry about it." Her mouth was set in a firm grin.

Three mugs were set on the table. The sugar jar, some milk from the fridge and three spoons. Each mug had a tea bag of Earl Grey and a spoon in it. Sophia carefully poured the hot water from the kettle into each, letting the steam rise. The kitchen was cold, but Sophia ignored the temperature to sit opposite them. "All right, what's going on?"

Maria Elena clasped her hands in front of her on the table. Bright red enamel fingers clicked together at the tips as Maria Elena turned to Juan who was stirring sugar into this tea. He in turn said nothing. Leaning back in the kitchen chair, Sophia shook her head. "I can't read minds so one of you will need to speak." She blew on her hot tea and slurped it carefully. Maria Elena nudged Juan with her elbow, "Go on tell her. I didn't follow you over here in the freezing cold to just sit here and have her stare at us." A frown appeared across Juan's forehead. "I'm thinking of the best way to start. Give me a minute." Sybil's door flew open with a thud as it hit the adobe wall. She flew across the floor straight to Juan. Her arms wrapped around his neck and shoulder, "Yes! Yes! You brought dessert!" She stood at the end of the table to stare at the three mugs, sugar jar and the milk. "Where is it?" Then she smiled, "It's in the fridge, right?"

Juan stood up pushing the heavy kitchen chair back behind him. "No, Sybil, I haven't brought dessert. I do need to speak to your mother alone if you wouldn't mind?" Sybil hurried to her mother's side, "Hey, Mom and I have no secrets from one another. We're a team. A team of Pino's, women strong and courageous, right Mom?" Sybil started to pull out a kitchen chair beside her mother.

Quickly, Sophia stood to put an arm around Sybil, "Right, dear, but tonight I have a feeling you need to go and take your shower and get ready for bed. You might want to check on your sister, too. She wasn't happy about being asked to leave either." Oscar ran from Sybil's bed meowing to jump on the kitchen table. He slid half way across it until he was picked up by Sophia. "Take this fur ball with you as well. Sorry, Kid, but us grownups need to share." Sophia kissed Sybil on the top of her head. Clutching Oscar to her, Sybil gave each one of the adults a nasty frown, "O-kay, I'm gone. I'll be with Donna. Bye." She waved Oscar's paw at Maria Elena.

Juan returned to sit in his chair as he pulled it up to the table. Sophia sat back down, "You both have me seriously worried. What's going on?" Juan placed both of his hands palms down on the kitchen table. His face appeared older, defined and wrinkled, "We felt it was important for you to know Maria Elena visited your brother Granger when he was in prison. Granger was telling Maria Elena what herbs to get from Malakai to help with her bad spine issues. Maria Elena didn't want you to find out through the sheriff or the police about her visits and believe the worst. The only reason she visited Granger was for medical reasons and medical reasons only."

Sophia stared at Juan's hands as they twisted round and round on the table. Then she stared at Maria Elena, "Is that correct? Granger can be very manipulative at times. Is it true you only went to see him for medical care and not to do his dirty work for him?" Shonac ran into the kitchen from the back bedrooms to lie down by Sophia's feet. He started licking the dirty boots. Sophia shoved him away.

The tea mug was right in front of Maria Elena. Her black eyeliner was smudged under her eyes and her bright red lipstick was clumped in the corners of her mouth. Lifting the spoon, she continued to stir the tea bag round and round in the mug without lifting her head. "No, I only asked Granger for help with my spine and my neck. I didn't ask him for anything else. It is just what Juan said." Her voice was soft almost a whisper.

Sophia leaned forward, "Maria Elena, what I asked you was did Granger require you to do anything for him? Did he ask you to do something for him while he was stuck in prison and you were free to do his task?"

Abruptly, Juan jumped upright from the chair. It flew back to hit hard on the wooden floor. His eyes were wide. Quickly, he reached down to retrieve the chair. His voice became harsh, "What do you think Granger wanted her to do? Kill! What would Maria Elena do for Granger's help, huh? Sophia, how dare you ask my sister such a terrible question!" His strong hands lifted Maria Elena up by her arm, practically dragging her out of the chair. His face red with anger, "My sister is not for sale! She did nothing wrong! How dare you! I thought we were friends! I thought we trusted one another."

Spittle shot out of his mouth, "I looked after your girls and didn't ask anything from you! What do you do? You accuse my sister!" Pulling her jacket from the back of the kitchen chair he threw it around his sister,

"Come on! Let's go! We know when we aren't wanted! Come on! Go!" Juan shoved Maria Elena in front of him. His hand flat on her back as she hurried down the hall and out the door into the cold night air.

Sophia followed. "Juan, it was a perfectly innocent question! Why are you so upset?" Juan slammed the door behind him almost hitting Sophia in the face.

"Mom! Mom!" Sybil and Donna were running down the hall to her. "What happened? What's wrong?" Sybil hugged her mother around her waist. "We were listening around the corner. Why did he get so upset? You weren't angry or threatening!" Sophia put her arms around the girls, "You don't know how people will respond do you?" She let them pull her back through the dark hall and into the kitchen. There on the floor under Maria Elena's chair was the bag of tea she had offered. Donna reached down to pick it up. Sophia stopped her, "No, let's put it in a baggie and call Clementine. There's something about this bag that has me suspicious."

Sybil ran to the phone in the hall, "I'll call her. She likes to hear my voice. At least that's what she said." Donna pulled a big plastic bag from the drawer to hand to her mother. Sophia turned it inside out to carefully lift the herbal brown bag with the gold and red seal into the plastic bag.

The phone was quickly hung up as Sybil walked into the kitchen. "Clementine is with Roberto at his old house. They are going through things to give away or to take to the dump or stuff he might want. She said to bring the bag to the department in the morning after you drop me off at school."

Sophia stood at the kitchen window with the sheet pulled up at the corner. "Maria Elena appears to be giving Juan a good talking to in our driveway. He's shaking his head. Evidently, that question seriously upset him."

"Mom, Mom!" Donna pulled on Sophia's sweater, "Mom, didn't you say that when people are guilty they get mad when they're confronted? Didn't you say that about Dad, too?" She kept pulling on the sleeve of her mother's sweater. "Mom, you're prying. It isn't polite to pry, right?"

Lightly pushing Donna's hand away from her, Sophia answered, "They're on our property, in our driveway and I was the one who was told off. What do you suppose they're talking about? They're under the Hangman's Tree. Donna go into the front room and see if you can hear anything. Juan is all but yelling at his sister and she appears just as mad. She's not taking it from him."

Sybil and Donna raced into the dark front room. They cautiously slid open one of the aluminum windows. Donna squatted down while Sybil stood tall both with their heads turned, ears at the ready. Then suddenly Maria Elena slapped Juan hard across the face. He lifted his hand, but then put it down again. He walked to the side of the barn and hopped over the fence to his house. Maria Elena yelled, "Cabron!" at him and walked up the driveway to her car parked on Alcon Road.

The aluminum window was gently closed. Jumping in fright as Sophia put her hands on the daughters' shoulders, "So, what did they say? Could you hear anything?" Sybil turned slowly with a smile on her face, "Not until we get three cookies each, right, Donna?"

Bone chilling cold seemed to have oozed into the house as the three females sat at the kitchen table with the heater going full blast. Sophia had her mug of tea, the girls had three chocolate chip cookies and some tea with milk in front of them. Donna had decided since she was the youngest with the most capable ears since she had not ruined them with loud music or anything other, she went first. "Juan mumbled something to Maria Elena and his tone was accusatory. He seriously felt she had done something someone would find out about and she would be in serious trouble. Then, he yelled that she was a stupid cow and would deserve to die for her actions." Donna took a sip of her milky tea, "That's when she slapped him.

"Right," Sybil munched on her cookie, "He told her that she had used Granger's herbs for her benefit not for what Granger had wanted her to do. Just because the 'old lady' was still in the hospital didn't mean Maria Elena should use the gift Granger gave her for her own personal benefit." Sybil swallowed, "He said she would go to Hell and he was glad he wasn't involved with her choices. That's when she slapped him hard. That's going to leave a mark. Let me tell you!"

Leaning back in her kitchen chair, Sophia pulled an blue book from her carry case. Reaching deeply inside the case, she held a mechanical pencil. "All right, let's write this all down for Clementine. Or do you believe we should call A.J. now to come out right away before someone else gets killed?" The blue book was opened. Sophia started writing down what the girls had told her. The two girls leaned forward over the table to read what she was writing. Sybil tapped the page, "You should write down that Juan was the one who was angry not Maria Elena. She was cool and collected. After all she was the one who slapped him. Juan was upset with her, but she was one cool cat."

"You know what, girls? This isn't a murder mystery novel. This is real life and somehow you two are seriously good at figuring stuff out." Sophia finished writing. "Now who do you think Maria Elena was involved with and who she wanted dead?"

"Mom, this is a no brainer." Sybil shook her head. "I have to take a shower and get ready for tomorrow. We're going to decorate the gym and I am anxious to look so good for you know who!" Turning her wrist,

Sophia read her watch, "Whoa, it is after ten o'clock. Donna, you need to get ready for bed as well, sweetheart. But first can you help me feed the cats and Shonac. Good thing we fed the horses already, huh?" Donna stuck her tongue out at her mother, "You can feed the cats and Shonac. You don't need my help. I'm going to bed for my beauty sleep."

A loud banging was heard at the front door. Sybil raced into the bathroom with her long blue towel. "I'm not getting that! Maybe it is Juan with dessert since he was ugly to us. No way am I going to eat anything from those people again! I'm in the shower, bye!"

Donna put her hand on her mother's shoulder, "What if they've come back to kill all of us?" Sophia shook her head, "Don't worry, our killer dog under the table won't let that happen." Donna raced into her room to slam and lock her bedroom door. Shonac came out from under the table either because he heard his name or because he was concerned. He trotted down the hall to the front door. Sophia followed him. Shonac wagged his tail. "Great, you're friends with all the neighborhood killers. Aren't we special?" She bent to rub his head.

Before Sophia could reach the door knob, it turned and the door was pushed open. She gasped and jumped when she saw Clementine, "What?" She knelt down to rub Shonac's ears. "Did you think it was Halloween and I was here to Trick or Treat? Really, Sophia, Halloween isn't until the end of the month!"

In the kitchen, Sophia plugged in the water kettle. The cat dishes were placed on the counter as the cats howled and wrapped their way around her ankles. Clementine was studying the baggie with the tea bag Maria Elena had brought with Juan. Pointing with the wrong end of the cat food spoon, Sophia said, "The blue book on the table has the written conversation of Juan and Maria Elena that the girls heard. The two siblings were yelling at one another in the driveway right outside the front room. The girls heard most of the conversation. Go on, read it. Tea will be ready soon."

The cats were fed on the low table in the kitchen's corner. Shonac received his bowl in the hall by the home phone. Sophia carefully watched Fergus for he tended to scarf down his food to steal everyone else's. He was picked up and placed in Clementine's lap as she read sitting at the table. The kettle clicked off as Sophia took a box of tea from the cupboard. "Say, what kind of tea would you enjoy this cold night?" Clementine laughed, "Any tea that comes in a box. Don't think I will be drinking any tea from a bag in a long time. Are there any cookies left? I see cookie crumbs on the table."

The two women sat opposite one another as they sipped tea from warm mugs and ate cookies off a plate. "This is pretty damning. Maria

Elena worked for Maisy and she wanted the job that Rosa was given. Even Charlotte knew Maria Elena from the school cafeteria and evidently had her over to help make the dyes the day Charlotte was poisoned. We don't have any proof yet, unless we find something in this bag she brought over for your tea." Clementine took another cookie, "What's your take on this, Sophia?"

The hot mug of tea before Sophia on the table steamed, "There are two things that are strange. The first is that I am no threat to any of these people. Not one iota. I have no hold on Maria Elena and if her relative on the rez hadn't told me she visited Granger I never would've known. The second question I have is why Granger gave these herbs to Maria Elena in the first place?" Sophia watched Clementine wiggle out of her coat to fold it on the flat seat of the chair beside her. Clementine shook her hair free after she pulled a rubber band from her ponytail. The brown-red hair fell softly down to her shoulders. The freckles covering Clementine's face were noticeable on her pale face. Sophia continued on, "Both girls picked up on Rosa's death. Certainly, Maria Elena wanted Rosa's job. But why Maisy and why Charlotte? What had they done to Maria Elena?"

A deep growl came from the back hallway. Both women heard the side door opened to let in a blast of cold air. Both women turned to watch Shonac as he crouched, moving backward toward the kitchen. His haunches were up and his teeth were bared. He continued to growl as he slunk low to the floor boards and moved forward to the open kitchen doorway. Donna's door opened a crack and then closed with a click of the lock. Sybil could be heard singing in the shower.

Clementine dropped low off the chair to her knees. She pulled her revolver from her back where it had been tucked under her sweater. She waved to Sophia to go to the hallway door. Whispering, she asked Sophia as she came closer to her, "Engage in conversation."

Sophia stood to put her hand down as she approached Shonac, "What is it, boy? What's got you so bothered?" Shonac kept still with his head down. He growled again as she moved closer to him. Then she turned to face the hallway door, "Juan? What a surprise to find you here at the side door? You could've knocked or come in the front. What's up? Are you here to apologize?" Sophia didn't move out of the doorway, but leaned casually against the door frame. Clementine was on her knees in the kitchen behind Sophia. She hadn't moved either nor was she able to see Juan.

Juan's voice was soft but firm, "Where are the girls?" He pointed to the bathroom door when he heard Sybil singing. "Where's Donna our horsewoman?"

"She's in her room, getting ready for bed. Why? Juan, what's going on with you? Why be so quiet? Juan, are you all right?" She started to move toward him, but something had hold of her pant leg and held her firmly in place. "What happened to your face? It's all red?"

Juan leaned against the inside of the door that was now closed to the outside. "Hey, I saw you have company. Where's you company, huh?" His eyes were wide. Sophia smiled, "Clementine came for a late night cuppa of tea. Hey, would you like a cup now that you're here?"

He shouted at her, "NO! Enough with your tea! I saw Clementine's cruiser out front. So where is she? Why isn't she out here with you?" His eyes were wide and his jaw was set firmly.

Now standing free from the doorframe, Sophia stood upright, "Clementine is in with Donna. She's reading a book with Donna. Clementine is a lover of horses as well and she brought a book for Donna. Why? Aren't we all friends?" Sophia started to move forward, but again Clementine grabbed the back of her pant leg to stop her. Sophia fell back against the door frame. "Please, Juan, you're acting very suspicious, what is it that you're doing here?" She put out her hand to Juan, "Why all the anger? Juan, tell me what's up with you?"

"Can I come into the kitchen?" He pointed to the doorway where Sophia stood. "Now come to think of it, it is cold and I would love a cup of tea. The cold really gets to me. Can we go into the kitchen now?" Juan started to move forward to Sophia. She put her hand up, "Juan, really, it is late and the girls need to get to bed. Tomorrow I have an early class and why don't you come back tomorrow evening earlier and we can have dinner? You can bring one of your great desserts. Tomorrow would be better."

He moved toward her quickly. He grabbed her forearm on her right-side and pushed her into the kitchen. Pulling out a chair, he shoved her into it. "No, I want tea and I want it right now! Where is the bag my sister left here? Where is it?" He ducked down to look under the table. Shonac followed him still growling with his tail down and his ears back.

Sophia put her hand out to the dog, "Juan, Shonac is ready to attack. He's picking up on your adrenalin. Please, what is it that you want?" Tilting her head down, she peered under the table and then searched around the kitchen. Both Clementine and the bag were missing. She noticed Clementine's old coat was still folded on the kitchen chair. Juan picked up the coat and flung it at Sophia.

His hand slapped the kitchen table top hard. "Where's the tea bag my sister brought in here?" Juan searched the chairs, pushed open the fridge and bent down to look into the cold oven. "Sophia, I know she left it in here. She called me. She told me she dropped it under her chair. I know you have it! Damnit! Where is it! Where's the damn bag!"

Sophia attempted to stand, but Juan pushed her shoulder down as she abruptly sat in the chair. Lifting her hands, Sophia started to speak, but Juan cut her off. "No! Don't give me any excuses. She left it here. Sophia, I don't want to hurt you or your girls! Where is the damn tea bag! NOW!" This time he pulled out a switchblade knife from his pant pocket and with a click it opened. A sharp glistening blade was swung in front of her face. As Juan waved it around in front of Sophia, he slapped her shoulder with his free hand, "Where in the hell is the bag! I'm not going to ask again."

Shonac leapt up, biting Juan's wrist. Blood squirted out all over Sophia's face as she yelped with Juan's blood covering her face. Juan kicked Shonac hard in the abdomen and then smashed his fist on Shonac's head until he let go of his wrist. "Goddamn Dog!" The knife hand now freed he lunged at Shonac. Sophia kicked Juan in the knee as hard as she was able. Down he went.

Clementine jumped out of Sybil's room with the gun held firmly in both of her hands. "Don't move. Don't think about it." She side stepped around Sophia who was on the kitchen floor holding Shonac who was bleeding from the neck. Clementine's voice was firm and quiet, "Drop the knife, Juan. Drop it now." Juan put the knife on the kitchen's wooden floor with his index finger and thumb still holding the base.

Clementine stood over Sophia, "Move away from the knife. Juan, no more games. Move away from the knife!"

Juan leapt forward with the knife straight for Clementine. The gun went off. The sound reverberated around the kitchen's thick adobe walls. Deafening everyone in the room until there was silence. Juan was leaning back against the kitchen counter by the sink. Sybil raced into the kitchen with her blue towel wrapped around her. Donna pushed her sister behind her. A crutch was firmly held in front of her. Sophia was huddled over Shonac whose blood was pouring out on the old wooden floor. Clementine moved to the far side of the kitchen table. The gun still held firmly in both of her hands. "Girls, take your mother and Shonac into the hallway. Call an ambulance. Tell them someone has been shot. They come faster if you don't tell them by who or for whom. Go!"

Donna ran into the bathroom returning with several towels. Sybil held the large blue towel around her dripping body as she spoke on the phone. Kneeling on the floor, Sophia cried as she held and rocked her beloved dog. Donna wrapped towels tightly around Shonac's neck. Clementine watched Juan as she pulled handcuffs from her waist belt. "You're not going to die tonight, but you came close!" She shoved the gun back down under her sweater as she approached him with the handcuffs.

Blood pulsed from a hold in Juan's shoulder. As Clementine approached Juan, he pulled the switchblade from behind him. Lunging directly at Clementine, she jumped to the side. Reaching back for the gun took Clementine only a moment, but in that moment Juan was down the front hall and out the front door. Sophia was at Clementine's side as she slumped to the floor. "Damn, I thought I got him better than that! He wasn't supposed to be agile! Damn, that's what happens when your friends with the perp! Damn!" Clementine rocked forward holding her side. "This really hurts, but look there's hardly any blood? That's good, right?"

Sybil lifted the house phone and this time she called A.J. He told her to stay put, he was on his way. Clementine's tears muffled her voice, "This is bad, really bad! I should've shot him square, but I didn't. I shot him in the shoulder! How did he still have the damn knife? Huh? I thought it was on the floor!" Sybil was now dressed and tightening the towels around Shonac's neck. The dog's eyes were glazed over and his breathing was rapid.

Sirens woke the neighborhood. The ambulance arrived first. Donna met the E.M.T.'s and brought them immediately to Shonac. His blood was pumping out covering the hall's wooden floor boards. The young E.M.T. knelt beside him as the other medic worked on Clementine. "This isn't deep just a flesh wound. Let's get you in the truck and get this cleaned up. How're you doing over there, Phil?"

Shonac gave a jerk and then his head fell back. Donna held the bloody towels tightly around the dog's neck. Sobbing, she gently lifted his head onto her lap. "Mom, Mom, oh, Mom, Shonac's gone! Oh, Mama! Mom!" She screamed a loud painful scream. Sybil was now dressed and beside her little sister, holding her gently and rocking.

The heater went off. The only sound was of sobbing and sadness. Sophia held Clementine as she leaned against Sophia. The two medics left to return with a gurney and two warm blankets. "Sorry, Ma'am, but we believe we should take you to the Emergency Room just to be sure you won't need sutures. What happened to the shooting victim?" Clementine shook her head, "He's gone into the wind. Let's go before my boss arrives."

"Too late." A.J. walked into the kitchen. He patted one of the E.M.T.'s on the shoulder. "You two probably know almost everyone in this room. Get her to the E.R. and send the sheriff's office the bill. She's special this one." He nodded to Clementine, "Go, get checked out. I'm sure Sophia and the girls will fill me in on everything. Go." He stood aside as the gurney was lifted. "Oh, be sure to have the sirens blaring. We want everyone to know about this event! Go!"

Clementine sat on the gurney, then rolled onto her side. Blankets were put on top of her. "Call me. Let me know what happens. Oh, Roberto is renting me his old house on Fourth Street. Some good news." Then she was down the hall and gone.

A.J. picked up kitchen chairs as he moved to Donna and Sybil. Sophia had somehow managed to get upright. Squatting beside Shonac, A.J. asked, "All right, now someone tell me what happened here?" Donna started shaking, "Shonac saved Mom's life." Tears fell to mingle with the blood on the floor, "Shonac's dead, A.J.! My puppy's dead!" Sybil helped Donna slowly stand as Shonac's head was delicately placed on the floorboards. Taking Donna by the arm, Sybil whispered, "Let's get you washed up, come on." Donna fell into Sybil's arms as she let all her sad pain flow against her sister's embrace.

A.J. took one of the bloody towels and placed it over Shonac's still body. "That's a brave dog." Over his shoulder he called to Sophia, "Are you all right for a moment? I'm going to take Shonac the Brave outside to be under the stars."

Standing behind him now, Sophia quietly answered, "Yes, how kind of you. Thank you. I'll bring out a clean blanket to cover him. It is very cold out tonight."

A.J. took one of the cleaner towels to wrap around the dog's body. Cautiously he carried him to the hall's door where Sophia opened it for him. Shonac was placed gingerly at the base of a smaller cottonwood tree between the farmhouse and the barn. Sophia hurriedly brought a camping blanket to cover the body. A.J. stood to hold her in his arms. "It's o-kay, you can cry. Let it out. We're here under the Great Night Sky. Just let go." Sophia stared at him and then she sniffed to fall onto his shoulder. "Damn it! A.J., no one was supposed to die! Oh, no, my daughters were put in harm's way, too! I'm a terrible mother! Sybil was singing in the shower!" She laughed and then cried.

A.J. finally pushed her back, "All right, where is this Juan Calderon fellow? Isn't he hurt, too? Come on, let's go back inside. You're shivering and my feet have gone numb. Also, we need to check on the girls. The dog is safe. Come on." He held her elbow as they moved into the house. They heard Sybil singing to Donna with the shower going.

Sophia nodded to A.J. as she went into her bedroom. He knocked on the bathroom door, "How is everyone in there? Are you girls all right?" Sybil answered, "Donna's still crying, but she's getting clean."

He pulled his cellphone from his belt to call out a search for Juan Calderon and gave his address in Alcon. The metallic smell of blood filled the two rooms as Sophia came out of her bedroom with a clean shirt. Squatting on the floor, she tried to mop up the dog's blood with the already saturated towels. A.J. plugged in the kettle. Two mugs were broken on the floor by the kitchen table. Sophia took two of the bloody towels into the cold bathroom on the other side of the kitchen. She washed them out in the old tub and ran water over them until they were clear of blood. Walking back and forth, she slowly cleaned most of the puddles of blood from the wooden floor. A.J. leaned against the counter watching her. "You know the best way to get the smell of blood out of wood is with lemon juice and apple vinegar. Maybe once the girls have gone to school tomorrow."

Turning her head to him as he continued to wipe the floor, "I have to teach tomorrow as well. Where do you believe Juan would go for help?"

Holding his hot mug of tea in his hand, he shook his head at her, "Sophia, we have sheriffs searching his home, Maria Elena's home and of course everyone in his family's home. According to Clementine, he was shot straight on in the shoulder. I can't find a bullet in the kitchen wall, maybe you could stop that now and help me look for a bullet casing."

She tossed the wet towel over the blood stains. Her left cheek had Clementine's blood smeared on it. On her hands and knees, Sophia searched the lower cabinet doors. Pointing her index finger at the hole in the cabinet door, she said, "There. The bullet must have gone into the mixing bowl cupboard." Pulling out the mixing bowls, she handed them up to A.J. without even looking inside them.

He put out his hand to stop her, "Yes, here it is. You can stop now. Sophia, you are in a state of shock. Don't you think you could sit down or lie down for a moment and get your balance?"

"No. There is too much to do." She stood with her hand on the counter for leverage. "No. I need to take care of my girls. Why don't you sit at the table and read what the girls and I wrote in the blue book. Go on, take your tea and read." Sophia jerked her hand toward the table. "Go, read!"

A.J. shook his head. "You need to let go for a moment, Sophia. All right, I'll read. You need to know I'm not going anywhere tonight. I'm staying here with you three. All the doors are locked now and the windows are double checked. I'm here for the night and NO you're not staying up with me. Now, I'll sit and read. Do whatever it is you need to do." He pulled out a chair and sat.

Sophia pushed open Donna's bedroom door. The two girls were both in the bed with all the covers pulled over their heads. "Hey, you two, what do you think about staying home tomorrow? Or going to the zoo or the movies?" She rubbed her hand over the covers, "Are my two brave daughters in here or is there a Halloween Ghost who has moved into this bed with Donna?"

"Mama, we should go to school." Sybil's voice was muffled under the covers. "We need to try and keep our lives normal. Donna and I were talking about it. She wants to talk to Griego and I need to help decorate the gym for Halloween and, Mom, you need to teach your classes. You've missed too many as it is, right?"

Sophia sat down on the bed. She studied her hands. They were wrinkled from water and her wrists were caked with blood. Her fingers pushed back her short curly hair, "Yes, although right now I could use a stiff drink and a trip to Europe. You know what I was thinking? I think we should move." The covers were flung up into the air and two girls sat upright. "Really? We can move! Yes! Yes! Let's move tomorrow!"

Sophia gathered them into her arms. "Not tomorrow, but soon. We have to fix this place up and sell it and then when we make a fortune, then we can move. Now, Sybil are you sleeping in here or in your own bed?" Donna grabbed her sister's arm, "She's sleeping in here." She took the covers and the two girls disappeared under them. Sophia laughed, "I'm going to turn off the light then because you both need to sleep if possible. A.J. is going to stay the night and protect us so don't be scared if a strange man is in the bathroom." The girls giggled as she turned off the light and softly closed the door.

Pacing the kitchen, A.J. was on the phone. When Sophia came into the room, he lifted his hand, "Here she is, let me ask her. Sophia, does Juan drive an eighteen wheeler? Do you know what make or model?" Staring at him, she thought for a moment, "Yes, he does drive an eighteen wheeler and he was going to drive late tonight to Denver through Raton Pass. I don't know the make or model of his truck, but it is metallic blue on the side, like a tall wave and the back of the truck has an insignia of a flying horse. Does that help?"

He gave her a thumbs up, "Cruz, did you get all that? What about Maria Elena? Has she been found?" A.J. was quiet as he walked back and forth across the kitchen floor. Sophia waved at him as she disappeared into the bathroom. The floor was soaked and so were most of the towels. Sophia left her clothes on the floor and jumped into the shower. There was hot water.

A.J. was still on the cellphone when she returned to the kitchen in her bathrobe and her hair in a towel. "What's the latest news?" Sophia plugged in the kettle. A.J. smiled, "Well, you're looking better at least now you're up for tea. I swept the floor. Got up all the mug shards that fell. Still I'm upset he killed your dog. There was no need for that at all and the girls will be traumatized for life!"

Sophia turned her head as she listened for a sound coming from the back hall, "What's that?"

"The washing machine. Thought the towels should be washed before the blood set in them. Also, I found some lemon juice in the back cupboard and some vinegar. The mixture was poured over there. Might take some more, but thought to give it a start while it was quiet." A.J. smiled, "Trying to be useful here, don't you know?"

Laughing Sophia gave him a hug, "My goodness you're the man to know around here! Thank you. Has anyone found Juan and Maria Elena yet?"

"Not yet, but Cruz went to her home. It appears she packed in a hurry. Clothes all over, half open suitcases, all the lights were on and her car is there. So however she was going, she wasn't going in her car. She may have gone with Juan since the two of them were in cahoots in all of this. Juan's house had bloody towels in the sink, blood drops throughout his tiny home and his horse was fed extra alfalfa. The front door was unlocked as if he's not coming back. We have an APB out for his eighteen wheeler, but no luck as of yet."

The kettle turned off. Sophia took her mug of tea to the table, watching A.J. pace back and forth. "You can sit down, you know? I'm trying to relax here." She nodded to the chair opposite her. A.J. pulled it out and sat down, "Where is the tea bag Maria Elena brought tonight. I can't find it anywhere. This is making me crazy. Do you believe Clementine took it?"

Nodding toward Sybil's empty bedroom, Sophia said, "Clementine was in Sybil's room when all the excitement started. Oh, God, we were almost killed over Granger's stupid tea! Granger, always Granger! Damn him and now he wants' to kill my mother!"

A.J. went into Sybil's empty bedroom. He turned on the light and searched the room. Pulling back the bed covers he found a book on Dracula and under it the plastic bag with Granger's tea bag. He returned to the kitchen holding up his find. "Well, here it is. I found it under a Dracula book on Sybil's bed. Your oldest has some interesting reading in her room." He sat at the table to pull open his chirping cellphone. Quickly, he stood and walked back into Sybil's room. His voice was low and guarded. As he came back into the kitchen he noticed the pile of dirt on the floor at the base of the doorframe. "This place needs some serious work." He kicked the dirt. "An eighteen wheeler was located traveling at a fast and dangerous speed just south of Raton Pass." He shook his head, pulled out the kitchen chair and sat down. "The Pass is closed. Over twenty inches of snow fell over the last week. Not good, this is not good. An eighteen wheeler of that size with that amount of weight if he was indeed carrying the inventory on his spreadsheet, not good, not good at all." He looked around the kitchen, "Do you have any cereal or anything I might eat for dinner? Lunch seems like a long time ago."

Sophia stared at A.J. with wide eyes. "Yes, I can fix you some fresh scrambled eggs and bacon with homemade bread toast. Do you believe Juan will attempt to drive the Raton Pass?"

"Hell," he stood and went to the refrigerator to hand her the basket with eggs. "I have no idea what a desperate man might do. While you were in the shower, Clementine called." Shaking his head, he continued, "You two women are as thick as thieves. The fingerprints on the knife pretty much connect Juan to Mrs. Mary Peters' death. Charlotte's tea bag found in her cupboard have Maria Elena's fingerprints all over it." He put his hand on Sophia's as she was about to scramble the eggs. "No, just fry the eggs. Three eggs sunny side up, if you please."

Sophia handed him the spatula, "Here you do it. You know what you like and I can't stop shaking."

He took the spatula from her hand, "The crazy thing is all those men taking bad enhancement drugs. The drugs had all expired. They have no idea where those drugs came from or even why those men would need them. Some of those guys are younger than I am and I don't have a problem, huh." He pushed the sizzling bacon around in the neighboring frying pan. "Where's the bread?" Sophia pointed to the bread box.

A.J. shook his head, "Damn shame. All this killing. That poor dog out there never did anything wrong to anyone. Damn shame, that's what it is!" He flipped the bacon with the spatula. "You know if he goes off the road with that huge eighteen wheeler there'll be a herd of Search and Rescue out there trying to find him and maybe even his sister Maria Elena who might be in the truck with him. Some of the rescuers may even get hurt of worse. Where are the plates?" Sophia handed him one.

The hall clock chimed midnight. The girls were both sound asleep in Donna's bed. The sheets in Sybil's room had been stripped and new ones tucked in for A.J. Sophia snuggled under the blankets in her bed, pulling the covers up to her chin. She held her diary in her hand unable to write anything. Four cats slept next to her. The wind blew hard against her bedroom window rattling the pane of glass.

15

Birdsong woke Sophia to roll over and stare at her bedside clock. It was almost nine in the morning. Voices could be heard coming from the kitchen. Slowly, she sat upright. There were no cats on her bed. There was no Shonac by her bed. "Oh!" A soft knock on her closed bedroom door brought her to stand. "Come in." Donna pushed open the door with her foot carrying a silver tray with a full breakfast "Here, Mom, we made you breakfast with A.J. Do you know he slept in Sybil's messy room and he didn't even have nightmares?"

The silver tray was placed on the foot of the bed. "Where's your sister and A.J. now?" The hot mug of tea was lifted off the tray.

"Mom, you remember Shonac was killed last night? How he bled to death in my arms?" Donna lifted her cast, which was now pink in color. "Well, we wrote something to say at Shonac's funeral."

Sophia slurped her tea, "Is the house secure? Did you get any news?" Donna fell into her mother's embrace, "Mom, we don't want to stay here anymore! Can we go away and stay at Grandma Margaret's? Can we pack up what we need and go to Margaret's please?" Sophia hugged her daughter with her one free arm. "Let's talk about it, o-kay. Now, I need to get dressed and get out of this room. It has been a very long night."

In the kitchen, A.J. was on his cellphone. Sybil was in her bedroom trying to tidy her mess. The sheet over the kitchen window was lifted and nailed to the wall. Sophia could see the horses were all in their stalls and appeared to be eating. Sophia turned to Donna, "Did you go out and feed the horses? You didn't go out there alone did you?" Shaking her head, Donna answered, "No, A.J. went with me. This morning is bitter cold. There's no wind and they're no clouds. Just freezing cold air. Not even the birds are flying or singing. They'd turn into popsicles!"

Putting the tray on the kitchen table, Sophia ignored A.J. and ate her breakfast. The cats were roaming around under the table. The heater was on full blast and for once the kitchen was actually warm. Putting his cellphone in his jacket pocket, A.J. turned to Sophia, "It is done. Now, everything is over and it is not good." He turned to Donna, "Would you mind helping her sister in her bedroom? I need to speak with your mother privately." Swooping Silky cat into her arms, Donna went into Sybil's room and quietly shut the bedroom door. No dirt fell.

"The worst imaginable has happened." A kitchen chair was pulled out and he sat to face Sophia. "Juan drove directly off the road and flew off the cliff, after plunging through the metal guard rail. The eighteen wheeler must have gone airborne before it crashed and rolled down the embankment." Leaning back in his chair, his long legs were straight out in front of him, he shook his head. "Damn shame! A huge ball of flames burned as an inferno and all was gone in an explosive moment. Boom!"

The half eaten plate of food was pushed away from Sophia. Her hands were trembling. "They're dead? Both of them?" Her eyes welled with tears as she stared at A.J. He continued to shake his head, "Boom!" Then under his breath he added, "Search and rescue spent all night following the path of the truck's downhill path. No survivors. No inventory. That's going to cost his relatives a pretty penny, let me tell you." Fiddling with his jacket pocket, he pulled out his cellphone, "They found luggage strewn on the way down. A woman's suitcase with cosmetics and clothes. Nothing of Juan's. Not a damn thing. There won't be anything left of them with that amount of heat." Still shaking his head he glanced at her, "Boom!"

A knock on the kitchen window made both of them jump. Clementine's happy freckled face glared at them through the kitchen's old bubbled glass. Standing quickly, A.J. said, "I'll let her in, she's probably got a lot to share about all of the good looking docs who took care of her at the E.R. last night. You know, I think it is time for me to leave." He put his hand for Sophia to shake, but instead she stood and gave him a warm hug. Whispering in his ear, she said, "Thanks for being a dear friend."

Clementine ran down the hall and into the kitchen "It's over! Finally, its over!" She grabbed Sophia to hug while spinning her around the kitchen. "We're all alive, it is over at last!" Sybil and Donna, upon hearing her voice came into the kitchen. "What? What's over?"

The funeral was in Alcon at the Catholic Church. There were a few family outsiders who attended. Sylvia, Donna and Sophia were present. Margaret in her wheelchair sat at the end of their row of chairs. They brought flowers and a casserole for Griego and his mother Reina. This was a sad event in too many ways. Dr. Peters said he might come, but he didn't appear. He was found innocent on all charges. Evidently his wife Mary had self-prescribed herself with the belladonna. She had used it for health reasons and to become more attractive to her husband. Charlotte was given Granger's tea of poison by Maria Elena at the school. There was an aura of peace at the funeral, although Sophia kept looking over her shoulder for Granger.

Thus ends this story, but will Granger make a comeback?

READERS GUIDE

1. Why did the author include several scenes not related to the main plot of the story such as picking up her children from school, fixing dinner, watching her daughters ride horses, etc.?

2. What are the major differences between Sophia and Granger that relates to their relationship with their mother?

3. Why did Sophia believe Granger was behind the poisoning of Rosa? How did she go about trying to prove this?

4. How did Clementine react to Granger when she first met him? Did Clementine believe Granger's alibi? Why not?

5. What was A.J.'s reaction to the many murders? Do you believe he tried to stop some of them? How?

6. How did Geoffrey explain to Sophia about the debt he owed Sophia's father? Do you believe he was telling the truth?

7. Was life better for Donna with Sophia or should she have been taken to Foster Care? Do you think the daughters were safer with their mother? How so?

8. Do you feel Margaret has dementia? Is she blindly loyal to Granger and not to Sophia? Give examples.

9. Why was Granger so anxious about getting his Mercedes back? What purpose did it have for him?

10. Do you believe Granger had manipulated the killer for a purpose or was it her own doing? Explain.

www.ingramcontent.com/pod-product-compliance
Lightning Source LLC
Chambersburg PA
CBHW010747310726
48980CB00004B/389
* 9 7 8 1 6 3 2 9 3 7 0 2 5 *